Christine McCarthy

Thomas Kelly is the author of the novels *The Rackets* and *Payback*. He lives in New York City.

Additional Acclaim for *Empire Rising*

"With its rich characters, expert pacing, and pitch-perfect dialogue, *Empire Rising* ratchets Kelly's work up a notch. . . . Cinematic in scope."

—*The Plain Dealer* (Cleveland)

"The poet-laureate of hard-hatted working stiffs."

—*Men's Journal*

"Like Richard Price, Kelly isn't interested in action for its own sake. Stories about crime are the means for understanding what makes cities tick. . . . In Kelly's case, the ferocious struggle for survival has rarely seemed so entertaining."

—Dan Cryer, *Newsday*

"Thomas Kelly knows how to tell a story. *Empire Rising* is a vivid, evocative, enthralling tale of gangsters, pols, an enduring New York mystery, and the hard, joyful work of building the Empire State Building. This is historical fiction writing at its best."

—Kevin Baker, author of *Paradise Alley*

"Compelling . . . *Empire Rising* is a richly entertaining yarn."

—*The Dallas Morning News*

"The New York of Thomas Kelly's imagination is a tumultuous, toxic Eden, teeming with great promises and fresh starts, pervasive and overpowering temptations, and harsh punishment for transgressors. But also with love stories and hard-hat heroes . . . It is a tribute to Kelly's gifts for juggling that he makes them all fit into this sprawling, brawling circus of kiss-offs and payoffs."

—*Daily News* (New York)

"*Empire Rising* is a page-turner that cheerfully abandons all pretenses to high style. Call it historical pulp fiction, engaging and action-filled enough for a day at the beach, but set against the forging of the crown jewel of Manhattan's gorgeous skyline."

—*Baltimore City Paper*

"Cinematic and completely enthralling. . . . Think Dostoevsky with a hard hat and a lead pipe."

—*The Village Voice*

"*Empire Rising* is, at bottom, a love story, told by one of my favorite authors: a writer of candor, grace, wit, and skill, who writes about the characters who make New York what it was and always will be: a place where the unique spirit of the Irish hovers over every sidewalk, building, street, and alleyway."

—James McBride, author of *The Color of Water*

"[Kelly's] best . . . It's a great historical thriller, filled with grit and atmosphere from the 1930s. It's also a brilliant love story about a building and a city. . . . *Empire Rising* takes his talent to another level."

—*The Globe & Mail* (Toronto)

"A fascinating tale that captures the cadences and decadence of art deco New York."

—*Publishers Weekly* (starred review)

"Great buildings, like great stories, are created layer upon layer. While the Empire State Building rises to dominate the New York skyline, Kelly gives vent to human loves and disappointments in this, an American story that will be recognized everywhere."

—Colum McCann, author of *Dancer* and *This Side of Brightness*

"The famous skyscraper has found a worthy literary legacy. . . . [A] gritty metropolitan tapestry."

—Associated Press

"Few who start this white-hot novel will fail to finish it."

—*Kirkus Reviews*

"Tom Kelly's labors recall those he chronicles in the creation of New York's signature skyscraper, piling mind over matter and then matter over mind until we reach striking heights."

—Edward Conlon, author of *Blue Blood*

"A thrilling tale . . . This is a superior action novel and a great love story that will appeal to a wide audience."

—*Library Journal* (starred review)

"With a score of hot-blooded, multifaceted characters, Kelly has vividly reconstructed the messy mix of class, race, religion, and politics that was New York City."

—*The Historical Novels Review*

"*Empire Rising* is vivid, vibrant, and raw, a story about beauty and corruption, idealism and violence, as intricate as New York City itself."

—Lauren Belfer, author of *City of Light*

"Riveting . . . Kelly successfully melds actual historical figures and fictional ones, but in the end, it is New York City itself that emerges as the central character here: a place that makes people the way they are."

—*Booklist*

"An audacious and compelling narrative by a master storyteller: tough, tender, and beautifully imagined, this intensely American tale is universal in its scope."

—Joseph O'Connor, author of *Star of the Sea*

THOMAS
KELLY

.

PICADOR

FARRAR, STRAUS AND GIROUX

NEW YORK

EMPIRE RISING

www.picadorusa.com

Picador® is a U.S. registered trademark and is used by Farrar, Straus and Giroux under license from Pan Books Limited.

For information on Picador Reading Group Guides, as well as ordering, please contact Picador.
Phone: 646-307-5629
Fax: 212-253-9627
E-mail: readinggroupguides@picadorusa.com

Title page image by Lewis W. Hine, 1931, from the Photography Collection, Miriam and Ira D. Wallach Division of Art, Prints and Photographs, The New York Public Library, Astor, Lenox and Tilden Foundations

Designed by Gretchen Achilles

Library of Congress Cataloging-in-Publication Data
Kelly, Thomas, 1961–
    Empire rising / Thomas Kelly.
        p.   cm.
    ISBN 0-312-42574-0
    EAN 978-0-312-42574-6
    1. Empire State Building (New York, N.Y.)—Fiction. 2. Skyscrapers—Design and construction—Fiction. 3. Construction workers—Fiction. 4. Irish Americans—Fiction. 5. New York (N.Y.)—Fiction. 6. Women artists—Fiction. 7. Nationalists—Fiction. 8. Immigrants—Fiction. 9. Criminals—Fiction.   I. Title.

PS3561.E39717E47 2005
813'.54—dc22
                                                                2004008580

First published in the United States by Farrar, Straus and Giroux

10   9   8   7   6   5   4   3

FOR MY MOTHER,
CATHERINE LOPEZ

.

This one, they say, will stand forever.

Michael Briody digs his bootheel into the muck and listens as hotshots in crisp dark suits speak of marvels. All around, in the gaping desolation where the Waldorf-Astoria Hotel so recently stood, are tangles of cables, beams, uncoiled air hoses, heavy trucks, and stacks of muddy lumber. The speakers huddle on a slapped-together podium and take turns salting the morning air with superlatives: grand, gigantic, epic, magnificent, unrivaled, biggest, best, momentous. They trace imaginary arcs in the air and all agree. The Empire State Building will dominate the Manhattan skyline, dwarfing all pretenders to the crown of tallest structure in the world.

Briody looks about at the gangs of his fellow workmen, who he knows can't wait till this is over. Next to him Armstrong lifts his shoulders and bounces on the balls of his feet. "Christ," he mutters. "Look at them. A flock of weasels. Ten seconds on a work gang would put any one of them in a hospital ward." Armstrong lets you know he started as a rivet punk on the Woolworth Building back in '13, that he has banged up steel on more skyscrapers than he can count. "Who needs these dipshits?" he asks. "I seen this city change shape beneath my feet. I'm the goddamn rivet king of New York."

On the sidewalks surrounding the excavation gawkers pause. They crowd five and six deep, jostling for views through holes cut in the wooden fence. Others mass around the entrances of ramps that lead down into the site. Some gather hoping for work, thinking, Hey, why not me. Men rise on their toes, angling for clear sight lines. Children perch atop parents. The air has the tinge of carnival, a funfair. Opportunists in shiny suits work the crowd selling postcards and trinkets commemorating the event, shouting about the eighth wonder of the world.

Cameras still and moving record the ceremony. Mayor Jimmy Walker, spiffy as a Broadway prince, each hair exact, steps to the microphone. He looks over the assembled, smiles widely, and starts to speak but is interrupted by an unholy screech of feedback that careens off the foundation's stone walls and assaults the gathered, causing them to slap hands to ears, wince. Walker, an old pro in a new medium, rides out the noise, and when it subsides says, "I didn't realize Fiorello was here too." The crowd roars. There isn't a goo-goo vote for blocks. Walker smiles again. It's the kind of smile that lights up rooms, douses ire, and lets him get away with so much.

Walker knows the drill. He pays homage to the project, its scale, and to those making it happen. He steps back in line, his head fuzzy from way too much champagne the night before. He swoons toward reminiscence. Back before he entered politics he was a Tin Pan Alley sport, a writer of songs, and on more than one occasion he tossed a sawbuck to Chuckles Larue, the house dick, and frolicked away an afternoon in the grand hotel with a chorine. Those were the days.

Now it is no more. The papers told all about it, how the destruction sparked a million memories, all those echoes of lost celebrations. People called asking for keys to rooms in which they had honeymooned. A socialite in Denver called demanding a ballroom mirror, a length of bar was hauled down to a speakeasy in the Village, chandeliers were hustled to uptown drawing rooms. Then the demolition gangs swung their wrecking balls and hammers and knocked the grand hotel into a pile of junk that was carted away and dumped into the briny sea just off of Sandy Hook. Like the corpse of some refugee nobody cared to claim.

Briody is not surprised that none of the swells on stage mention the six men who died demolishing the old hotel. Not surprised in the least. He considers their ugly endings, the crushed and broken bodies spirited away like just more rubble, their names already forgotten. Their stories untold. He shifts his weight from foot to foot, is anxious to start work. His fellow workers watch with dull stares.

They have no interest in the staged spectacle. They mutter and joke under their breath until one of the concrete crew makes a loud noise, like a ripe fart, and the superintendent swivels his fat head around and glares at them as if they were recalcitrant schoolboys. They fall silent. They want the work. The next stop is the bread-line.

Al Smith, red-faced and stout, strides to center stage as a round of applause rises against the swirl of the wind. He rolls his cigar over his teeth, tosses it aside, doffs his brown derby. He wraps a meaty hand around the neck of the microphone and cracks a wide smile that flashes gold. He sweeps a hand across his front, indicating the foundation. "I know it don't look like much today. But trust me. The same way I came out of the Fulton Fish Market to rise to governor of this great state, so too will this site be transformed. A year from now we'll be drinking tea a quarter mile high in the air and looking down on Walter Chrysler's nifty little tower." Smith accepts the shouts and cheers of the crowd and talks about the project, its magnitude, its importance, as if he were still trying to convince himself that the raising of a skyscraper is a serious enough task for a man who so recently was his party's candidate for president of the United States of America. He eases the gathered into a few awkward verses of his theme song: "East Side, West Side—we tripped the light fantastic on the sidewalks of New York."

Briody knows the story—how Alfred E. Smith came up from the docks of the Lower East Side, how he clawed his way to the top, made governor, how he looks out for his own kind. And while he no longer occupies the office, he holds the title still. They say he champions the little man, the average joe. But center stage in his suit and vest, his tight shave, his diamond stickpin catching the morning sun, he is a long way from the reek and stifle of the cargo hold.

There is to be a ritual first rivet and Briody, with his tall Celtic features, has been told by the superintendent that he is the ironworkers' poster boy, like it or not. Dust rises in little swirls as the wind blows through the site. The dignitaries vie for position in the throw of the camera's strobe while out on Thirty-fourth Street someone leans hard on a car horn. A hush falls over the crowd. The sky is clear. Briody comes forward and smiles stiffly. His colleagues have a hoot at his expense, but he doesn't mind. He looks up and sees the office workers crowded at their windows, staring slack-jawed, heads resting on shoulders, women peeking through men's elbows, noting the event so as to pass it down to the generations to come.

The Governor, his crooked smile wide, shakes Briody's hand. "I'm a card-carrying member of the bricklayers union." Briody feels the warm fleshiness of his palm and says, "Ah, that's grand, Governor. A brickie." He imagines that the last billion bricks or so in the city have been laid without the man's help.

Skinny Sheehan cranks the bellows, flaring his coke fire. The rivets are bright orange now and Sheehan spits gently into the heat, his saliva hissing into steam. He nods and Armstrong plucks a rivet out of the heater. Acrid smoke stings the air. The officials push forward, moths to a light of recognition. It is not enough to merely be present. They must be seen to have been there, their attendance entered into the official record that is the city's tabloids. Their movement kicks up more dust, causing a few to produce handkerchiefs and blow the muck out of their noses.

Briody hooks the pneumatic hose to his rivet gun, securing it with a quick turn of the wrist. The column is held steady by a derrick cable. Al Smith nods the go-ahead, waves the crowd silent as if this is a moment for reverence. Armstrong puts the scalding steel nugget in place, Delpezzo bucks it up, and Briody drives it home, securing the column to an anchor plate. The tool barks like a Thompson as a golden flame erupts around the rivet and sparks shoot in dying arcs from each side of the steel.

A roar goes up from the men of commerce. There is fear in these men now, maybe for the first time ever, so they need this day, want the energy and optimism that the construction of this behemoth will take—want it all to rub off on them. The politicos make a point of glad-handing the union officials who showed up. Every vote counts. The Mayor backslaps the boys: the ironworkers, the laborers, the derrick men. He puts his arm around the son of a man he knows from his old Greenwich Village neighborhood. But as soon as the cameras are put away the crowd disperses until it is just the men and the work.

The ironworker foreman, Hard Nose McCabe, strides toward them. At six feet five inches he towers over most of the men and he can barely contain his disgust over the work delay caused by the ceremony. "All right ladies, now that your mothers are gone it's time to get this modern marvel built," he shouts over the carpenters pounding apart the podium.

Briody leans back until his head is parallel to the ground. He stares up into the vast blue expanse of the New York sky and tries to project how far the steel they are about to throw up will reach. To what point in the heavens he and his crew will ascend, where they will meet the ether, where the Stars and Stripes will be mounted at the topping-off ceremony. There is nothing in sight to scale it by.

"Great country, hey Paddy?" Armstrong slaps his back.

His head is heavy with blood so he rights himself. For once, he doesn't even mind being called Paddy. He nods. "So they tell me," he says.

Nothing gets built in Gotham without a kickback. When the Empire State developers were ready to turn their crazy dream into concrete and steel they had turned to Johnny Farrell. Now Farrel stood in the foundation hole admiring the scope of the project he had helped make possible. He pulled his fedora snug and stepped lightly across the dirty construction site. Up on Thirty-fourth Street he slid into the backseat of the Mayor's jade green Duesenberg, where Walker was busy wiping his shoes with a handkerchief. They rode in silence through scattershot city traffic, skirted trolleys, horses, jalopies, and trucks, the dashing and darting populace. The driver worked his horn and siren to little effect.

"Did you see Smith? In his glory with the finance men, his new pals. He's a long way from his boyhood on Oliver Street, our old friend. Next thing, he'll be breaking bread with Episcopalians, or joining the Union Club, maybe running for redemption on the Republican ticket." The Mayor dropped the soiled handkerchief on the floor between his feet. "Do me a favor, Johnny Farrell, when I am out of the politicking business, don't let me sully myself so."

"I'll make a point of it, your honor."

"And he gives me grief for enjoying the nightlife, the odd showgirl."

"It's easy to be self-righteous with a full belly."

"Is it?"

The Mayor placed his homburg on the seat between them, leaving his hand atop it. Farrell noticed the thinness of his fingers, the nails immaculately buffed, the skin pale and smooth. If ever a man was born to a particular job in a particular place and time it was Jimmy Walker, Mayor of New York. Farrell wondered how the Mayor saw his career. Was this his last stop? He clearly loved his position, reveled in the power, the pomp, the burn of the spotlight, and while he never expressed interest beyond his present office, who knew? Walker lived his life on two stages—one for the world and one for himself. Farrell's success often depended on his ability to read the Mayor, to anticipate his moods and whims, but it was never easy.

Walker stared out the window and said, "So, Deputy Commissioner of Buildings, did the little code changes make my constituents happy?"

"Pleased as punch." Farrell smiled at the rare use of his official government title.

"A small price to pay for the ability to construct such a monument to their own greed."

"Business as usual."

"Well, it should keep the lads happy in this time of need."

Farrell broke down the kickback in his head, distributing the loot, working his mental abacus. The Mayor, as usual, would take far less than he deserved. In these matters he was strangely reserved. A small percentage, a "commission" he called it, a fee for his services. Which Farrell was entrusted to deposit in one of the fourteen bank accounts the Mayor had going, or sometimes to the Mayor's good friend and financier, Sherwood Wilson, who would squirrel it away God knows where. There was a lot of talk of overseas accounts and blind trusts. Walker tended to keep his distance from graft. Still, he knew better than to try to stop it. The system had acquired a dangerous momentum and woe to the man who interfered with its dark commerce. Farrell had no qualms about taking his share, and occasionally bits and pieces of others'. And why not? They ran the show and to the victor go the spoils.

Johnny Farrell popped a mint into his mouth, adjusted his cuffs, and wriggled deeper into his seat. Even so, this was by far the biggest score he had ever worked on. The developers needed two changes in the building code to make the Empire State Building feasible, never mind profitable. Steel gauge and elevator speed. Two simple adjustments in the way skyscrapers were built that the Mayor had vetoed twice without comment. Farrell had played the developers beautifully, had created supreme leverage.

His assurances that the Mayor would be swayed had led to the massing of capital and the forging of steel in the burning cauldrons of the Monongahela River Valley, to the commitment of the money boys, to the transformation of an idea into a million tons of fact. And Farrell had secured the Mayor's signature, after doubling its price, of course, to a nice round one million dollars. And that was just the beginning. There were to be dozens of subcontractors on the job who would have to pay for the privilege, not to mention ancillary work like sewer lines, roads, and a sparkling new subway station. Plus, someone had to meet the gambling and policy needs of several thousand workers. Farrell controlled all of it.

"It's just a bigger scale than usual. Any contractor knows how this town works."

"I am sure you educate those who don't."

"The reformers can't fault us on this one. Even when the Organization is out of power, nothing gets built without a tribute. It only makes sense that the biggest building in the world calls for the biggest payoff." Farrell knew he did not need to spell it out for Walker. Kickbacks were as constant as the roar of the elevated. Whether the government was machine or reform, Democrat or Republican, made no great difference. No hammer could swing or derrick hoist or saw rip without an arrangement, and whether you were pouring a slab of sidewalk or erecting the eighth wonder of the world, you paid and paid accordingly.

"Slopping the hogs?" The Mayor tapped the briefcase that sat between them. It held the second installment of the kickback, crisp bills of large denomination. "What if they decided not to pay off?"

"Life would get hard for them in many ways. Levers would be pulled, antibusiness scenarios played out. A lot cheaper and smarter to stick to the deal, to be gentlemen."

"I shudder to think who and what you deal with, Johnny Farrell. The Organization's man for judges and jackhammers."

"Judges and jackhammers." Farrell liked the description, liked the juice that came with control over two vital elements of the machine's power.

"Speaking of judges, what the hell is going on with this Vitale mess?"

Farrell chose his words carefully. "It's an unfortunate turn of events, but I feel it is contained."

"What kind of clown of a magistrate sits down to play cards with the Italian racket king?"

Farrell suppressed a smile. "He was, let's not forget, joined at the table by three city detectives—first grade—and an alderman."

"And seven men with guns were foolish enough to rob that game?"

"They wore masks."

"How'd the papers get it?"

"It is an attention-grabber."

"How did they find out Vitale was indebted to the dearly departed Arnold Rothstein?"

"We have top-notch reporters in this town."

Walker shifted in his seat and let it pass. "It's going to be a long day, Johnny. Who do you think we should visit first?"

Farrell was grateful for the change of subject. The Vitale case was a bad omen. Crooked cops were almost expected. Crooked judges caused people to sit up, to doubt their democracy. Times were going sour and as a student of the machine he knew it was about time for a reformist upswing. Crooked judges splashed across tabloids were just the kind of thing that emboldened their enemies.

"We have what, two hours before the parade? I were you, I'd see McManus. Hell's Kitchen was your highest vote, right?"

"Really? Maybe I should go where they love me the least. Reach out, build a bridge."

"I doubt the reformers on Park Avenue want to see your mug on St. Paddy's Day. Most of them find a reason to be out of town today anyway."

"Funny coincidence, that. Speaking of which, how are your in-laws?"

"Out of town, of course."

"Pity. They'll miss a hell of a parade."

"Some people, they just can't appreciate the grandeur of it all."

"Well, keep your ears open around that crowd, Johnny. Gather intelligence. Listen and learn. Helps to know what your foe is thinking. They'll never forgive us, will they?"

"Forgive?"

"All because we landed on these shores and forced them to confront their commitment to such high ideals as 'all men are created equal.' They really did not want to cut anyone in, did they?"

"I guess we did rain on their parade."

"Well they rained right back until we put a stop to it."

Johnny Farrell did not respond. He lacked the grudge-holding capacity of most Irish. His eye was on the future, the past be damned. He was true-blue American, no matter his parents crossing the ocean in steerage. While he appreciated his background, that's all it was.

The car sped underneath the Ninth Avenue El, through a kaleidoscope of light and shadow. Sidewalk strollers gaped in recognition, lifted tentative hands. Shoppers trailing bags shouldered in and out of stores. A pair of young bootblacks squared off, ready to exchange blows over turf. Sparks showered down as a southbound train passed overhead, and drops of oil drizzled the windshield. Johnny Farrell winced from the noise and caressed his satchel, rubbing the smooth cool leather the way a child might a newly won prize at an arcade. Their driver swerved to avoid a tipped horse cart and the screeching peddler trying to ward off housewives who considered spilled vegetables fair game.

The driver braked in front of the *McManus Midtown Democratic Club* and a crowd engulfed them. Farrell struggled to get his door open, forcing back a wave of fleshy exuberance as a band, on a platform, stopped "Galway Bay" mid-note and quickly swung into

"Will You Love Me in December as You Do in May?" Hell's Kitchen was Walker territory and the entire neighborhood had filled the street in anticipation of his arrival. Bulky men in fedoras began to ease the crowd away from the car using elbows, shoulders, knees, and bellies to clear a way for the man of slight frame emerging from the car. A woman in a bright green dress, sporting a matching flower in her hair, slipped past them and planted a deep kiss firmly on Walker's lips. "We love you, Jimmy!"

The Mayor rubbed his jaw, smiled, and said, "Well hello, Hell's Kitchen. I see it's as hot as ever here." A great cheer went up, then a bloom of tiny American and Irish flags, green and blue and red and orange blurring together. Everyone was dressed in their holiday best, cops and firefighters, nurses, local merchants, hooky players, killers, clergy, the milkman, most of them Irish, but some darker, Spanish and Negro, others Jewish and Italian, all believers in the power of the machine, the giver of jobs, and bail, and life, of the cradle-to-grave lookout and all the trials in between. Just turn up on Election Day, the machine will handle the rest.

McManus himself, a tall man just shy of forty with a thick mustache and a warrior's bearing, came to the door followed by his brothers, seven of them, all dressed in sharp dark suits, green carnations pinned to lapels, hats pushed back. Cheers anew went up at this meeting of the municipal and local powers, throaty and raw, beer mugs thrust aloft, foam spraying about. The band picked up the tempo and switched to "The Sidewalks of New York" as the club members pressed in to touch the Mayor, to slap his back, to grab at his sleeve, to bask in his presence, "Jimmy boy, Jimmy lad!" because he, with his wit, and his smarts, and his good looks, and his success, was living, breathing proof that all the decades of striving and clubbing and scratching had paid off and that the city was theirs as much as anyone's.

Walker hoisted a mug of beer and then drank deeply to more cheers. McManus embraced him, bear-hugging the Mayor into the air.

Farrell, clutching the leather case, followed the Mayor, keeping a respectful distance. He watched the reception, the bellow and love of that crowd, thinking, This is not for me. He wanted many things but mass devotion was not among them. He was tight with Walker, knew all the district leaders, paid homage to the other sachems, called Al Smith a friend. He could name every commissioner and assistant commissioner in the city, every precinct captain. He knew where the bodies were buried. He'd also reached out to the enemies, the good-government types and even the Bible thumpers, to the point where they all thought they had a friend in the Hall. He knew the uptown crowd. Every beat reporter in the city had his private number. He was a class A operator. What Johnny Farrell wanted was to be the Boss of Tammany Hall. He would thrive in the shadows, exercise power with nods and whispers instead of speeches. Then, even the great and beloved Walker would have to bow to him.

McManus began to lead Walker through the sidewalk crowd toward the club. Farrell struggled to keep up. Somebody in their enthusiasm bounced into him, splashing beer over his shoulder and chest, and knocked the satchel out of his grasp, and as he bent to pick it up he was pushed, caught in the surge toward the club. He saw a glimpse of his bag through a dozen legs. He stood up straight and fought his way toward it. His mind flashed on the possibility of one hundred thousand dollars being lost. He began to flail against the tide of flesh and rancid breath. "Excuse me! Make way! I'm with the Mayor!" He threw elbows, ducked his shoulders, and pointed over heads. But in the chaos he was just another flushed-faced hooter and hollerer. Finally, the crowd passed him by and he stood curbside breathing hard and glancing about the street, now quiet except for the slow smoky crawl of truck traffic. He looked up and down that avenue and as the El smashed by overhead he let out a roar.

Grace Masterson woke to the klaxon of a fireboat rushing up the East River, its motors droning at full throttle as it scampered to some dousing. The wake jostled her houseboat and she lay for a moment in a tangle of her hair. Her breath was cold and white and sour in the cabin and she pulled the blankets up around her and huddled in her own scarce warmth as the sleep lifted from her, freeing her from the unease and dread of her dreams. Her mouth was dry from too much bad wine. She felt a dull ache spread in her stomach and remembered this date, March 17, another anniversary of woe, another holiday in the calendar imbued with dark significance and ill tiding, another bad-luck number. Valentine's Day, Easter, and now St. Patrick's Day: all her private horrors came on days of public celebration.

She threw off the stack of blankets and rolled out of bed, fighting an urge to stay under the covers and hide from the day. She wore Milo's union suit and a fisherman's sweater over it and could feel the cold floor through her woolen socks. She pulled on a pair of canvas trousers and pulled her hair back into a ponytail and secured it with a rubber band. She slipped her feet into a pair of moccasins that Milo had brought back from Alaska and moved into the galley.

The galley was long and narrow with an iron stove and a sink, a counter that ran along the wall. There were pots and skillets hanging from ceiling hooks. The floor was wide plank, notched and grooved, worn from years of padding feet. Milo had won the houseboat in a poker game over in Jersey and had had it towed to Brooklyn after the Great War. The walls were adorned with dusty relics of his misadventures in exotic lands: crossed Samurai swords, a constellation of frightful African masks carved from hardwoods, a lurid painting of a tropical sunset. There was a pair of shrunken heads that she had banished to the storeroom.

She fed hard dull hunks of coal into the stove. She filled the kettle and emptied a half jug of wine so she would not be tempted to drink it that evening, watched it pool in the sink and swirl slowly down the drain that emptied into the river below her. What a waste, she thought, but better not to have it around. She was looking for the gauzy escape of liquor too often these cold nights.

When the water boiled she added it to her teapot and let the brew darken to nearly black, then strained a cup and added just enough milk and sugar to take the edge off. It was good Irish tea and the smell of it always recalled her childhood, rainy afternoons and turf fires, a world that was lost to her in so many ways. She wrapped her fingers around the cup and carried it to her studio, which was an extension of the bridge Milo had built for her to draw and paint in, a room fifteen feet square, with the wall facing west made of thick glass. She came up the ladder and stood for a few moments. The city was laid out before her across the sweep of the East River, washed in a soft early light, a city of pink quartz, its bustle unimaginable from this remove. Although she had lived on the boat for three years, the view still stunned her, and on this day it was the one thing that could bring a smile to her lips.

When she was ready to work she sat and stared out at the scene before her. The river had a constant pulse that was the blood of the city, a working conduit that carried cargo and bodies, scrap and refuse. This morning was no different. A half dozen ferries from midtown to down past the Brooklyn Bridge were churning across to berths on the far shore as if in competition with each other. Barges pushed or dragged by squat tugs spitting black into the unusually clean city air fought the rip currents of the East River. An old man, a rain hat pulled down on his ears, piloted a small outboard skiff bobbing like an empty can in the wake of all the other traffic. Down to the south, a three-master, a relic from a pre-steam age, was unfurling sails, hoping to catch enough wind to find open sea. The river always calmed her. This morning a flow tide brought clean water from the sea, surging north with force, inevitable.

She knew about the new building, the Empire State, and was eager to draw it as it rose, to document its ascension, capture and portray it. This was what she did. She painted and drew her new city, was compelled to freeze moments of it in time. Construction sites were one of her favorite subjects. All that energy directed to such a finite and exact purpose, the spinning of the steel into the sky, the shells and facades, the elaborate touches; gargoyles, spandrels, columns, and friezes, and the men—hard and quick, they went about their work with controlled intensity, all muscle and sweat and so physically assured, so distant from the men she came across in the jazz clubs and art houses, the offices where she freelanced. She had clipped a saying that proclaimed building skyscrapers was the closest peacetime equivalent to war. She was inclined to agree.

But the Empire State would have to wait. She spun on her stool, anxious, working up the focus to paint. She cocked open her easel, propped up a stretched canvas. She mixed her colors, then she placed the photograph out on the stand next to her, an animal of muscular, savage beauty, its head pulled back and high, staring down with what appeared to be true disdain for both the man beside her and whoever was taking the picture. This was her bread and butter, a simple painting of a foolish rich man standing beside his racehorse.

She worked steadily until the Angelus rang out the noon hour, surprising her. She set the canvas aside and dropped her brushes into empty cans, then poured fresh spirits till the horsehair was covered, the fumes stinging her eyes and nose. She went down to the galley, pulled cold meat from yesterday's chicken to cobble together a sandwich.

While she ate she flipped through an old issue of *Harper's Bazaar* that she had sketched for. On the cover was the quickly fading flapper. She finished her lunch and took the scraps out on the deck, setting them down, and waited as a black cat sauntered up and began shredding the meat with careful swats. There were many riverfront cats that fought with the rats and pariah dogs for survival, but this one, a female she called Black, had turned up the week after she had heard Milo was missing and she had adopted it, feeding it every day. Although the air was crisp, the sun was surprisingly warm and she turned her face up to it, sat on the bench she had put on the boat, and dozed briefly. When she woke Black was curled at her feet and she bent to stroke her neck, but the cat as usual sprung away.

Milo had promised her there would be no more upheaval—that as long as she loved him, he would demand nothing from her, would live life on her terms. As if that was what she had wanted. But now he was two years late in returning through the door, disappeared somewhere in the Pacific, reported missing in Manila. He left his ship for a night of revelry and stepped into oblivion. Since there was no corpse and no physical proof of his dying, her friends insisted he might still be among the quick. But no. She knew these things. She was born with the caul over her head, and while it did not bring her the luck it gave her an ability to see things unknowable to others. This belief she held to as she ran from other superstitions. Milo was another dead male in her life, the others dead in front of her. At least this one had the decency not to die in her arms.

Back in the boat she marked another day off her wall calendar. One wall of her studio was a map of her life. A personal atlas spread out that started in Ireland, a stop in London, to Spain, Seville, across the sea to Havana, then Tampa, north to the Bronx, and now Brooklyn, where she was anchored, in an eddy, a place they said had been a pirate cove long ago. She was living a tinker's life stopped on the edge of a continent. The boat somehow gave the impression that she was still on the move, still unsettled, and this comforted her.

She needed to go up to the candy store on Manhattan Avenue and place a phone call to Farrell. Tonight she would not see anyone. She knew Johnny Farrell would not be happy, but that was too bad. Tonight, she needed to be alone with her loss, to commune with her ghosts.

Armstrong calls you a donkey, ignore him. He yaps, but he ain't a bad guy. Besides, best ironworker I ever knew. Works like a demon."

Briody, tired and dirty from the day's work, rode along the Third Avenue elevated listening to Skinny Sheehan. As the train curled around the uptown bend he felt a jabbing in his back and turned to see an old woman with skin creased so deep she seemed to be carved out of some ancient rock cropping. She clutched a soiled burlap bag brimming with the refuse of pushcarts: bits of vegetables and squashed fruits salvaged from the gutter, scraps of rancid meat, and the head of some ancient monstrous fish. He nodded his head at Sheehan and wiggled a few feet away.

"He'll give you a hard time 'cause he figures you're a greenhorn, but you handle yourself well, I can tell."

"Armstrong is the least of my worries. Delpezzo seems sound enough."

"Nicest guy. Hard Nose McCabe you gotta watch out for. Company man through and through. I call him Hard Noise. Gives me headaches, the ways he screams."

The car was packed with those lucky to be employed. After a year Briody was still amazed at the variety of people riding along in the rush-hour crush. There were those like the old woman who seemed barely part of the twentieth century, and others like the trio of businessmen to his left, camel-hair coats, tight clean-shaven faces, and easy laughter as they retold old stories on their way toward houses and leafy gardens. At the next stop no one got off and a dozen people clambered through the doors, pushing everyone harder against one another.

"Jesus, you'd think this was the last train on earth."

Briody turned and found the old woman jammed against his chest. He wrinkled his nose and recoiled from the malodor. She craned her head up to hiss words in an unknown tongue. Jesus lady, don't blame me. Still, his pay envelope was thick in his pocket and as the train careened into the 138th Street station he peeled off a bill and pressed it to her hand. Out of nowhere she spit up into his face, the saliva hot and rheumy. Instinctively he clenched and raised his fist, felt a rage roil inside him, but noticing the stares of others, he backed off the train, wiping the vileness from his cheek.

Sheehan followed him out of the car saying, "I'm a peaceful guy, but you should've smacked the last tooth out of that animal's head."

"Hit that little old creature? That's what I get for trying to be a big shot."

They descended the stairs and walked toward Willis Avenue, past several boarded-up stores and a derelict three-story structure that sagged toward the street. A gang of adolescents chased a cat around the corner, throwing stones and yelling.

"Too bad you didn't know this place when I was a kid. It was real nice then. We'd swim, go fishing all day. My old man worked for Haffen's Brewery up on a Hunnerd-fiftieth—all the free beer we wanted. New York was like another world."

It was shift change at the Alexander Avenue precinct house and day-tour cops were spilling into the street in their civvies, cheap knockoffs of fine suits, all with fedoras pulled down at rakish angles, ties knotted tightly to thick necks, but their shoes, scuffed from beat pounding, gave them away as gussied-up working stiffs. They shouted and jostled and fled the precinct like inmates from a jail. They were big lads for the most part, with faces that would not have looked out of place back in Kilnaleck. They moved with the physical assurance of armed men who know they have the odds in their favor. Despite their Celtic features they provoked unease in Briody.

"You up for a drink, Skinny?"

"Oh sure. I got eight kids and number nine in the oven. I get home five minutes late she starts sending them out one by one to search the neighborhood for me, like Indian scouts. I'll see you Monday morning."

Sheehan turned north on Alexander Avenue. Briody fingered his pay envelope and debated hitting the gym before stopping for a glass or two of beer. The hell with it, he thought, it's payday. He weaved his way back down the sidewalk, passing the candy store with its flinty, boisterous truants hanging about, past the butcher shop where defeated housewives coveted sumptuous cuts on display in the window, knowing they'd have to settle for mean hunks of meat dragged from the back of the store. A hearse, buffed black and low-slung, pulled to the curb and he watched the driver, a squat bald man dressed in livery, hustle used funeral displays back into a flower shop that gave out the cloying reek of the hothouse. He sidestepped two mongrel dogs lying in front of a cabstand as a stream of curses followed an indignant drunk out to the sidewalk. Briody vaguely recognized the man, who stood and turned back to the door, puffed up his inconsequential chest, and shouted, "Why you rat, you no good bunch of rats," in a fading Galway lilt. A staccato burst of laughter came in response.

Briody shouldered his way into the Four Provinces, into noise and heat, a room thick with smoke where workmen and the unemployed sucked down glasses of beer. Every barstool was taken and the drinkers were standing four deep behind them, some quietly enjoying their beer, but most were engaged in lively debate with those around them, shouting to be heard over the din. He nodded at the doorman, Mannion, then walked down the steps through the crowd and the stink of beer acknowledging friends and acquaintances, doing his best to avoid the truly sloppy. At six feet two he was taller than most of the patrons.

He spotted Danny Casey at the end of the bar surrounded by some of his fellow transit men and shouldered in behind him. Casey held a mug of beer with the two fingers left on his right hand and poked the air before him with his left. They had worked some missions together during the civil war back home and Casey had mishandled a stick of gelignite one night while they were preparing to blow a bridge in Kerry. Briody remembered the flash and the bang; the smell of melted flesh, Casey running back to him with his clothes scorched off, face blackened, his hand mangled. Despite this, the man was laughing, his eyes shining like new coins. They retreated to a safe house and cauterized the wounds with a branding iron. The following week they were captured and interred in the Curragh prison camp, where three months later Casey led a spectacular breakout and escaped to America, to the Bronx, freedom, and sporadic work with the IRT. Briody had not been so lucky.

He listened while Casey held court and signaled the barman for a beer.

"So the lady asks me how to get to the Brooklyn Museum and I say, Lady, I haven't the slightest idea, which is a fact. Now usually I make up something if I don't know. Just send them on their way down the line like, maybe they find someone who knows. But I've not worked in six days, I've not slept in two, and I've been showing up shaping every day and not being put to work and I'm in no mood for this stuck-up Yank giving me the business." Casey paused for a sip of beer, looked up, and waved at Briody. "Ah, here he is my trusty boarder, the mighty builder of the new Tower of Babel. As the country sinks into despair the grand tower shall rise above it all."

"Beats shaping for the IRT, so it does," Briody said.

Casey shrugged and went on. "So she says, You can demonstrate a little courtesy, young man. I look at her, she's no older than I am, and I take my stub, this one here"—Casey waves one of the abbreviated fingers of his right hand—"and I jab it into me nose. You should have seen the look on her. She staggers back like I pulled down my trousers, and off she goes, finery flapping in the wind."

There was a general chuckle. Like most of the men there, Briody had briefly shared that same predicament. Forced to beg for work at low pay, they were often dumped on by the public they served. Briody had shaped with transit when he had first arrived. He was lucky to have got on with the ironworkers. Lucky, and further indebted to Tough Tommy Touhey, a man who liked all debts to be in his favor. And though the job had been set up as cover for him, he was really enjoying the work, looked forward to it.

"What happened?"

"Sure enough she informed on me. The company policy is I must go to her house and apologize before I can go back to work. No exceptions, none."

"She'll want to feel those elegant wage-slave fingers caress her plump upper-class bottom."

"Aye. Maybe she'll invite me in for tea and a tumble."

"Why not?"

"I think she'll run screaming. I doubt she'll support the IRT on that policy."

Briody placed his beer on the bar. He took out a crisp five-dollar bill from his pocket, rubbed it between his dirty fingers, and placed it next to his mug. The bartender came down and Briody indicated the semicircle at the end of the bar and said, "Get the lads on me." The Four Provinces was patronized by all types but the after-work crowd tended toward Irish Republicans who had fought or at least railed against the treaty signed with England—the losing side of an intimate and ugly civil war. Like all the bars in the neighborhood it was technically illegal, but an envelope picked up once a week by the local-precinct bagman assured the uninterrupted flow of booze.

"How's the biggest building in the world?" Casey was staring up at Briody, a hint of a smirk on his smooth face.

Briody thought that was one thing about Casey: the man had

not noticeably aged a day in the decade he had known him. If all the stresses of his life, the feeding of six kids, the clandestine efforts at war, affected him at all, it was not obvious.

"It wouldn't be the biggest building in Cavan Town yet."

"Soon enough, soon enough. Men starving on breadlines and millions going into that monstrosity."

Briody tapped the money on the bar before him. "Well at least we're getting a little bit of the pot."

"You've a point there, boy. Don't know how we'd manage without the rent you pay us."

Fifteen feet down the bar, a man pitched forward, his forehead slammed on the bar, knocking over a half-full mug of beer, which spread in a foamy semicircle away from him. No one moved to clean him up. No one seemed to notice.

Casey nodded. "Packy Farrell from Kildare. His son is a big-wig down at Tammany Hall, not to mention Tough Tommy Touhey's great pal. You would never know it though. They say he never comes to visit the old man, or his consumptive mother. They live above the butcher shop. I guess the son has gone high-hat. A pity."

"Do you have a file on everyone in the neighborhood?"

"Jesus lad, you been here a year now. You know it's just like the villages back home. Everybody needs to know everything about everyone. God forbid you miss out on a juicy tidbit."

"A fast year, really." Briody sipped his beer and decided to send his mother some money. As he sat at the bar he had eighty dollars in his pocket, more than he had ever made in any month of his life, all for a single week's work. He felt an odd sort of charmed. One day he was scraping by shaping up with the Transit, a cold fear about money dogging him. The men trying to start a union on the sly which the company fought viciously. He was lucky to get a week's work out of a month, occasionally picking up day laboring, even a shift here or there on a new water tunnel being built.

The Empire State job was a godsend: months of work for good wages at a time when jobs were scarcer than ever.

"All the money in this bloody country and just take a walk

down Willis Avenue. More hungry children on one block than you can count. It's as bad as home, worse."

Casey had Red leanings, the touch of the anarchist in him. Destroy to build. Briody's politics began and ended with Irish Republicanism. Casey, his eyes bright, wanted to remake the world.

The door opened and a tall man with bright cheeks slunk in, a face from the neighborhood, a Cork man fond of drink and braggadocio. Mannion the bouncer rose, not a good sign, and Briody felt a current go through the bar. The Cork man settled himself on a suddenly empty stool.

Now Casey leaned into him, his breath thick with beer and conspiracy. "Time for a little theater, Mike. A show. Your man has been seen meeting with the wrong crowd."

The bartender, who shook his head with a genuine sadness, pointed to a sign behind the bar. It read NO BEAKIES ALLOWED. The customer pulled up straight and blanched, his fingers gripping the oak before him. Briody knew that beakies were spies for the subway and trolley companies who were paid a dollar a day extra to inform on any union-organizing activity.

The beakie turned his head quickly from side to side, searching for a kind face, an ally. But there was no one for him. There was only Mannion coming down the stairs. Briody wondered at the intelligence that prompted this. The bouncer grabbed the beakie by the lapels and, smiling, drove his forehead into the man's nose. He let go and watched as the beakie staggered like a sodden drunk, then fell to one knee. Mannion then dragged the whimpering beakie like a piece of carrion and when someone held the door open Mannion gave him a kick in the ass that sounded like a cannon shot. Briody caught a glimpse of the bloodstained face, a mask of terror. The beakie rose to his knees in the dying light of a South Bronx afternoon. Tears mixed with blood. Pedestrians swerved past him. He probably had a family. But now he was a pariah, a Judas, a traitor beyond even Christian forgiveness. He would have to move.

"He can take his rat money and drink elsewhere, the no-good informer," Casey shouted.

Packy Farrell stirred and yelled, "Whiskey!" then fell back to the bar. The crowd laughed and ordered more drink, their thirst stirred by the sight of another man's humiliation.

Briody wondered how many of them harbored secret fears that someday desperation might lead them to a bloody comeuppance under a sour South Bronx sun.

O n the first day of spring, Grace rode the ferry from Greenpoint across a choppy East River to Twenty-third Street. It was mid-morning and the boat was nearly empty. A woman in a long black coat kept her six children in line with hard stares, muttered threats, and the odd slap. One of the boys, a towhead about seven, took a blow and winked at Grace. It had rained earlier, and though the wind was up the air was soft and had a sweetness to it. She had learned to enjoy this time of year knowing that soon enough the stifle of summer would descend and the river would give off vile odors.

As always, she rode in the front of the ferry so she could watch the city loom up before her like some great hand-carved edifice— the cluster of towers around Wall Street, the squat warehouses that lined the midtown shore, power plants, their smokestacks punching the sky, the new apartment houses looming over the river near the Queensboro Bridge, the shiny peak of the just-finished Chrysler Building—she loved all of it because she knew there was nothing like it anywhere else in the world. The tide was coming in strong, the pilot angling to elude its northward pull, the engines throaty and hot. The river spray shot up onto the deck, causing the children to squeal with excitement. The ferry docked hard, banging off the pylons.

Grace stepped quickly onto the pier. She moved along with a cap pulled down over her eyes, wearing pants, construction boots, and a faded workman's jacket of tan canvas. Her hair was piled up under her cap and she carried an easel and small folding chair under her arm. She was accustomed to her attire drawing miffed glances, stares, occasional taunts. She did not care.

On fair afternoons she would go down to Washington Square

or up to Central Park and draw the tourists for a dollar a pop, or she might gussy herself up and perch in the lobbies of the grand hotels and capture the swirl of the hoity-toity. Most of the doormen were Irish, and if she presented herself well no one seemed to mind. She'd also talked her way onto construction sites and into tunnels being built and caught men in their labors. She had made herself familiar. Many of the foremen had taken a shine to her. She would sketch them, always careful to add extra brawn, portray them as heroic, makers of a city.

On Thirty-fourth Street she ducked into the lobby of an insurance concern and waved to the doorman, who was from Cavan, not far from where she was born. His smile was wide and bright. He nodded to the elevator man, who wore the same burgundy-and-gold-trimmed uniform, and the car was held open for her. The operator leaned on the motor lever and whisked her up to the top floor. "Good luck with the art stuff, miss." He lifted his cap as she passed him into a hallway lined with fading portraits of the company's long-dead founders.

At the end of the hall she pushed through a door and took the stairs one flight to the roof. The light was dazzling and she squinted as she crossed to the parapet. The view was perfect. She stared down into a maw that used to be the Waldorf-Astoria. The hole sank four stories below street level and covered the entire block back to Thirty-third Street. It was as if the grand hotel had been razed by an artillery barrage and its remains scraped away. A number of steel columns already rose from the floor of the site, sturdy beams, jutting upward, that would anchor the entire building, a thicket of metal.

She whittled her pencil with a pocketknife, the curled shavings falling about her feet. She sketched, capturing the frenetic movement, the steel being hoisted into place by the derricks, the men guiding, then connecting the beams. She drew the trucks arriving in a nonstop procession, disgorging material, then speeding off. Each sketch was just a moment in time, and when she finished she dated it, then started another. She heard a bleat drift up to her like a distant foghorn and all the men inside the fences moved as a herd toward Fifth Avenue, kicking up dust, clamping down on their hats as a breeze rolled across the site. She watched an earthmover with fat wheels as tall as a man drop a series of large metal mats over a piece of ground and pull back. There was another shriek of the horn followed by a *whoomph* and the mat lifted and hovered on the force of the blast, then dropped, and a cloud billowed out from beneath it. The men walked through the drifting smoke, determined, tools in hand and bent back to their varied tasks, while the earthmover dragged the steel mats to a corner of the site.

In the afternoon, tired now, she collected her gear and the dozen drawings she had executed. She swept the shavings up and on the way out gave the doorman a hug, causing him to blush deeply. It was her form of payment to these homesick farm boys she knew so well. To them she contained just the right mixture of the familiar and the exotic—being Irish herself yet of New York in a way they could not yet grasp. She ducked out of the building and crossed to the south side of the street. Teamsters stood beside their idling trucks smoking and joking as laborers unloaded planks, red bricks, terra-cotta blocks, copper pipe, and long gleaming pieces of small-gauge rail. One of the teamsters blocked her path holding his hands wide and leered, as if he was readying a lewd embrace. She skipped sideways and he laughed, revealing a set of crooked black teeth.

She took the subway to Twenty-third Street and walked toward the Gramercy Park Hotel. The day was still sunny and there were a dozen nannies gossiping as they pushed carriages and led the polished children of the wealthy in and out of the park. One of them, a dark-haired girl with round eyes, bolted from her keeper and was chased down right before she ran into oncoming traffic. Grace gasped at the near miss and at the horrid memory it triggered. In the hotel the doormen regarded her with respect because they knew she was with Johnny Farrell, golden-boy sachem of Tammany Hall, keeper of the secrets, a human link between night and day. No one with any sense wanted to get on his bad side.

She used her key to enter the four-room suite that Johnny kept for them. Her relationship with Farrell had started as one of convenience, a bit of her soul offered up on the altar of survival. He was handsome and generous and decent enough and had pursued her mightily. He was a good time, and after Milo, that was all she could imagine being with a man for. But somehow he had gotten under her skin, had become a comfortable fit. She stripped and lay on the bed.

She thumbed through a little volume of Byron that Farrell had bought for her. The man worked hard toward romance, which she'd give him. She heard a commotion on the street seventeen stories below the window, a garbled shouting over a parking space, she imagined, or a woman perhaps. New Yorkers were great ones for screaming at each other. She wondered what he had in mind for this evening, dinner, a round of the speakeasies, and a jazz club uptown most likely. She enjoyed the madcap swirl, the crazy energy of the Manhattan night, the escape from her solitude on the boat. While she cherished her independence, some nights came at her hard and smothered her with ghosts.

Farrell was a man on the make, a quick riser in the city. He was also a sentimental drunk, and when in his cups proclaimed a great and consuming love for her, offered promises of leaving his wife and children and sharing a life with her. Grace knew this to be nonsense. He could never face the censure abandoning his family would bring upon his head. She blamed him for none of that. If it was not for the wife, Grace thought, she would have nothing to do with him. His marriage made him safe enough for her. Creamy sunlight spilled through the window on a cool breeze. She considered how New York had changed her in that adultery was no longer something she recoiled from. She was in no mood to consider all the other ways.

Johnny Farrell, dressed in a handcrafted suit of Italian silk and linen, held a satchel full of municipal plunder on his lap and listened to Captain Jack Egan as his driver muscled them through midtown traffic.

"A hundred grand is a fortune, Johnny. Whoever found it will start throwing it around, sooner or later." Egan took a peanut from a paper bag and popped it, shell and all, into his mouth.

"A windfall like that, I'd take advantage, spend big."

"They'll want to impress their pals."

"Not to mention the broads."

"Play the big shot, sure."

"This stays between you and me."

"Doesn't everything, Johnny Farrell?"

Farrell watched Egan leave the car and walk up the steps to the 18th precinct house. Egan, whom he had known since they were kids, was his cop, his pipeline to the streets. Farrell did not share Egan's optimism but he was not going to let it get to him, not today. A hundred thousand was a fortune, but Farrell saw that much money in an average week. It was just a matter of robbing from Paul to pay Peter until he came up with a way to replace it. Besides, there were real problems to worry about. Magistrate Vitale's indiscretions were the kind that could lead to the all-consuming scandal. It showed the wider world connections best left in the shadows.

In front of the Gramercy Park Hotel he patted his driver on the shoulder. "Don't bother waiting for me, Bill, I'll cab it from here."

A hotel attendant pulled open the car door with a flourish, bowing slightly in his direction. "Mr. Farrell. Good afternoon, sir."

Farrell peeled off a crisp ten-dollar bill and slipped it to the man while shaking his hand.

"Pete, come on. How many times I need to tell you, call me John. Or Johnny. Knock off the mister crap. I'm not your science teacher."

The doorman bowed again and preceded Farrell to the door. "Yes, Mr. Farrell."

"Jesus. Is my friend here yet?"

"Yes, Mr. Farrell. She arrived at three o'clock. Sharp."

"Good man, Pete."

The lobby was busy with new arrivals from out of town whom Farrell judged by their flat accents to be midwesterners—prairie people, God-fearing. Stacks of luggage were being sorted and loaded onto bus carts by hotel staff. He shifted the calfskin case to his right hand and waited for the elevator. He caught his reflection in the wall mirror between the car doors, and noticing his pocket square was askew, righted it. A couple stood next to him, plainly dressed, he in an ill-fitting suit and she in a worn navy dress crowned by a lace collar and more makeup than she needed—fake lashes like spider's legs, full lips painted blood red. Farrell winked at her and she blushed. He stepped aside and gestured to the open car.

"Johnny. How's things with the big boys?" the elevator operator greeted him.

"You know what they say, Bruce. Be nice on the way up, you never know when you'll be on the way down."

"About a hundred times a day for me, boy."

Farrell laughed. "Plenty of practice then."

Bruce let the couple off on three and then took the car up to the penthouse floor. Farrell dug in his pocket for his key, padded down the soft red carpet of the hallway, and paused at the door to still his breathing.

"Sweetie?" He was greeted by silence.

He passed through the parlor into the bedroom. There on the bed sleeping was the object of his febrile daydreams. Farrell peeled away the covers and found her ass displayed, offered up to him like a sacred feast. He leaned over and planted a kiss on her buttock, softly. He put the satchel on the bureau and covered it with his jacket. He placed his hat beside it, removed his tie, fumbled open his shirt buttons, and plunked his silver cuff links in an ashtray. He hung his suit up and stripped out of his boxers and undershirt.

He considered that of all the women he had bedded during the sexed-up twenties, none came close to Grace. None came anywhere near. They were quick, sloppy screws, and adios, illicit couplings followed by mild disgust. Grace he cherished. He stood quietly, admired her dazzling beauty—smooth white skin, her wavy chestnut hair cascading down her back, the birthmark like spilled burgundy on the small of her back, just before the swell of her buttocks, the tiny translucent hairs at the nape of her neck which were visible only when the light caught them just right. His breath was ragged now, fast.

Coming up from sleep, Grace rolled onto her back. He climbed on the bed and knelt between her legs. He trailed his fingers along the inside of her thighs. He nudged her legs farther apart. He cupped his hand across her sex and began to rub, feeling the heat of her. She started to move against his hand as she rose slowly from her slumber and then she opened her eyes and smiled in greeting and that was as much preliminary as he could stand. Farrell slid inside her. He felt, as always, like something whole, like something complete, like something he could never let go of.

From somewhere Grace heard an oboe playing and she felt a sadness come over her.

"Why won't you take the apartment? We'll be able to see each other more."

They lay entwined in the damp sheets, Farrell smoking quietly. The midday sunlight had left the room and in the late afternoon gloom Farrell rubbed her stomach, scratched it lightly. The smoke curled up to the ceiling.

She rolled onto her stomach. "You mean when you're not running to the wife and children on Fifth Avenue?"

"Ah Grace."

"You just want me at your beck and call."

"Points out the fact that I got brains."

"My boat is a sanctuary. It's all mine."

"Until your dead sailor comes back."

She scooted away from him on the bed. "He's not coming back. It's my boat now. Why are you so uncomfortable there, always sniffing the air like it's beneath you?"

"It's not sanitary living like a pirate on a boat, that stinking river."

"Jesus. This, from the son of a washerwoman and a drunkard."

"Watch it."

"You run so hard from your past you must get dizzy."

"I take it that's a no."

"You knew before you asked. Why torture yourself. Even Johnny Farrell doesn't always get what he wants."

"It's more a case of what I need."

"So now I'm supposed to be flattered?"

Farrell rose and dressed. He was meticulous in his manner,

fussy in a way she had seen in other handsome men—an awareness of their good looks mixed with insecurity about them. He picked lint off his pants, smoothed the creases between two fingers, shot his cuffs in a way that was both deliberate and delicate. She thought his thick brown hair might be his one true love. He ran his fingers through it so slowly it seemed he wanted to stroke each hair individually with a reassuring caress. He stood before the mirror longer than anyone she ever knew, women included, rubbing the skin under his eyes, massaging his cheeks as if he could press the wear and tear of his nocturnal existence off his skin.

He pulled on his jacket and rolled his shoulders, ran his fingers once more through his hair and turned to her. "Enough about your pirate life. I need you to do me a favor."

"Sleeping with you isn't favor enough?"

"You're cracking wise with the best of them today. I'm serious."

Grace propped herself up on a pillow, brushed her hair behind her ear, and waited. Farrell popped his knuckles loudly, something she had never seen him do before. He was not his usual cocky self today. He came around and sat on the edge of the bed. "I can trust you, right?"

She wanted to be honest and say no, but she said, "Of course, Johnny."

"I want you to make some drops for me. A little banking. It's all up-and-up."

"Up-and-up, is it now?"

"I'm going to give you an envelope once in a while. First you go around to some banks, different ones, and get safe-deposit boxes. I'll let you know which banks. Then you just make the drops, okay? Nothing illegal. I'll pay you a hundred cash for each drop. How about it?"

She sat up. "Johnny, I know you think I stepped off the potato boat whole and pure and innocent. But I knew enough even then to know a hundred dollars a go for nothing illegal is a fairy tale, even on the golden shores of Americkay."

Farrell smiled. "Fair enough. In a lot of places it might be a bit shady. But Grace, by now you should know we run this mess of a town. I could just as easy get someone else to do these things. I just figured you might like it as a way to help finance your art career. Give you some independence."

"Come on, now." She laughed. "Johnny Farrell, you might want a lot of things for me, but independence? Please." Still, she had been left broke and alone more than once by men she loved. The chance to put away enough money to live life on her own terms had appeal. "I'll help you, Farrell, but let's not kid one another."

Now Farrell opened the satchel he had left on the dresser and pulled out a thick stack of bills. Grace noticed thousand-dollar bills, five hundreds, and a batch of C-notes. She had not expected this—a flurry of green.

"Thirty thousand." Farrell seemed to glow while he handled the cash.

"You call that a little banking?"

"It's only money."

She wanted to ask questions, but knew better. She hefted the loot. She was surprised so much money took up so little space in the world. Imagined what it could buy her—a new life, a new place. She entertained a thought of leaving New York, making a mad dash; she saw Johnny Farrell choking in rage. But she knew she could not outrun Farrell and his cohorts. They owned the cops, the press, and the gangsters too. They had reach, were a law unto themselves. They would catch her and exact a terrible revenge. She squeezed a wad of bills between her breasts and cooed, teasing him.

"A lot of big people are counting on this, Grace." He smiled, but there was no hiding the warning in his eyes.

"Are you going to tell me what this is all about?"

"Grace, I figured you were smart enough not to ask."

"Is that a no?"

"It's just the business of the metropolis. Consider yourself a good citizen."

"Will I get a ticker-tape parade?"

"I could arrange it. Be bigger than Lindbergh's."

"I know you could."

"You'll be looked after. No one can hurt us in this town."

She sat at the edge of the bed, naked, the soft cotton sheets still damp from their coupling bunched around her knees. A breeze lifted the lace curtains. He was so put together in his Savile Row suit and his spit-shined shoes, his go-getter airs. At least he had stopped wearing the spats. She had teased him mercilessly about those, called him Jimmy Walker Junior. He fingered his diamond tiepin. She took his hand, the left, the one with the band of rich metal that was supposed to signify an unbreakable bond, and placed it on her right breast. She looked up at him and held his eyes in hers until she saw his resolve leave him. He had places to go, this power broker, but not until she said so.

Briody's gang each had a hand on the column as Armstrong signaled to the crane operator with his forefinger and thumb.

"I never saw one like this," Delpezzo said.

"That's 'cause there never was one like this. One hundred and two thousand pounds—the largest column ever used on a building site." Sheehan shook his head in wonder. "Feel it. It still holds heat from the forge."

Briody walked carefully as the crane eased the behemoth along, stepping over dozens of beams that lay waiting for the columns to be set. Cables, planks, and loose rock made maneuvering tricky. The air was yellowed, heavy with diesel fumes. All through the blockwide foundation hole other crews planted the last of the steel columns, 210 in all. Tomorrow, they'd start with the beams.

"Christ, this thing toppled, it would wreck the entire site."

When the column was over its concrete pier, Armstrong signaled the crane to stop with his hand like a blade across his throat. Briody leaned his weight onto the column, and though it was hanging by cables in midair, he could not move it by himself.

"If you like your feet, keep an eye out. We're coming down." Armstrong signaled with his fist out, thumb down, and they lowered the column onto the steel grillage connecting plates. Briody and Sheehan bent over and using their spud wrenches lined up the holes, then quickly banged in temporary bolts to steady the mass of Pittsburgh steel.

When the column was secured Armstrong shimmied up its thirty-foot length, unhooked the cable, and swung out over their heads like a trapeze artist as the crane lowered him to the ground. He landed with a curtsy.

"We earned our lunch today, boys."

They strode through the forest of steel to the wooden ramp that led to the street. The wind picked up and they clamped down on their hats and squinted against the dust. On Thirty-fourth Street, they waited in line to buy sandwiches from a food wagon, then sat under the sidewalk shield on upturned tin buckets along with scores of other men. Delpezzo had brought food from home. He ate pasta from a deep ceramic dish.

Armstrong elbowed Skinny and pointed to the Italian. "Too good to eat from the roach coach like the rest of us."

Delpezzo ignored him, sipped homemade wine from a mason jar.

"Too good, or too smart?" Skinny pulled the top slice of bread off his sandwich. "Isn't the cheese supposed to be yellow and not the ham?"

"That's bad? You shoulda been in France," Armstrong said.

"I was in France, and you know that."

Briody kept to himself as they ate and bantered. He too had been in France, with the British army and he surmised for a lot longer than his American coworkers. He'd spent more than two years in the muck and the slime serving the British army with rats and dead men for company. He shook off images: piles of bloated corpses and limbs, the horrible false dawn of artillery barrages. He watched across the street as a woman wearing pants and a workman's jacket talked to the doorman. She flashed a smile and disappeared into the dimness of the lobby, the doorman trailing her like a puppy. He wondered what her story was. That was the thing about this city. Everyone, it seemed, was from someplace else, everyone had a story.

Briody finished the last bite of his pork sandwich, washed it down with root beer, and dropped the empty bottle into a wheelbarrow serving as a trash can. The story he presented about himself, that he was just another immigrant farmer looking to chase the American Dream, was an outright fabrication.

"Resting on your laurels?" Hard Nose McCabe appeared, scowling. Back to work. The foreman had more than thirty crews working under him and he rode them all as if their pay was coming out of his own pocket. As usual he wore a sport coat over an open-necked white shirt, corduroy pants, and believed that a boss should never get dirty. He stood, hands on hips, his black beaver-pelt fedora pushed back on his head, and broke into his sergeant major cadence. "Make no mistake—pissants. We're going to break all records. We're going to throw up more steel, each week, each day, each hour, than anyone has ever done, anywhere. You pricks are either with the program or you're down the road. There's plenty of men waiting to take your place." He indicated a line of haggard men standing against the fence, a line that wrapped around the block. Their faces were set with a type of grim hopefulness. This despite a number of signs indicating no hiring was to be done on-site. "Now let's move it," McCabe barked, and then he was gone down the ramp, to harass the next crew.

Skinny Sheehan wiped his hands clean with a white handkerchief before putting it back in his pocket. "They expect us to bang out a floor a day, things get rolling. Every damn day. My cousin's an engineer on this job. He tells me we're gonna throw up nearly sixty thousand tons of steel before it's all said and done."

"A floor a day?" Delpezzo took a final sip of wine.

"Kid's stuff." Armstrong dug muck from his boot with his spud wrench.

"I ain't never seen that kind of production. Three and a half floors a week, that's standard."

"Yeah, well it's a whole new decade, Skinny. This time around we separate the men from the girls."

Delpezzo finished his pasta and wiped his lips with his sleeve. "They gonna try to give us all heart attacks?"

"What about you, greenhorn, you think you can keep that pace?"

Briody took his gloves from his belt and slipped them on, punching his left palm, then his right. Armstrong had been riding him from the start. Part of this was standard, breaking the new guy's shoes, but it was starting to wear thin.

"We'll see, won't we?"

"Well Paddy, you're no Sean Reilly, that I can assure you right here and now." Armstrong pushed past him.

Sheehan spoke softly. "Reilly was fine when he showed up sober. Which was getting less and less. Armstrong ain't a bad guy, he just don't like change."

"Few of us do." Briody knew the story. Armstrong, Sheehan, Delpezzo, and Reilly had been a team all the way on 40 Wall Street, which after a yearlong dash into the sky had lost out to the Chrysler Building for title of tallest building in the world. Reilly was sent packing on orders of Tough Tommy Touhey to make room for Briody on the gang when work was increasingly scarce. Briody knew most ironworkers were superstitious, that once a rivet gang was formed they stuck together, learned to trust each other with their lives. If one man failed to show up, the whole gang took the day off rather than integrate a shaper for the day. Still, he could not afford to worry about who he had replaced.

"And don't let the greenhorn stuff get to you, either. I came here when I was two, don't even remember a thing about Ireland, and he still calls me Paddy. He don't mean nothing by it."

"I'll only put up with so much of that. My work will speak for itself."

It was no secret that this was *the* job in town. The best iron-workers were assembled, veterans of all the grand buildings of the twenties, poised for a manic ascent. They were one of the few gangs that had not been sent to the job as an established team. Over the last two weeks, despite Armstrong's constant ribbing, they had begun to jell as a crew. But this close to the ground there was ease and nonchalance that Briody assumed would disappear as they made their way into the clouds.

The steel had been rigged before lunch with temporary bolts; now it was time to rivet it in place, to make it a lasting part of the is-land upon which it stood. Skinny used the bellows to fire his coals, which were soon red, molten. Briody, the gunman, took hold of the rivet gun and set himself on the opposite side of the column from Armstrong and Delpezzo. Armstrong nodded to Skinny, who grabbed a burning rivet out of the forge with a pair of yard-long tongs and tossed it end over end in a glowing arc to Armstrong, who caught it in an old paint can, plucked it out with his own short pair of tongs, tapped it on the edge of the beam, and stuck it in the hole. Delpezzo used a short metal tube that grabbed the rivet, bucking it up from the other side. Briody swung the rivet gun onto the head, wielding it like a weapon at hip level, and with a yank on the trigger and a pneumatic blast that shot a rain of sparks, fused it in place.

The other crews were at it now, creating an infernal racket, a howl that drowned out all talk, all thought except—the work. Armstrong's gang moved along at a nifty clip, rivet after rivet, fast but deft, practiced in their endeavor. On a good day they might pound in five hundred of the inch-and-an-eighth-long rivets, more than one a minute. Briody felt the heat in his back and arms, the movement becoming automatic and ingrained. Muscle and steel and heat, working together to forge a skyscraper.

At two-thirty they stopped and sat for a ten-minute coffee break, their sweat chilling them as they sipped hot rancid muck. Armstrong walked along the beam on his hands, his sleeves rolled up to expose the ropy muscles of his forearms. He whistled as he made his way. When he reached the end of the cold steel he let his legs flop over his head until he formed a human arch and then sprung forward so he was standing upright again.

"Like a little monkey." Delpezzo waved dismissively.

Sheehan spit coffee in a long stream. "You know what's amazing?"

"What, your ability to yap like a girl?"

"The Fifth Avenue Association won't let them deliver materials on the street because it will mess up traffic. Everything except the steel's gonna come right in here and be off-loaded, then hoisted up to where it needs to go. You believe the nerve of those high-hat rats?"

"I care about the beam right in front of my face. They got college-boy pencils to figure the rest of that crap out."

"Come on now. Someday you'll be glad you worked on this one. The biggest building in the world."

"Ain't that what they said about the last one we put up?"

"This one's different, I can feel it."

"Christ, a clairvoyant."

"There ain't a single other building of any size going up anywhere in this town."

"The boom is bust."

"It won't last. Before you know it, they'll be going two hundred stories straight up."

"I just don't see it."

"The money's gone."

"I got eight kids to feed," Skinny said, returning to the bolt burner.

"Whose fault is that?" Armstrong called after him. "You can't keep the snake in its cage."

Sheehan's face glowed red, reflecting his fire. "Go screw, you bum. Just 'cause no one will have you."

Briody took up the rivet gun. In the job-site lull he could hear the city sounds of the horns and sirens above them. He squeezed the trigger and the gun jumped, barking in his hands. He was ready. Sheehan and Delpezzo stood waiting for Armstrong, who had walked off a dozen yards and was pissing. Briody thought it odd that both Sheehan and Delpezzo, like a number of other men, wore white-collar shirts and ties under their coveralls, as if they might strip off the outer layer and head to work in an office.

"Why do you wear that stuff under there?"

"Respectful, that's all."

Armstrong rolled his eyes at Sheehan's explanation. "Let's get it done, boys."

When the whistle blew at four-thirty all work stopped at once. Hundreds of men banging, tearing, hammering, drilling, raising a racket, and then—nothing, like a switch thrown, a stunned quiet that made the ears ache for sound. Briody thought that if he screamed his voice might echo off the walls of silence. Sweat started to cool on his skin. The crew dropped their tools in a gang box, a metal container on wheels the size of a small car with ARM-

STRONG stenciled in white paint on the top and sides. Briody took his gloves off and folded them over his belt. He windmilled his arms, working a kink out of his shoulder. Armstrong snapped a padlock shut on the gang box and slid a small pewter flask from inside his boot, uncorked it, and sipped. He offered it to Briody, who waved him off.

Armstrong shrugged and sipped again. "Paddy, another ten, fifteen years you might even be able to call yourself an ironworker."

Briody regarded him. "The name is Michael."

Armstrong sipped from the flask. "Plans for the evening?"

"Not a thing."

"Good, you might want to take that rivet gun home and get some practice."

Briody grabbed the flask and tipped it to his lips. The whiskey was good and strong, burning all the way to his belly. He handed it back and walked, caught in a stream of men up the ramp to Thirty-fourth Street. They moved along, a ragged and muscled bunch: laborers, drillers and blasters, muckers, electricians and carpenters, a couple of concrete gangs, a scrawny water boy, tin knockers, and canteen men, brickies, hod carriers. Some carried their tools, belts dragging along. Men smoked and cursed, bragged and anticipated the night's revels. They raised dust as they moved. It swirled up among them and Briody was covered in it, his skin and hair whitened.

Up on the sidewalk they overwhelmed the passersby, the commuters making an early dash for Pennsylvania Station, the casual shoppers, the odd tourist. Pedestrians darted into traffic to escape the scrum of workmen as it moved toward subways and local watering holes. At the corner Briody leaned against the fence surrounding the site. He jumped up and down and flapped his arms, kicked his legs about like a mad bird trying to loose the dust, slapped his hands against his body and along his limbs. He took off his hat and ruffled his hair, beating the hat against the fence. Coughing, he loosened bits of thick dust, burnt carbon from the rivets, all that was grating the wet flesh of his throat. He spit on the sidewalk. Satisfied, he made his way toward the IRT at Thirty-third Street.

A year ago this city had seemed like nothing more than crowds and chaos. Now there was logic and a rhythm to it, and he was starting to enjoy the place. The light was behind him now, casting long faint shadows. The street was picking up, office workers starting to spill out of all the other buildings, so many of them new and magnificent and built during the previous decade. He scanned the faces of the people who passed him walking into the light squinting, women with hands held over their eyes, so many of their lips painted bright red, men with their hats pulled down for shade, shouldering their way deftly along. The faces were their own geography, a map with a thousand distinctions, features that spoke of every corner of the globe. It was the thing that struck him the very first day he walked on this island.

He pondered this and his pace quickened. The day's labor seemed to make him stronger, to increase his vitality. He felt the roll of his muscled shoulders, the bounce along his strong legs. He bought a pear from a corner vendor, rubbed it on his thigh, and bit into it heartily so the juice ran down his chin. He almost felt like running home to the Bronx.

Roosevelt pulled his diminished self out of the plump, fair servant girl and rolled onto his back. He reached for the cigarette case on his end table, took one out, then insinuated it into the ebony holder and lit it with a flourish. He felt a creeping shame, then pushed the feeling away like the silliness it always was—a Catholic or maybe Jewish affliction. Puffing on the cigarette, he traced a line along her side. The girl would have to go soon enough, but he enjoyed the lingering, her warmth and fleshiness, her musk. These afternoon idylls, these romps, were sadly rare.

As he smoked the cigarette down, she dressed right out in the open, shamelessly. When she was back in her uniform she helped him into his trousers, pushing them over his braces, kissing his knees before covering him up to the waist. Finally, she bent and laid a soft kiss on the top of his head, then picked up her feather duster and went back to her less sordid duties. He finished dressing, swung himself into his chair, and looked over the reports his investigator had compiled.

The '32 campaign was fast approaching, and while he publicly disavowed interest in running, he had already made up his mind to do so. Only Eleanor knew of his plans. He had to find a way to politely distance himself from the Tammany machine. No Democrat had a chance of winning the White House without strong support down South, and Smith and Tammany were poison below the Mason-Dixon line. The Happy Warrior—phooey. He regretted ever putting that phrase into circulation. Smith was more like the Irish Hack. Everybody was forever praising the man for his smarts and his administrative prowess. Smith seemed to think that meant it was perfectly all right to stick his nose into state affairs, offering his experience. Well, his experience included 1928, the worst humiliation a candidate could take in a national election. Roosevelt smiled at the thought of it. Things did have a way of working out for the best.

There was a polite knock at the door and the barber entered, pushing a cart complete with towels, razors, and piping hot water. Roosevelt flipped over the reports and wheeled himself around the side of the desk.

"Jenks, how is life treating you?"

"Never better, Mr. Franklin."

Jenkins deftly wrapped a towel around his neck and draped him in a barber's shawl. He closed his eyes and leaned back. First the shave. He relaxed as Jenkins removed his glasses and smoothed his face with a hot towel. Smith. Ditching the old machine man was just a part of his strategy for winning the White House, where he as a Roosevelt knew he belonged. He long ago began thinking Mayor Walker might have to go. The Democrats of the South might be bigots, but he needed their votes, even so. Jenkins whistled softly while he worked the razor up his neck, carefully pinching the skin when need be.

He could easily win over the reform crowd if he could just knock out the embodiment of Tammany excess. In his strivings, his deepest ambitions, he had always known he would be elected president. He had paid his dues and made all the right moves. He had played nicey-nice with the Tammany gutter scum for longer than he would like to remember, sat through countless speeches at innumerable banquets and county dinners where he had to struggle to stay awake, glad-handed and backslapped and roared with hearty false cheer. He convinced them that he liked them, that he admired them even. 'Thirty-two would be his year. The time was nigh. The country was howling for change. The Republicans had destroyed themselves with their greed and stupidity, their heads buried in their posteriors. Hoover was vulnerable. He could taste victory.

The shave finished and his face wiped clean, Roosevelt reached up and caressed his chin, appraising his steward's fine work. Walker and Smith provided him with perhaps his biggest dilemma. He needed those Irish yahoos in Tammany, needed the vote-manufacturing power of the machine, but he could not rise to national prominence with the stain of big-city corruption on him.

Jenkins splashed bay rum. He produced a pair of scissors and began to snip away.

The question was how could he dump Walker yet maintain the support of the Tammany army? How to distance himself from Smith and yet win Catholic votes? He had no strong dislike for Walker and secretly admired the man's honesty: he did not try to hide his transgressions, publicly paraded his mistress, and laughed off any attempts at chastisement. That took a twisted kind of guts. He knew Walker at times enraged Smith but there was an odd papist competition there. If Smith possessed a tenth of Walker's flair and charm and good looks he would be president, Catholicism or no Catholicism.

Jenkins finished and held a mirror up. Roosevelt admired his profile—one of a born leader, he thought. "Excellent, as always, Jenks." Jenkins removed the bib, the towel, gathered his tools.

"Will you come with me to Washington, Jenks, should I move to a certain house on Pennsylvania Avenue?"

Jenkins smiled, shook his head. "That's a long ways from home, Mr. Franklin."

"Do you doubt my prospects, Jenks, my ability to vanquish the jowly Hawkeye?"

"I don't doubt no single thing, Mr. Franklin."

Roosevelt wheeled himself down the hallway toward his office, past the portraits of his gubernatorial predecessors. In truth he loathed Smith, especially his Self-Made Man spiel, for while he did not come from money, he came from the machine, which was a far greater springboard to politics than any old River family ever was. Spare me, Roosevelt thought. Here I am, crippled, dealt a blow like this in life, and we are all supposed to admire Al Smith because he had the misfortune to grow up with the stink of the streets on him.

He wheeled with purpose, now determined to show the world who the better man was. In his office, Egan stood twirling his hat. Roosevelt admired the cut of the man, his rock-jaw seriousness. Egan went through life on the balls of his feet. His shave was perfect, his shoes buffed to the point of reflection. They had been kicking things around for a few months. He loved these little private sessions, unknown to even his closest advisers.

Egan took his hand and started right in. "The problem with the Mayor is—he's no fool."

"That's public knowledge."

"I think we need to attack at the margins, his periphery. My sources say Walker is not really interested in more than being, well, than being the Mayor."

"You telling me he's not lining his pockets, battening at the public trough?"

"I would not go that far. It's more that he allows others to plunder. And he is slick enough to keep a distance, to maintain buffers."

"Others?"

"His Tammany cronies. The usual suspects. Commissioners, judges, district leaders, precinct commanders."

"Old news, Egan. Get me something that will stick. Something that will turn heads."

"The money, sir."

"Money?"

"Yes. If we can follow the money, we'll have something. Anyone who does any business with the city pays kickbacks. Judges buy appointments. A subcontractor who breaks a square foot of sidewalk pays for the privilege. All that money ends up somewhere. Walker's salary is forty thousand a year but I hear he has at least a dozen bank accounts."

"A dozen bank accounts?" Roosevelt wheeled himself over to the bar and poured from a bottle of gin into a tumbler. "Care for a cocktail, a Bronx perhaps, a nod to your place of origin? Gin, sweet and then dry vermouth, and orange juice, correct?"

"Never touch the stuff."

"Not sure what to say to that." Roosevelt finished with the ingredients, plunked in ice, shook. He poured himself a tall one. "People seem to almost admire Walker for that. Don't they? It's as if they see him as a modern-day Robin Hood, like they don't make the connection between their hard-earned tax dollar and the Tammany plunder."

"Maybe."

"Maybe, Egan?"

Egan kneaded the brim of his fedora. "In good times. But now things are changed. When people are hungry, they get angry."

"Sure they do. But who do they blame? Walker is still theirs. I don't think they'll abandon him anytime soon."

"That's my job now, isn't it? To turn the tide against their beloved mayor."

"I never asked you, Egan, why? I mean you come from there." It tickled him to no end to be using one of their own against them.

Egan donned and squared his hat. "One reason is that I think Tammany has lost its way. Like most successful people, they have become what they once hated—fat and happy."

"There's more to it than that, surely?"

Egan paused at the door, debated the telling. "You ever see a one-armed carpenter?"

"Not that I recall."

"My father, he was from the other side. He comes to the Bronx and he is so happy to be in a place where he can be his own man. He is a master craftsman, a real top-shelf finish guy. Works in the most beautiful, the richest homes in the city. The one thing he hates is a guy telling him what to do. You know how things work come Election Day. You're supposed to vote the star ticket all the way down, you're supposed to go along to get along. My father has a problem with that. They talk to him, they lean on him. But my father, he figures he did not leave one place to come to another where he is told what to do and when to do it. He votes how he likes. One day the district leader decides he better make an example out of Eddie Egan. They give him a beating, jump him right outside our building on Alexander Avenue. They break his right arm so bad the doctor has to amputate. One-armed carpenters don't do so well. What they do is drink themselves into the gutter and have their kids put on orphan trains."

Egan grabbed the door handle. "Does that explain a guy's motivation, Governor?"

"Quite satisfactorily, Captain."

Egan found his car and started the long drive back to the city. He took a flask from his glove box and tilted it back, pulling long on the Canadian whiskey. Roosevelt, what a character. Still, he did believe the man was going all the way, was going to be running the big show soon enough. Not a bad guy to have owing you a favor. If all went well they would both be replacing a Hoover come early 1933. Director of the Bureau of Investigation, now that had a nice sizzle to it.

Egan knew that if it happened he would have his dead brother to thank. Pete, a state trooper, had been Roosevelt's driver until he was killed in a car wreck just after dropping the Governor off for the night. FDR had quietly arranged a generous private pension for the family. At the funeral Egan had told him if there was anything he could do for him in the city, he'd be happy to. A year later, he came home from work to find the Governor sitting at his kitchen table on the East Side. The conversation had been blunt. Would he be willing to dig dirt on Tammany? Why the hell not?

Outside of Yonkers he stopped for gas. He thought about Farrell's one hundred thousand dollars in the trunk. It had taken him less than three minutes of sap work to get it from the clown who had picked it up and waltzed into a Cadillac showroom on West Fifty-seventh Street an hour later. He topped off the tank, checked the oil, kicked the tires just to be sure. Back on the highway he felt the wind in his face. He'd sit on the dough, another card up his sleeve.

G race entered the Corn Exchange Bank Trust Company on Fourth Avenue and sat in reception waiting for a manager to help her. Presently a man in a suit, smelling of talc and mouth rinse, extended his hand. Grace stood. Though the suit looked expensive, there was a stain on the right sleeve, another on the tie, mustard perhaps. He appeared to be holding himself together with a stiff effort. She wondered how badly they were faring what with the market crash. She introduced herself as Mrs. Francis Moran and explained that she and her husband had need of a safe-deposit account.

"Mr. Roland. I'm the account manager. I was told to expect you. Please come this way." He led her to a room beyond the tellers. The door was solid oak and he pushed it open, then closed it behind them. The furniture matched the door and she imagined it was cut from the same grove that outfitted the staterooms of swank ocean liners. The banker stood next to her for a moment, his eyes moving up and down her. He seemed to be doing it without any lecherous intent, as if appraising the worth of her clothes. She had dressed for her role in a long brown dress cut conservatively; she wore her hair in a bun but carried a small handbag stuffed with an amount of cash that would surely make this banker wonder.

"Please, sit. There are just some forms for you. A pity your husband couldn't make the trip with you."

"He's a busy man."

He indicated the chair by his desk and she sat, splaying her hand with the fake wedding ring she had taken to wearing on these banking missions, and he seemed to shift his manner, become more officious.

"Well, he's a lucky man as well."

Roland produced the two forms, one an application for the account and the other a beneficiary sheet should something happen to her or her husband of the day. She filled in the names and realized she had forgotten the address she was supposed to use. She looked up, smiled. "I'm sorry. Can I use the ladies' room?"

He said nothing but lifted his right arm and pointed to a door in the corner of his office. Inside, she ran the faucet and pulled a stack of bills from her purse with a piece of paper strapped to it, read the address, and washed her hands. She waited a moment and flushed the toilet. Back at the desk she completed the forms while Roland stared out the window onto the street. When she was finished she had to call his name twice before he turned back to her and led her to the safe-deposit area. He pulled open her box, laid it open on the table. "Here you go, Mrs. . . . ?"

"Moran."

"Moran. Right. I hear Ireland is a lovely spot, despite all your troubles."

"Ah, it's grand, Mr. Roland."

"I hope you and Mr. Moran continue to prosper in these times."

He handed her a key and then retreated with a nod. Grace took the bills from her purse and dropped them in the box. She stared down at a fat green pile of dirty money and wondered at its origin. She riffled through the stack with her thumb and fought the urge to take a quarter inch off the top and put it back in her purse. She was seeing so much money these days. Could she ever just take it all and run? So much of her life was lived on the margins of poverty, it was easy to imagine this being the one chance to make a score. Johnny Farrell would tire of her one day and then where would she be? She felt a quiver of fear and looked around the small airless chamber. Of course, she was alone. She locked the box and left the room. Out on the street, she took a deep breath and walked south, squinting against the midday glare as she angled her way through the lunchtime crowd. New York had made her many things, but she was not a thief, not even when it came to stolen money. Still, she would hedge her bets. From now on she was going to keep a little journal, a diary of her banking duties—an account of their illicit accounting.

Needing to pound something before going home, Briody stopped at Gus's gym on Willis Avenue. A crowd around the main ring had gathered where a young heavyweight from up Fordham Road sparred with the hulking Italian contender, Primo Carnera. The younger man, also big even for a heavyweight, did not know how to move. The Italian strongman looped overhand rights like a bar fighter looking to get lucky. Briody was stunned by their lack of skill, but then a haymaker landed with a noise like a dead man dropped onto the pavement and the novice went down like he was trying to catch up with that sound. A whoop went up from the assembled fight fans and hangers-on—men in thin suits out of work and out of prospects who came to the gym because they were sick of staring at the walls in their furnished rooms. The pigeons, Gus called them. They pressed against the ropes to examine the fallen boxer's pain up close, to see someone having a worse day than they were, while Carnera retreated to his corner and spit blood into a bucket.

"Come on, Mike. Get ready, you can move around with him." Gus was at his elbow, a cotton swab tucked behind his ear. His breath was sweet with the dark rum he sipped throughout the day, but his eyes were clear, his voice firm. "Just gotta move and stick with this guy, move and stick."

The dressing room was five rows of wooden benches aligned with a dozen or so gunmetal lockers. All the chlorine that was splashed over the place daily could not hide the stink of sweat, and more. Before the gym, the building had housed an abattoir, and as Briody pulled off his dusty clothes, still damp with sweat from the ironwork, he tried to shake the feeling of death about the place, the images of bloodletting and primordial terror. He piled the dirty clothes in his locker and stood naked on the icy concrete, then pulled on shorts, laced up his boxing boots, and yanked a sweatshirt over his head. Three featherweights spawned in nearby tenements burst into the room like quicksilver. They roughhoused and laughed. One sported a grotesque shiner that had turned the color of a rotting banana.

Ringside, Gus taped his hands and helped him into gloves, lacing fast and sure. He pulled a worn and smelly leather headgear tight and fastened the strap until the brass buckle bit into Briody's chin. He stuck the mouthpiece in, smeared Vaseline over Briody's nose, cheeks, and brow. "Like I says. Move and stick, this palooka." Clearly there was some history here, a grudge festering. Unsure what that might be, Briody nodded, leapt to the ring apron, and ducked through the ropes, moving left, right, shaking his arms, snapping his head, getting loose. Carnera stood and watched him, disinterested. The bell rang.

Carnera stalked straight ahead, unwavering, his huge arms cocked up at the elbows, chin tucked in between the gloves, his head like a fat pumpkin. His first punch was one of those ugly rights and Briody glided away from it, sticking a jab that caught the Italian giant on the end of his nose. Carnera was like a truckload of bricks moving down an embankment. All you needed to do was stay out of the way. Briody moved and stuck repeatedly, presenting angles, offering no real target. Occasionally Carnera trapped him against the ropes, and then Briody felt the weight of him, his flesh hot and wet.

In round two Carnera pulled back and Briody weaved left, and then moved laterally in an attempt to come up and land a right to the side of that massive head. But he walked into it—a punch of unknown origin, one that lifted him up onto his toes and filled his head with hot white air and noise, then a flickering of darkness and light. He crouched and threw several weak blows until the darkness passed and then he buried his face in Carnera's chest, trying to wrap his arms around that bear of a man.

Carnera smacked him hard behind his ears—cheap shots, he dimly heard Gus yelling from ringside. Briody pushed off, angry now, things on the edges still a little blurry, like seeing life through a rainy window. He feinted and when the palooka went for it he landed a perfect three-punch combo—jab—straight right—a crushing left hook. The blows stopped Carnera and stood him up straight and dopey, his hands coming down. Briody ripped three more to the belly, each one shooting for the spine, each one intent on crushing organs. Carnera bent over him, a weight on his shoulders, his breath ragged. They were wrestling now. Briody tried to squirm away, but the lummox would not let go.

Somebody barked, "Time." Briody pulled back, his hands in the air. The Italian stumbled forward, sweat rolling off him. Blood dripped from his broken lips, splattered softly on the canvas. Briody heard sharp, murderous words and looked to the corner. A man dressed in a gray suit, his fedora pulled down to shade his eyes, had Gus backed against the ring apron, and was jabbing his finger like a man shooting a pistol. Briody could tell by the way Gus was bent back away from his accuser that he was very scared of the man dressing him down.

Briody moved around the ring, shaking out his arms and legs, the stickiness clearing from his mind. The man with the fedora finished with Gus and tilted his head up and stared at him. His shoulders were slight, and he was not very tall at all, but there was real power in that face, a dark force that would not be denied. The man spun and was trailed out the door by six of the biggest, ugliest men Briody had ever seen.

Briody left the ring and let Gus unlace his gloves. The sweat poured from him. Gus was still muttering, "These goddamn racket creeps. They think everything is for sale." Gus snatched off his headgear. Briody sat and began to peel the tape off his fists.

When he looked up Tough Tommy Touhey, the local ganglord and hot-wired owner of the Four Provinces, was heading for him. Briody had not noticed he was there. Touhey was thirty years old and built like the light heavyweight fighter he once was. His snap-brim fedora was cocked just so.

"You sure know how to pick the wrong guy to piss off."

Briody looked up at him. "Who? The big Italian?"

"You wish." Touhey tipped his hat off and twirled it on his finger. His hair was golden blond and slicked back hard. His eyes were the bluest Briody had ever seen. They brought to mind the glacial lakes he'd seen in Kerry, cold and unfathomable. "Case you didn't know, that was Owney Madden, the Killer. Racket king of Manhattan."

Briody shrugged. "Wasn't him I was punching."

"No, only his latest meal ticket." Touhey sat next to him and placed his hat on his knee. "You see, your buddy Gus, he takes all this serious. It's lots of things to him. It's a calling, an art form, a way of life. Some type of warrior code. He puts as much time into working with you or a mutt off the street as he does a hot pro prospect. Why? He doesn't like money, doesn't want money. It sullies his great love. Now, Owney, the Killer? To him money is all it is. Entertainment designed to make him more of what he already has a lot of. He thinks two men fighting in a ring is stupid unless everyone gets paid. Knowing Owney, he thinks doing anything without getting paid is stupid."

"That's a wonderful philosophy on life. But it has nothing to do with me, so. I'm just a fella looking for some exercise." Briody unwrapped his hands, flexed his fingers. The sweat was cooling on him; his shoulders were heavy from the day's work and the sparring, but he felt great, strong and alive. He wondered what Touhey wanted. He always got the feeling the man was analyzing him, sizing him up for some task yet unnamed. He always spoke about motivations, that if he knew what yours were he had you solved like a puzzle and could bend you to his will. Briody figured it was what made him different from the Maddens and the Schultzes and the other racket guys he had come into casual contact with. With them it was terror, stark fear of grisly endings. Not that Touhey was a slouch in the mayhem department. His body count was the subject of rumor and whisper. But those other guys were small men who wanted you to know they were tougher than you were. Touhey already believed that about himself. What he wanted you to know was that he could outsmart you too.

"How'd you like to fight at the Garden?"

Briody laughed. "Headlining will I be?"

Touhey was a fixture at the gym, was said to own it as he did most enterprises in the neighborhood. He controlled some of the more promising young fighters as well as a stable of journeymen willing to take dives for a few bucks. He had them all, all the ones running from something: blacks up from the cotton fields, bohunks tired of the gut-slick killing floors, thick-necked Polacks who had mined enough anthracite, wiry street Jews, Mick and guinea gutter fighters looking for a score, ocelot-quick island boys. All the hard young men who thought taking a beating for some coin was a step up in life. Touhey parceled out hope to them until the obvious became obvious. The odd one made a nice run of it, maybe headlined a bill at the Garden and took a walloping from a champ. The rest he set up in jobs. Some he made cabdrivers, some he sent down to building sites, others went to the warehouses in Mott Haven. Some became his sappers and shooters, his garrote and ice pick men. They all had nice things to say about Tough Tommy Touhey.

"I'm serious. They're throwing a benefit for the NYPD Widows and Orphans Fund. Fighting the Boston cops. We'll bring you in as a ringer. The Garden, great place to fight. The crowd—a thing like this, it's just like a championship bout."

In the ring, Gus goaded two of the featherweights into pummeling each other. Touhey nodded toward the ring. "Looks like they hate each other, right?"

"It's boxing," Briody said, considering how to say no to the man.

"Well, they ought to. They're brothers. Nobody hates like brothers." He put his hand on Briody's shoulder. "What do you say? I'm only asking 'cause I'm a little light on heavyweights, these days. These kids don't get enough to eat, stunts their growth."

"Work's got me pretty worn out."

Touhey laughed. It was loud and genuine laughter, full of charm and good humor. Boxers paused to glance over. "You don't really want me to solve that for you, do you?" Touhey moved right past the threat, as if he had not actually voiced it. "It's a nice thing, for a good cause. I know you don't want to let the widows and orphans down."

Briody stood. He and Touhey were eye to eye. Two big men who could handle themselves, get things done. "Sure thing, Tommy. Just give me the details."

Touhey stepped back and cocked his fist, grinned. "Thatta boy."

Briody went to his locker, stripped, and stayed for a good long while under the steaming hot shower. Why not fight? It was just a smoker, three rounds. Touhey was the kind of guy that liked to have his hooks in everyone and everything. Briody figured as long as he kept them from getting in too deep, what was the harm?

As soon as he walked in the door the Casey kids were on him, a swirl of arms and legs and shaved heads as pale and spare as the bleached skulls he'd seen in surrendered enemy trenches. Briody fought off that image and grabbed as many of the children in his arms as he could and lifted them squealing. "Where'd you get those fancy haircuts?" He put them down and rubbed their heads one at a time as if for good luck.

"We got the cooties."

"Is that so? Are you going to give them to me?"

Briody joined Maggie, who sat at the kitchen table plucking a chicken with such speed that her hands were a blur. Feathers drifted in the air around her and every time one of the kids ran by they would spin into miniature twisters of down. "Instructions came from the school nurse. Head lice. A whole building full of baldies. Happens at least once a year since we come to this country."

The children scurried back to the radio in the living room and huddled over its glow, six clean pates mesmerized by murmur.

"Where's yer man?"

"Is that a trick question?" She was tired, drawn, but managed real warmth for him. Briody slipped her a twenty and she took it, avoiding his eyes. The back of her hand was splotched and red from bleach. Though his age, she seemed a generation older than when he knew her in Kerry. The money was a secret bond between them. Most afternoons she scrubbed floors for the doctors on Alexander Avenue, usually having to drag a few of the kids along. Casey hated the fact that his wife had to work, and would never accept a hand-out. Briody rented a room from them and what with the steady work was glad to overpay. In the year he had been in this country, he had eaten nearly every dinner at the cramped Casey table. He had arrived with pennies in his pocket and Maggie never once com-plained about another mouth to feed, so once he started work he made sure to compensate. He put his hand on her shoulder.

"He might surprise you one day."

"Nah." She waved him away. "He's too busy plotting the glori-ous revolution that's going to break us free of our shackles and our worries. The sewers will run with honey. Heaven right here on earth when he and his comrades rise up. Meanwhile, we're lucky to eat anything but slop. Do me a favor, Michael. Go down and drag him out before I do."

He bounded down the stairs, past Mr. Daly on the second-floor landing. The old man, a retired sandhog, stood bent at the waist, gasping for air, his hand, large and knobby, gripping the banister. Without looking up he managed a "Michael" in greeting and Briody patted his back and passed on, knowing to leave it at that. The tunnel work had filled Daly's lungs with death, but he wanted no sympathy.

The night had fallen and was cool. On 138th Street he walked past rows of brown brick buildings with the storefronts dark. Up above people hung out of windows hollering, it seemed, for the sake of hearing themselves. The side of his face was starting to swell from Carnera's uppercut and he could taste a coppery trickle of blood in his throat. Fat Walsh the beat cop was leaning against the drugstore window tapping his club on his thigh.

Unlike the ones downtown, many of the faces here brought to mind Cavan and the countryside of Ireland. These were the Irish who had fought and lost, who had left the isle because they had to, not because they wanted to, the great republican exodus after a dirty civil war. Here in America they dreamed of an Ireland united, at peace, and conspired to achieve it. Though Briody figured that most would never see the place again. They had left before the Free State had started to solidify, before so many of their old comrades had compromised. He did not have their belief that it was just ahead of them. He knew in his heart that the dream was receding, the fight getting harder as the days piled up. He kept this to himself. He figured most of them would die in this new strange place and be buried far from the vales of their youth. Still, he was committed to the fight. It was why he was here.

He ducked past Mannion the bouncer into the Four Provinces. The place was slower than usual and those at the bar watched a pig dart about chasing pickled eggs the men threw. Flags hung from the ceiling and there were paintings of Ireland, poor smudgy oils done probably by lost patrons. Black-and-white photographs of Easter Sunday, of Al Smith on the campaign trail, of Jimmy Walker leading a parade up Broadway and many of the Yankees and Irish footballers and hurlers. Being tall, Briody noticed that not much above eye level ever got dusted.

Briody indicated the pig. "New customer, Mr. Casey?"

"Fits right in, he does."

"Another Free Stater."

"Saturday night is going to be greased pig night now. They slick him up and pay ten dollars to the man who can capture him. This is just a training run, see how evasive he is."

"And the pig?"

"Oh, you get him too. Plenty of rashers for the victorious."

"Sounds like quite the night out."

"An emissary from her highness, I presume?"

"Correct. You see the wee ones?"

Casey's eyes flashed, but he forced a rueful smile. "The land of opportunity. No need the vermin should be excluded. Have a seat."

"She's in a state." Briody knew Casey would sit there all night if he could. Not for the drink so much as the conspiratorial company. Between trying to organize the transit workers into a union and running guns to the lads back home, Casey was up to his eyeballs in clandestine activity.

Briody accepted a glass of beer. Casey leaned in and said, "A shipment's going on Thursday night. I'll need you to make the move around ten." He ran his finger along the side of the mug.

"Back in business. Good. I've been getting awful antsy." Briody sipped his beer. There was no question involved. Casey had arranged for his safe passage to the States and Tough Tommy Touhey, who supplied the ordnance, had set him up with the iron-workers union. He felt a nervous flutter in his stomach and was glad for it. He had been inactive, his last gun run had been before Christmas. He was anxious for action.

"Thursday will be grand." He raised his glass and looked Casey in the eye. "Up the Republic."

Casey raised his glass. "Up and away, all right."

"Your man came by the gym today, put the arm on me to fight down the Garden. Benefiting widows and orphans."

Casey was quiet for a moment. "Did you say?"

"He reminded me of my employment status."

"Never a bad thing, raising of money for widows and orphans. Is it? We do plenty of it ourselves, Michael."

"Might be a lark, boxing in a place as big as the Garden." He knew that Casey felt he needed Touhey because Touhey helped the cause. It was only natural Touhey then needed Casey to do something in return. Briody finished his drink. His own needs, he knew, were not really of concern to anyone right now.

As they walked back to the apartment, Briody ducked into the candy store just as it was closing and bought a bag of sweets for the kids.

"You'll spoil them to death, Mikey."

"Thank God I can even attempt to."

"God and Tough Tommy Touhey."

"That's what I'm afraid of," Briody said.

They turned onto Park Avenue and made their way uptown, gliding along in the Manhattan dusk. Grace settled into the lush leather seats and let Farrell massage her thigh. She had barely eaten all day and was looking forward to a big, outrageous meal.

"Hungry?"

"Could eat like a pack of wolves."

"One of the things I like about you Grace, you don't eat dainty."

"The other things?"

"Too long a list."

They stopped in front of Jack and Charlie's "21," outside of which stood a doorman with happy eyes who waved them right through the door with a hardy hello for Johnny. A buxom girl with long red hair checked their coats and Grace noticed that Farrell handed over his case as well. She wondered if it was stuffed with cash money this night. Farrell put a hand to her elbow and steered her toward the interior. She liked the clubbiness of the place, the dark wood, admired a George Bellows painting of two fighters exchanging blows that hung on the wall next to the stairs. Johnny glad-handed his way along the dark red carpet toward the back bar. Ceiling fans circulated air that was hazy with cigar and pipe smoke smelling like cherrywood. Something about the place spoke of deals being cut, of money.

Farrell introduced her to several notables, a coked-up chorus girl, a gambler of dark renown, a former police commissioner. Babe Ruth, the ballplayer, was expansively drunk and had cornered a petite socialite who seemed charmed by the mauling attention. As she sipped a sour cocktail, Johnny held a conference of whispers with a writer from the *Daily News*. He spun away and embraced a West Side district leader, all the while tossing off nods and waves to passersby, occasionally reaching to shake a hand, squeeze a shoulder. There was a glow about him, the ease of a man well on his way, who reveled in the charged air of the place, the rush and swell.

She excused herself and climbed the stairs to the ladies' room, cursing her high heels. She fixed her makeup, used the toilet. When she came out two women who appeared to be sisters were slapping and clawing at each other, screaming about a man. Grace saw blood, sidestepped the mayhem, and made her way back to Farrell's side, lacing her arm through his as he guided her to a corner table. He sat with his back to the wall. She sat by his side.

The food was rich, heavy: gamy meats from Adirondack hunting forays, vegetables dripping in cheese sauce. Farrell ordered two bottles of the best Châteauneuf-du-Pape. Grace matched him bite for bite, swill for swill. Farrell was in good cheer. He regaled her with saucy tales about other patrons. "That guy over there, the brown suit, the bald guy?"

Grace looked and nodded, her mouth full.

"State senator from the Upper East Side, loves plump house-boys. Goes through them like most men go through socks. That little fellow over there? Jockey drug fiend. He'll fix any race for a snootful of cocaine. At that far table, the starlet? I'm sure you know her. Four failed suicides to date. How miserable can you be? And the guy whose ear she's licking? He's a novelist, so called. His wife actually churns out his potboilers." Farrell signaled the waiter for another bottle of wine by lifting the empty slightly off the table.

"You keep quite a catalogue of weaknesses, don't you, Farrell?"

"You kidding me? In this town that stuff is money in the bank. Solid gold."

She watched as Babe Ruth entered the dining room and stood looking as if a jungle king over his domain; his eyes were hooded, his head was large, his arms hung low. Apparently he'd lost his so-cialite. Hulking, a menacing presence, more gangster in appearance than any of the dozens of racketeers she saw all the time when out with Johnny. Despite Ruth's finery, there was still something very much of the gutter fighter about him. He stood for a minute, then something, sadness, or a deep disappointment she did not expect, crossed over his countenance and he turned and walked out. He seemed lost. Johnny had mentioned once that Ruth had been an or-phan. She thought this was easy to believe.

"How's the vittles?"

She spoke with her mouth full. "The best, Johnny. Aces."

With a flick of his wrist he summoned the waiter, who whisked away his empty plate and was back in a flash with cognacs. He leaned to her, careful to keep his elbows off the table. "You don't have a problem making those drops, do you?"

She shook her head. "Easy money, Johnny. You'll spoil me." In-deed, she had already made three drops that week, three hundred dollars—crazy money. Somehow it made her feel less the whore. At least she did something for his cash.

"Well, I'll probably be keeping you busy for a while. They'll be trips a little farther afield, too. Time to time."

"Best work I ever found." She felt safe enough. She did not figure she had much to worry about while working as Farrell's courier. Her Johnny was wired into the top. She sipped her cognac, felt its smoky bite on her throat. She wondered if this might lead to something, if there was a bigger score in it for her—something that would set her up for years to come—something she might fall back on. "I'm your girl, Johnny."

After quite a few drinks a man came and stopped at their table, his eyes lingering on her breasts as he shook Farrell's hand. Grace knew him from her cigarette-girl days—the Judge. His hair was parted in the middle and plastered down to his skull. His nose looked like it belonged on one of those Roman coins and his skin was burnished from the sun. Only the puffiness around his eyes betrayed his wantonness. He had bedded more than a few of her colleagues and possessed a certain sexual renown.

"Johnny Farrell. How's the pride of Mott Haven these days?"

"Judge Crater. Never better, Judge. Where'd you get the suntan?"

"Stole a week in Palm Beach. Rode the Limited. Encountered quite a few of your friends on the way down, not to mention back up, as well."

"Some guys have all the luck. Do you know Grace Masterson here?"

"I don't believe I do. Sorry to say."

He sat and proffered his hand and Grace obliged him. He held her hand a little longer than he should have.

"I envy you, Johnny. All seems well with you."

"I have some people that need to see you, Judge."

Grace felt the power shift, Farrell pulling rank now, taking control.

"Well, Johnny. That's our, well, arrangement." The Judge smiled like a man trying to sell a used appliance.

"They'll expect to come away happy. They'll expect to get what they want."

"I am not averse to this."

"They won't be denied."

The Judge leaned back in his chair. He looked about the room. He regarded his empty glass. All he said was "Fine."

"And Judge? This Vitale thing? You need to be careful. Lowly magistrates one day, Supreme Court judges the next. Our enemies will be snooping around, trying for leverage. Use caution."

"I was bred for caution, Johnny. It's a hallmark of my faith."

Johnny stood, a smile, a chuckle. "Jeez, it is always good to see you, Judge. Always."

Crater stood and nodded at Grace. "Pleasure to meet you." As he shook Farrell's hand he said, "Just tell them, Not in my chambers. Please. It is unseemly."

"No problem, Judge. Not at all. We can't have unseemly. Unseemly, no, never."

Farrell watched him weave through the crowd. After a time he said quietly, "I own that man."

Later, after more to drink, Farrell helped her into her coat. As they passed into the cool night, she noticed he had not retrieved the satchel. She ducked into the waiting car wondering just what she had gotten herself into.

On Friday mornings the men were handed numbered aluminum pay tickets with their brass ID checks. Briody waited in line, took his from the paymaster, slipped it into his pocket, and went to work. The frame was up in the air now. Sheehan was rattling on as Delpezzo and Armstrong stared glumly over the tangle of materials that were constantly dropped at the site. Sheehan showed up every morning fully alert, wired like a man halfway through his day, while the others were still trying to shrug off the night's sleep. "Ten million bricks, boy. Ten million. I was talking to my engineer cousin. This ain't just another skyscraper. It's the eighth wonder of the world. We'll be able to see six states from the top, you believe the press releases."

Briody bent and tied his work boots. He had slept poorly and fatigue settled as a dull ache behind his eyes. He took the spud wrench off his belt and scraped the dried muck from the sides of his shoes. A biting wind swirled down across the site, blowing refuse in small spirals.

He stood and said, "It's a bitter wind."

"No kidding, this is crazy weather so late."

Armstrong tightened his work belt. "Where in Ireland you say you're from?"

Briody stared at him. Armstrong had lightened up on him lately, but he was wondering where this might lead. He noticed Sheehan edge closer, ever ready to make peace. "Cavan."

Armstrong nodded as if he knew where it was. "Where's that at?"

"In Ulster."

"Oh, the English part."

"No, England is in England."

"Whatever you say. I'm part Scotch Irish on my father's side, German and English on my mother's. Pure American though."

Briody took an apple from his pocket and rubbed it along the side of his pants to warm it. He bit into the fruit and while chewing said, "Pure American."

"That's me, through and through. I got nothing against you guys coming in though. Keeps the niggers in their places. Least youse speak English."

"Glad to be of good use."

Delpezzo rolled his eyes. Sheehan laughed out loud.

"Hey, you think I'm kidding. Those bastards are scabs at heart. They come in and work for a dollar a day they had half a chance. They live like animals."

Briody smiled and nodded his head. The complexities of American tribalism still baffled him. The work bell tolled and he tossed the other apple to Armstrong, who said, "Come on. Let's get set up."

Armstrong put his fingers to his teeth and let out a shrill whistle. Delpezzo and Skinny Sheehan chose the elevator. Boardman, the rigger, worked a cable around the crossbeam and hooked it to the crane. "All right fellas, the express is leaving." Briody and Armstrong stood on the steel, holding on to the cable as they rose up above Thirty-fourth Street in the wind, twisting slightly from left to right as they climbed. Briody felt the sluggishness leave him just as it always did when work began. He felt blood pump through his veins, warming his muscles. He slid a hand down the cable and was stabbed by a loose strand. He turned the palm up and saw a small dark bubble of blood rise. As he stepped off the beam onto the fifth-floor setback he sucked the blood from the wound. He put his gloves on.

The four elevators, which had been salvaged from the old Waldorf-Astoria to ferry men, arrived on the floor in quick succession, each with its own distinct screech of metal, like the separate howls of dogs. The gangs spilled out and moved with ease over the scattered materials to their workstations, their tool belts clacking at their waists. The looming escape of the weekend lightened their steps. Briody was looking forward to the time off. He'd made no plans, anticipated having a beer at the end of his shift and sleeping in for two days, taking a long leisurely run on Sunday.

He crossed the site to the tool shanty and fell into line with the men getting their equipment for the day. He gathered a rivet gun and ran a pneumatic hose from it to the generator, checking to make sure it was secure. Gun over his shoulder, he scrambled up the temporary scaffold, straightened up, and took in the view, which changed every day as their labor took them skyward. Today the sun cut through gunmetal clouds and caught the new stainless steel spire of the Chrysler Building eight blocks north, lighting it like a newborn star.

Skinny Sheehan pulled himself onto the deck with a grunt and said, "Jesus, will you look at that. There has never been a building that looked like that."

Briody nodded, "It's a sight, all right."

Briody smelled the burning coals and knew it was time to work. He brought the rivet gun into line and pounded the bolt to station. Soon he was caught in the frenetic rhythms of the workday. Rivet after rivet after rivet was melded to the steel as they moved along, forming an assembly line in which the workers moved, not the product. Armstrong shouted, urging them to greater speed. In the fleeting instants between rivets, Briody watched down below his feet as an endless line of trucks disgorged material onto the site, each roaring off empty to return to plants and warehouses and river barges.

The men smoked quietly at coffee break. Trucks still came and went like clockwork, belching smoke, grinding gears. Sheehan pointed to the lineup. "There's gonna be five hundred a day when this job's going full tilt."

Briody laughed. "I doubt there's five hundred trucks in all of Ireland."

Delpezzo sipped black coffee he poured from a thermos. "Where the hell's all this stuff coming from?"

"Right from the piers. Steel goes from Pittsburgh to Jersey by rail, then they load it on barges and float it up to the docks, drop it on these trucks, and shoot right across town. Piece of cake."

Horns blew beneath them, shouts floated up, the clank of steel being lowered fast to the ground where it rarely stayed for more than a few minutes. The labor of the construction gangs was the end result of dozens of processes: of mountains scraped of pig iron, of mines stripped of anthracite, of granite blasted and quarried, timber felled, mud baked into brick, copper squeezed and shaped into tubing, cinders crushed into blocks, silica fired into window glass. They wielded their tools, transforming the raw into finished, participating in the great industrial frenzy of America that conspired to raise this building into the New York sky. Here, at the end point in this convergence of muscle and material and technology, they worked as hard as they could, moving ever higher.

"The idea is to make sure we ain't never standing for a second, doing nothing."

"The way it should be. Day drags, you don't stay busy." Armstrong slipped on his gloves.

They watched as one of the checkers, a slim young man of twenty wearing a skinny tie, approached, carrying a clipboard. He cleared his throat and looked away when he said, "Gentlemen, your ID checks please." Briody, Delpezzo, and Sheehan dutifully reached into their pockets and presented their brass tags, each stamped with a number. It was a twice-a-day ritual to prevent gold-bricking and ghost jobs and they were well used to it. Armstrong ignored the checker, smoked deeply from his cigarette.

"And you, sir?" The checker looked at Armstrong's chest, not sure enough to make eye contact.

"What, kid?"

"Your check, please." It came out as a whine.

"You some kind of apprentice pencil?"

The kid started smacking his lips. The sun cleared the clouds and the harsh light forced him to put a hand up for shade. "I'm, I'm only doing what they tell me to do."

"Scram, pencil. The name's Armstrong, you got a problem, run it by the super. Everyone in this business knows who I am. I ain't about to prove it to you, ya company rat."

The checker flushed red and turned to the other three. Sheehan shrugged and waved him off. "You're better off moving on, kid. We vouch for him."

Briody bit his tongue, but Armstrong's bullying did not sit well with him. They bent and picked up their tools. They were in a race with the other gangs. Who could throw up the most steel in a day, a week, in a month? There was competition now and they held their own against the best gangs: against Hope, the storied Norwegian and his cousins, against a crew of wiry Calabrese, against Hard Nose McCabe's own handpicked gangs, many of whom were Newfoundlanders referred to as fish. There was even a gang of Mohawks who had learned their craft during the raising of Adirondack bridges. On Monday mornings every ironworker put two dollars into a pool to be paid to the winning gang on payday. All of them strained to be the best, for even as the men worked they knew this one was different and they shared a reverence for the project and their complicity in it. In the beer halls and speakeasies ironworkers from other jobs, or from no jobs at all, regarded them with jealousy and awe. Even the youngest among them knew that they would look back decades from now and say, "I built that," and if they did nothing else of note in their lives it was more than most people could claim.

The other crafts chased them into the sky. Some days the ironworkers worked so efficiently they seemed to be dragging the rest of the trades upward with them. On others the wire lathers and concrete workers were clicking, placing so much mud so quickly they were nipping at the ankles of the steel men. Then the others came behind them, the cement finishers and carpenters and masons and electricians and tile men and asbestos workers and tin knockers and steamfitters and plumbers and painters, sucking the sheer mass skyward, creating a relentless momentum.

Briody steadied his legs and back and torso and arms and clenched his jaw against the rattle of the pneumatic gun. His muscles were fluid one second with movement, static the next to drive the rivet home, a contracting and easing of his brawn that over the weeks had become as regular as breathing. The gang moved in perfect sync as four parts of one whole, advancing nonstop from beam to column to beam. The sun was out now, overhead and hot. The morning chill was gone. Sweat poured down their backs. Briody watched their rivet punk walk along a beam with a burlap bag full of bolts slung over his shoulder, his hat askance. He was seventeen and glided along the six-inch-wide crossbeam with the assurance of the oblivious.

Suddenly, as on all good days, it was noon. They ate sandwiches and drank bottles of near beer. The company was building canteens on various floors to avoid the logistics of hundreds of men going off-site for lunch, but for now most of the ironworkers lunch-pailed it and ate on the sidewalks outside the building. Armstrong's gang stayed up top on a crossbeam, legs dangling. Soon they would be higher than all the surrounding structures, up alone in the air. They waved at the office workers who filled the windows across the avenue. In one, a solitary figure raised her shirt, unhooked her brassiere, and pressed her fat white tits against the glass, keeping her face hidden behind a shade. The men shouted approval in half a dozen languages, then clapped for an encore, but none was forthcoming.

"Look at that wacky broad."

"Crazy dame. I was working on lower Broadway when they had that parade for Lindbergh."

"Who?" Briody enjoyed playing the stupid immigrant around Armstrong. He took off his porkpie hat and poured some water onto a bandanna and draped it around his neck. Sweat cooled on his back.

"You're kidding me, right? The pilot. Biggest parade they ever had."

Delpezzo nodded. "I was a rivet punk on the job."

"You're still a rivet punk."

"Go screw."

"We all sat on beams and watched the man pass right beneath us through more ticker tape than you can imagine. Broadway and Wall. It was like trying to see through a blizzard, or a cloud. The broads were crazy for that flyboy. They were throwing their underwears at him. I was spitting down on the heads of all the swells when they went by."

Delpezzo opened a jar of marinated artichoke hearts and offered them around. He found no takers and began eating them with his sooty fingers, olive oil dripping off into space.

"How can you eat that crap?" Armstrong was up and pacing back and forth.

Sheehan produced a folding knife and began trimming his fingernails. "I saw Jack May at my sister's yesterday. Says they got no jobs coming in at all, says this is it and we should all slow it down. We'll be eating pigeon for Thanksgiving, 'stead of turkey. I agree with him."

"Yeah, you would, you Red. I'm surprised you wasn't down at Union Square getting your head smacked with the rest of the commies the other day."

"I'm a socialist."

"Commie pinko, pure and simple."

"You'll change your tune when you're standing on a breadline, maybe selling apples to feed your kids."

"I'll always find work. Besides, I ain't got no kids."

"You sure?" Delpezzo thrust his jar around again.

Across the way, Miss Tits was at it again. Sheehan said, "Armstrong, tell your sister to quit teasing us."

Briody took an artichoke heart and held it between his thumb and forefinger, examining it as a jeweler might a gem. He bit into it with caution but found he liked the savory flavor and the texture of it. Delpezzo stood over him, awaiting approval. "Not bad, right?"

Briody swallowed and reached for another. "Not at all."

"Watch it, Paddy, you'll end up half a dago, eating that crap."

Hard Nose came along carrying a cup of coffee. "Let's go boys, my money's on you. Don't disappoint me. You too, Irish." He slapped Briody's back as he passed.

Briody wiped olive oil on his pants and hopped back to work. He did not mind Hard Nose calling him Irish. In America, at least on the job site and up at Mott Haven, his Irishness was seen as an asset. It had been different in England, where he'd spent several years working on the buildings, lying low while awaiting a call to action. There was open disdain in London for the immigrant Irish, so he'd kept in the shadows, cultivated blandness, strove to pass unnoticed, nursing his wounds and grudges in private. His service in the English army might easily have gained him some respect, but he never revealed it. He was not there to make a life. He was a weapon to be summoned when the time was right.

"Mikey, give me a hand." Sheehan had hold of a ten-foot plank and Briody grabbed the other end. They banged together a brace that hung over the edge of the building so they would have something to stand on while driving the rivets. When it was done Briody stepped onto it, holding the column while testing its strength. Satisfied, he picked up his gun and the rivets flew.

His hunger strike had lent him renown in the movement. He was chosen to lead a cell of six men. They had some success in acquiring weapons—rifles from Russia, volatile gelignite from a contact in Belgium, a sporadic supply from America. Missions were planned with escape routes and maps, dark strikes at the heart of the empire. But they were in disarray, riddled with spies, dazed and beaten from fighting not just the British but the Irish Free Staters as well. Petty power struggles distracted them from their objectives. The Special Branch leaned hard.

He kept moving, changed names, sought refuge in the back rooms and basements of sympathizers. They blew up a rail bridge, managed to shoot two soldiers outside a barracks. They stole rifles, robbed a bank. One day when he was returning to the safe house he watched as two comrades were dragged down the steps of the building and beaten. Briody pulled his hat snug and passed unnoticed, close enough to hear the pleas of the men as they were pistol-whipped. He kept walking all the way to the rail station where he had stored some clothes and a forged U.S. passport. He boarded a train to Liverpool, then crossed the Atlantic in steerage, nine days of storms and sickness, wondering about the fate of his friends. Later, he learned one had died in custody, bleeding to death from a ruptured spleen.

Casey met him at the Hell's Kitchen docks and took him to the Bronx. It was a happy reunion, and after a long beery dinner Casey described their activities in the city, mostly procurement and reprisals against British agents and Free State spies. Briody's war would never end.

A derrick man guided the I beam into place. Briody watched the connecting gang rise up the column, like monkeys going up a tree. He remembered the long stretches, the Curragh POW camp, the relentless damp, and then the crushing grayness of Mountjoy prison, a place that seemed designed to kill the spirit, the so-called food, the cruelty and indifference of the screws, who liked to deprive the prisoners of everything from letters to cigarettes to laundry. And the clergy who refused them the sacraments because they would not denounce the movement as if the Bishop could deny Christ his followers. And finally the hunger strike. Forty-three days.

It began with determination, the highest sense of devotion to a cause, and once the pains of hunger ceased it was endless days of low-level delirium, of resolve that manifested itself so he endured while all the others faltered. His own death became a reality, something he was determined to use if it might break the will of their enemies. But then the command buckled, the strike was called off. They won nothing. His months of recovery were far more difficult. He had to learn to eat and to walk and to shit and to live while his body was born again.

Here above Manhattan it was easy to feel as if all that had happened not to him but to a lost acquaintance. That part of his life seemed so remote here in the bright blue sky over America. He slid down a secured column and moved to the next station. He wondered if he could bear any more prison time.

Briody waited with his crew as the paymaster, joined by two

armed guards, sorted through the envelopes. "Armstrong, Briody, Delpezzo, Sheehan. Here you go boys, spend it wisely. Save a few bucks for the family," he said, taking an aluminum ticket from each man in exchange for his pay. He turned and the men with guns stepped gingerly over beams and tools, following him across to the next gang.

Armstrong tore open his envelope, kissed the bills. "Tonight, I'm going to make this pile grow like magic."

"A fool and his money."

"No, no, you rats, don't jinx me now. Tonight's the night. I can taste it."

When the whistle sounded the carpenters arrived and slapped together gaming tables out of plywood and two-by-fours. Green felt was glued down. A roulette wheel was taken from a gang box, set up, and spun. Dealers donned eyeshades and stacked cards for poker. Barrels of beer secreted in fifty-five-gallon drums were rolled up on the narrow-gauge rail that ran through each floor, a daytime conduit for brick and block, steel, heating pipe, and insulation, concrete, mortar, and now a delivery system for booze.

"A casino with a view." Armstrong had traded his entire pay packet for chips and was riffling them from one hand to the other.

Briody noticed that Mannion, from the Four Provinces, and a couple other of Touhey's sullen boys sat on chairs at the edge of the floor, watching the action.

Sheehan nodded in their direction. "Look familiar to you?"

"Tommy Touhey's men."

"Mannion and the McGowan brothers. Real batsoes those two. Note the pistols stuck in their belts. They don't play games. Touhey controls all the gambling down on this job, plus the policy. He gets the okay from his buddy Johnny Farrell from the neighborhood, who's now a bigwig at Tammany Hall. We all grew up together on a Hunnerd thirty-eight Street."

"You grew up with them, how'd you avoid becoming a racket boy?"

"I had an ambition to see thirty, who knows, maybe even forty."

"Who tells who what to do?" Briody wondered at the way all these little New York worlds were connected.

"You mean, who's the boss? I gotta say Johnny. The Organization still runs this town."

Briody traded a ten-dollar bill for quarter chips and took a seat at the roulette table, content to try his luck with the red and the black. Sheehan and Delpezzo both played one hand of blackjack, won, and then left for home and family. Within the hour Briody hit twice on 19, his mother's birthday, and the chips were stacking up before him. Armstrong came over, plopped ten dollars on red, and squeezed Briody's shoulder as the silver ball whispered round and round, finally settling on red 3. Armstrong shook his fist and then took his winnings back to the craps table, where fortunes rose and fell at a greater velocity. Briody sipped beer and won more than he lost.

Around midnight, a bricklayer came in trailing a passel of good-time girls dressed in fancy hats whose perfumes drowned out the familiar work-site smells. Men with beery eyes took girls to darkened floors. Armstrong stayed intent on his craps. Briody switched to poker and won a couple weeks' pay extra. He loved being here away from things, just a working stiff yukking it up with his fellows. They had been tracking a man, an executioner for the Irish Free State, who was in New York trying to gather intelligence on their fund-raising. Briody knew it was coming. They would look to him to be the triggerman, to finish the thing. He stuffed his winnings into his pocket and poured another beer from the keg. The man was out there, asleep in a city foreign to him—a city in which he was going to die. Briody wandered over to the craps game, picked up the dice, and rolled a 7.

It seemed too soon, but dawn broke out over the reaches of Long Island and the men hooted and cheered as a pink fissure of light cleaved the horizon. The darkness was rising. Briody decided to go. As he said goodbye to Armstrong only the serious gamblers were left, men whose hunger and fatigue were etched into their faces. He rode the elevator down with three carpenters who were going home exhausted, glum, and penniless. The night watchman, a squat drunk missing one eye, twirled his keys and waved them into a city rose-colored and at peace. The air was sweet and clean. Briody walked over to Fifth Avenue and flagged a taxi. As he rode home past the mansions of sleeping rich men he pulled the greasy wad of bills from his pocket and fingered through it, laughing at the notion that on this dawn he was richer than he'd ever been.

Farrell watched Pamela line up the children and fuss over their outfits, repeating an Easter Sunday ritual she had been subjected to as a child, a final inspection on the way to Episcopal service. The children beamed and so did Farrell. They were not old enough to consider rebellion, not yet. The three girls—eight down to six— and his son John Junior, who at three had an eerily precise replica of his own head at that age, seemed to enjoy the pomp. He watched Pamela, sterner now, a little thicker, but still when the light caught her just so, he remembered why he fell in love with her. She had been a young firebrand whose politics were forged in Village salons, a suffragette, a feminist, a radical socialist, and still, when they met in the early twenties, a rebel against her family, her upbringing, every taint of her Prescott heritage. And although he thought her politics a bit extreme, he was content to bash her class right along with her. The children had changed all that. It was almost chemical, and he knew that on some level she was troubled by it. It was as if the act of birthing had transmuted her into her mother. She still belonged to the Heterodoxy Club, still read left-leaning publications, called herself a socialist when prodded, but that was it. Her life was all about the children to such an extent that it was another thing that had come between them.

She pulled him into the next room. "You can't make one Sunday and set an example for your own children? On Easter of all the days?"

"To go to your church."

"Please, we agreed when the children were born."

"The city doesn't take the Lord's day off."

"Your mayor takes half the year off. Where's he today as the breadlines grow? Palm Springs? Miami? With a belly full of illegal gin?"

"My mayor."

"Please, John, let's not persist with the delusions. It's embarrassing."

"To who? Your father?"

"Among others."

"Him and his cabal that sit on their piles of 'skulls and gold,' your phrase. What happened to you? I wonder that a lot late at night these days."

"Like you can even think late at night—these days. I grew up, John. You might want to try it someday. It's not something to be afraid of."

"For Chrissake."

"Not in the house. Save that talk for your speakeasy floozies."

"My mayor prefers whiskey—Irish—the real McCoy."

"Nice item in the *Times* yesterday. Four-hundred-pound lifeguards working at city beaches."

"No reason to exclude the wide-bodied."

"Who don't know how to swim?"

"All that lard, they probably float like a charm. You just latch on."

"Clerks who cannot read?"

"The *Times*, huh? They report on any teenagers with black lung on the city payroll? Or is that just in your family's company towns?"

Pamela spun and walked back to the foyer. Farrell sighed, then followed her. At the door his children chimed in unison, "Goodbye, Father," and Farrell swallowed a grimace. It was an affectation his wife insisted on that sounded to him like nails on a blackboard. Father. It should be reserved for priests.

Farrell kissed the children goodbye and watched as Pamela shepherded them into the waiting car, insisting that they ride the four blocks to the Church of the Resurrection rather than walk because she liked to make an impression. He thought for a moment of his own childhood in the Bronx, how his mother used to drag them through the crowded neighborhood streets to St. Jerome's, all those immigrants seeing the church as a way to keep their past alive, and for a moment standing in his Fifth Avenue apartment so far from the warrens of his youth he could smell the incense and hear the Latin intonations and feel his mother's rough hand holding his. The woman had lived in fear. And that fear had instilled in him a hunger, an ambition, and a need to never settle for anything, and now this is where that need had brought him—an elegant and spacious home among the city's elite where his own children were total strangers to him. He grabbed his coat and hat and headed out into the day.

When the taxi got stuck in traffic at Twenty-fifth Street, Farrell paid and made his way on foot down to Union Square. The April air was thickening, a storm was coming. He passed a gaggle of applemongers, the newest manifestation of the economic troubles hitting the city. They beseeched him to buy their pitiful produce. While most were sheepish, humiliated at the depths to which they had been knocked, one man, of spry middle age, pushed his fedora back on his head and thrust forth a polished McIntosh. Farrell recognized the suit. It was wearing thin but must have set the man back two months' salary at Dunhill's when he was flush.

He spoke in a clear and educated diction. "Excuse me, Mr. Sharpie; won't you help your fellow man in his hour of need?" This is what spooked Farrell the most. So many of the unemployed were university men, were guys who had believed their futures and their good fortune was a lock. They had earned madly for a decade, had heeded the optimistic prophets of the age, bought on margin, spent like drunken princes. Then poof, it was gone, all gone. Farrell looked into his eyes and saw it—the fear and the defeat that belied the man's eager smile. Feeling a creeping sense of guilt, he purchased a half dozen, stuffing them into various pockets. The man displayed a grin of such earnestness that it appeared to be the onset of dementia. As Farrell started away the man called after him, "Hey partner, they used to call me the Wizard of Wall Street!"

Farrell crossed the square and entered Tammany Hall, the wigwam, tossing the apples into the garbage. Drury, the guard, watched him pass. "Goddamn shame what's going on in this country. Damn shame. The good captain is waiting for you upstairs."

Farrell nodded and took the stairs to his office. He had his own problems. Still, he loved coming here on Sundays when it was cool and hushed. Despite what his wife might believe, it was usually a busy day for him. Etched in glass on his office door was "John P. Farrell Political Director." He pushed through the door, considering that the politics these days he left mostly to the district leaders except for the weeks leading up to an election. Most of his duties at the Hall were troubleshooting and greasing the wheels, being a master fixer.

Captain Jack Egan sat on the couch, leafing through a newspaper. The room was twenty feet square, dark-wood-paneled with ivory floor tiles that shone from daily buffing. The walls were lined with pictures of Farrell standing with a who's who of politics, power, and celebrity: Woodrow Wilson when he was in town trying to sell the ill-fated League of Nations, Lindbergh on his victory lap, to his favorite, a shot of him leaning over the back of Silent Charlie Murphy's chair, ear cocked, while the master, hand over mouth, whispered up at him. Egan looked up at the picture.

"Never been the same since Murphy dropped dead. Walker said it best—the brains of the Organization are buried in Calvary Cemetery."

Farrell sat. "Come on now, Jack, should I take that as an insult?"

"I'm referring more to the big guy a few doors down."

" 'Yes, no, and I'll look into it.' That really is all I ever heard Silent Charlie Murphy say regarding a contract."

"And from those responses flowed the power of the mighty metropolis."

"As for the current boss, we just need to do our best to minimize the effects of his dim-wittedness."

"No easy job."

"Find my hundred grand?" On his desk were a pile of telephone messages from the last two days. As he waited for Egan's reply he leafed through them quickly and stopped at one from Miss Masterson. Grace was canceling on him for the third time in a week. Damn it. There were three from Mr. Touhey.

"Not a trace. I got men all over the neighborhood searching for signs of a windfall. Whoever picked up that bag is either A—from someplace else—or B—smarter than your average West Side mug."

Farrell considered that the loss of a hundred thousand dollars was not yet cause for panic. He could almost afford to lose that much. Almost. It was the embarrassing way in which he had lost it that caused more concern. If that story got out.

"I know you're keeping the details to yourself."

Egan looked at him and said nothing. Farrell flipped through Touhey's messages again. His boyhood chum was becoming a pain. There had been a time, not long ago, when their careers were arcing upward in lockstep, when their partnership was exclusive and beneficial. But now he was wondering if he had backed the wrong horse. Those were the exact words of an Italian gentleman with whom he was conspiring of late.

"What's new on the Vitale mess?"

"We been taking the judges aside, one by one, and reinforcing the idea that silence is golden. Nobody talks, this thing dies a quick death."

Farrell stood up and walked across the room to look out onto Union Square. A crowd had gathered around a soapbox orator. Red flags fluttered. Mounted cops gathered on the margins, waiting.

"I'm curious, Jack. What's my summer going to be like?"

"Machine-gun fire, blood in the streets, strikes, the odd riot or two."

"That's your forecast?"

"There is a lot of rumbling about big-time beer wars. The young Turks feel they're not getting what's due them. Place is going to seem a lot like Chicago before it's settled."

"This can't be nipped in the bud?"

"Johnny, you been around long enough. That much money at stake, it won't stop until one guy gets strong enough to end it. Right now, I'd say there's a dozen contenders."

"Ours?"

"Mostly theirs. They're a little hungrier. And let's face it. Outside of Owney, the smart Irish have moved on. They're selling oil or bonds. You got nuts like Diamond and Coll but I doubt either of those dopes sees another Christmas."

Farrell figured the future was surely going to be less dominated by the Irish in both politics and crime. New blood is vital to any organization. That was one of the lessons he had learned from the late great boss Silent Charlie Murphy. Was he to let old allegiances hold him back? That made no sense. He had busted his ass and kissed others' far too long for that to be an option. He considered the paucity of new construction contracts and cursed the economy. The Crash was killing everyone, but construction had nearly stopped. It was one reason he was branching out, making new contacts and performing unsanctioned fixes. Tough times demanded innovative thinking.

He considered how far the racket boys had come. When he went into law school at the end of the war, they were where they had always been, on the street. Now, they were players on a major scale in the city and had the ability to affect even the machine. Their lack of inhibitions when it came to violence was now backed up by real money, by real power. True, most were crazed pistoleros bound to meet predictable ends, but some were apt to be factors in the city for years to come. He saw it as his duty to corral their potential and direct it in ways that would benefit the Hall, and of course, Johnny Farrell.

He pulled out two cigars, handing one to Egan. He poured glasses of Jameson Irish whiskey from the bottle he kept in his bottom drawer. They smoked and drank. Farrell picked up a framed picture of his wife.

Egan nodded his head. "How's that going?"

"It's marriage."

"I never asked you. You get on with the family?"

"You know, proud Episcopalians. They consider themselves open-minded people because they made nice with the richer German Jews. Not too crazy about papists though, or poor Jews. They tell warm stories about Grandpa Cornelius, like he's a fuzzy curmudgeon who built the family fortune by virtue of spit and hustle, quick wits and business savvy. They leave out the swindling and butchering of Indians, a brisk trade in black slaves, his blood coursing through mulatto bastards consigned to oblivion, and the numerous children who died in his mines." He put the picture down. "And they call this place a nest of vipers."

"Amazing how money cleans itself up."

He used her father to gauge the mood of the Protestant money crowd. The old man had been dropping hints, lately. He wanted his daughter to stay clear of scandal, had offered Farrell various positions in the Prescott family concerns. He'd be a junior captain of industry, travel the world. How little they understood me and where I am from, Farrell thought. He kept his distance. His pompous in-laws could shove their blood-soaked mining interests. He was his own man.

On his desk there was a smiling photograph of him and Boss Murphy, taken the day he had graduated Fordham Law School. None of his family had bothered to make it for the ceremony—his father too drunk, his mother too sick, and his siblings too jealous of his success. The Boss, there as a guest speaker, had singled him out. Murphy dropped dead two weeks later. Nothing has been the same since, Farrell thought. He moved another picture, one of him and the new boss, Curry, to the side of his desk.

"Decisiveness," Farrell said.

"What's that?"

"That's what I miss the most about Murphy. His ability to cut to the bone of an issue."

"Cut? More like bludgeon. I remember one time, I used to walk the beat down on Second Avenue and I passed Silent Charlie on his corner. He'd see guys turn the block, and if they were getting a no Charlie would just shake his head before they were within ten yards of him, and they'd pull up and turn away."

"They'd go home."

"They'd skedaddle."

" 'Cause once Charlie shook that head . . ."

"It was over all right."

Farrell blew smoke, straightened his tie. "Curry dithers."

"Dithering is not a good trait in a boss."

"It's not a good trait in a plow horse. Sometimes I envy the way the racket boys depose their kings."

Egan gave him a knowing look. Farrell smiled to indicate he was joking. Was he?

Farrell polished off the glass and poured two more. He noticed a message slip on the floor and picked it up. It was from Frankie

Vamonte, the Dago himself, and read, "Tuesday night, same time, same place."

"Things sure have changed since we came up. I don't know if I can count ten district leaders in this city that actually run their wards anymore. Used to be gangsters were nothing but muscle, gutter thugs and dock wallopers hired to bust up Election Day."

"Goddamn Prohibition."

"We got street kids running around like feudal lords. And the same people that gave us a dry country are blaming us for the monster they unleashed."

"Money has been made."

Farrell laughed and made a point of checking his Moët diamond watch. "A few bob. We just need to keep things from getting totally out of control."

He decided he was not going to get back in touch with the Dago either. Let him stew. He put his affairs in order, scratched out condolence cards with his gold fountain pen, stacking them in his out-box.

"What's with so many people dying?"

" 'Tis a terrible year for it."

"It's maybe a sign."

"Don't go superstitious on me."

He checked his watch again. The man was late. He stubbed out his cigar. He left Egan to his whiskey and paced down the hallway, his shoes clicking on the polished marble floor and echoing softly off the plaster walls. Though the building was only a few years old, it seemed to hold its share of ghosts, as if they had followed the Organization up from Fourteenth Street. Oil portraits of past leaders, white-haired men of gravitas and theft, gazed upon him in the dim corridor. There was the feel of a temple about the place, a temple for paying homage to past glory, but also one where power was still seated. Farrell reveled in it.

He pulled a key that he was not supposed to own from his pocket and eased open the door onto the deep and wide expanse of the Boss's office. There were framed election posters, two six-foot-tall Indians carved from redwood, a present from the Boss in San Francisco, a thousand citations, proclamations, the clutter of prominence that seemed about ready to rip the paneling off the walls with their weight. He settled himself behind the barge of a desk, propped his feet up. He picked up the phone and placed it to his ear and saw himself barking directions, commanding the legions of Election Day, chewing out senators, cowing the odd banker. Farrell put down the receiver and used the private bathroom off to the rear of the room. When he was done he flushed and, leaving the office, said to the silence, "Screw you, Boss."

Back in his office the man he needed to see was seated next to Egan. He had placed his fedora on the table before him and was pondering a tabloid through the pungent smoke of a Monte Cristo. He looked up at Farrell's entrance and folded the paper. Farrell sat and the man took a thick envelope from his pocket and secreted it within the tabloid. He gave it a push with his fingers across the desk. "Four down, six to go."

"Everything is going smoothly?" Farrell dropped the newspaper and its contents in his satchel.

"More or less."

Farrell sensed the man was not happy. "Anything the Commissioner can help you with?"

"There is a man. Claims to represent something called the Northeast Truckers Association. He's talking problems. Flat tires on the turnpike. Traffic jams. Headaches and slowdowns. Drivers so stupid they end up in Buffalo on account of accident. He's breaking shoes with his hints and winks."

Farrell regarded his nails. He tapped his satchel. "This covered zoning changes. Elevator speeds, gauges of steel. Things you needed to make this project happen. We never discussed hints and winks, Brian."

Brian slapped the satchel, a little harder than was necessary to make a point. "Like I said, four down, six to go. We can break shoes too."

Farrell smiled broadly. "Brian. Do you think you should threaten us? Here we are with a business arrangement that made all involved happy, right? And you bring this other crap into it."

"We understood it to mean we would not have problems."

"A rather broad interpretation."

In the silence that followed Farrell realized the smart thing to do was look into it. He could guess who was behind it all. "All right. I'll ask around. We'll do what we can to bring these hinters and winkers to heel. But Brian, you know as well as me, this town ain't what it used to be." He waved out the window, handed Brian a cigar. "There's only so much—"

"Another thing. There is a subcontractor on the Empire State, Redondo Brick. They're being struck on a job on Twenty-third Street. The worry is that the strike might spread to the big job."

Farrell raised an eyebrow at Egan. Egan sipped his whiskey and nodded. He was not a man you needed to fill in the details for.

Brian sucked the cigar aflame, let smoke ease out of the side of his mouth. "Some of the fellas have been speculating. The Governor knows about this?" He pawed the money bag.

"Smith or little Franklin?"

"The Soldier for Rome."

"I doubt the man would be such a happy warrior, he knew. Then again, he's been around long enough to know how things play out in the big city. He might even have ventured a guess. Who knows? Just don't expect he'll be able to help you with the winking hinters."

"Sure they're not hinting winkers?" Egan smiled.

"Whatever you call them, just please, make them vanish from my life."

Farrell watched him leave. He realized he could not avoid the Dago, after all.

"Politics can get really complicated at times."

Egan looked up at him, exhaled a long blue cloud, and shrugged. "That ain't exactly news, Johnny."

Briody, dressed in workman's clothes, walked into the back room of the Four Provinces and there was the crime lord himself seated at a table with his sleeves turned up, exposing his meaty forearms.

Touhey tipped his hat and indicated the chair. "You work down there. Who's running the book?"

"I wouldn't know now. Not much for the gambling," Briody said, but he knew Touhey was being disingenuous. It was common knowledge on the site that Touhey split all the gambling and loansharking rackets on the site with the Italian, Vamonte, who was known as the Dago.

Touhey nodded as if this was the answer he expected and it did not upset him.

"Tell me you've been training for the fight."

"I've been training for the fight."

"You're never gonna get rich, humping steel."

"I'll never get prison time either."

"Lot of opportunity for tough young guys like yourself."

"I'm happy hanging steel."

"You guys, you Irish, you just-off-the-boat mutts. You'll walk the streets of New York with a bag full of heaters for nothing, not a plug nickel, but a chance to do something similar and get yourself a nice payday, make out okay for yourself, somehow you look down on it. I can't figure you guys out."

"Don't mean to perplex you, Tommy."

"The same kind of thing you're doing here I can put you on the payroll, you'll make a nice buck, set up a nice future for yourself."

"I'm not doing this for the money."

"Oh right. The principle of it, being a good soldier and all that. You know I understand that. I have respect for that. But, I mean, you do these things. I mean, I'm all for Ireland united, all that jazz. But isn't the war over for you guys? Now no matter what they might tell you, you put yourself at risk. They want you to think they got it all sewed up like it's a big game and everyone is playing it. It don't always work out quite like that. You might get pinched by the wrong cop, or maybe someone hears you're carrying certain items they might want for themselves. Things happen out there, on the street, this city, not all of which can be controlled. You can end up in a lot of tight spots. Places where nobody can reach out for you. You need a sponsor."

"I'm really not interested. Besides, my war is not over. Now, I appreciate your offer. Don't take my refusal the wrong way. We appreciate all your help."

Touhey said, "I am not easily dissuaded." And then he laughed again, that buddy-buddy guffaw of his. "You guys. Where's your partner in crime been? Ain't seen him."

"He landed steady work, graveyards. And the wife is keeping a close eye on him these days."

"Ask around down that job, who's running the numbers. I hate to think it might be the Sicilians."

"They need to eat too, Tommy."

"Not if I can help it. I don't mind them taking the sanitation, the garbage routes. Fair enough. They're born for that stuff. But they need to leave the mathematics to us or the Jews at least."

Touhey smiled and Briody wasn't quite sure if he was serious or not. Touhey never seemed to limit his association to the Irish. While his inner circle was mostly relatives, he had plenty of other kinds in his employ, licit and otherwise.

"I ever tell you the story about Joey the Jap?"

Briody looked at the clock and shrugged. He wanted to get on with the job. His back was sore from work and he needed sleep. Thing was, you had to work on Tough Tommy Touhey's schedule.

"Joey the Jap. He was actually Chinese, from Mott Street. Chinese with an Irish grandmother to be precise. But the stupid hayseeds named him before I got assigned to the unit. They wouldn't know a Jap from a Swahili, those cow bangers. Anyway, Joey the Jap, the Chinese kid from downtown, had balls the size of a rhino. Over there we used to send guys out to draw fire from the enemy lines."

"We wondered at your enthusiasm." Briody considered that insanity. After endless months in the trenches they wanted nothing more than to get home in one piece. The Yanks showed up when everyone else had had enough.

"I don't know about youse, but we did it mostly on a volunteer basis. Some guys never went and some guys went on a reasonable my-turn rotation. Joey the Jap volunteered every single time. It was like he thought he was bulletproof or invisible. He'd leap back in the hole like he had just come back from a walk down Broadway to buy flowers for his girl. We used to get to talking, me and Joey the

Jap. The other guys steered clear of him, were spooked by the guy gliding through the tracer rounds like it meant nothing, like they were raindrops. We used to swap stories about New York, the good old days all that crap. Joey the Jap was wired into the Tongs downtown. His uncle was a big deal. We talked about setting up a little operation when we got home. We used to make real big plans. Hanging around with Joey the Jap, I started to feel invincible. We volunteered for crazier things. Guys were being turned to shit and blood in the mud all around us. Me and Joey the Jap, not a scratch. Not a scratch.

"One day, this captain, a punk rich kid fresh in from the Point, a kid from Boston, wanted to do a little recon, get his uniform dirty. He took two imbeciles with him. A hundred yards out and a mortar round drops right in on them, eighty-eights, big bastards. Splat. All we could hear was that captain wailing for his mother. Nobody wanted to make a move to help him. So I follow Joey and out we go. The two guys had taken the brunt of it and the captain was covered in blood, brains. He had an ear stuck to his helmet. I remember that. A perfect human ear. Anyway, me and Joey drag him back to the trench, rounds coming after us, tracking us. The earth shaking, the sky was that gray that lasted for weeks on end over there. The guys were screaming, urging us faster, till we tumbled down on top of them. We settle the captain and the corpsman comes over, checks him out. There wasn't a thing wrong with him. All that blood was somebody else's."

Touhey leaned over the table. The muscles along his jawbone bulged. Briody saw the strain in his eyes, a weariness he had not noticed before. A subway rumbled beneath them. The lightbulb overhead swayed. "I'm only telling you this because you were there. That captain put me up for the Silver Star. Just me. Not Joey. 'Cause he was a Chinaman."

Briody wondered at this level of intimacy.

"You know what killed Joey the Jap?"

"No."

"Influenza. One day he was smiling, dodging ordnance. Next day he's shivering and puking, turning blue about the lips. Day after that, he was dead, Joey the Jap. A lot of guys died that month. I never once got sick. I started to think Joey the Jap had rubbed off on me."

The door opened and a man sporting a plump outdated mustache came in, nodded at Touhey, handed him a brown bag, and slid back out. Touhey pulled the bag close to him, resting his forearm on it. "When I got back home, first stop I made was Chinatown, even before the Bronx. Joey's mother, I gave her my Silver Star." Touhey emptied his glass in a long pull. "They threw us some parades, we got back. Me, I couldn't wait to get out of that uniform for good."

"They didn't throw parades in Ireland for them that fought in the English army."

"Yeah, why did you do that?"

"You remember being fifteen, don't you?"

"Scars to prove it."

"I was big for my age, they needed bodies."

Touhey stared at him for a moment and then called out and the door opened again and two men appeared. Both were stocky and had the quick eyes and bouncy step of street fighters, the type that enjoyed kicking a man after he was down. There was no humor about them. "They'll give you what you came for." Touhey went toward the bar, stopped, and said, "That captain, the one me and Joey saved? They found him one morning with his throat slit. Ear to ear." Touhey, who rarely stated anything flatly, presented an enigmatic smile. "I had a half a dozen Joey the Japs, I'd run this town forever."

Briody watched as one of the men went through the basement door and brought up a wooden box that he hefted onto the table and opened. Inside were a dozen U.S. Army–issue Colt .45 pistols. Briody examined a couple, dislodged the clips, sighted. Everything seemed fine. Touhey claimed to be a big supporter of the cause back home. Briody wondered at this. He took an envelope of cash from his back pocket and laid it on the table beside the box. He placed a duffel bag he had been carrying on the table and transferred the guns to it, first wrapping each in a small towel. The weapons smelled faintly of kerosene.

It would not make for much of a hiding, but according to Casey he was not to worry about cops. The two gunsels regarded him with flat eyes. The one nearest, who wore a bright blue tie, picked up the cash.

"I don't need to count this."

"But sure you don't." They were great for staring, these Yank gangsters. All liked to look at you like there was something about you they could tell. Judging your worth like it was as visible as the cut of your suit. He stood and hefted the bag, let it hang by his side.

"That's more than thirty pounds of metal you're carrying there, Paddy."

He walked out past the men at the bar. No one even turned to look. He noticed Tough Tommy Touhey watching him in the mirror. On the street he moved along with a rolling gait. In London just the fact that he was Irish brought scrutiny. Here it was easy to blend. It was one thing he already loved about the city. For the first time in years he had a feeling of moving along unobserved, not suspected, not maligned, not watching over his shoulder. Anonymity was a powerful feeling. He made his way down Third Avenue under the El; the night had turned cool and the street was quiet, the cobblestone slick from a recent shower. The shops were closed for the night. He heard laughter, then shouting, radio sounds drifted down from above, echoing off various surfaces, no way to judge precisely where the noise was coming from.

At 138th he climbed the stairs to the platform. He paid his nickel and pushed through the turnstile; just another working stiff headed for a graveyard shift. There were a couple dozen people waiting for the train. Most watched their shoes. He was relieved to see no cops on the platform. He watched the spotlight from the first car lead the train, screeching, into the station. He took a seat next to the door and caught flickers of the Bronx night before the train curved onto the bridge and presented him with the razzle-dazzle of the Manhattan skyline, the flat roofs and church spires of Harlem giving way to the still-lit towers of the south. Somewhere down there was his building, not yet jutting high enough to be discerned from this distance. He pushed back in the wicker seat. He figured he would never fail to be stunned by that view.

He waited in the appointed diner across from the piers. At the counter three old and drunk stevedores hunched over cups of coffee, studiously ignoring each other. The counterman perched by the cash register. Whenever someone sat down at the counter or took a booth seat he flipped his towel over his shoulder and shuffled along to take the order.

Briody sipped his coffee. The bag was beneath the table at his feet. Twelve pistols. Seemed like a hard way to wage a war. But he knew everything helped. Casey was lining up contacts. He lit a cigarette and smoked deeply. Sympathizers abounded, in the military, the police, the underworld. Next would be explosives. They were stockpiling for a bombing campaign, wanted to shake the Brits right where they went to bed at night. There was also talk of a huge shipment to be exchanged for cases of whiskey. Briody thought Prohibition was an interesting notion. In New York it seemed to be entirely a joke, a way to enrich the racketeers and their political cronies. There was the odd raid for show, but the booze never stopped flowing, not for a minute.

He looked up as a woman came in trailing two children, odd at such a late hour. They were dressed in the soiled remnants of what looked to be maintenance-man uniforms, cut roughly to fit. With their desperate eyes and hard sheen they looked like the men coming out of thirty days in the hole on bread and water. He was shocked at the amount of despair he saw in New York. He had believed in all the myths, the stories of staggering wealth. His own father had left County Cavan to work on the building of the subway and come home with enough money to buy the neighbor's farm. He sung the praises of Americkay to the day he died—rivers of gold, the fat good life for anyone who would work for it, opportunity and plentitude. Briody wondered at his father's capacity for exaggeration.

The woman was insistent, beyond shame, nearly shouting in broken English, "Food, for my babies, now, please."

The few patrons stared, waiting. The counterman moved quickly. He produced a club, smacked it sharply on one palm, and made his way toward the beggars faster than Briody imagined he could. The woman stood her ground. The two boys pressed themselves to her cadaverous thighs, cowering. She muttered something in a foreign tongue and the man pulled himself up short and threw his arms in the air. Somehow she had claimed a small victory. He went over to the counter and took a handful of pastries and thrust them at the woman. She clutched the pastries, then slunk like a thief back into the chill night of the waterfront.

Briody watched as a man of about twenty-five came in dressed in the manner of a longshoreman, in dungarees and a brown canvas jacket with a watch cap pulled down to his brow. He looked quickly around the diner and focused on Briody. He moved toward him, his shoulders pulled back, that Yank cockiness about him.

"You got a package?"

Briody nodded and the man sat across from him. As he sat his feet hit the bag below the table. "There we go."

He signaled the counterman by pointing at Briody's coffee cup. The counterman brought him over an empty cup, placed it down and poured, then topped off Briody's coffee, filling both precisely. The longshoreman rubbed his palms together and bummed a cigarette. "But Christ it's chilly, for spring."

The door opened and Briody looked up to see a burly cop with a bulbous nose making his way in. Briody stiffened. The longshoreman noticed and turned around to see the cop. "Relax. The fat bastard makes any trouble for us he'll be taking a boat to work."

"A boat?"

"Jesus, you are some greenhorn, ain't you. Staten Island. You think he got to be that much of a lard ass off a cop's jack? Chump change." He turned. "Hey Jimmy, you prick. You eating again? Save some for the rest of New York."

The cop whipped out his nightstick and cracked it on the counter. "Keep it up, you sewer rat, and I'll use this on you instead of your mother."

"Ah g'won."

The longshoreman slugged down his coffee and stood. "Well I'd love to stay and chat, but I gotta get back to the job. Let's go."

Briody stood, uncertain. He had never been to this pier. A truck rumbled past outside, shaking the window.

The longshoreman shook his head, smirked. "No pal, I don't carry the load. You do."

Briody reached under the table and picked up the bag, hefted its weight. He felt strange with the cop standing there, exposed. New York was a funny place.

As they walked past, the cop said, "Special delivery, boys?"

"Mind your own business."

"He with you?" The cop was eyeing Briody, making an inventory.

"Yep."

They crossed Twelfth Avenue. Briody bent to the wind off the river, wet, cold. An Irish wind. A guard shack stood at the head of the pier where four men sat on crates smoking thick cigars and playing cards. One, wearing bottle-lens glasses that lent him the look of a moron, glanced up and smiled, then made a wave motion with his cardless hand. Behind the shack two men lurked in the dimness. The shorter of the two stepped forward and took the bag from him. "All set now," he said in a distinct Dublin accent. Briody nodded, then headed back to the street. He thought of flagging a cab but decided to walk.

He made his way up to Thirty-fourth Street and headed east. Despite the chill he decided to keep walking, right across town to the Lexington Avenue line. He felt lighter, relieved that the job was done. It was good to be back in the game. He strode across town past rows of apartment buildings spotlit as taxis discharged dolled-up residents returning from dinner or shows. Doormen, uniformed and white-gloved, spoke in brogues and escorted them into the grand lobbies. He moved along invisible, anonymous. He passed Pennsylvania Station, and then the darkened hulk of Macy's department store where the window mannequins draped in whites and pastels anticipated the summer.

At Herald Square he could see the frame of the Empire State stark against the night sky. The gloom had cleared, a balmier wind blowing away the clouds. Presently he came upon the job site, quiet and dark. A few watchmen lounged inside. The building shot a dozen stories above the street, the steel frame just a few stories higher than the granite-enclosed floors. It was only a fraction complete. Still, cars slowed so people could gawk, their heads jammed out windows, necks craned for a vertical view. He felt a well of pride. He'd be back in a few hours and could not wait. Pedestrians stopped to peer through the gates, then stepped back and tilted their heads to the now-sparkling sky as if they were imagining the building complete, rising so high it obscured the stars. A man described its grandeur to his fur-clad date in tones hushed and reverent. Briody fought an urge to divulge his complicity in its creation, to point out the very steel he had erected that day. Instead, he headed for the Bronx and sleep, under a moon so bright it was like a cold sun.

Just past noon Grace rolled over and came alert with a heavy head. The bed beside her was empty and cold but still held Farrell's scent, although he was long gone. She drank deeply from a pitcher of water on the nightstand, then showered and dressed. She was spending too many nights in this hotel. She needed to get back to her painting, her boat, and the small routines that gave her structure and comfort. She took the envelope Farrell had left on the nightstand with the name and address of a bank in Brooklyn written on it. Today, she would be Mrs. McGuiness and she would open a safe-deposit box for her husband. She leafed through the stack of new bills and though they were crisp the money actually looked dirty.

She rang for a chicken sandwich and took it down to Gramercy Park, letting herself in with a key Farrell had provided. The day was pleasant so she sat on the ground and flipped through a newspaper while chewing her sandwich. A few nannies pushed prams around the park and she caught stray gossip as they neared her, rumors of illicit sex and complaints about bosses. A tall man in an overcoat was trying to coax a squirrel out of a tree, proffering a type of nut in his outstretched hand. According to the *Daily News*, beer wars were raging about the city and men were being gunned down all over town. Just yesterday suspected members of Legs Diamond's gang had aerated a funeral home with machine-gun fire, killing three and wounding twelve.

She finished eating and lay back, looking straight up through the budding branches of the trees to the pure blue of a spring sky. Not a single building marred her sight line and it was easy there, with the cool grass beneath her and the soft perfumed breeze of the park, to believe she was very far away, in a place lacking anxiety and despair. She shut her eyes and the sun warmed her face and for a moment she forgot all of her bad choices.

She made her way toward the ferry, walking east to Third Avenue past the ornate apartment houses that reminded her of elaborate cakes. She could not shake her hangover guilt. She was drinking too much, not working, smoking too much, and sleeping with Farrell far too often. God, these little offenses loomed so large in her mind. The residue, she knew, of her Catholic upbringing. Blood of the lamb. He suffered for you. Died for you. Achh, go away. She was no slouch on the suffering front.

She walked in the shadow of the El and as she approached Twenty-third Street a battered black panel truck skidded to a stop so close to her that she jumped back from the curb. The back door banged open and a scrum of men spilled out, muscled and grim, carrying ball bats and ax handles, and as their faces caught the sunlight they seemed to shine with malice. Grace followed them around the corner just as they set upon a group of men carrying picket signs and chatting idly.

They started swinging then, their weapons describing brutal arcs in the spring air. Grace winced at the horrible noise of the attack: cries, bones snapping, skulls cracked, thuds like cleaver strokes on meat, deranged laughter. She stumbled closer, leaned on the wall, pressing one hand against the rough stone, the other to her mouth. She fought down bile. She wanted to do something, but she tried to scream and her throat was closed tight. Cars slowed on the street. People called out. Faces hung slack. No one dared intervene. One worker had grabbed a club and was holding his own, taking short fast cuts at the strikebreakers. He looked to be a teenager. The strikebreakers regrouped and went at him as one, the first of them taking a whack across the chest for the group. The kid fell beneath dozens of blows and then they piled on him.

A cop watched from across the street like he was ringside at a prizefight. Finally, he pulled his whistle up to his thin lips and blew three times sharply. The truck that had deposited the men swung around on cue and the attackers jumped aboard. The last one kicked a man in the face who was on his knees pleading. "Ya commie!" he shouted, and then had to chase the truck until he leapt and was pulled in by his cohorts. The truck swerved and receded, speeding toward the East River.

As a crowd gathered a man crawled along, sobbing and searching the ground for his teeth, which lay scattered about like yellow pebbles. Another leaned against the wall of the building, looked around him, blood leaking from his ear, mumbling, "What happened? What's going on?" One man lay on his back, his eyes staring vacantly up at the sun, atop him a sandwich board that read "Redondo Brick Unfair to Workers." Bright splashes of blood now added to their work jackets, shirts, pants, and soft hats. Grace saw what was left of the boy who had put up the fight. She again swallowed bile and knelt beside him. She put her hand to his neck, trying for a pulse. His skin was hot but still. She picked up his wrist hoping to feel a heartbeat, but there was just flesh and bone, nothing quick. She stood and moved away as the ambulances started to arrive. She turned and bumped into the cop who had watched from across the street, her cheek brushing against the rough wool of his uniform. His breath was stale from beer, his eyes indifferent. She pulled back and said, "You."

He pushed her aside. "Move along. Police business."

She came back at him. "You allowed this." She waved at the dead and the wounded, the staggered and broken.

He looked down at her as if seeing her for the first time. His smile was genuine. He leaned over as if to say something in her ear and kissed her hot and sloppy on the lips. She brought her knee up, but he was ready for it. He grabbed her leg and before knocking her over said, "Beat it, you dumb gash."

She landed on the small of her back, the impact jarring her. She swallowed rage. From the sidewalk she calmly noted his badge number: 674. Screwing Johnny Farrell was finally going to pay off.

· · ·

She found her neighbor Harry fishing from her boat. He sat with his legs hanging over the edge, a bottle of bathtub gin glinting in the sun next to him. He wore a leather aviator hat and a dirty brown jacket. His shoes were repaired with rope. He was whistling a tune she recognized as one by Stephen Foster, a ballad for the forsaken. Grace leapt onto the boat and he looked over his shoulder at her for a minute, the whistle stopping on his lips.

"What the hell happened to you?"

She stared back at him, uncertain. "What? Me?"

"Your hands. What's that, paint?"

Her hands were streaked red with the striker's blood. She held them up, turned them over, then shook them as if she could loose them from her wrists. She scurried into the boat, tripping over the threshold. She did not bother with water. She poured turpentine right from the can, took a paint-smeared rag, and scrubbed hard. The turpentine bit a nick on her thumb, stung her eyes. She scrubbed vigorously. She just wanted to be clean of the blood. She felt she had taken something of the boy with her, that she had violated him. She kept scrubbing until Harry said over her shoulder, "It's all right now, Grace. They're clean now."

"God, it was horrible. Horrible."

She dropped the rag and turned her hands over and over. They were rubbed raw. But the blood was gone.

"Come on now, you can use a little air."

She followed Harry outside and sat with him while he resumed fishing. It was low tide and the water was stagnant and oily. There was a faint smell of sewage. Trash, various flotsam and jetsam gathered around the hull of the boat, broken vegetable crates, empty tins, a child's doll bobbing, sinister in the black water. She described the violence and he shook his head.

"That's just the start of it. Way things are going we're gonna see a whole lot of hell. They say this recession's a lot worse than 1921, 1907, 1893, even. Let me tell you, those were not good times. People change, things get bad. People turn mean when they're hungry, just like pack dogs. Those fellows beating those strikers were mutts, but I'll bet they were paid chump change for their services."

"They looked like they were enjoying themselves."

"People need to have someone to dump on."

She closed her eyes and saw the boy and remembered her own broken dead. Harry stood and then squatted down, bouncing lightly on his haunches.

"You here for the influenza?"

"No." Grace looked out over the water. She had been in Ireland, where it had been bad enough. She did not mention this. She did not mention her dead.

"People forgot all about being neighbors. People stopped even talking to each other. There was nothing but fear and terror, a darkness in the land. Men were killed over there wasn't enough coffins. There were riots over that. Imagine? A lot of people thought it was the end of the world and for a good while you would not have been crazy at all to believe them." He sat back down and spit tobacco juice in a long line out into the water. "I think this whole thing is going to be a lot worse before it's over."

Harry pulled in his line. The hook was baited with a slick wiggle of pig intestine. He looked at it and shrugged, then with a flick of his wrist sent it out a few more feet. A fat sleek rat swam past with eyes beady and determined. The wind shifted and Grace caught a whiff of the slaughterhouse across the East River, imagined the gruesome activity, the howl of the damned. It was no different than what the strikers had suffered. Her mood darkened further.

She was twenty-seven now, childless, her family scattered around the globe. She felt a surge of self-pity, rare in the daylight. Tragedy followed her. First her father shot dead in Ireland. The force of that single bullet collapsed her family. Her mother sent the kids off in different directions, just wanting them away from that stricken country. Two brothers went to England, three to America, two to Australia. She went to London, then to Spain and to work as a domestic in a villa on the outskirts of Seville, where she was seduced by the oldest son, a man nearly twice her age. She married at seventeen. Francisco's family played it out like a medieval blood opera, hysterics, renunciations, and threats.

They were exiled to Cuba to oversee the family's cigar-making interests. She was startled by the oppression in that strange humid place but fascinated by its rituals, its stew of cultures and colors. She bore a son and was waited on hand and foot by the kind of servants she had so recently been. She could not get accustomed to that. She was constantly giving them paid days off, slipping them extra pesetas, conspiring to make their lives a little easier, and though it incensed her husband, who insisted she was just making them lazy and indulgent, she did not care. Sitting on the bank of the East River, she could recall the smells of the sea outside Pinar del Rio, the quality of light on a winter sunset, the taste of jungle fruits she had with breakfast: mango and papaya and the sweet gritty juice of coconuts. Mostly then, life was good.

She had Francisco and the baby Sean and her painting and she was happy. His family must have sensed their happiness for they were ordered to Tampa, a dreadfully dull place, malarial and controlled by tightfisted true believers who thought of themselves as a kind of Anglo vanguard in the hinterlands. It was her first experience in America. She became pregnant again. Then things just started going wrong. Francisco, a healthy man of thirty-eight, came home from work one night and collapsed onto the marble floor of the foyer. A heart attack, massive, dead before he hit the ground, the doctor assured her as if somehow that made everything all right. A month later she bore a second son, whom she named Francisco. Another month later he went to sleep one night as a hurricane approached and did not wake up. She buried him next to his father. Cut off by her husband's family, she fled Florida, took the new railroad north from Miami up the Atlantic coast to Pennsylvania Station in New York with Sean, age six now, and moved to the Bronx, a flat that looked directly out onto the Third Avenue El. It was a noisy, cold place of boisterous strangers. She went back to cleaning up after other people.

She had watched out the window as he came running toward her, toward home and supper. He did not see the taxicab. She hardly spoke for two years afterward. She left the church. She wandered around the city as if she was the only soul in it. She was trying to disappear herself. She sketched and painted horrific scenes, was consumed by bleakness. When things got a little better she would take the paintings out and look at them. It was as though someone else had created them. She started boozing, which she had never done, and was caught in the craziness of the time, wanted to obliterate herself, to kill the hurt.

She took work in a series of speakeasies, hatchecking, cigarette girl, became a night creature. She resisted the idea of taking things further, of sleeping with the men for money. They tried—every type: the fat men, the old men, fresh-faced, sports, husbands, financiers, racketeers, men with ugly hungers, men who swore love, men that drooled, actors, lawyers, cops and doctors, tourists and desperadoes. She shot them all down. She chose her lovers far from the tumult of the speakeasies. She slept with a man she met in the library, another she met on the ferry home. She controlled them. When they got too close she shook them loose, discarded them, felt none of their pain.

Then she met Milo in a waterfront dive. He was no matinee idol, possessed the kind of a scarred-up face her father used to describe as looking like a well-slapped arse, but he was gentle and understanding and left her to her moods. He was the only man she ever met who was nonjudgmental. He demanded nothing but her company, would laugh and say he was her safe harbor in a storm. And that was exactly how she felt about him. He was the kind of man other men followed. Every few months he would ship out and sail to some far-flung port like Rio, Hong Kong, or Bombay. It was a perfect arrangement. Time alone but with the security of a good man. Milo was a touchstone, a lifeline. Now he too was gone.

Next to her Harry yelled and stood up. His hat fell off and he tried to catch it and was almost pulled off-balance by whatever was on his line. He grabbed the pole and set his feet. His pants slid off a bit, exposing the crack of his ass. Grace laughed, caught in his excitement.

"Moby goddamned Dick!" He worked the rod back and forth frantically, reeling hard, then letting it play a bit. "Get the net!"

Grace leapt and retrieved the net hanging on the wall of Harry's boat. Harry backed up a few steps and, straining, put the rod down and stepped on it. He took the net and leaned out over the river, swooping into the water and out of sight. "Jesus Christ, what the hell I got?" When the net broke the surface again it held a snapping turtle the size of a manhole cover. Harry, his neck and face bulging from the effort, wrestled the beast onto the deck. "Turtle soup!" The reptile was still for a moment as if contemplating its defeat through its ancient cold eyes. Then off it went, moving with surprising speed, motoring across the deck. Harry yanked, slipped, and fell back on his ass. The turtle crashed back into the river and was gone, dragging the net and pole with it.

Harry gasped for breath. "Sweet Jesus. That monster turned the gotdam table on me." He snatched up his cap and slapped it on the deck. "My pole and my net." He looked to be on the verge of tears. "Now what?"

Grace convulsed with laughter.

Harry regarded her with hurt. "Ha, ha. Now I'll hafta go hungry."

"I don't know how you eat anything out of that slop."

"The voodoo insurgents and malaria down the Philippines couldn't kill me, you think a little river slop will?"

She watched Harry drink deeply of his homemade gin. "From the depths of hell that sucker was."

"Don't worry, you old goat, I'll feed you." Grace laughed again. Harry's tango with the turtle was the funniest thing she had seen in weeks. She ducked inside her boat to find something for him to eat and in the stillness of the cabin she remembered that today she still had to go and do Johnny Farrell's banking.

Sundays Briody always ran. He never had a plan or a route. Just out the door and go. Some Sundays he'd run down to the Willis Avenue Bridge and into Manhattan, all the way to the bridle paths and ponds of Central Park and back. Other Sundays he'd meander through the Bronx finding strange neighborhoods, exploring his new home. This time, he went north. He jogged up Third Avenue, wearing a hood pulled over his head, his boots slapping the pavement. People came out of a bakery laden with boxes of cakes and pastries. A fat red-faced man stood next to the door, his lips turned white by powdered sugar, watching Briody speed past with a look that said, What are you running from?

He saw some of Touhey's hard boys gathered in front of the candy store replaying the previous night's beer garden brawls. They threw mock sucker punches, laughed at pain inflicted. One sported a welt of a shiner.

As he went beyond the confines of Mott Haven the storefronts reflected the population shifts; there were pizza stands and Minno's pork store and, a few blocks up, Eckstein's schnitzel, and then up by the Grand Concourse where men and boys in yarmulkes gathered outside Golfedder's kosher meats. He turned a corner and came upon a gaggle of blacks congregating on the steps of a Baptist church. The men, starched and polished, huddled in grim consultation with the pastor. The women wore bright flowered dresses and wide-brimmed hats of brilliant color. Their children cavorted on the sidewalk. Some girls played double Dutch, their jump rope and Sunday shoes slapping a quick beat on the concrete. Briody was past them in a flash.

He ran hard. Last night's beer poured from him in a drenching sweat. His lungs burned. He made his way up to 161st Street. At the bottom of the hill Yankee Stadium sat stark and white, rising from the streets of the neighborhood like a modern-day coliseum. The ball season had begun and it was game day. People spilled down the elevated stairs, cars with Jersey registrations idled in traffic. Boys scampered about selling peanuts in brown bags. An old man sat on a barstool outside a soda shop with a monkey on his shoulder, selling oranges two for a nickel. Cops leaned against light poles twirling their clubs. Stragglers from the opposing team walked down from the Concourse Hotel past a phalanx of guttersnipes hurling insults.

"Go back to Beantown, ya creeps."

"Thanks for the Bambino, you dopes."

"Ya sissies!"

"Hey, your sister's a lard ass."

Briody noticed that despite their bravado the kids looked upon the big leaguers with reverence. One of the players took a baseball from his pocket and tossed it high in the air. As it rose above the elevated platform it seemed to hang in the Bronx sky and the boys went for it en masse, pushing and knocking each other to the ground.

Briody rounded the corner as one of Touhey's cabs pulled to the curb and out stepped the man with a blonde not his wife. Touhey watched as Briody passed, shouted, "Thatta boy, Mikey, roadwork on Sunday." Briody waved, picked up the pace, and ran through a cloud of smoke coming from a hot pretzel stand.

He ran south, back toward home. His mind cleared and he considered the trip he would make down to the piers that evening. Revolvers, this time, two dozen six-shooters to be taken across the Atlantic on a freighter bearing Model T tires. He was beginning to wonder. He was having a hard time keeping up his revolutionary zeal with things going so slowly. Ireland was beginning to feel far away and his other life, the workaday existence that was designed as cover, was something he enjoyed more than he would have ever thought. He needed to focus.

At Graham Square there was a gathering. Briody, moving more slowly now, approached the margins of the crowd. A man stood on a small wooden platform addressing a few dozen teenage boys and men. It reminded him of the rallies back home, impromptu gatherings in market towns; RIC men taking notes, priests staring in distaste. Still, ideas took hold, led to action. Here the crowd was less rapt. But some gazed, their jaws slack with want of a scapegoat.

Briody recognized some faces from the Four Provinces. Some brandished signs proclaiming "Death to Commies!" "Reds Out!"

The speaker held his hands up, arms spread wide. "That's right my fellow citizens. How many of you lack for the simple decency of a job, a pay envelope to feed your loved ones with? Let me see a show of hands."

Almost everyone raised an arm into the air.

"All of you. Each and every one of you, all hardworking men with a commitment to a pure and proper work ethic, and none can find employment. It's wrong, I tell you. It's not right, I tell you. Why? you might ask. Why is this so? What are the causes of this malaise, this abomination upon the land? Well, just look around you. Look at this great city, this great nation, and how it is being laid to waste, led to ruin. By who? By the foreign agents of a Red peril, that's who."

There were whistles and catcalls from the crowd. The speaker was louder now, stabbing the air in accusation. "That's right! A Red menace, a Red conspiracy of moneylenders that strikes at the very heart of what this nation stands for!"

"Go back to Rubeville, Okie!"

The speaker made like he did not hear. "United we can fight back. You must be aware, you must be on guard. We must fight back!"

The listeners pressed in. Cars rattled past on the avenue, their engine fumes filling the air. Some of the drivers leaned on horns. The orator shook his fist above his head, his voice was louder again, its pitch higher. His face, smooth and handsome and reassuring just moments ago, was purpling with anger.

"How many of you cannot find work?"

A dull whoop from the crowd.

"The Red serpent is everywhere!"

"Yeah!" A man located in the middle of the crowd raised his fist. And the proselytizer focused on him.

"Look at those shops! Who runs those shops?"

"You said it, brother."

"Agents of Lenin, of Marx, of Stalin!"

"Kill the bastards."

"Who are your landlords?"

"Sheeny kikes!"

The back-and-forth between the speaker and his most rabid supporter prompted a round of twittering. From the edge of the crowd a bottle traced a lazy arc toward the podium. The speaker watched it fly, sidestepping as it clattered along the platform and spilled over the side, smashing on the sidewalk.

"I am here to tell you that all your suffering to this day has been nothing compared to what's coming. We are at war, my brothers, in sustained battle with a ruthless and wily foe, a sneaky adversary that will stop at nothing to destroy all that we hold dear."

Briody noticed that while some of the men seemed mesmerized, most smoked or sipped from pocket flasks and looked like mildly curious passersby out for a Sunday stroll. As the man ranted on Briody noticed a trio of police vans rounding the corner at 138th Street. A dozen cops got out and gathered to watch from a distance, their clubs at the ready. He took this as a signal to move on. He jogged lightly away from the gathering, past the filling station Touhey owned on the corner, where two grease-covered mechanics had disassembled an old steam engine car and were standing bewildered amid the wreckage they had caused. Gasoline was listed at nine cents a gallon. He thought that in the short time he had lived in the Bronx these naysayers and doom announcers were becoming a common sight. Agitation was in the air, but here, unlike at home, it was diffuse, sporadic, the targets and villains shifting with the winds.

He jogged the last few blocks home. Young Danny Casey was sitting on the stoop waiting for him. Briody rubbed his stubbly head and settled himself next to him.

"Is it bigger than a mountain yet?"

"What's that?"

"Your building."

"No. Takes time, Danny. I'll bring you to it. You'll be able to see it from the roof here before long."

"Our roof?"

"That's right, boy."

"Really?"

"I wouldn't lie to you, would I?"

Danny shook his head. "I learned a new word today."

"Did you? What's that?"

"Fuck."

Briody stifled a laugh. "Where did you learn that?"

"Fat Walsh the beat cop said it. He called it at—"

"Well, maybe he did, so. But it's a very bad word, Danny. The worst. Whatever you do, don't use it again. Especially don't let your mother know. If you can promise me that, I'll take you down to the building, the Empire State, and I'll bring you up to the top and we can look for your bedroom window from there. Okay?"

"When can we go?"

"When you finish school. How come you're not off playing with your friends?"

"I wanted to wait for you."

"All right. But now you should run off and catch up with them. What's that?"

"What?"

"Behind your ear." Briody had palmed a silver dollar and now he reached behind Danny's head and pulled it from his ear. He held the coin up and Danny took it.

"Thanks, Uncle Mike." Danny rubbed the coin between his palms. He had his father's name but his mother's looks, Briody thought. The blond hair and the wide strong face, blue eyes streaked with yellow. At eleven he was nearly as tall as his dad.

Briody stood. "Remember now, never use that word." He watched Danny run up Alexander Avenue in the bright daylight, his shadow chasing him toward the playground. He wondered at having kids in a place like this, wondered about what different people they were bound to become here among the concrete and the elbowing crowds. It was so far from what they had known as boys: the tiny villages and dark green fields that held few secrets, where you knew everyone and they knew all about you. Here, it seemed, you might turn a corner and disappear forever, lost in the multitudes.

He climbed the stairs. He needed a shower. Then, he had guns to collect and deliver.

Hard Nose McCabe and the superintendent stood toe to toe, their faces darkened, neck veins throbbing, spittle flying, and only a thin thread of civility keeping them from exchanging blows instead of words. "Punches fly, my money's on Hard Nose," Armstrong said. "I'll tell ya, this ain't like other jobs. Other jobs was bad, but this one is bad and worse. The pressure is going through the roof."

Delpezzo concurred with a toss of his plum pit off the nineteenth floor. The gang sat, legs dangling. A truckload had arrived from the Pennsylvania mill that morning with unmarked beams and girders. That simple screwup had sent the job spiraling into chaos. Whatever held up the ironworkers stopped all the trades following them up into the Manhattan sky. So now you had concrete workers and masons sitting on their asses and if it kept up there would be leisure time for the electricians and carpenters, then the tin knockers and plumbers, right down the line to the finish men. The Empire State was an assembly line where the people moved and if one stopped, eventually they would all be stopped. There were rumors of engineers and architects and job runners having nervous breakdowns. Still, Briody and the gang enjoyed the respite.

Armstrong pointed to the Chrysler Building. "That was gonna be the biggest building in the world, too."

"My brother did six months on that one. Hated that foreman. A real daddy's boy. Brother told me he almost threw him off the forty-eighth floor one day."

Skinny laughed and spit tobacco, the brown juice trailing into the space over the street. "Yep, I know that prick. John Smith. Not a jury could have convicted you, that prick. He hates the Irish, too."

"Hey, I don't hate no one. Except the pencils."

Below them engineers with blueprints huddled, then moved about the truckload of steel, sorting, marking, and shouting, while trying to fit together the pieces of a puzzle.

Briody took out his pocketknife and cleaned the dirt from under his nails. He felt the fatigue of a poor night's sleep. The gun drops down to the docks were starting to weigh on him. He always carried out missions with aplomb, considered himself to be steely of nerve. It occurred to him that being in America, where the old antagonisms and grudges meant little, might be weakening his resolve. Maybe he was just burning out. Or maybe he was just tired.

He got up and walked along the beam, two hundred feet above the street. The air was warm and cloudless. Walking toe to heel, he proceeded to the Sixth Avenue side of the site and looked out over the North River, a golden pond under the spring sun, and beyond, to New Jersey and the horizon. The others said that on a day like this you could see clear to Pennsylvania. Briody wondered about the America out there. Since arriving, he had left the city only once, to go to a Casey family christening outside Philadelphia. He figured that someday he would like to venture west, see the country.

He rose on his toes and shot his arms out straight like a man ready to burst into a swan dive. Below him, cars, black forms with sun glinting off their windscreens, inched along in thick competition and people marched along the sidewalks like legions, starting and halting in response to traffic cops, whose whistle blasts floated up to him like faint notes. No matter how high they climbed into the sky, the heights did not worry him. He loved his job, looked forward to waking every morning and coming down to this place and rising into the air, higher each day. Days like this he wished it would never end, that they would rise forever, never topping off.

He leaned forward a bit, looked between his toes, sighted on the traffic standing still on the avenue. He imagined falling. What must those who have gone over the edge have thought as the ground sped closer? Were they relieved? When the end came? The wind changed and he rocked back on his heels, then turned and rejoined the gang.

Armstrong, scratching a large *A* on a girder with the point of his spud wrench, watched Briody return. "You're a real skylarker, ain't you?"

"I like the heights all right."

"A natural. I known guys in the racket twenty years, still got to coon their way along a beam."

"I'm one of them," Sheehan said. "Better safe than sorry." He folded his copy of the *Daily Worker*. "Says here they expecting more than two hundred workers to be killed building the Empire State. You believe that?"

Armstrong flipped into a handstand. "Only the strong survive. Who gets killed on these jobs? Dummies."

"Don't say that," Skinny said. "My brother died on the job.

Wind knocked him down. He fell forty stories. Freak accident, they said. Company sent a thing of flowers to my ma."

Down below the puzzle was sorted out and the cranes kicked out puffs of oily black smoke and swung into action, grabbing steel off the flatbed trucks. The gang pulled on their gloves.

"I wasn't referring to him," Armstrong said. He looked off to the distance, where bunches of skyscrapers stood. Each had its ghosts. The gang fell silent, a nod to Skinny Sheehan's dead brother and to the fact that any one of them might be next.

G race worked feverishly and still she could not get it right: the striker's eyes, light and cold at the same time, as if he was still there and not yet aware that he was dead. It was as if the sudden and violent nature of his demise had arrested his soul. Most of her dead had died like this man, boy really. Her father, Francisco, her little Sean, and Milo she was sure. With their shoes on and their eyes open. She ripped another sheet off and let it drop to the floor. She sketched compulsively. She tried again, worked on the shape of the face, the incipient rictus of the jaw. All was perfect until she came again to the blank stare, those eyes and what they did or did not see. She tore the sheet off and let it fall.

She sank into a chair surrounded by dozens of faces dead and incomplete. The sun was gone over the city, the last light fiery beyond the skyscrapers. It always looked as if the sun set in the south, not directly west across the river from her beyond the middle of Manhattan, but downtown behind the Woolworth Building, as if something was askew, as if the world was crooked on its axis. Darkness came fast. She imagined the boy's family receiving the news. First the shock, then the keening, and the futile lament followed by the biggest question of all, Why?

She reached down and picked up one of the sketches. At least they did not have to see him dead on the sidewalk. She wondered why death followed her and why she had been chosen to witness it. She felt drained. She contemplated her loss of faith, how all the tragedy in her life proved to her that no God worthwhile could be presiding over this earth. Still, while she never prayed for herself she did for others, not wanting her own lack of belief to condemn someone else. Superstitions, rituals, die hard.

Farrell was picking her up later. She should get ready. She liked him, was amused by him, entertained. Certainly she collected his baubles and spent his cash and got a thrill out of plying the night city with him. She knew she was a whore in an exact sense. But she saw only him, did not run the gamut of sports as so many of the other girls did. She lay down with this one man. He did not try to see any further into her than she allowed. He was safe. He returned to his wife and children faithfully every night, no matter how fierce their frolic.

The boat listed to the left and she rocked gently, feeling a touch of vertigo. Someone had come aboard. She had been on this boat for several years and still that feeling unsettled her. She stood.

"You Irish hussy!"

On the deck was Anna. "Where have you been?"

"San Francisco. With Mario, the spaghetti mogul. He cooks for me and sings Italian love songs and he has quite a sausage on him, thick as my wrist. How I love a swarthy man." Anna was dressed in trousers and vest, a black coat and a red beret. She wore workman's boots and her long black hair flowed down past her shoulders. She carried two large canvas shopping bags emblazoned with advertisements for a California market.

"You look like you're ready for the revolution."

"Warm up the guillotine and let the festivities begin. To tell the truth I am too well fed and well laid to be agitating on a fine evening like this. You need a little deprivation to revolt over, or a little boredom, at least. I am in the mood for a fiesta though, that much I can tell you. Here, give me a hand."

Grace grabbed one of the bags. "What did you bring?"

"I present souvenirs—meats, cheese, and contraband wine from the best vineyards west of Burgundy. You and I can throw me a coming-home party."

"Oh Jesus. I've got company coming. Johnny's coming to pick me up. We're supposed to go out."

"The big Tammany man?" Her tone flattened.

"The one."

"Good, he'll lend an air of respectability to the party. Some Manhattan cachet."

"Easy on the sarcasm. I don't think he likes my boat."

"Well, the hell with him. If he's too fancy for us he can find another party to go to."

Grace made some coffee and they sat sipping the hot Spanish brew and watched the river traffic. A tug pulled a garbage barge past them in the dusk, its wake lapping gently against her boat. Barking seagulls wheeled above, then dove and rose, clutching scraps of refuse in their beaks. A bargeman moved along the deck, ignoring the storm of feathered scavengers. Across the oily river the city lights blinked.

Grace described the incident on the picket line and showed Anna some of the sketches. Anna placed her coffee cup on a checkerboard side table and shuffled through them quickly, lingering over several which she then placed in a smaller pile on her lap.

"These are excellent. I don't know what you think you saw or what you think you're missing, but these are haunting. I love this one." She held up one that showed the boy taking his last swing before he was set upon. "I mean the look on his face, as if the fear and the defiance are fighting for supremacy. That confusion is so real. Damn you are brilliant."

Grace took them and placed them on the table. "I just can't shake it. The goons seemed to be enjoying it, like kids playing ball. The sounds were horrible, the cracking of skulls, the men moaning. They never had a chance. It was all so matter of fact."

"There was a big strike in Frisco when I was out there that turned into a three-day riot." She sipped her coffee and stared out at the city. "They called in the militia, who wasted no time opening fire on peaceful demonstrations. At first I was livid, but then there was no real response, people just ran scared back to their little lives. The newspapers whitewashed everything, described it as a few radicals getting what they asked for. Now I can't help feeling the hell with it. Like I want to just have fun and everyone else can rot. Everybody is out for themselves. Why not us?"

Anna picked up the pile of drawings again. "All this time I've known you, I never asked. Where'd a rube Irish farm girl learn to do this?" She held a picture of the dead boy, pushing it toward her. Grace had to turn away.

"It's just something I picked up as a girl."

"I come from the West Side of Manhattan, Grace, and I've been around you Irish immigrants most of my life. I don't think you just 'picked this up' over there."

"I was lucky I guess." Grace poured another black coffee from the small enamel pot and swirled in some sugar. "Back home, my family worked on one of the estates, the Bells. They were Protestants, but well liked by most people. My father looked after their horses. My uncle ran the farm. My mother was the head of service. The old woman was a watercolorist and she just kind of took me under her wing, like, and taught me. I used to sit in her studio with her and watch. She was always kind to me. One day, she asked if I'd like to give it a go. She told me I was a natural. I would go to her after school and she would teach me. We kept it secret from everyone, telling them I was cleaning her studio for her."

Anna looked at some of the work. "She taught you this, the country gentlewoman?"

"God, no. If you looked at her work you would think Ireland was the most idyllic place. Her work was all about garden parties and rolling landscapes in full bloom, splashes of color. A Gay Old World. She was good, don't get me wrong. But she painted a world they wished for, a world that had passed them by. One day I had painted a scene I remembered from when I was about five years of age. An eviction. It was awful, the landlord egging on the constables, the family outside, the mother keening. Eleven now-homeless children crying while the husband just sat on the ground, his head in his hands. I never saw such defeat. I made him the focus of the piece. Mrs. Bell picked it up and went on about its brilliance. She put her hand on my head. I can still smell her lilac, her powders and scented oils. She strode over to the fire and threw it in, then came back and said, 'Not the sort of thing anyone wants to see, though.' "

"Why'd you leave?" Anna was wrestling the cork out of a jug of wine.

"My father was shot dead."

"That's it, shot dead?"

"It was during the wars. I'd rather not go into it. After that, Mrs. Bell paid to send me to London to work for her relations. I was not happy there, so when I heard about jobs in Spain from another Irish girl, I left."

"I had no idea."

"Achh. Was all a long time ago. Let's have us some fun."

"After that tale of woe?"

"What woe? I'm here to tell you about it. How woeful can it be?"

"That's looking on the bright side."

"It's the only side worth looking on."

Grace went to the toilet, then stopped in her bedroom. She should get dressed for Farrell. On her bureau was a picture of her father. She kissed her finger and then touched it to the glass over his face. A pile of money from Farrell sat on the bed, dirty green tribute to corrupt times. She pulled the door closed to block Anna's view and slid the bed from over her hidey-hole. She used a letter opener to pry between the worn floorboards, then lifted the top off. She looked down at the growing pile of cash and the two dark, blunt pistols Milo had kept there, her journal where she recorded her bank stops—dates—names—amounts. She added the bills and closed the trapdoor. She slid the bed back over. She sat in front of her mirror and when Anna called out she beckoned her into the room. Anna stood behind her and pulled her hair back, working it into a long braid.

"This hair is amazing. How does it stay so lustrous?"

"I'm too lazy to wash it enough to dry it out."

Grace watched in the mirror as Anna bent over and pressed her nose to her head.

"Smells clean enough."

Anna's rings caught the light and dazzled while her hands braided. Grace figured Anna was probably her closest friend, someone with whom she shared even her grief over Francisco and her boys. She was not one to lament publicly, carried her dark burdens deep inside of her. But she felt comfortable telling Anna because Anna brought that out in people and while being a vicious gossip knew where to draw the line. She seemed to respect the difference between the embarrassing and the humiliating, between that which caused a blush and that which caused real pain. It set her apart from the immigrant Irish Grace had lived with when she first came to New York, many of whom had packed their begrudgery into their valises along with their humble belongings. She had confided much to Anna. But no, she figured she had better keep her dealings with Farrell to herself. For now.

They took a bottle of wine to the deck. Anna flipped through her sketchbook. "Nice stuff for a Catholic girl from County Cavan. You just keep getting better and better. These I like a lot." Anna showed her a couple of the Empire State.

"I just wish I could get inside the place."

"I bet you can. Have you ever met Lewis Hine?"

"The photographer?"

"He's been commissioned to document it in pictures. I hear he has full access. Comes and goes as he pleases. If you knew him, I bet you could get on the job."

"Really?" Grace was excited. "Maybe Johnny can help me with this."

"You can put him to good use, finally."

"I'll ask him. But do you think this Hine will go for having a woman around?"

"Well, the one thing I bet can be said for your Johnny is that he's good at getting people to do what they might not want to do."

"I think that is why he likes me so much. I rarely let him set the agenda."

"Men are just nuts. But you're right. You get too pliable, you lose your allure." Anna tossed the empty wine bottle into the river. It sank and then bobbed to the surface, moving south with the tide.

"Right you are."

"Why don't you let me draw you? I haven't done any work in weeks."

Grace led Anna into her small sitting room and propped up an easel and drawing pad for her friend. She sat on the couch, letting the robe fall away from her. Anna said, "Come on, give us something provocative."

Grace lay on her side, a hand propping up her head, her legs crossed at the ankles. Anna and she often drew each other nude, using their bodies to hone their craft. Sometimes when Anna stayed on the boat after an evening of wine and work they would hold each other in the night. At first this was awkward and Grace had wondered at her friend's intentions. But while each of them was curious, neither dared to move beyond playfulness, to jeopardize what for them had become a strong friendship. The nights she shared her bed with Anna were chaste and she enjoyed them just for the heat of someone who was not compelled to impale her.

Grace was amazed that she wore her nudity so easily. She had posed often for portrait classes, dressed. When a model did not show up one day and Anna suggested she fill in, she had laughed. It never occurred to her that she would do something like this, much less be comfortable doing it. Now it seemed natural and easy and when she posed all the prudishness ingrained in her youth fell away as completely as the robe.

Grace watched her scratch away at the paper before her, biting her lips as she worked at rendering an image. She looked down at herself, at the stretch marks from birthing that were now faint striations, ghostly reminders of other places, other lives. Sometimes that was all she had to remember her babies: her children, her two beautiful boys. Because some days, she just could not conjure up the reality of them. It was as if they were part of a fleeting and lost dream. Some days she was dead to the past and this frightened her.

Later, how much she wasn't sure, Grace looked up to see Johnny Farrell standing like a mannequin in the doorway, the light drained from his face. She had forgotten all about him. Johnny stared at her with a look of distaste. Grace laughed, could not help herself. She slipped off the couch, grabbed her robe.

"For God's sake get dressed. This is disgraceful."

Anna laughed. "Ah, it's more like the full Grace."

Farrell shot her a look. "Shut up, you."

Anna saluted. "Yes sir!"

Grace laughed again and brushed past Farrell into the bedroom. She dressed quickly and came back into the room. Anna sat on the couch drinking wine and smoking. Farrell clutched his pearl gray fedora in his hand; without moving his lips, he said, "Let's go outside."

Out on the deck there were shrieks, music, and gaiety coming from other boats. The river reflected lights off its oily surface. The air was cool. Grace hugged herself for warmth.

"What the hell is going on?" He squeezed her arms. "Hey. You were supposed to be ready to go out."

"Anna stopped by, Johnny. My friend." She heard herself slur and did not like the sound. He tightened his grip, his fingers digging into her biceps.

"You coming with me or you're staying?"

"Oh Johnny, you're so . . . " She lost her thought and laughed again.

"So what?" Her giggling angered him. "I said, I'm so what?"

"Just so, Johnny, you're just so, Johnny."

She went back in and told Anna she was going. "Keep an eye on the place."

"You sure you want to leave with that creep?"

She said, "It's okay," but she wasn't sure. She could not even tell why she was going. She walked arm in arm with Johnny out onto Quay Street. Rats ran alongside the abandoned brewery and she felt Johnny shudder. "Christ, do I hate rats." Three river dogs watched them pass, their eyes red from the light, sniffing the air as if looking for weakness. He held the car door for her, slamming it as soon as she was seated. Grace kept the window down and the salty air sobered her a bit as they roared through industrial Brooklyn. Johnny railed against her "choice of friends."

"My father died a long time ago. I make my own mind up."

"For Christ sake, Grace, they're riffraff, bohemian scum. Was there one person on any of those boats with a job? I bet they all sit around complaining how awful this country is, knocking the system, woe is me and all that jazz. Well, the hell with them. They should take baths and hit the bricks looking for work like real Americans instead of Red radicals."

"Ah Jesus, Johnny, would you ever shut up?"

"Where would I be today if I had an act like that? I'd be sleeping on my mother's couch in the Bronx, that's where. Nobody gave me nothing in this life, nobody ever will. You want something, you go out and get it. It's the best system there is."

Grace laughed loudly.

"That's funny? I'm funny?"

"Jesus, Johnny Farrell, to listen to you you'd think you were mining coal morning, noon, and night instead of grafting your way through life. Do you think I'm that daft?"

She watched his jaw tighten, a grimness come over him, and she realized she probably had gone too far but she was too drunk to care. They drove in silence for a while. As they pulled onto the roadway for the Williamsburg Bridge Farrell spoke in a calm and measured tone that lost calm and measure with each syllable. "Where would your people be without Tammany, Grace? Have you ever considered that? Or are you too busy being hoodwinked by those dope-fiend anarchists you like to frolic around with? How about this car, Grace, and the meal we're going to eat and that necklace you're wearing, the one with the diamonds and rubies that would cost five years' wages back in that dreary hellhole you crawled out of?"

She had heard enough. "Stop the car."

"What about the money you make going to the bank once or twice a week? How bad is that? There's nothing wrong with honest graft. The system was set up long before we got here, Grace. What's wrong with us getting what we deserve?"

"Stop the car!" She shouted this time and he looked at her in alarm. She had never raised her voice with Johnny before.

"What for?"

"I'm going to be sick." She put her hand to her mouth, knowing this would make him pull over. God forbid his prized ride was sullied. She was out of the car before he fully stopped. Other drivers leaned hard on horns as they swerved to avoid the car. She ran to the railing and climbed over onto the pedestrian path. She pressed herself against the outer railing and looked down to the black water far below, breathing deep the cool air, then up at the city that rolled north all the way to the upper reaches of the Bronx. The factories on the Brooklyn shore sat, quiet blocky ghosts surrounded by pools of darkness interrupted only by the weak light of the streetlamps. To her left, the towers of Manhattan, the Woolworth, the Municipal Building, the Cunard, and the shiny new Bank of New York, pierced the night sky and she wondered at the activity in the glowing windows at this late hour, pictured cleaning crews going through the motions and desperate men behind closed doors worrying numbers trying to stave off ruin. In the distance the dull red emanation from Times Square suggested a city aflame. She stood on the lower bar of the rail and, leaning forward, lifted her arms to the sky. A fresh wind blew down the East River. A train smashed along behind her, bursting through the night. Grace turned and watched a mosaic of faces, swing-shift workers heading home to cold midnight dinners, sleeping families, fading hopes. She'd known that life once.

"Grace, let's go."

She ignored him. She traced the outline of the Queensboro Bridge, remembered reading about it in Fitzgerald's book when she was on the train coming to New York for the first time. It was glorious at night, engineering as art, cold steel aglow from the sweep of headlights that dazzled like rough diamonds. She felt a chill and pulled her sweater closed.

"Grace. Please. I love you."

She turned and saw his anger was gone. He stood beside the open door of his car offering it to her. He looked like a schoolboy pleading. She took his hand and let him lead her back to the warmth of the idling automobile. The only thing she had over him, she knew, was her unknowability, his inability to fathom her. The power would shift to him the minute he figured her out. But she could rest assured that this would never happen.

Judge Joseph Force Crater took in the show at O'Halloran's. He sat ramrod straight and sipped bourbon over cracked ice, his panama hat on the table before him. A dozen girls moved as one, barely dressed, tassels taped to cover their nipples, sequined and spangled in shorts so tight that little was left to the imagination. Left they swayed, then right, forming a smiling jiggling chorus line of flesh and exuberant temptation, beads of sweat gathering at the edges of their made-up faces, their lips so ruby red and glossy they looked to be made of glass. But one stood out. He had a hankering for the third girl from the left, a spunky redhead with long legs and stupendous breasts. He'd seen her around, knew she had a fondness for liquor and power brokers. He sipped his drink, swirled the chilled whiskey around his mouth, savoring its smoke, and imagined her naked and pliable. She brightened his mood considerably.

He needed distraction. That buffed-up ghetto barrister Johnny Farrell had called him that morning, pimping for one of the racket boys as usual. There was a murder case coming up that they frowned upon. Maybe the Judge might see things their way, might conjure up a technicality. The little papist monkey had no shame. Crater knew he did owe a certain debt. Ways of the world and whatnot. He had paid a year's salary in advance for his judgeship and it was worth every penny. Still, he had expected to toss out the odd case—domestic disputes, civil trifles, not to let bloodthirsty murderers saunter out of his courtroom sporting the smirks of the invincible. He nodded to the waitress, indicated his rocks glass, and watched her sashay to the bar. The dance number ended, the crowd brayed its approval, intermission commenced. The Judge stood, squared his shoulders, and made for backstage, where he stood twirling his panama hat until the door opened. The dressing room was no more than a back room stacked with cases of booze where every two girls shared a chair to hang their things on, and he caught a glimpse of flesh and sparkle, a whiff of sweat and perfume. The door closed again. He was prepared to wait. The flowers had been delivered along with a tasteful invitation to ride to dinner in his Nash coupe. She would know of his reputation, his ability to deliver the goods, his standing in communities of both light and dark.

Farrell had also mentioned again the growing brouhaha surrounding the Vitale mess. He heard not so subtle threats as Farrell stressed the importance of shedding no light on the inner machinations of the Organization. He had been insulted by the pointing out of the obvious.

Her colleagues filed out in twos and threes, eyes averted, sweat drying on their skin still flush from the show. Bundled up now, their fleshy assets hidden, their faces wiped of paint, they looked to him like college girls on their way to a pep rally. They pulled hats down to their brows for disguise. They shared giggles and whispers and pushed past him to the back-alley door where a bodyguard would see them to the curb unmolested by overappreciative fans.

He checked his pocket watch. She was taking her time. He liked that—a little cat-and-mouse, a little game that showed sass, initiative. He leaned against the wall and signaled a waitress to bring him over another drink. When she finally came out she smirked but he could detect her desire behind it. He was not a judge for nothing. "Well your honor, to what do I owe the honor?"

He donned his hat, proffered his elbow. "Please, Vivian, call me Joe."

Briody, dressed in shorts and boxing boots, sat on a table while Gus wrapped his hands with trembling precision. The room was thick with the stench of sweat and stale cigar smoke and the old Jew worked the gauze in between Briody's fingers, then took pieces of medical tape and finished each hand with it, making tight white clubs. He then held his old hands aloft and open and let Briody pop the palms, one two, one two.

"Good. Good." Gus was satisfied.

Briody looked at his fists. "Nice work, Gus."

The trainer smoothed his thin hair across his pink scalp, pulled a yellowed handkerchief from his back pocket and blew his nose until his face was dark with blood. "Most of these guys are pier six brawlers, of this I'm sure. You box like you know how, this will be a walk in the park. Just don't let your donkey temper get the better of you, you get clocked. Just move and jab, jab, jab. You got nothing to prove. Nothing. You hear me?"

Briody nodded.

Gus smoothed his hair again and said, "Come on, get up and move a little. You eat today?"

Briody stood and jogged lightly in place. He raised his arms over his head.

"Egg sandwich for breakfast, piece of beef and some potatoes for lunch. A cup of ginger ale."

"Good, you'll have some gas. Lot of guys have trouble eating day of a fight."

During the Irish wars, two days before a mission his stomach would start to roil and he could not eat a bite. A few hours afterward he was ravenous and would gorge himself as if the mission had drained all the vitality from his being. But boxing, in a ring with a referee and judges and doctors nearby; what was there to worry about?

Then he stepped into that arena and was stunned by its vastness, and by the size of the crowd. The place was an undulating cavern of blurred screaming faces. A shudder rolled through him. Most of his fights had been in prison before screws and inmates, where at most the governor brought some friends for the show. He shook his legs to dissipate the nervous energy coming over him. The Emerald Society pipe band came in bleating, drums pounding. People were clapping and screaming to the sounds, on their feet, pumping fists in the air, maddened now with bloodlust.

Briody stood in awe. "Jesus Christ," he muttered under his breath. They started a slow retreat from the ring to the strains of the pipe band playing "The Rising of the Moon." The crowd was frenzied. There were cops, firefighters, laborers, trainmen, street sweepers, and ditchdiggers, all those that made the city go, and they filled the cheaper seats that rose all the way to the rafters. Briody knew their kind in France, those that will fight and die in wars. Closer, in the sections that ran back briefly from the ring, the swells and sports congregated, well dressed, natty, half of them turned to watch the raucous mayhem above them. Across the ring stood his opponent, the Bostonian.

Briody bounded about the ring, the hood over his head, and started to throw easy combinations, left, right, uppercut, hook— getting the feel of the canvas, moving laterally, switching directions, pivoting, bobbing. He bounced on his toes. The ring floor was firm, which would benefit him for he was quick. He was announced as a sergeant in the 40th precinct. He snuck views around the place. In the front row, he noticed Babe Ruth and Jack Dempsey, their broad primate faces surrounding cigars. Just behind them was Walker, the mayor, his mistress by his side talking to another couple. The man was thin-faced, well dressed, and looked like a big-city sharpie. Briody threw combinations faster, trying to work up a light sweat. He hated to start a bout cold. He studied the woman that was with the sharpie. Her dark hair was piled on her head, and as she was talking to her man she turned and her head tilted back with laughter, and even at a distance her warmth was something he could feel. She looked up at him and Briody felt his breath catch. Did he know her? Even in the ringside crowd of sports and their glamorous escorts, she sparkled and the harsh light and smoky air of the arena did nothing to diminish her glow. Gus pulled his robe off. Briody looked at her once more and she smiled ever so slightly, the corners of her mouth rising just a hint. He turned back to the fight.

"Just do what you know how to do." Gus was speaking up to him.

The bell rang. The other fighter, a chunky six-footer sporting bluish tattoos, was all barroom savagery. He threw bunches of wide chopping punches that were mostly all arm and lifted his chin while he attacked. Briody simply moved laterally and started pasting his face with jabs. He knew what the man was going to throw because his arms would start backward first as if he was grabbing something behind him to hit with. Briody stepped to his right, landed a heavy double jab, and spun. He was in back of the ripsnorter now and the crowd appreciated the move. The Bostonian bled from the nose. He came at Briody behind a flurry of sloppy shots, desperate to inflict hurt. Briody caught the blows on his elbows and shoulders and hammered back, landing at will. He could hear the crowd gasping at the sound of the concussions. The bell rang.

Gus poured cold water into his mouth and down the front of his shorts. "A brick wall for a head, this guy."

Briody breathed easily. He tried to pick out the woman from the crowd and could not. He spit into the slop bucket. "Go for the breadbasket, Michael. You'll break your hands on that head."

Briody spent the first half of round two moving, sticking jabs, waiting. The Boston cop's eyes were full of hate and defeat. He gathered himself and came at Briody, a wide left, a wide right. Briody bobbed underneath the punches and landed four cannon shots to the man's gut. The cop grunted with hurt but managed to wrap his arms around Briody and hang on. The ref came in to break them and when he did the cop threw a crushing uppercut to Briody's groin. Despite the cup Briody felt the punch sear through him like a flame. He felt nauseous. His knees buckled and when he doubled over the cop thumbed him in the eye and threw a quick elbow to the point of his nose. The official had seen nothing. Briody tasted his own blood. The bell rang.

Briody walked gingerly back to his corner, his left eye swelling with each step. The pain was turning into something else. When Gus swung his stool into the ring Briody kicked it out through the bottom rope.

"Don't lose your head, kid. The fight is all yours. Just box, stay outside. He's a dirty copper bastard. Don't sink to his level." Gus splashed his chest with a sponge and wiped the blood from his face. Briody watched Gus wring the pink water into the spit bucket and said nothing. He stared across the ring at the smirking face of the Boston cop and was reminded of all the lousy prison guards who lied and cheated and abused the little power granted them by the state. The sounds of the Garden grew muted and distant until all he could hear was his own breath. The lights seemed to shine brighter. When the bell rang Gus slapped him on the back and said, "Just stick and move." Briody had other ideas.

Before the cop was a foot from his corner Briody was on him. He landed a left hook to the side of the man's fat head that snapped it around, spraying sweat and blood three rows deep into the audience. Then Briody stepped back and waited for the man to come forward. He would take his time. For the next minute he threw only jabs—swift, cruel shots that began to cut and swell the cop's face, occasionally dipping his shoulder to land one to the solar plexus. The cop, all stupid rage, kept coming as Briody knew he would. Briody started to throw his right, landing it at will but not really loading up on it. He saw the consternation of the cop's cornermen. He feinted a jab and when the cop went to swat it away he nailed him square in the jaw with a right, feeling the concussion back up his arm and down to his toes. The cop buckled and his eyes rolled up in his head. Briody saw the trainer lift the white towel of surrender and throw it over the ropes. As the towel sailed softly through the air Briody ducked and threw three murderous hooks to the man's gut. The last drove him to the blood-splattered canvas, where he curled up and vomited weakly on the referee's shoes.

When the referee raised his hand in triumph the crowd was on its feet roaring. Briody looked for the woman again, but she was gone.

A line of dolled-up partygoers stretched down the block and around the corner onto Eighth Avenue. The men, restless, loitered in flannel and wool suits that sported razor pleats and flashy silk ties knotted tightly while the women laughed beneath the brims of stylish hats, slinky in the latest cinched-waist dresses. Everyone smoked. Tipped flasks caught the streetlamps, sparkling in the city light. They affected poses that said, We belong where the action is, not here on the dirty Harlem street. An earlier shower had cut the humidity and left the city air smelling fresh. Farrell had his driver pull right to the front, jump out, and hold the door open for them. Grace took his hand and as she alighted from the leathery confines of the Cadillac she marveled at Johnny Farrell's capacity for showmanship. Lines meant nothing to him.

The doorman, a tugboat in black cashmere, greeted him with a bear hug. "Always a pleasure, Johnny. Every time. You too, miss." He offered her his hammy hand. A few odd jeers came from the crowd. All she saw was a wall of faces that in the rush to the inside took on a fun-house look. Johnny flashed his smile and Johnny nodded and shook the man's hand. Grace knew something passed between them, a bit of cash, grease. "You gotta duke 'em," he was fond of saying. The city was one big kickback circus to Farrell. She thought she might like to trace just a single twenty-dollar bill's ricochet around the metropolis for a week. They were whisked past the line of gapers and gawkers, those not in the know.

Inside they climbed the stairs to the second floor and were greeted by the maître d', who very nearly snapped his heels. "Mr. Farrell, we've been expecting you."

Their coats were removed with surgical precision and they were whisked to a prime table, a corner banquette fit for a platoon. She slid in before Johnny, who put his arm around her and asked, "Oysters sweetie? You want to start with oysters?"

"Sure, Johnny. You know I love oysters."

Farrell held her hand on the table and nodded toward the waiter, who was standing at a polite distance awaiting his summons. "A dozen oysters, two dozen, and some champagne, the best you have."

"You're in a good humor."

"Why not? Life is short and I have a beautiful woman by my side and a pocketful of money. Most men go through life never having either, the poor chumps. How'd you like the fights?"

"More than I expected, so."

"What did you think of the Irish heavy?"

"Who's that?" Grace asked but she knew exactly who he was talking about. The tall Irishman who fought last. Even from the distance of her seat she had been struck by his masculine good looks. What a build on him.

When the oysters came plump and silvery in their juices Farrell and Grace polished them off without speaking. Johnny smothered his with horseradish. What a waste. The salt tang of the sea reminded her of home and autumn trips to Galway Bay when she was a young girl. The champagne made her flush and she watched as Farrell, ever the mover and shaker, rose and made his way to the toilets, pausing twice to hold court.

She was content to sit and watch, sip her bubbly, considering how she would paint the crazy movement of the place, the characters. Every table was full and had a small lamp. Lovers at two tops leaned close to each other, whispering, holding hands across the cloth, or attended to each other underneath, hands unseen. At the larger tables parties of night creatures slugged illicit brews and talked loudly, laughing, hooting, blowing smoke rings. A waiter snaked his way through the crowd carrying a birthday cake, dozens of candles glowing, the tiny flames swaying to the beat of his movements. The dance floor was a vibrating mass of revelers, arms and legs akimbo as they danced to the electric beat of the Harlem River Quiver, brows sweaty, shirts and dresses clinging to their bodies in the humid air of the club. She lit a cigarette.

Johnny came back, grabbed his slick glass, and took up his sport of pointing out a who's who, but she'd worked in some of the better speaks, had been around long enough to know all the types. There were the moneymen, lenders and financiers, scions of metal and machine and oil fortunes, speculators, and the show people, dancers and writers and players, all kinds of razzle and dazzle, and of course the racket boys, some grown so fat and soft as to be indistinguishable from the moneymen, others granite-faced delinquents, still gutter-thin but dressed now in garments of rich men earned by mayhem. The only blacks she noticed were either playing onstage or busing tables. She sucked her flute dry. She watched weary-eyed newspapermen, politicos, and merchants who contrasted with those boys born rich, fresh from leafy campuses, who wore it all so easily. She catalogued the gamblers and losers and all the retired Indian killers and veterans of wars and private feuds, dreamers and fakirs and con men—many who had played large roles in two centuries and were supping in the Manhattan night. She needed to draw, to paint. She fidgeted, dug in her purse for a pencil.

"Is the Mayor coming?"

"You bet. Him and the lovely Miss Compton. She's fond of you, what the Mayor tells me, a big fan."

"Really."

"So he says. She's some number, but she doesn't hold a candle to you." While he said this he scanned the room.

"Ah, Johnny."

He turned back to her. "How's your picture painting going?"

He always called it that, as if she was a schoolgirl with a hobby. Farrell took nothing seriously that did not result in the instant flow of cash or the amassing of power.

"It's grand, Johnny, but now that you mention it I thought you might help me with something."

Farrell went back to scanning the crowd. " 'S that?"

"Do you know a fella, Lewis Hine?"

"The do-gooder guy with the camera?"

"Yes."

"Yes. No, but yes, I know of him. Seen him once or twice around town. Why?"

"They say he's been commissioned to document the Empire State Building with his camera, take pictures of the construction."

"So?"

"I was hoping you could get him to take me on the site, as an assistant."

He patted her hand. The band played a waltz, causing a sea change in the dance floor crowd. "What would you want to do something like that for?"

"So I can keep painting it."

"I can't figure you out. Can't you just go to the park and paint trees and the flowers like other women? The guys on those sites are pretty rough-and-tumble. They'll eat you alive."

"Maybe I should be like other women and stop running around town with a married father?"

He looked at her, his thin lips pointing down. "That's a cheap shot."

"Well, if you can't arrange it, I understand. I'll ask around." She knew the challenge to his ability as a fixer would goad him to action. Johnny Farrell believed there was nothing in New York he could not arrange.

"All right already, I'll call a guy."

"Who will call a guy."

"You're learning, kid."

"Might as well be from the best." She leaned back and let the waiter refill her glass. She was excited now, had something to look forward to. The site.

There was a commotion and the band stopped mid-note. Necks craned. Lovers broke their gazes. A nervous, expectant twitter rose in volume until the band swung into "Will You Love Me in December as You Do in May?" and Mayor Walker, tuxedoed, and Betty Compton, dazzling in fur and pearls, glided onto the dance floor, beaming. Walker hammed it up, dancing a little soft-shoe to the song he had written as a young man dreaming of a life far from the dirty game of politics. The crowd headed for the dance floor, everyone trying to get close, until the Mayor and Betty were hemmed into a tight circle, a spotlight shrouding them in golden light. People clapped and stamped, whistled. Walker's presence confirmed something for them: This was the place.

Walker soon begged off the floor, but it was a full fifteen minutes before he made it through the adoring throng to their table. Grace thought what a tiny percentage of men ever knew such adulation. Walker was made for it. She was aware of his youthful show business aspirations and thought there were only two professions where he might have been happy. She watched Farrell stand and glow, the acolyte greeting his master. But first the Mayor leaned in to kiss her on the cheek. "Grace."

"Mr. Mayor."

"Johnny Farrell."

Grace watched the crowd watch them. She had to admit she did get a bit of a kick out of all the attention.

Dozens of people stopped by the table to pay respects to the Mayor. He sat like a sultan receiving tribute, acknowledging every one of them with that dazzling smile. A large man with a shock of white hair leaned over the table and, unable to get Walker's attention, offered a pudgy hand to her. "Evening, John Roscoe, Board of Aldermen."

The Mayor turned at this announcement and said, "What a co-incidence, I'm bored of aldermen, too." There was a spitfire of laughter and the alderman did his best to chuckle along as his fat face bloomed. Jack Dempsey, trailed by a forlorn starlet with watery brown eyes, stopped long enough to playfully cock his fists. "Jimmy, top of the evening." A pair of blond and busty Minnesotans approached demurely, asking for an autograph. The Mayor obliged.

After a while the Mayor stood up and, trailing Johnny Farrell, walked to a door in the corner where they and a group of solemn-faced men disappeared. Betty leaned over and lit a cigarette with the candle. "Johnny's a doll. The Mayor thinks he's hot stuff."

"Red hot. You're in a new show, Johnny tells me."

"It's called *Three's a Crowd*. A real corker. I'll leave you some tickets you want to come down."

The two of them sat smoking, sipping from their flutes. Men stared with hunger, but kept their distance.

"You like New York guys too, huh?"

"Seems to be a lot of them about."

"Loads."

"They all married?"

"Please. I can't believe what you get away with in this town. Where I come from? Forget it sister. My cousin, Shanna? Real pretty girl, nice too. She started sneaking around on her husband, which believe you me, if you knew Shawn, you might too? Starts seeing this fella on the side, some writer—they damn near ran her out of town on a rail. She is forever shamed."

"The stuff in the newspapers doesn't bother the Mayor?"

"Him? No." She laughed and Grace saw how truly beautiful she was. "Not James J. Me? Heck yes. He has an amazing ability to shrug things off."

Grace pointed to the door through which they had gone. "What do you think goes on back there?"

"Don't know, don't want to know. Jimsie says the 'business of the metropolis' and I am content to leave it at that."

Grace smoked, wondered if the Mayor knew of her own involvement in the "business of the metropolis."

Betty excused herself to the ladies' room and Grace sat alone and watched. She was amused by the spectacle and enjoyed the rich food and wine, the pulse of the music, the ambient energy of the dance floor. She marveled at just how far removed from the actual life of the city these people were, how carefree and above it all they seemed. She was a voyeur, an interloper, a transient on this scene, and somehow she was grateful for this, for the chasm between the haves and the have-nots was so large it was perverse, unbridgeable. Johnny, she was sure, was intoxicated by access and proximity to the throb of power.

Betty returned, her lips fiery red. "Here they come."

When they sat back down the two men seemed pleased with themselves. She felt Johnny's hand, furtive, on her knee, a caress that crawled up her thigh until she squeezed and stopped it between her legs. She took him by the arm and said, "Come on, let's dance." Johnny was a decent dancer, lithe and nimble of foot. They moved about as the orchestra played, pressing flesh, flushed with drink and the heat of the night, exertion, the air full of sexual charge and release. They moved in and out of couples, some dancing with grace and easy rhythm, others flailing about madly, just happy to be moving in the New York night. Next to them a skinny man with bad skin maneuvered a bloated perfumed old sot around as if he were piloting a dirigible. Johnny pointed out that she was an heiress involving food. As Farrell spun her about the room in perfect sync with the music, she felt a slight delirium. Her breath came fast as she let herself be put through the paces.

She was surprised when the Mayor cut in. He waltzed her around the floor, precise and practiced. He kept his hands where they should be. After a couple of numbers he led her by the hand back to the table, turned that smile on her. His charm was something you could feel, it had weight to it. "Thank you my dear. Have you ever been to Castlecomer in Kilkenny?"

"Not that I can recall."

"My father was from there. A beautiful place. I wonder if it is like Cavan."

"It's only a small country."

"Why did you leave?"

"War, hunger, begrudgery, and rain. Not necessarily in that order."

"Each and every one reason enough on its own. Well at least you were smart enough to end up in our splendid little town."

At the table, the Mayor let Betty nuzzle his ear. He grinned slyly and nodded, yet he managed to keep his attention turned outward to the madness around him.

Long after midnight a group of men came in and Grace watched a subtle concern slide down Walker's face. Beside her she felt Farrell stiffen. She watched the men come toward them, moving on the balls of their feet with an animal grace. One man, obviously the leader, she recognized. Tommy Touhey. Behind him, she realized with a start, was the fighter from earlier. He followed Touhey looking about at the scene and she saw that there was a melancholy described in those dark eyes, a sadness she would not have expected after seeing the way he had brutalized his opponent. The whole room was watching them. There was power in the way they moved, something that said these were men of consequence. She sat up straight and slid her hand out from underneath Farrell's.

Tough Tommy Touhey led his men right to their table. She thought that crossing that room you had to offer up a hundred "excuse me's," but people just got out of Touhey's way. Farrell reclaimed her hand and squeezed harder. He shot a glance at the Mayor, who was already standing, trying to coax a bleary Betty to her feet. Grace could feel the history of these three men but she focused on the boxer, who stared right at her, just a hint of smile at his lips. Somebody had gotten him to a tailor. He looked splendid in a double-breasted suit.

Touhey backslapped the Mayor. "Your honor. Where you going? I voted for you five times in the last election."

"That's what I was afraid of." The Mayor said it with a wide smile.

"You're not going to buy me a drink?"

The Mayor's security detail, three men in dark suits who had been keeping a polite distance, started to close on the table. "Ah, Mr. Touhey. If only you had gotten here sooner. I have to escort this young lady home. I'm sure your old pal Johnny Farrell will oblige you."

"Least you can let your guard dogs stay out, enjoy the night."

"They're professionals, Tommy. No time for gallivanting." The

Mayor gathered Betty and departed to an abundance of smiles and handshakes.

Touhey wasted no time taking the Mayor's seat. "Real character, that song and dance man. A dandy from the Village—now look at him."

Touhey looked about and then turned his gaze on her. His eyes were blood-rimmed, but he did not seem drunk. He put his huge forearms on the table. "Grace. Meet a fellow Mick. Say hello to the fighter of the night. Mike Briody."

"Brady?" Farrell did not like losing control of the conversation.

"Briody."

"Hey, you say tomahto we say tomato."

"That's a Cavan name. I'm from Cavan. Grace's my name. Grace Masterson."

She extended her hand and Briody took it. "Is that right? Whereabouts?"

"Mullahoran."

"You serious? I am from Kilnaleck."

She laughed. "Jesus, we're practically related then. What do you do when you're not half naked and beating people up?"

"I'm putting up the Empire State Building." He turned his hands up to her and she looked at the thick ridges of calluses, fought the impulse to run her fingers over them.

Farrell laughed, trying to play the sport. "Now you did it, Mike. She's some fan of your work. Loves that building."

Touhey put his arm around Farrell's neck and pulled him into a headlock. "Johnny boy." He mussed Farrell's hair and she watched as Farrell pulled himself away, forcing a smile as he smoothed his hair back into place. Touhey watched him pat his hair down and as soon as Farrell dropped his hands he did it again and burst out laughing. She knew Farrell was seething.

"We go way back, me and slick here, lady. Way back. So it hurts my feelings when I don't hear from him." Touhey smiled, but she saw no warmth there.

"You're a real character, Tommy. You done playing hairdresser?"

"I'm just breaking your shoes, Johnny. Don't get touchy on me."

Briody sat next to her, all heat and muscle. She felt a connection to him, made no effort to move away. Was it because of home? Or was it something else entirely? Farrell's obvious discomfort with the intrusion amused her. On the bandstand Cab Calloway broke into "Happy Feet." Farrell held his face in a rictus of a smile, his lips pulled back as if stuck there by a massive stroke. Touhey cracked his knuckles absentmindedly, the sound like rocks bouncing along the gutter.

"Swell joint here. You know a kid from the Bronx, he should be careful about letting his head get all swelled up, goes all fancy maybe he forgets where he comes from, what and who he owes his good fortune to. I know Johnny Farrell ain't a fella like that. But we both know guys like that, and what become of them, don't we Johnny?"

Grace watched as Johnny leaned back. "It's good to see you, Tommy. You're right, I been running around so much, I ain't even been back to see my mom lately." He waved over at the waiter. "Get you a drink, Tommy? Some of this champagne?"

"Yeah John. I'll drink one with you for old times. Why not? Then maybe you come up the Bronx you get a minute and I'll buy you one."

Farrell indicated to the waiter that he wanted a fresh bottle and more glasses.

Grace listened to them make small talk about the days growing up in the Bronx. She knew little about Johnny's past and she found this conversation revealing. He was always vague, glossed over it, said he was a college man, affected an upper-class manner, except when he was drunk and railing against his family. Touhey scared her. He seemed stitched together by violence, had the look that said he enjoyed doling out pain.

"Johnny ever tell you the time we robbed that payroll, the gas company, up on the Grand Concourse?"

"Johnny doesn't tell me much about his youth." Farrell squeezed her hand, a warning.

Touhey drained his glass. "Ask him sometime about what a lit-

128

tle street punk he used to be. Before he went high-hat on his old pals. He was a wild one. He ever take you to meet his wife and kids on Park Avenue?"

"Tommy, Tommy. That's uncalled for, come on."

Touhey laughed and mussed his hair again. "I'm only joking you."

Johnny's face hardened but still he squeezed out a smile.

Grace was suddenly uncomfortable watching him be bullied, felt surprising compassion for him. "It's Fifth Avenue," she said, then excused herself and went to the toilets so they might hash out whatever they needed to.

At the bar a number of men held dark counsel muttering to each other, seemingly oblivious to the madcap night around them. One of the bouncers swung his arm as a barricade and she watched Owney Madden, accompanied by a beefy entourage, head into the night. There was a surprisingly short line for the ladies' room. Sweaty women, fresh off the dance floor, fanned themselves with their hands.

She sat on the toilet and, feeling a recklessness brought on by the champagne, spread the crisp white dinner napkin across her lap. She was sure she wanted to see this Briody again. She used a drawing pencil to do a quick sketch of the Empire State Building and wrote "start" next to it. She outlined Manhattan Island and then an arrow pointing to the Williamsburg Bridge, which she sketched to span the East River. She outlined a quick grid of the industrial neighborhood, a few blocky buildings, and labeled Kent Street with an arrow pointing north and then a turn onto Quay Street. She drew a small precise version of her boat with a woman standing on the deck, hand to brow, searching the distance, and next to the boat she placed a large X. She studied it and laughed. Someone banged on the stall door. She wrote, "I'll be there all week," folded it in half, then quarters, then eighths, a small compact square.

She stood at the sink and washed her hands while a duo of showgirls shared some cocaine. A pale-faced woman next to her painted her lips the color of bruised cherries and Grace asked for a loan of her lipstick, applying it thickly. She opened the map and pressed her lips to the space next to her boat, leaving a perfect red kiss. The woman looking over her shoulder asked, "What's that, a treasure map?"

Grace laughed, handed back her lipstick. "Of a sort I guess it is."

Owney sent a bottle of champagne over but did not bother to come by himself and in the calculus of the underworld this was at the very best a polite slap. And the worst? Who knew? Touhey looked across at Farrell and there it was: the flicker of his knowing. Farrell was doing his own reckoning of the slight and how it affected him. Touhey understood the dynamic, how the tiniest of actions might spiral out and finish in swamping waves of destruction, the ultimate victims bloodied and bowed and wholly ignorant of the forces that had landed on them. Things took on their own velocity. Touhey felt the shift at the table. Farrell was not stupid. Touhey drank Owney's missive, savored every sip. This was bad. He might go it alone, but he would not last long with Owney lined up against him. He was not about to let Farrell know he was worried. "Johnny, let's have another drink. For old times."

Back at the table she offered Briody her hand. "Let's dance. These fellas seem to need to catch up."

Briody looked to Farrell, who waved them off. As they walked away he said into her ear, "Sure, I did not expect to meet someone like you here."

"Didn't realize you were a gangster, so."

"Neither did I."

"If we judge you by the company you keep."

"The pot and the kettle."

"Johnny Farrell merely tends to the business of the metropolis."

"Murky business at that. Why don't you leave with me?"

She laughed. "Don't underestimate Johnny's potential for difficulty. Jeez, you've two left feet. You'll do nothing to add to the Irish reputation as good dancers."

"They get me around all right. They might even do a fine job of taking me to see you, if I knew where to find you."

"I drew you a map."

"At the end of which is a pot of gold."

"That would be a rainbow. This is only a map."

"A treasure chest then. Where do I find this guide?"

The song ended and she pushed him away. "Try your pocket."

The drummer beat out a one two one two and the band was off again and Briody grabbed her by the arm and spun her. She saw beyond him a man with a gun and then she heard the crack of the shots going with the music. She saw Touhey pull Farrell to the floor and flip over their table and then he was holding his own gun in his left hand and sparks were jumping from it. The music started to fall apart, not all going silent at once but piece by piece as each player realized what was happening, first the trombone, then the drums, next the guitar, until the bass beat out a few lost notes and the screams became the music. Then she was up and in the air, her legs kicking, and she realized Briody had lifted her and they were moving for the door. He knocked a few slow-reacting patrons to the floor and they were down the stairs and hit the street and the warm air. He bent forward and placed her gently against the wall and knelt to pull her dress to where it should be. His hand brushed her calf and she felt a tremor.

When he stood he was not even breathing quickly. "So, there you are, all in one piece."

People were running out of the club, fleeing with terror-struck faces. Sirens pierced the night. She lit a cigarette and blew the smoke through her full lips. A lock of hair fell across her face and he reached up and pushed it behind her ear. Briody placed his hand on the top of her arm. She moved away.

"Johnny Farrell has eyes all over this town."

"I believe it. But how'd you get involved with the likes of him?"

"Now, that's a long story. But involved, I am."

"I'd like to know how it ends, that story."

"Stick around long enough, you will too."

Farrell and Touhey came toward them, moving quickly. There must have been a back door. Touhey nodded to him. "I'm headed for the Bronx, Mick. You all right?"

Briody nodded and watched Touhey jump into his car. Farrell's driver swung across the street and lurched to a stop. Briody read the poster on the wall of the club announcing Cab Calloway, John Bubbles, Josephine Baker, Victor Lopez, and an all-star jazz revue. More cops arrived, ran into the club, all herky-jerky, guns drawn. He did not want to see her get into that car, wished she was going home with him. In the backseat she turned and raised two fingers, her face vacant, and then the driver stomped on the accelerator and the car shot away and she was gone. He walked west until the corner of Broadway, then he reached into his pocket and took out the dinner napkin. Indeed it was a map. Apparently she lived on a boat on the East River north of the Williamsburg Bridge. He folded the map carefully and put it into his pocket. A parade of sanitation trucks swung up from yards near the river, each with two wiry men hanging off the back. When they reached Broadway the trucks went in all directions. Briody watched them knowing he had only one place to go. As daylight started to bleed into the eastern sky, he walked the ninety blocks south to the job.

W ell if it ain't the aristocrat." Sheehan was tying his boot and looked up as Briody came off the lift still wearing his suit. "What's with the fancy pants? You the boss man now?"

"The night, it went on a bit."

"Good thing you made it. I can't miss a day's pay." Sheehan pointed at his feet. "You can't work in those shoes."

"Lucky I left a pair of boots in the gang box." He changed his shoes, grabbed his battered porkpie which he had left there as well and slapped it on his head.

When he felt the drag of fatigue, he'd think of Grace and the vision fueled him. At morning coffee Armstrong said, "Saw you fight last night. I ain't calling you Paddy no more. Why didn't you point out the fact you can fight like that, hit like that?"

"That usually speaks for itself, sooner or later."

At lunch he sat alone in the shade of a lower floor and watched a concrete gang maneuver one Georgia buggy after another filled with concrete into place, then tip the contents and spread it around. Three men with shovels, two with rakes and one a skinny Portuguese in a red shirt, worked the vibrator, a thick horse cock of metal at the end of an electric cable encased in rubber that he flopped about, dropping into piles of concrete and forcing the stuff slowly out in all directions. Their foreman stayed on top of them, barking over the racket. Briody closed his eyes and nodded off, his hat pulled to the point of his nose. In a dream he was back in Ireland, sneaking in the back window of the house in Kilnaleck hunting he knew not who, only to find it empty.

Sheehan was shaking him. "Mike, come on. Four more hours. You can make it, right?"

Briody stood, pushing his hat back and blinking at the hard daylight. "Not a bother."

Two hundred earsplitting rivets later he could barely carry his gun down to the gang box. He grabbed his jacket and his dress shoes, and too tired to contemplate the jostle and crush of a subway car, he took a cab home. The entire way he studied the map Grace had drawn for him, tracing the trail to its conclusion on the Brooklyn waterfront. He could not wait until he might follow that trail himself.

The skinny Irish kid sat with his hands underneath his ass as if he had just been caught stealing. Farrell watched as Touhey stood behind the chair and placed his hands on the kid's shoulders. "Hey Johnny, you imagine this one? Kid's three quarters an inch short of the police height requirement. Ain't that a shame? You do something on this?"

Farrell shrugged and shook his head. "Not a brain in his head, cross-eyed, bowlegged—that's fine, Tommy. I could make a call, sort the thing out. But you are either tall enough or you are not. Sorry. Rulers don't lie."

"That's a shame. Ever since I known little Denny Monahan here, all's he ever wanted was to be a flatfoot. Ain't that right, kid?" Touhey patted the police aspirant's shoulder. "Now his mama comes from outside of Bantry, a little place called Goat's Trail? You believe that? Boy, is she going to be disappointed."

"Maybe she should have married a taller fellow."

"You got a point there. Hey Denny, what time is your appointment downtown?"

"In an hour." He hugged himself and leaned forward as if he was in pain.

"An hour?"

Touhey moved to the back wall and picked up a short section of board. He hefted the wood, felt its weight. He returned behind Denny's chair. "Well, I'll tell you what, Denny. I say you go down there anyway."

"But Mr. Touhey . . ."

Touhey raised the board and brought it down flush on the top of Denny's skull so hard Farrell winced. The kid was out of the chair howling, jumping up and down, whimpering and cradling his head in his hands.

"Now sit your ass back down."

"That hurt. Why'd you hit me, Mr. Touhey?"

Touhey waved him over and put Farrell's hand on the top of Denny's head. A lump was sprouting through his brown hair. "What do you think? Got to be at least an inch."

Farrell felt the knot. "That should do it."

"Now get downtown before this thing melts on you."

"Hey Mr. Touhey, you're the greatest, wait till my mom hears about this."

"What every mother likes to hear, that I'm whacking her kids' heads with boards."

Touhey walked Denny Monahan out of the back room of the Four Provinces and came back with a growler of frothy beer and two iced-down mugs.

"You take care of the Judge?"

"As per usual."

"That's good, Johnny." Touhey lit a cigarette and offered the pack to Farrell, who declined. "I forgot, you're trying to give them up." Touhey lit another match with the flick of a thumb, watched it flare and burn down. "I get the feeling you gave up a lot of things, Johnny, moving downtown and all. Marrying that skinny Protestant broad."

"Nothing but the smokes I gave up, Tommy. Watching your own mother with the consumption, hard to keep smoking. Still like a cigar, though."

"Right, cigars. Well, I hear things, whispers, idle chatter. We, you and me, we go back a long ways, Johnny. But I have to admit. I start to worry sometimes. I have to call you three times before you get back to me? It was never like that before, Johnny. Never. We made a bond, a pact, based on account of we known each other since we was born, since the cradle, for Christ sake, since we did not even know we was together. You got comfortable downtown, is that it?"

Farrell sipped his beer, nodded. He was in no mood to go down memory lane. "You see this Vitale mess in the papers?"

"How about the time we stomped that cop caught us breaking into Mazzeo's butchers? I got caught, you got away clean on account of I kept my mouth shut, meanwhile you were the guy that broke the chair over his head, nearly killed the guy. You don't forget things like that, do you?"

"Come on, Tommy."

Touhey leaned over and grabbed the lapel of his suit, rubbing it between his thumb and forefinger. "That's some smart suit you're wearing, Johnny. I wonder about your chances of going to Fordham Law School if you had been pinched back when, if you had to spend a couple of seasons at Coxsackie along with your street corner pals." He did not let go of the cloth.

"Tommy, you know I owe you a hell of a lot for a lot of things. What are you getting at?"

"You ain't dropping your old pal, are you, Johnny?"

"Tommy. Things, the way the city is going. We got pressures now we never had. Sometimes I don't get messages like I should. I get back always. Always I get back as soon as I get the message. It's pretty hard to get back to a guy when I don't even know he's looking for me yet. Right? Maybe we should buy a carrier pigeon." Farrell affected a laugh, good cheer, familiarity. "Come on, Tommy. I know where I come from."

"I hope that is true, Johnny."

"Hey Tommy, it's me here, Johnny." He pulled up the lapel of his hundred-dollar suit away from Touhey's grasp. "This ain't me, Tommy." He dropped the lapel and slapped his chest three short times. "This is me. My heart is still in the Bronx."

"Well I hope so, Johnny. I hope so, because I for one really believe, and this is, I swear on my mother, forgetting where you come from is the biggest sin of them all."

Touhey leaned forward. His sleeves were neatly turned up to his elbows. Thick veins bulged blue along his forearms. His knuckles were swollen and rough like large hailstones. Farrell had always been afraid of him, all the way back, as far as he could remember, afraid of the violence in him. But he had long benefited from it. Even as boys, he rarely had to fight just because everyone knew he and Tommy Touhey were fast friends. Not that he lacked nerve. When they pulled the crazier stunts, whether jumping from the Hell Gate Bridge or riding along the tops of subway cars as they smashed through darkened tunnels, he was certainly Touhey's only equal in the neighborhood. But when it came to physical violence Touhey had no peer. He was the kind of street brawler who spent days picking fights with the biggest toughest characters he could find, often pounding three or four kids into bloody piles at the same time. And that was before he'd ever picked up a gun.

"You know, a lot of the old crowd, my wife even, they ask me all the time, whatever happened to Johnny Farrell? They seem to think you sold me out."

"Even Tricia? Tommy, that just ain't square."

That little bitch had some nerve, Farrell reflected. He was the one who had introduced them right after Tommy came back from the war. Those were the days they had vowed the city would be theirs. For a while things had gone according to plan, Touhey was the muscle and he was the plotter, the schemer, the smooth talker, and as the twenties rolled on they ascended, achieved a certain renown, he in politics and Touhey in the rackets, two circles that in

New York overlapped considerably. But Tommy had decided to stay in the Bronx, to limit his rule to a familiar slice of the town. His loss.

"How is she? The kids?"

"See, that's just it, Johnny, this is not the kind of thing you should need to ask. You know where we live. I never left a Hunnerd thirty-eight Street."

"Truth, Tommy, I don't see my own kids much."

"A guy makes his choices."

Farrell believed that his old friend had shot and missed, was not up to the next level, did not have the same ambitions. Maybe he was the wrong horse. Still, he did not want Tommy Touhey as an enemy. Besides, Touhey might be used in ways that would be good for the two of them.

"I know exactly where I come from, Tommy."

"I can't think of the kind of fate a guy like that deserves."

"The worst." Farrell just wanted to agree and get back to Manhattan.

" 'Cause you and me both know we're under attack and now we need more than ever to be together."

"Thick and thin."

"These dago guinea wops and these Jews, these European mutts—they want what's ours."

"They'll die trying." Farrell attempted a hearty bravado.

Touhey stared. "Think so, Johnny? Last time you did a piece of killing?"

Farrell strained to hold Touhey's gaze. Those eyes. He felt the little hairs on his neck dance in the coolness of the saloon's back room. He glanced away, swallowed. "Tommy, we each got our own thing to do. You handle your end, I'll handle mine."

Touhey suddenly smiled. He reached over the table and rubbed Farrell's face with a meaty hand. "Come on, Johnny, now that you decided to grace the Bronx with your presence, why don't we go over to Mulrow's and hustle us some pool. For old times' sake."

Farrell grabbed Touhey's hand and squeezed it. "Right, Tommy. Old times' sake. And for our bright future." He raised his glass.

Touhey laughed and stood, finishing his beer in a long swallow. "Just remember, Johnny, the world is my oyster. Not yours, you little prick, mine. Go on out, I gotta take a piss. I'll meet you out front."

In the bathroom Touhey retrieved his revolver from under the sink and nestled it in the small of his back. He turned on the faucet and splashed his face with cold water. He regarded his reflection, thinking, Do I look like an asshole? Our bright future, says Johnny Farrell, the slickster. He straightened his tie thinking, Johnny Farrell better watch who he screws around with. Because if he forgets where he comes from, Johnny Farrell's future is gonna be about as bright as a drum full of concrete at the bottom of the Hell Gate. Boyhood pal or no.

So this was Brooklyn. Briody followed Grace's map down the oily streets of the Williamsburg waterfront and turned north. It was a strange place, a forlorn stretch of real estate where hulking warehouses crowded the streets with shadows. The sun was down but it was not yet night. Things lurked in those shadows, dogs moved along, feral beasts that studied his every move. Juiceheads lounged in doorways. The river gave off rich odors of decay. He wondered at her living on a boat. Across the black water the rising Empire State stood out, a dark structure delineated by the lights high on the derricks. Gusts of sticky wind buffeted him. He ducked his head slightly to keep his hat from turning into a kite. He carried flowers, uncertain about what she expected and even more uncertain about what he did.

He found the dock and the dozen ramshackle boats and walked out the pier toward the last one on the left. At the boat before hers he saw the glow of a pipe and a disembodied voice growled, "What the hell you looking for, fancy boy?"

Briody stopped and watched as a liverish man emerged from

the doorway of a broken-down vessel. He wondered at its ability to stay afloat. The man peered out from under great white bushy eyebrows and said, "I ain't gonna ask you twice." He hit the pipe hard again and its flame lent his face a demonic glow.

Briody stifled a laugh. "I'm after seeing a woman named Grace."

"Grace who?"

Briody was taken aback. He looked at the last boat. Unlike the others, which were all various drab wood, it was painted in a riot of bright colors. A row of sunflowers stretched along the bow like a collar. He was certain it must be hers.

"Masterson. And who are you?"

The old man stepped closer. "That's smart, real smart. Turn the whole thing around so you get to ask the questions."

Briody exhaled. "I'm only paying a social visit."

"Well, there's no one here to visit. I suggest you take your dopey ass back to New York City."

Briody had not realized he had left the city. He looked again at her boat. It was dark. There was no use standing there and arguing with this yellowed old man. He handed the flowers to Harry. "Tell her, someone from home called in."

"From home, my eye."

Briody, feeling foolish, turned away and retraced his steps along the forsaken piers, wondering if her interest had been some phantom he had conjured up.

The ride out to pick up the machine guns was a revelation. Briody was surprised at how soon they left the city behind, how quickly the landscape changed. They passed through a great swampy expanse of nothing but marsh grass and greasy water that stretched for miles. The Buick rode low to the ground and its V-8 thrummed as they easily overtook the older cars and slow-moving trucks loaded with produce and junk that crossed the Jersey badlands, the faces of the drivers blurs of light. Briody smelled a piggery long before they came upon it. That singular stench—it transported him back to Cavan and his youth, to days before violence, days before exile, working with his father and brothers in misty dawns gathering in market towns to engage the Irish countryman's mix of good cheer and simmering peasant resentments. Touhey and his driver recoiled in disgust, hid their noses in their hats, the Yanks. Briody found the reek comforting. Casey sniffed the air, shrugged.

They passed the smoky city of Paterson, its steeples and chimneys stark against the clear blue sky of northern New Jersey. Then they were into the woods, rolling fields. A dozen miles past Paterson they stopped at a filling station and took on gas and water. Touhey knew the proprietor from his bootlegging days.

The owner was sandy-haired and rangy, wore canvas shoes, and pushed his straw hat back on his head. "You fellas out for a little fresh air?" He carried a crescent wrench and stuck it in his pocket, wiping grease on the front of his coveralls.

Touhey embraced him. "Yep, out to see the country."

"Ain't much to see."

Briody got out and asked for a bathroom. The man laughed and pointed to the bushes. He walked past the hut that served as the station, where crates of apples, potatoes, and onions were laid out on a wooden bench that ran along the front wall. Metal signs tacked to the wall advertised cigarettes and soft drinks. Around the side were stacked racks of empty soda bottles, blown-out car tires, and cardboard boxes of used oil cans.

Two boys, who could only be the owner's sons, played catch with a dirty baseball and eyed the city slickers with quiet awe. Touhey was talking up the good old days with the gasoline man, who shouted something that caused the ballplayers to drop their mitts and scramble past Briody and around to the back of the garage. They returned in a flash with two bottles of brown whiskey. Touhey accepted the gift and slid back in the car, his driver pouncing on the accelerator before the door was shut.

"Guy used to pull liquor across the border for me, down outta Canada. Built trucks that could really fly. Best grease monkey in the world, that guy. If it has a motor, he can pull it apart and make it better than new. Boats, cars, trucks, washing machines, any goddamn thing that whirs. Don't matter. The best, bar nobody. I tried for years to get him to move to the Bronx and take care of my fleet."

They drove along a lake road until it ended and then drove some more on a dirt track. When they came upon a rise the driver stopped and said, "I don't want to risk it. Getting this son of a bitch stuck again."

Touhey shrugged and got out of the car. "Let's do it." He carried a bottle of the whiskey in each hand and started walking with care down a rocky slope. At the bottom was a large green field. A tractor was parked in the center with a flatbed attached to it. Three men sat, legs dangling.

Briody trailed behind Danny Casey, stayed in the background while the greetings went on. He saw that all the crates were still nailed shut and marked USMC. They were in a valley, surrounded by dense forest on all sides, and black, jagged hills rose above them, casting the field half in shadow. Briody figured the three men waiting had to be American. Two were dressed in work clothes with caps and the third wore a gray pinstriped suit but they all projected that Yankee confidence, heads cocked up watching their approach. The one in the suit was the lawyer O'Brien, the Clan-na-Gael man. Even here, deep in the woods, he was dressed for spirited exchanges with opposing counsel. His diamond pinkie ring caught the sun as he shook hands all around. He sported a silver crew cut and looked like he'd enjoy outrunning you. Briody saw that he had covered his shoes in paper bags.

"Men, what we have here is an excellent addition to our arsenal. The procurement process is proceeding apace." He nodded and one of the others, a stocky lad whose leer hinted at a reformatory youth, leapt onto the flatbed and creaked open one of the cases with a pry bar. He reached down and pulled out a machine gun. He carried it over to O'Brien, holding it aloft on upturned palms, like an offering. O'Brien grabbed the gun and made a show of examining it. He turned it over and sighted along the barrel. He nodded to the other man, who ducked into the cab of the tractor and came back with a drum magazine.

"This is a Thompson M1 1928 submachine gun. A tommy gun. A Windy City typewriter. It possesses a firing capacity of seven hundred rounds per minute with a muzzle velocity of two hundred and eighty-one meters per second." O'Brien picked up a magazine and attached it to the gun. "This drum contains fifty rounds of .45 caliber ammunition. Needless to say, this weapon has an excellent capacity for damage. Step aside, gentlemen. I'll demonstrate."

O'Brien shouldered the weapon, sighted, and squeezed through the magazine in three long bursts. A sapling was cut in half, the stump left smoking in the sunshine. "That's what I call firepower."

Touhey pulled on the whiskey and passed the bottle along. O'Brien regarded it as if it was offal. "Ordnance and alcohol, a fool's cocktail."

Touhey threw him a mock salute and reached for the gun. O'Brien let him have it and looked on while Touhey worked the weapon with assurance, spraying hot lead down the length of the clearing.

Briody was reminded of the Yanks showing up in Europe. They were loaded with gear, fresh-faced and full of fight. It didn't take long for the reality of that hellhole to dampen their gung-ho enthusiasm. When Touhey was finished shooting, Briody took over the Thompson. He set it on the flatbed and let it cool for a minute. The stocky kid tossed him a magazine. Casey stood by, his eyes bright.

"Jesus, Mikey. Now we're in business."

"I'd say it's a step up from revolvers. This will make them sit up."

O'Brien put his camel-hair overcoat back on. He slapped his kid gloves on his thigh and watched Briody. "Learn that at the Somme?"

"No, back at home we managed to come up with one. Somebody's cousin brought it from Boston along with his golf clubs. In France we did not have the toys you Yanks had."

"We like to send our boys in prepared to fight, to get the job done."

Briody nodded. The Thompson was far better suited to inner-city beer wars than to combat. O'Brien had a gleam to him, a spit-polished shine that betrayed the type of armchair fanaticism Briody despised. It was the kind that got other men killed. There were many Yanks supporting the cause of Irish Republicanism. Some were serious, others dilettantes, most somewhere in between, often inspired by damp-eyed allegiance to dead or elderly relatives. Briody would not doubt O'Brien's commitment, but his motives were suspect. He would guess he was in it for the gamesmanship, the murky intrigue.

They decided to wet-fire all the guns. Casey argued that they did not want to discover one was defective in the middle of an operation. O'Brien concurred. The seven men stood in a row, weapons poised. O'Brien indicated a fat maple tree that had doubtless stood on the edge of the grass for a century or two. O'Brien, assuming the role of field marshal, gave the order. They all let rip and the tree fell as if struck by lightning. They went through all the Thompsons and, finding them shipshape, repacked them.

O'Brien had organized a picnic, rations for his troops. He spread sandwiches out on the flatbed, encouraged the others to help themselves. He produced a pocketknife, snapped it open, and sliced his bratwurst on rye in half. He sidled up to Briody. "I'm glad we finally got to talk. I always wondered what possessed a man to fight for his enemy."

Briody selected ham and Swiss. He'd been explaining away his stint in the British army for years. It had been the same in Ireland, especially with the Dublin crowd. Had not anyone else ever been fifteen and stupid? "Best way to learn how to fight against him."

O'Brien studied him, waved off a fly. He wiped his thin pink lips with a handkerchief, folded it, and slipped it back into his pocket. He jingled some change. "Good enough reason I guess."

Briody opened a bottle of root beer with his teeth and spit the cap on the ground. "Worked like a charm so far."

"So they tell me. I have excellent reports on you, Briody. I think we can work well together. As long as you realize that on this side of the pond, it's my show." He tipped forward slightly, rising on his toes. A chin thrust, the little man in charge, asserting his authority.

Briody nodded and took another bite. While chewing he said, "Sure thing."

O'Brien's eyes narrowed but he smiled and patted Briody on the arm. "Look forward to it, boyo." He turned and took a large brown envelope from inside his coat.

The gun seller took the envelope and nodded solemnly. "These are going out of the country, right, overseas? You promise me that, I'll promise you we'll be meeting like this on a regular basis, get to be pals. These turn up killing some pedestrian, a couple of tourists, in some beer-war shoot-out, we're all gonna have big problems."

Briody did not trust O'Brien. Being of the officer corps, the little man fancied himself a leader. And like nearly every officer Briody had known, this man would think it his duty to sacrifice others for the objective. He would expect his orders to be followed. But Briody knew this was not conventional warfare. There would be no cavalry charges. It would be about moving weapons and money and occasionally the type of intimate killing that was a lot harder than shooting into the distance. He hoped O'Brien would just handle the politics and the fund-raising.

On the ride home, Touhey sat in the back next to him. "Remember guys like him over there?"

"I was thinking that exactly."

"Lot of good kids never left Europe, pricks like that. I'll bet a dollar to a donut he never came within two miles of the front."

Briody cranked down the window and let the air blow in his face. "Would've wrecked his shoes."

"God forbid." Touhey lit a cigar, offered one to Briody, who declined. "You think any more about coming to work for me?"

"I think we have our hands full for now, Tommy." Briody assumed the topic would come up. It always did.

Touhey leaned his head back and drew mightily on his stogie. "Yeah, you'll learn, you'll learn."

When they crested the ridge above Paterson they had a clear view to the east and on the horizon the Empire State Building stuck out, rising above the nubs that surrounded it. Casey pointed out the windscreen. "Look at it, Michael, hasn't grown an inch without you there to see it done."

Briody stuck his head out into the wind for a better look, amazed that from so far away it already made an impression.

ey, let me show you something," the doorman Fergal said, and took her up on the elevator to the twenty-sixth floor. She carried her easel under her arm and paint and brushes in a canvas bag slung over her shoulder. As they walked down the long tiled hallway Fergal whistled an Irish song softly and Grace found herself whispering along to it although she did not know the name, caught in reminiscence. She thought of her uncle John Joe, who often sang that song as he worked the fields at home. At the end of the corridor, Fergal paused before a door bearing the sign "Applebaum Surety," inserted a key in the lock, and opened it inward. The office was empty except for three wooden desks and some odd files scattered about the floor.

"Looks like someone left in a hurry."

"They're all leaving in a hurry these days, Grace. Way things are going, this whole building will be empty by Christmas."

There were three windows stretching nearly floor to ceiling that looked straight out at the construction site, which seemed closer than it was, so close she might reach across Thirty-fourth Street and touch it. Daylight cut through the glass, splashing the room.

Fergal stood as if presenting a child with a present. "This way, Grace, you can do your artwork rain or shine."

She hugged him and he blushed.

"Here, I made you your own key. Place will be all empty a long time, way things are going."

"It's brilliant. I can't thank you enough."

"No thanks are needed, none at all."

She put her bag down and unfolded the wooden legs of her easel while Fergal watched.

"How are things in the Bronx these days?"

"Fair enough. Filled with Paddys, sometimes it's as if I never left home at all."

"Come on now, so. How many blocks of tenements are there around Cavan? How many cars and trucks, and where are the elevated trains?"

"Not to mention the Italians and the Jews and the god-awful stink of the niggers."

Grace pursed her lips, let him register her disapproval. "Don't be like the rest of them, Fergal. It's one thing to miss home. It's another entirely to walk around with your head up your own arse, making believe you never left."

"It's a comfort to be with your own kind."

"Really? And what's the other kind? Orangutans and walruses and zebras at the zoo? It's a great thing to be forced into company with others. You realize how much we're all alike. Take advantage of it."

Fergal was silent for a moment. She dumped her tubes of paint out on one of the desks.

"Jesus, Grace, you been here a lot longer, you're used to things being different. Besides, after I sock away a good few bob, I'm on the first boat home."

Grace stared at him and then smiled. We all need our delusions, she thought. They get us through the day. "You're a fine lad. Now let me get some work done." She rubbed his arm and kissed his cheek.

When he was gone, she positioned her easel. She wondered whether the market crash or the noise had driven Applebaum from this bit of real estate. Twenty-six floors below, trucks were constantly stopping and starting, honking, roaring about, the windows humming from the sound. A thin coat of dust covered everything. She pressed her hand to the cool glass and felt the vibrations from the rivet guns, the motors, and the incessant hammer blows. Looking across to the site was like looking into the belly of a factory where the movement never stopped. Each floor she could see was its own hive of action and motion and industry, with men attending to their varied tasks. She sketched different floors from her perspective, and since they were still windowless and without walls, each presented her with a perfect frame containing a different activity. Right across from her a bricklayer on his knees wielded his trowel with the deftness of a baker icing a cake, the wall rising so quickly he was soon crouching, then stooping and finally standing. A floor above, the concrete men were hanging recklessly, holding on to the building with one hand while using pry bars to strip plywood from freshly cured concrete pillars.

She began to paint. The sunlight coming through the windows heated the room and she had begun to sweat as she worked, had to wipe her face with her sleeve. She stopped and poured herself some water from her thermos. The workers closest to her she painted as flesh and blood, the ones beyond moved in shadow. When the men broke for lunch the noise just stopped and she felt her whole body relax.

Fergal came back and they ate ham and butter sandwiches and smoked. He was too shy to look at her face so he sat at an oblique angle, occasionally stealing glimpses, which she found touching. They shared a thermos of tea and he went on again about his mother in Ballyjamesduff and of his scrimping and saving toward a triumphant return home. How he would buy the neighbor's farm and lord it over them all. She stared at the side of his pimply face and knew with a cold certainty that he would die here in America without ever seeing Cavan or his mother again. Quickly, she sketched him, softening his features a bit. She wondered why so many of them were mad to flee the one place they had ever been where they could finally be themselves. She stubbed out her cigarette and handed him the sketch.

"Ah now, Grace, thanks so much. I'll send it home to me ma. Fergal in America. She'll love it."

After he left, she finished her painting and set it aside to dry, then went up to the roof with her sketch pad and started drawing the ironworkers hanging steel above her on the edge of the highest floor, which by her count was the twenty-seventh. The day had turned balmy and several of them worked without shirts, their ropy muscles exposed. She watched one, who was taller than the others, take off his hat and slap it on his thigh, and when he looked her way she realized with a jolt that it was him. Briody. She watched as he walked alone toward the corner of the building, signaled to someone on a lower floor, then rejoined his crew.

Suddenly the sky darkened as a wall of black clouds descended but no storm came from them. Against that backdrop the tossed rivets glowed brightly as the burners sent them sailing through the air to the catchers. On the top floor dozens of the rivets flew, trailing showers of sparks, a choreographed meteor storm. Transfixed, she just stood and watched until the clouds passed and the sky lightened.

She executed several drawings of the men working as a team to rivet the beams in place, then she concentrated on Briody as he straddled a beam, reaching to the sky. The only thing between him and Thirty-fourth Street was oblivion. His hat was pushed back on his head and he looked to be enjoying the work. Even from across the street she felt vertigo and imagined the great heights to which the ironworkers had yet to climb. When she had a few drawings she liked she put her pencils away and went back down the stairs to get her things. She decided to leave her easel locked up in the office and grabbed her jacket. She wanted to see Briody again.

Waiting for the shift to end, she made small talk with Fergal in the lobby, his blush going purple once again. At twenty minutes after four the construction racket ceased and soon afterward the men started piling out, dozens, then hundreds of them, trailing a cloud of dust, laughing and joking into the midtown streets, overwhelming the pedestrians in their way, elbowing, cutting up. They moved en masse like a conquering battalion spilling into a town square, bunches of them stepping into the traffic, confident with their muscularity that they now owned the street. No driver dared to honk, they just sat smiling stupidly, trying not to provoke, their motors idling while the builders knifed through the lanes.

Grace felt dizzy trying to pick Briody out of the crowd of hats and shoulders and dirty faces. She remembered his being very tall so she scanned the heads that rose above the rest, hoping to spot him. It was useless. She stood on her toes and looked about. Men smiled at her, tipped their hats, whistled. A hand smacked her ass and she turned but there was no way to be sure who had violated her. When the crowd started to thin, she caught a glimpse of a man she thought must be Briody and she tried to shadow him, but soon she was jostled to the sidewalk and he was gone.

She walked on toward the subway, feeling silly about her desire to see him, like a schoolgirl with a crush. For so long she had been in control of her feelings for men, had set the agenda. This iron-worker from Cavan had stripped away so many of her defenses and she had barely spoken two words to him. Maybe it was just a yearning for her lost and distant childhood or for a place, Ireland, which she had run from so precipitously and had tried to forget. Since moving to the boat, she had made a point of spending as little time as possible with fellow Irish, striving to be American, to lose her past. Anna, with her fondness for Freud and psychoanalysis, would have an interpretation.

She stopped for the light at Fourth Avenue and was overtaken by a crew of men from the site. They surrounded her, a wall of muscle, sweat drying on their shirts as they waited for a break in the traffic. She stepped to the side to get clear of them. They smelled of work and dirt. When they crossed the street she decided to turn uptown and walk to Grand Central. On the sidewalk a half a block north a man walked on his own and she knew just by his stride that it had to be him. She hurried and caught him on the corner.

She tugged on his arm. "Hey, boxer. I know you."

He pulled back and looked down at her, surprise on his face and then a big smile. "Grace. I came looking for you. Met a nasty old geezer instead."

"Oh, that's Harry. He didn't mention it at all, the river rat. I thought you'd given me up."

Men pushed past him, bumping him. One of the men slapped his back. "Who's the dame, Briody?"

Briody stared down at her. "No. I wouldn't do that, sure."

"Get to know me you might sing a different tune." She pulled her cap off and let her hair flow down past her shoulders. "You have time to buy a girl a cup of coffee?"

He looked around the street. "Loads of time."

"I know just the place, up by Grand Central Station."

They strolled easily along the sidewalk talking, her shoulder occasionally brushing his arm. She felt an odd sensation that this man was no stranger at all. "You've a funny accent for a Cavan man."

He shrugged. "Moved about a bit. Was in Europe for the war. Spent time in Kerry after, with relations."

"A Cavan man in the British army? Fighting for the crown?"

"Not much for the royalty. I was a young lad, a stupid boy who had read too many books. Thought it would be a lark. I'd come back a hero."

"Are you?"

"Hardly, now."

"How are you after finding America?"

"No rivers of gold yet, but good work at a union wage. No bother."

"I don't think that will last, the look of things. Soup lines and shantytowns. Not much of an American Dream."

"Problems anywhere you go. But at least you can walk down the street here and be . . ." He indicated the sun-splashed sidewalk before them as if grasping for some idea.

Grace nodded and said, "Anyone you want to be."

"Exactly."

"You don't think I'd get away with this outfit in Cavan Town, do you?"

Briody looked down at her masculine attire, the paint-splattered shoes with their wash of color. "No. Not likely. Plus it would take me three months to earn the same as a week over here."

"What did you do in Kerry?"

His silence was a physical thing, a presence between them. She realized she should have been careful. He was of the age, so many coming over in the last few years were running from things as much as to them. They had histories, were participants in horrors private and public, all that ugliness.

He stopped walking and stared at her. Horns blared on the avenue. A woman came out of an apartment building walking an outrageously tiny dog. Briody laughed. "It's about the size of half a rat."

They resumed walking and he said, "Bits and pieces. Some

farming. Took care of things for an aunt. Beautiful country. Outside of Kenmare."

"Do you miss it at all?"

"There are days. Yourself?"

"Never. Even when I was a girl, I wanted to be somewhere else. Read too many books myself, I suppose."

The coffee shop was in the basement of the Lincoln Building across from Grand Central. She ordered tea, Briody coffee black. A man in a threadbare suit sat at the counter going through the help wanted ads with a pencil, tsk-tsking his way down the page. The porter came by and she spoke quickly to him in some language.

"Italian?"

"Español."

"Picked that up in Cavan, did you?"

"Had my own European lark."

"So much in common."

"That we do, Michael."

Grace spread four of her drawings on the table before them.

"Jesus, that's pretty impressive stuff. They look so . . . alive."

He took one that showed his four-man team in the act of securing a crossbeam. She watched him study it, pleased that he liked her work.

"That there is Armstrong leaning too far back, as always, flirting with danger. He's a madman for the work. The detail is amazing, Grace. This is Skinny Sheehan, he always wears the one glove looped over his belt just like you have it here and every morning he wraps the electrical tape over the bottoms of his pants legs. The last fella here is Delpezzo, an Italian, grand he is, and you got him just right. I almost expect to hear him speak. These are brilliant, Grace. There's just one problem."

"What's that?"

"Surely I don't have muscles that big."

"I'm after flattering you a bit. No harm."

He smiled. "No, I suppose not."

Briody waited while the waitress refilled his cup. Steam rose from the coffee. The job seeker at the counter let out a cackle.

"So you know what I do. Is this your livelihood, making these pictures?"

She wiped a bit of tea from the table before her and fought a ridiculous impulse to blurt out her complicity with Johnny Farrell. "It's a scratching by, it is. Least I don't have a boss to answer to."

"I know what you mean. Mind if I buy these from you?"

"Achh, go away. They're yours."

Briody finished his coffee. "No, Grace. I insist. How much does someone as talented as yourself get paid for something like this?"

She realized it was futile to argue. "Five dollars for the lot."

"Fair enough."

He grabbed his hat from the table and went to the counter and paid for the drinks. She watched him walk, the roll of his shoulders, but there was something there, a body that had been through too much. There was more to him than the farm boy he was pretending to be. When he came back over he handed her a five-dollar bill and scooped up the drawings.

"I do have a meeting tonight. Union thing," he said.

"That's too bad. I'm in no hurry at all."

"It's been a pleasure doing business with you, Grace from Cavan." He stood at the entrance to the train. "I don't suppose you have a telephone?"

"No." She was relieved that he wanted to contact her. "You?"

"Not even one in the building yet."

"I know where you work."

"I know where you live."

"No excuses then, do we?"

"I'll find you."

"Why don't I find you on, say, Tuesday. I'll wait right across from the job. I'll take you to dinner."

"You'll take me? The pants is one thing."

"You're not in Ireland anymore."

He wondered at leaving the way he had. For some reason he was not yet sure of, he wanted to be honest with her. He was so used to the lies. Still, who was she? Not many Cavan girls were fluent in a foreign tongue. Their enemies would try anything. But she would have played the farm girl role. He dismissed silly paranoia. There was a spark—she had distracted his thoughts since he first met her. But he needed to be smart to stay focused. He could not afford a relationship.

The meeting was in Mike Quill's apartment, a drab two-room flat he shared with his brother. Briody sat on a radiator and listened to the back-and-forth as the Clan-na-Gael men argued about the wisdom of opening a speakeasy to finance weapons procurement. He thought it was a decent idea. Fund-raising was falling short since the Free State started pressing the U.S. State Department to rein in dissidents. BI men had been showing up in Bronx neighborhoods, casting about. Men were followed. Mail went missing. Two recent shipments had been intercepted, one a box that Briody himself had brought to the docks. Efforts were being made to tie them to the Communist Party. There was fear of double agents.

O'Brien, the lawyer, held up a hand and the bickering ceased. "Gentlemen. What we need more than anything right now is to avoid bad press. It is paramount that we are not cast in the light of the Reds, or the racketeers." He was dressed in his usual three-piece suit, his white hair precise. He rubbed his manicured hands together. Briody figured he knew his influence was waning. The Irish civil war vets were young and aggressive and asserting themselves. Many resented O'Brien's control, his moneyed ways. Briody thought none of that mattered. As much as he dismissed him as a soldier, he knew they needed men like O'Brien. He could pick up the phone and place a call to D.C., could sway policy makers. He could call off the dogs.

Danny Casey was up, waving his mangled hand like a red badge of courage. "And where exactly, counselor, do you think we get our ordnance? Who, in fact, makes it possible to ship the goods home? That's our racket boys. And as for the Reds, they haven't turned their backs to us like the AOH, and the Friendly Sons of Ireland, not so very friendly to us now, are they? Who then, the church?

The priests are no different here than in the hills of Kerry. Those great institutions of Irishmen are nowhere for us. They look at us like lowlifes. They're a long way from the cause back home. And a long way from helping the working Irish right under their noses."

There was a murmur of agreement.

O'Brien waved off the noise. "That might be so, but let us not confuse our causes. This organization is about Irish freedom, not about working conditions on the IRT or selling proscribed alcohol. We do the cause no good by associating openly with the outlaw. Of course we get our weapons from them. We cannot ask the army for them directly, or the police. People can understand that. A speakeasy is the next step, it's indefensible."

"So, what now, a cake sale?"

There was laughter and O'Brien, to his credit, smiled. "I am cultivating a couple of philanthropists, big moneymen, with ties to the old country and a correct sense of nostalgia. In the meantime, let's focus on why those shipments were intercepted. From now on, you will be contacted the day of. Take pains to be sure you are not followed."

As the meeting broke up men milled about making small talk. O'Brien motioned to him and Briody followed the lawyer into the back room. They stood between the two twin beds and O'Brien spoke quietly, even though they were alone. "We will be lifting your man shortly. When we do, I want you to handle it."

O'Brien stared at him intently. Briody felt the cottony air heavy in his lungs. He stared right back at O'Brien and simply nodded his head. O'Brien grabbed him by the bicep and squeezed. "Good man."

Out on the street Casey and Briody walked along Willis Avenue with Mike Quill and J. P. Adare.

"I get the feeling it's all a hobby for the man. He's taken us up like his peers take up hunting or polo, or however else they fill their days."

"We need him," Briody said.

"Do we? Touhey has been as good as O'Brien when it comes to supplying us. And he gives us further cover with his contacts downtown. O'Brien talks a big game and then it's let's go easy now fellas."

"He came up with the Thompsons."

"Touhey says he can get them."

"Touhey is trouble and you know it."

"Achh, you sound like O'Brien now. You and Touhey were going on about his deficiencies on the way back from Jersey. Mocking
his officer airs."

"That doesn't mean we don't need him. Besides, Dublin wants
him, so we have no choice."

"Dublin. What good has Dublin ever done but let us down?
You of all people, Michael, know what the Dublin crowd is all
about. They're too comfortable to do what needs to be done.
They've no incentive for risk."

Briody wondered how he got in the position of defending
O'Brien. They needed his contacts, something he guarded with
vigor. O'Brien was smart enough to know where his true power lay.
The night was warm and they all agreed a beer was in order. Briody
begged off. As the others ducked into the Four Provinces, he kept
going.

He stopped in the apartment and took his gym bag and a fresh
towel and went for a workout. He skipped rope and hit the light
bag for a few rounds. The gym was empty except for Gus and a
couple of his old wino buddies playing dominoes. Briody beat the
bag with a steady rhythm. When he was done he took a scalding
shower and slipped into clean clothes. He sat alone in the locker
room and looked at the picture Grace had drawn that day. He
folded it and put it away and thought about what O'Brien had said.
As he left the gym he knew that his next mission was going to be a
great deal more serious than taking guns downtown.

Farrell figured why not go see the Dago. It was merely a business
meeting between two hustlers on the rise whose interests were
coalescing. Happened all the time in the big town. The room
was small and cluttered with crates and boxes, barrels of wine and
oil. The man spoke softly so Farrell had to lean over, his forearms
resting on the cable spool that served as a table, so close that he

could feel the man's breath. "We can both profit from some accommodation. There are things you can do for me, and I for you." He studied that face, famous for having been caved in during a botched assassination attempt, a long cold night of torture. He had survived and now he was angling for power.

"So far every time you lined me up with something it paid well for both of us, no? And there was no messiness, nothing in the papers to reflect poorly on you or your people."

Despite the fact that he was at the center of chaos, there was nothing bellicose about the man. He was not prone to rants and violent outrages that resulted in spontaneous carnage. There was precision to his violence and each gesture was aimed at a very specific objective. He possessed an inexplicable serenity with that goddamn hint of a smile playing always at the corners of his mouth and eyes. And now he was reaching out, looking to broaden his base, to make alliances, to capitalize on a decade and a half of reputation-building audacity. Farrell was beginning to realize he could not deny the man much longer. It was true, they both could benefit, and how.

He rubbed his hands together, pursed his full lips. Farrell often heard talk about Vamonte's outsized ambitions. How he wanted to be king. But he could not achieve his goals without the machine on his side and Farrell could not achieve his without real underworld muscle. Madden did not seem open to the possibilities, was content with his bootlegging and more legitimate enterprises, taxis and laundries, the same for Big Bill Dwyer. The rest were mutts too volatile or insignificant to consider a union with.

"There is a man in the Bronx, a man you know well. He is resistant to change."

The Dago regarded him, let it sink in. Johnny Farrell knew it was coming. "I get your point."

He meant Tommy Touhey, his boyhood pal. It was a test. Set up Touhey and we'll see you're serious. The air seemed to grow tighter as if the suggestion of such grave betrayal burned its own oxygen. It was left unsaid. It did not matter. The Dago was content to let conclusions form on their own. Farrell decided on time, maybe a counteroffer. "I'll think it over." He took his leave of the back room.

Outside, the sun was high and warm. Farrell skirted a truck, contemplated the forsaking of a lifelong friend. He felt his stomach flutter, his heart beat fast. This was one of those crossroads. He imagined the time when he would consolidate power. He checked his watch, ran his hand along the fine cut of his suit. He was late for Grace. He flagged a cab and told the driver to step on it.

At high noon on a Sunday, while his men went to work, Tough Tommy Touhey stood in front of his cabstand smoking a cigar, making small talk with three detectives who had happened by. Touhey had his foot up on the bumper of his Pierce Arrow, knee bent.

"You know fellas, as a businessman I got to say the way things are going I might have to pull up stakes and relocate, find, what's that called—greener pastures. A guy can find it hard to make a buck, what with these foreigners all over the place. I don't mean the Irish. I mean—hey—my people are from the Kingdom, right outside of Tralee. It's these dagos and sheeny kikes, the odd Kraut and Zulu."

Two of the detectives smiled widely, the third smirked. The tallest one said, "Well Tommy, maybe you should join the better business bureau."

"Ha! I am the better business bureau. That's the problem, see. The worse business bureau is trying to take over."

The cops pulled back and rough laughter jostled the air. Touhey checked his watch and put his foot down on the dirty Bronx cobblestone. Right then, he figured it was all going on, and God willing, smoothly. He knew he was operating with little room for error. He had planned all along to be loitering here in front of his cabstand idly crafting a sound alibi when the detectives happened to come along, making it the perfect alibi. The sun shone. Cars moved past slowly in the thick traffic. The detectives were decent sorts, the two Galway men at least. They did not begrudge a man an honest living outside the law, as long as certain boundaries were respected, the proper tribute paid. The third, Halloway, had a sour reputation, was known as a bit of a crusader. That was all right. If he got too zealous they could always use a new man in Central Park, looking out for the well-being of squirrels, or out on the beaches of Staten Island.

Touhey pulled open his jacket. "Gentlemen, cigars?" The two Galway men bent to the flame that Touhey offered. Once again Halloway stood off just a bit, looking down the street as if hoping for a reason to produce his pistol. Touhey would keep an eye on him.

"You hear they got two of Larry Fay's boys?"

Touhey shrugged. He was practiced at admitting nothing. The two gunsels had been snatched, tortured, ice-picked to death, and then, in a particular affront, dumped on Fay's lush Long Island lawn.

"It's gonna be a tough summer for you guys. I'll bet a dollar to a donut that you earn your money." Touhey checked his watch again, puffed on his cigar, and tipped his hat to a trio of passing housewives who smiled at the gesture.

The McGowan brothers argued over who was going to row and who was going to shoot. Buzzie, the older and smarter brother, won the argument; now he sat enjoying the sun with a sawed-off Remington twelve-gauge across his lap while Twitch, his younger by eleven months brother, struggled against the Long Island Sound tide. Buzzie figured the plan was neat and simple enough. Vito Scalasi, the greaseball his boss wanted killed, was some kind of fitness nut who swam every day out from Orchard Beach. So they had commandeered a boat from the Parks Department and donned swimsuits to pass themselves off as lifeguards. Buzzie reclined in the bow, enjoyed the sea. His brother was grunting and sweating as they rounded the bend at Duck's Point. Off to their left, the beach, blanketed with oiled sunbathers, shimmered in the distance. Schoolkids frolicked in the water. Seagulls barked hysterically as they wheeled overhead. Buzzie told his brother to knock it off and they drifted back a bit while he scanned the water. The boat rocking was soothing and Buzzie thought he might get one for himself someday. Take up fishing, a way to unwind.

"What kind of half-assed job is this?"

Twitch's breath was coming hard and his face had turned the color of blood. Buzzie shook his head. "You always got a complaint about everything."

"What's that supposed to mean?"

Buzzie watched as his brother's eyes narrowed and his chest puffed up as it did about fifty times a day. Their entire lives, Twitch had taken every thing as an insult, a provocation. Buzzie often marveled at the fact that Twitch was still alive at twenty-three. Hell, he himself had almost killed the wiry little bastard a dozen or more times.

"You want to question Tommy Touhey? You got a better idea? This is the one thing the greaseball does; he ain't surrounded by a dozen goons. You prefer that? A shoot-out with twelve guys, or this, where all you do is row a boat and play navy for a day?"

"I just hate the water. You know I can't swim."

"Who's swimming? The greaseball—but not for long. All's you got to do is row. Any half-wit can handle that. Quit your crybabying."

Twitch looked off to the distance, another of the things he did, as if it was some kind of punishment that he wouldn't look you in the face. Buzzie sighed. A powerboat came roaring by, all polished teak and brass, a fat man at the wheel grinning maniacally, a statuesque blonde at each elbow trailing streaks of golden hair in the wind. The wake rocked their boat so hard that Buzzie gripped the sides and Twitch screamed curses at the offending craft. When the boat settled Buzzie trailed his hand in the water and looked forward to spending his share of the prize. Tommy Touhey was a stand-up guy and of all the various mugs that approached him for his services, Tommy was the only guy he would do the big job for.

Soon, a solitary swimmer left the crowd at the water's edge, propelling himself with deft and sure strokes into the open seas of the sound.

"There's our man." Buzzie tried to calculate a path to intersect the target. "Come on, get going, galleon slave."

It took twenty minutes of Twitch's grunting, cursing, and rowing to intercept Scalasi. When they pulled alongside the Italian bootlegger Buzzie told Twitch to keep rowing so they kept pace. Finally Scalasi stopped and, treading water, looked up annoyed. The sun reflected off his goggles and rivulets of water snaked down his bald head.

Buzzie smiled grandly. "Excuse me sir, but there's been reports of sharks in the water today."

Scalasi looked around like he would enjoy a fight with one. "Stay out of my way, assahole."

"Ass a hole. You must mean asshole. You're not from around here, are you? Funny accent like that."

The man slapped the side of the boat. His hairy back looked like a pelt. He glistened in the sun, scowling.

Buzzie laughed. "Hey you hairy bastard, anyone ever tell you, you like one of them harbor seals?"

Twitch started barking and clapping his hands. "Like in the circus."

The greaseball looked up through his goggles, his eyes dark with fury. Buzzie raised his gun, and as the man dove he opened up with both barrels, a roar of hot metal. Blood mushroomed up and then suddenly he was in the air and the sky was rolling over his head and he hit the water thinking, Shit, Twitch can't swim. The sound was colder than he expected and as he treaded water he realized he had lost the gun and that the greaseball like a wounded animal had upended the boat. He saw the mark fifty yards away still swimming, his strokes weakening, a windup toy running down, trailing reddened water. He pulled to a stop, raised his head, and sank. Buzzie spun in the water, thrashing, and Twitch floated past him, his neck twisted and broken, his soft blue eyes glaring into nothingness. The greaseball had killed while dying. Buzzie began to swim for the far shore.

. . .

Maurice Cohen, wearing a black homburg and nursing a gin hangover, gathered his toy poodle in his arms and carried the slobbering dog to the fourth-floor elevator. He stared out the hallway window at the lushness of Bronx Park where children ran and played games while their parents congregated over grilling meats. It was a quiet Sunday and he was enjoying the day off. No matter how irregular his line of work, he made a point of taking each weekend off as if a straight enterprise employed him. His boss was not happy about it but could not really complain, for he lacked the business savvy to keep his enterprise in operation. His boss had his talents, mayhem and fearmongering prime among them. The elevator arrived. He got on. Maurice Cohen fully understood his usefulness. He passed through the lobby and when he reached the sidewalk he bent and let the poodle down, scratching it under the chin. They proceeded across the street to the park. He could easily afford to live in a posher part of town. But he liked the Bronx, liked the hustle-bustle, the immigrant striving, the park, the remove from the dirty air of downtown. His neighbors paid him little heed.

Cohen lit a cigarette and played out his dog's leash. He strolled. There was much merriment in the air as the children screamed and cavorted but he took no pleasure in this. Children for the most part annoyed him. He had none of his own and was glad because to him children were nothing but scheming, drooling, shitting little connivers that required much too much attention. Especially American ones. He let Googie lead him down the path toward the river where he stepped carefully so as not to muddy his shoes. He planned to meet some friends that night for dinner and a commemoration of his leaving Danzig twenty-five years ago. A quarter century. He found this hard to believe at times, that so many years had passed, that it had been so long since those awful days on the run out of Poland, where they were hunted like rats during a flaring of anti-Semitic fever. He shifted his money belt, which was stuffed with thousands. He wore it like a security blanket everywhere he went. He would never be chased through streets with nothing again.

He had mixed feelings about America. There was freedom, to

an extent, but also a suffocating crudeness, an elevation and cele-bration of buffoonery unlike anything he had imagined possible. Two patrolmen made their way along the river what, looking to roust stew bums from the weeds? He liked no one but especially disliked the fat-faced Irish cops and their love of petty violence, which recalled clearly the goyim animals of his youth. He had learned to wear a mask of gentility to hide his ruthlessness behind spectacles, conducted his business quietly. Despite this, he had achieved underworld renown because of his facility with nothing more than mathematics. He would never understand how numbers proved so mystifying to so many. It was simply fractions, division, multiplication, mere figures to be added and subtracted, all of which he performed in his head without any need of paper and pencil or abacus.

"T his uniform is itchy."

Mullin ignored his colleague as they strode along the park. He had memorized the picture of the kike, expected him any minute, out to walk his dog. He continued his lesson in killing.

"So what you do is you just aim for the middle of the chest, chances are good you'll hit him right in the pumper. Then you pull him toward you, by the throat, hook your leg around behind his, and put him down. Then, what I usually do is yank it out, and then shove it right up under his chin, wham, through the brain, till you feel it smack off the top of his skull. You got it?"

"I don't know what's so bad about a gun."

"Noise, plus I seen guys shot in the head, lived to talk about it."

"None I ever done."

"I used to be a garrote guy myself, but they always shit their pants. Everyone I ever did like that, they shit themselves—no ex-ceptions. I can't stand that smell. Plus it's work, choking the life out of some mug."

"I still like the gat. Bang and you're done."

"Right. Well, we're gonna give this a shot. You want to have a go at it?" He produced the weapons, wood handles, the long tapered metal points that caught the sun.

"Yeah, I do. Why not?"

"Oh yeah, and make sure when you pull the ice pick out of his chest, you ain't standing right over him."

"What for?"

"You hit it right, believe you me, the blood will be flying."

He took the weapon and made a few thrusts, a sword fighter. "I seen that Captain Blood picture. I kind of like this uniform. Those guys have the best rackets of all. Gun and a badge, it's a permit to steal and that's all. How many guys you know, grew up alongside of, now they're on the job and they make out better than any racket guy I know."

"There he is."

"So, let's go get him."

They strode together easily.

Googie squatted to do his deed and Cohen looked off. The cops were now coming toward him, smiling grandly, as if in on some private joke. One short, the other tall, they both had those red faces he hated. If they were out for sport they would regret it. The local commander was fattening at his bosses' trough.

"Hey mister!"

Cohen stopped and turned. He affected a smile. "Hello, officers. It's a nice day, no?"

The tall cop turned to the shorter. "Nice enough."

"Lots of sun."

"Good day to kill a dirty kike."

Cohen tried to turn away but the short cop was on him and he smelled the rancid breath and he felt the punches to his chest. His first thought was, How dare you strike me, don't you know who I am? The fat-faced Irish laughed at him as he jitter-stepped to the side and a bright spigot of blood shot into the quiet Sunday sky.

Then he felt dizzy and warm liquid was spilling down his front, something hot, sticky, and he was on his knees and saw his poodle in the arms of the tall fat-faced Irish and they were laughing at him and as he slumped on his side he thought of all the ways he might die this was the worst.

ouhey checked his watch. Three targets should be down or going down by now. "Bet your retirement fund on Carnera. It's an Owney Madden production, boys, and the outcome is as certain as the coming of night. That's as straight as you'll get."

"Can that animal actually fight?"

"Your kid sister would take him in less than three."

"It's a shame what you guys have done to the fight game," Halloway said.

"The man just gave you an opportunity to make a little bonus and you're gonna be the mother superior."

"Hey, bet his opponent, you want." Touhey laughed.

aul Costa leaned over the stove and sliced the garlic razor-thin. The onion was already melting into the simmering olive oil and he breathed the vapors. While the garlic softened he picked up three tomatoes, still sun-warmed from his garden that morning, and began juggling them the way he used to as a boy in Tompkins Square, pitching them faster and faster into the air until they were a continuous red blur. He had not lost his touch. He tossed them back into a bowl and quick-chopped some parsley, sprinkling it into the saucepot. He sliced open the tomatoes and seeded them, then squeezed them with his own hands, dripping the pulp onto the sizzling oils and garlic and onion and minced veal.

He went to the faucet to wash his hands and there was still no water. He punched the wall so hard he cracked the plaster and scraped his knuckles raw. He cursed and wiped the blood on his boxer shorts. He picked up his phone and called the only other one in the building.

"Hey, you drunken Irish! Where's my water?"

The super assured him the plumber was on his way.

"That right? If you're lying to me I'll march right down there and rip your dirty donkey Irish ears right off your skinny head." He hung up and began pacing his kitchen. The wife and kids were off to noon mass and he relished the quiet. It was the only day of the week he got out of bed before four o'clock, his one concession to family life. He took a bottle of Canadian beer from the icebox and pried the top off with his teeth and spit it in the sink. He turned on the radio, hoping to catch the game.

The super hung up the phone and seethed. Now he was glad he had agreed to help Tough Tommy Touhey. They promised they just wanted to talk to the Italian and that's what he told his wife to keep her calm, but he had to admit deep down he knew this was probably a lie. He was no greenhorn anymore. He knew how the ways of the world in New York worked, he did. But he did not care, not at all. It had been one heartbreak after another since coming over, and what with jobs so scarce, he more oftentimes wished he had stayed in Mayo. If you were going to be poor and miserable it might as well be in a place you know with people who cared whether you lived or starved. Here was easy money and that muscleman Italian had been breaking his shoes since the day he moved in, calling him a dirty drunken Irish pig right to his face, and in front of his kids, what's more. He was definitely a no-good hoodlum and was only getting what he deserved.

When the buzzer rang he went and let the two guys in, dressed in plumber's overalls and carrying tools. He made a point of looking no higher than their chests, so no matter what he could not tell anyone what they looked like, because he never saw them. The one handed him an envelope and he stuffed it in his pocket and went back to the kitchen. An hour later, when the fat wop wife and kids came back from the twelve o'clock at Our Lady of Mt. Carmel, he heard the screams. They were horrible and relentless and streamed down from above, echoing throughout the courtyard until they scraped his nerves raw. He looked up and Noreen glared at him and went back to the bedroom. He knew he had disappointed her in a way she would never forgive. That's how things went in America. He went down to the dingy basement and turned the water back on.

Touhey looked at his watch and decided to make the late mass. "Well fellas, I can't go a Sunday without the mass." He crossed 138th Street and ducked into St. Jerome's, where he sat in the front pew. The priest acknowledged him with a brief nod, then preached a homily about the rich man's difficulty in getting into heaven. Touhey did not mind the rebuke at all, especially since the good father might be called to confirm his alibi. He made a mental note to donate a couple of new Cadillacs to the archdiocese. The Reverend might have a problem with the murky source of his tithe, but the Archbishop did not. He went to his knees.

Grace sat in the dawn light gazing out upon the still black waters of the East River and painting her hangover away. It was Sunday, and there was little of the usual boat traffic. At quiet times like this, she wondered what Manhattan had been like before the Dutch swindled it out from under the Indians. She painted a verdant scene: hawks circling above, deer prancing along the riverbank, a plume of smoke rising from an unseen cooking fire. She imagined a people caught in the cycles of nature, of birth and death and life, a time before gunpowder and the incessant clank of machinery, before coal smoke and concrete. She mused for a minute that it might have been idyllic but then figured it was just a more personal savagery. Innocence lost. Different means to the same end. Bloodshed and stupid vendettas, squabbles over ground and trinkets and women.

Sometimes, when the dawn came and her mind was clear and she felt the grip of the night ease from her heart, she acknowledged certain things. She had not loved Francisco as much as she protested. She had been young and married for reasons unknown. Or maybe fully known. She had been lonely and far from home and absolutely flattered by his charms and attention, his Mediterranean wiles. He took her to shows in Seville, ignored the whispers and glares. She figured he had his own reasons. His marriage to her was a stab at his parents, a grab for independence. They were banished to Cuba. They had the boys. He laid other women in Havana hotel rooms that smelled of tropical rot. But she honored her dead, she nurtured them, and they grew pure in her memory.

She imbued the imagined island across the oily river with the livid greens of Cuba, worked quickly, fat strokes, globular. She darkened it, made it sinister, filled with betrayers. Creatures lurked, red-eyed and ravenous. Her pale hands were splattered with paint. She felt as if she had extended herself beyond a point she could sustain. She reeled her feelings in and kept them tight. She thought about the Irishman, the boxer. Something passed between them, something alive and real and scary and full of possibility. But no, she believed all true love was behind her. From now on it would consist of men to hold her and have her. But she thought of him often. Contemplated them naked and joyous together. It made her less interested in seeing Farrell, who seemed so effete and self-obsessed by comparison. Not that she knew the Irishman at all, really.

She washed up and rode her bicycle to the graveyard. She rarely went there on sunny days. These were somber occasions and she wanted the sky to reflect the darkness within her. She often brought drawings or little figures she made from clay. She sang softly his favorite song and apologized for leaning so heavy on him after her husband died. She smothered him sometimes. This she felt guilty for, it pierced her to her being. The few years he had were made darker by her need, her grief, her loneliness and hunger for love and safety. She picked the grass that had sprung along the headstone, tidied the grave. What had he done to deserve such an early death? She stood, looked down the rows of tombstones, at others gathered in grief and remembrance. She picked up her bike and rode away, toward home.

T he days got longer and the streets were filled with children playing after-dinner games. Briody sat on the stoop and watched stickball being played by boys with the accents of Connacht, Munster, and Ulster, intonations from the bogs and coastal wastelands. Inside the homes they were Irish, but on the cobblestones and dirty sidewalks and in the school yards they yearned to be Yanks, to fit in, to be like the kids they saw on the silver screens along the Grand Concourse and heard over the radio. Briody understood this urge, this need.

He leaned forward, putting his elbows on his knees. He was bone weary from the pace of the job. The superintendent had come around saying things were cranking up, that in July they would be nailing a floor a day. Briody figured he would be out of work long before Christmas.

Young Danny came to bat, pointing the broom handle up 139th Street, his face nearly glum with destructive intent, a pint-sized imitation of the Great Bambino. He batted left-handed like his hero and walloped the first pitch. The Spaldeen traced a fierce arc up above the tenements as the outfielders, arrested for a flash, gaped in wonder, then turned heel and dashed for the receding ball, hollering all the while as Danny trotted with studied ease around the bases. Briody clapped loudly, a one-man ovation, and Danny smiled over at him.

Maggie came out and sat next to him. "Drives his father mad, playing the baseball." She smelled of soap and a little bit of sweat. Her hair brushed the tops of her shoulders and when she tossed it back she looked for a moment like the girl he'd met at home.

"We can't all be hurlers."

Briody envied Casey his children, his wife, the dense familiarity of the cramped apartment.

"He hates having all these narrowback children."

"Just be glad you didn't go to England. At least here you can imagine a future."

"You'll get no argument from me on that. How's the job?"

"Gangbusters."

"I can't believe I can see it out the window now. Sticking up like a stub on the horizon. Could you imagine? America is a wild place, wild. I worry about the kids over here. There's so much bad that goes on right around them every day. It's funny, Michael. I think back home things were bad for the grown-ups but it was a great place to be a child. Here it seems the opposite."

Briody indicated the ballplayers. "They look to be having a grand old time at it now."

Maggie rested her hand on her chin. "Michael, what is Danny up to these days?"

Briody took a breath. Fat Walsh the beat cop came ambling around the corner looking for a way to brighten up his day. He stopped and studied the game with porcine eyes. Fat Walsh the beat cop recalled a screw that had given the men a hard time in the Curragh camp. Briody hoped Maggie would not press the issue. There was really nothing he was able to tell her.

"It's not particulars I am after, Michael. It's just a worry I have that's been eating at me more and more like a poison. I can't imagine raising all these children without a father."

Fat Walsh the beat cop started whistling and slapping his nightstick on his thigh. "Would you look at that eejit?" Maggie leaned closer and he felt the warmth of her against him. When she spoke again her breath brushed the side of his face. "I just don't know why you fellows can't just leave it all behind you."

Briody could say that it was because their enemies wanted just that, but knew it would not explain anything to her. The batter swiped at a pitch and fouled it off to his left. The ball careened across the street to where Fat Walsh snatched it in mid-flight. A smile worked its way across his expanse of face, and he began to toss the ball lightly in the air, higher each time he caught it.

Briody took Maggie's hand and felt its dry rough skin, its calluses. She was like so many, stuck between embracing a new land and rejecting it at the same time. Doomed to live on and never be fully a part of either place, caught in a transatlantic limbo.

The kids were yelling to Fat Walsh, begging for the ball back, when one of the outfielders barked "lard ass!" In response, Fat

Walsh calmly took out his pocketknife and began to saw the ball in two. Finished, he tossed the halves into the air. As he passed the stoop Briody fought the urge to stand up and slap the man, turning his eyes away when Fat Walsh nodded in greeting. When he was gone, Briody called Danny over and gave him a silver dollar. "Buy yourself a bushel of new ones."

Maggie watched her son run down the block. "I worry about him. And his father."

Briody squeezed her hand. "I wouldn't worry about either of the Danny Caseys. They're survivors." He sat in her company in the warm sun and knew this to be true. It was himself he was starting to worry about. He knew he was soon going to be called upon to kill.

There are rumors, son. Rumors, innuendo, and calls for action. Frankly, the powers that be have had it with that crowd you run with. And don't hit me with any of that Catholic-bashing horse crap. The Democrats are raping and pillaging this town. Avarice is ugly, young man. Incompetence worse."

Farrell sat and watched his father-in-law hold forth over bootleg brandy. His brow was furrowed, his jowls beginning to slide from his skull, and his nose would not look out of place on a greenback. The old skinflint was in rare form.

"What this city needs is a man of vision, a sweeping change, an age of enlightenment. By God, a good old-fashioned delousing." He was up now, wheeling and sputtering. "And believe you me, that day is nigh. I am hearing a lot of talk down at the club. Now listen, Farrell. You and I don't always see eye to eye on these things, but whether I care for it or not, my flesh and blood is tied up in all this. You're a lawyer man, an educated fellow. Can't you see the writing on the wall?"

"Doctor, I see you've been listening to the rants of the good Reverend again." Farrell topped off both their snifters. Prescott, as a result of throwing major money at a small mining college, had been awarded an honorary doctorate, so Farrell called him Doctor. The man took it as a compliment.

The Doctor waved away his assertion. "It's not just that. Can't you see? What with the market down, way down, they need a scapegoat, a witch burning. That pretty boy in City Hall is up against it. His gangster element can't save him now."

"Doctor, his honor is a committed and tireless foe of the bad guys in town."

Harrumph, a casual exhalation of smoke. "Committed? Hard to say. Worthy, not at all."

"How's business?" Farrell tried to steer the conversation.

"Shot to hell. But we're hanging on. Thank God I divested heavily last summer. Best move I ever made. Let me suggest something, John. Two words." The Doctor sighted down his cigar. "Los Angeles."

"Where's that, Texas?" Farrell would rather set himself aflame than move to California. He briefly flashed on himself parched, bored, old, and defeated in some arid valley filled with starving Filipinos. He'd seen a newsreel.

"You're a barrel of laughs. I have a solid connection there in City Hall, not to mention I have played golf with several of the Otises. Solid folk, God-fearing."

"Your God, I presume."

"Don't get Jesuitical on me."

"Old habits. Rose Hill and whatnot."

The Doctor slowly crushed out his cigar in an ivory ashtray he had brought back from a hunting foray to East Africa. "John." He leaned in for effect, dropped his voice an octave. "We have been jousting over these things since my daughter first dragged you in from the cold. We've had our fun with it, too. But times are different now. People are clamoring for blood, there is a new level to all this, a viciousness. Scalps will be taken. Mark my words. I will not sit idly by while my daughter is humiliated."

"What makes you so sure this is any different than all the other crusades?"

"You are making light of my concerns."

"That boy, the one that cried wolf?"

The Doctor leaned back. Farrell got the impression he was weighing a revelation.

"John, in the past it usually was people like the good Reverend, a few other excitables. Motivated surely by good solid moral grounding. Christian men mind you. But, certainly, pains in the ass to a certain extent. What I notice now is how, well, universal the sentiment seems. Men that rarely agree are speaking in one voice. They're reeling, and someone has to pay. Now you people have done well in politics, the law maybe. But it's not your town."

"Yet."

"Ambition is a charming thing."

Farrell wondered what it might portend. He rubbed his hand along the smooth leather of the Doctor's chair, sipped his brandy. He always suspected that the fact of his daughter screwing a Catholic was a source of grave disappointment to the man and that he never gave Tammany and the Democrats much of a thought until one was sullying his offspring. If he knew how seldom they actually coupled, it might ease his mind. Farrell would certainly mull the information over. He did not know what use it might be. There had been purges in the past. He considered his status as sacrificial. No, he was needed by too many people, had built a temple of graft and deceit of which he was the cornerstone.

Farrell stood to leave. "I do appreciate your concern, Doctor." At the door to the study he turned and said, "Thank you."

"And John, do me a favor will you? A fellow from the club, named Harcum, has some interest in city contracts. He's a transportation man. Solid enough."

Farrell fought down a laugh. "Of course. I'll see what I can do."

As he was pulling the door closed the Doctor shouted, "Los Angeles."

Farrell had to give it to the old coot. Business came first, no matter what.

■   ■ ■ ■

S he waited across from the job in a flower-print dress, her long hair spilling over her shoulders, the sun from over the new columns of the Empire State Building spotlighting her. Hundreds of people were rushing up and down Fifth Avenue but she seemed in a strange way to be the only one there. Grace waved him over and he shouldered his way through the crowd till he was beside her, in his ripped sooty shirt, his filthy dungarees and dust-covered boots.

"Told you I'd find you."

"I'm hardly dressed for a night out."

"Perfect. What happened to your face?" She rubbed his left cheek, which was bruised from sparring. He started at the pain, then felt the heat of her, an unexpected intimacy.

"I was bobbing when I should've been weaving. No bother."

"Horrible sport, that boxing."

"I don't take it serious enough for it to be dangerous."

"By the state of you, it's dangerous enough."

He laughed. They began walking south on Fifth Avenue.

"I know a quiet little place in the Village, nice food, good wine. Nobody will bother us."

"They let me in looking like this?" Briody indicated his work clothes, stiff with dried sweat and dirt.

"Are you joking? It's an artist hangout. They'll envy the muck on your trousers."

"So you're taking me to all the fine places in New York."

"Nothing but the best for a Cavan man."

"Taxi?"

"No. It's beautiful. Sure, let's enjoy the walk."

"A great place for walking, Manhattan."

They made their way down Fifth. She pointed out the variety of architectural styles, the wisps and curlicues and gargoyles of all the older buildings they encountered. They window-shopped idly along the way. Briody caught their reflection in the glass of the storefronts, liked the way they looked, like stars of their own picture show—she in her pretty dress, hair lifted by the breeze, he a head taller, thick-shouldered. People hurried past them, intent on getting home. No one seemed to think it odd that this well-dressed woman was walking along with a workingman. At Madison Square a dozen mounted police watched over a demonstration that had only managed to gather a handful of protesters against the rise of a political party in Germany.

"It sometimes seems there's as many protests in this city as there are people."

Briody pointed at the Great War monument and read the inscription on the base aloud. " 'For Our Heroes.' That's the one they should have protested."

"I'm sure someone did. I wonder if the dead feel they're heroes. I can't imagine what it was like."

"I was there and sometimes I can't imagine what it was like."

Grace hooked her right arm through his and with her left indicated the sweep of the square. "This is my favorite little piece of Manhattan. They say it used to be a potter's field. Can't you feel the ghosts? But look at these gorgeous buildings—the Metropolitan Life and over there the New York Life, look at that courthouse with the statues all over it, like something you might see in Rome, and my favorite, without a doubt, the Flat Iron. Isn't it gorgeous?"

Briody enjoyed her enthusiasm. "It looks like a ship, cutting uptown. I used to go there looking for work building tunnels. The sandhogs have their union office there."

"Do they? I always figured it was just a coat-and-tie crowd in there."

She led him into Marcel's, a bistro on Macdougal Street where the staff of mustachioed waiters met her with great warmth and familiarity. They were escorted to a booth in the back. Briody, despite her assurances, felt a bit out of sorts in his work clothes, but he liked the coziness of the place. "You certain they won't hand me a mop and send me to the toilets?"

"Don't be silly. I think you look like a million bucks."

"And you sound like a Yank, all right."

"Why not?" She picked up a menu. "Are you a meat-and-potatoes man, Michael, or are you adventurous?"

"The Italian fellow in the gang, Delpezzo, has me eating all sorts of things. Artichokes, and sardines, loads of garlic, monstrous stuff."

Grace laughed. "I'm sure he's not forcing it on a big strong fellow like yourself. So you trust me to order for us?"

Briody looked at the menu, which was entirely in French. "I don't think I have any choice, do I?"

"There's a keen fella. You okay with wine, or is it porter you need?"

"I don't mind a little wine, now and again."

"Good. They manage to get the best stuff here despite the Prohibition. Can you imagine trying to ban the drink?"

"Doesn't seem to be working very much in this city."

"It's a joke entirely."

The wine was brought to the table, uncorked, and poured. Grace raised her glass. "Here's to meeting someone from so close to home."

Briody clinked her glass and said, "So far away."

They sipped the wine and leaned over the small candle on the table. Her face glowed in the soft, uncertain light and he fought the urge to reach across and touch her, to feel her warmth. Before the food arrived Briody got up and went to the men's room. He stood over the sink and ran hot water and as he soaped his hands he stared at his reflection, at a face smudged with grease, at tired eyes, at deepening lines. No question, that face looked older than his thirty years. The past was presenting its bill. He washed his hands quickly and then roughly scrubbed his face. He noticed the half dozen small paintings that hung in the small windowless toilet, street scenes from Paris. He recalled the furloughs there, breaks from the front when they drank buckets of wine and kept the company of sweaty whores. Those sad-eyed country girls pressed into use. He dried his hands. This Grace made him feel comfortable in a way he was not used to. Not with women, not with himself, not with anyone. He considered that he needed to take it easy. She was, after all, Johnny Farrell's girl.

Back at the table a first course of mussels steamed in wine and garlic was waiting and they devoured them, using crusty bread to sop up the juice.

"You seem familiar enough with these," she said.

"We used to pull them off the rocks ourselves down near Kenmare."

"A fisherman on top of being a boxer, an ironworker, a soldier, and a farmer?"

"I bore easily."

"Does that apply to your women?"

"Only to ones taken by someone else."

Grace pulled back and stared at him. "Fair enough. But I am taken by no man. I am not something one stakes claim to like a piece of land."

Briody, surprised by the heat of her reaction, wanted to ease her ire. "I would not suspect you could be."

The waiter interrupted with the next dish and Grace, letting go, said, "Well, now we'll see what stuff you're made of."

Briody looked down at the plump golden lumps. "Garden slugs?"

"Escargots."

"I heard about these in France." He speared one, dipped it in butter, and slid it into his mouth. It wasn't half bad, tasted mostly of garlic. After swallowing he said, "Don't get too full of yourself, but I can honestly say you're the only person on the planet I would have done that for."

They spent most of the meal laughing, connecting all the rural Irish dots of common experience and place. They realized that at certain fairs and market towns of their youth they probably passed within touch of each other. She often went to Granard, as did he. The fair in Ballinagh, Christmas in Cavan Town. He knew the estate she was raised on; she knew his village, had passed it many times as a girl.

"We were always warned away from you lads," she said, and placed her hand over his.

He stared down at their entwined hands, looked away, then said, "Hell, look what good that did you."

"I was always a bold girl."

They shared a crème brûlée and lingered over the last of the wine. The place had filled considerably but the tables on either side remained empty. He held her hand a little tighter and she leaned down and kissed his.

"Why do I feel like I know you better than I should?" he asked.

"Don't know, but I feel the same. Odd."

"There are things, Grace."

She looked up at him, the candle flickering in her eyes. "There are always things."

He could not help but say, "I'm not exactly what I seem."

She pressed a finger to his lips. "None of us are. We covered a lot of ground tonight. Why don't we save some for the next time?"

Briody nodded and kissed her over the table and they gathered their things. There had been no talk of war or any trouble as if they both knew it well enough and pressed it into the dark and fading past. There was no further mention of Johnny Farrell, which was all right. She insisted on paying.

"A regular bohemian, are you?"

"Please. You can pay next time."

"I hope there is a next time." He watched as she pulled out a fifty-dollar bill and handed it off to the waiter. He wondered at her painting being so lucrative.

As they strolled through Washington Square, she laced her arm through his. They sat on a bench in the velvet air and Briody commented on how far this all seemed from the Bronx.

"I lived there for a while when I first arrived. Too many Irish for me."

"Through with us, are you?"

"Please, don't take it the wrong way. I just didn't want to be stuck in the same old life, the same old fears."

After a time they walked again and at Fourteenth Street she said, "Jesus, it's nearly eleven. I had better go."

"I was beginning to hope this night would last a bit longer."

"Just beginning? That's not very flattering."

"Don't want to seem too eager. I might chase you away."

"I doubt that, Michael. It's just that my life is a bit complicated right now."

"I'm a patient man."

"Good man. There might be hope for us yet."

She turned to him and they kissed. A taxi approached and he flagged it down, then kissed Johnny Farrell's girl once more before holding open the door. Once again he watched her in the backseat of a car, receding into the night.

On the Dyre Avenue train he wondered if this was what love felt like. He was surrounded by men and women with pinched hard faces that described some inner lament. Not he, not tonight.

One hundred thirty-eighth Street was quiet. Briody ducked into Bauer's speakeasy, wanting to avoid the usual stops. It was nothing but a dim grog shop at the back of a grocery, and the few patrons, mostly old men in need of shaves and work, were scattered along the bar and deep into their cups. They all turned at his entrance and stared through smoky eyes. Briody wondered at their scrutiny. He took a stool near the front and the barman came down and dropped a coaster before him. Briody ordered a beer. Next to him was a half-full glass and presently a man looking weary beyond his middle years came back from the bathroom and reclaimed the next stool. Briody recognized him at once. It was Packy Farrell, Johnny Farrell's father.

Briody, queered by the coincidence, stared straight ahead.

"Are you one for the ponies, lad?"

"No. Can't say that I am."

Mr. Farrell waved a *Racing Form* at him. "I'm from the Curragh and before I came to America I broke the yearlings. I know a thing or two about the nags. If I were you I'd take a good look at the third horse in the fourth race tomorrow at Belmont. She's a gasser."

Briody thanked the man and stared ahead. But Mr. Farrell seemed to need a companion.

"How long have you been over?"

"A year."

"A real greenhorn. I been here since '95. Never home once. It's a great country, Americkay. I've a son in Tammany Hall. Top man is he. Fordham Law graduate. Best friends with Jimmy Walker."

Briody wanted to add, And I was making time with his girl just an hour ago.

Presently Mr. Farrell got up and went for the bathroom again. Briody pointed to the man's glass and the barman who had been within earshot filled it and said, "The Tammany man hasn't been to see his da in nearly two years, nor the mother. Some son."

Briody relived the night in his head: her touch, her smell, the way she laughed. Mr. Farrell came back but stayed buried in his *Racing Form*. Briody had almost finished a second bad beer when the door opened and in spilled sour streetlight and Tommy Keating, one of Touhey's many cousins. Keating appeared happy to see him. Even before sitting down, Keating signaled the myopic bartender for two more beers.

"You ain't an easy guy to find. I've been waiting since suppertime. This joint is some dump."

Briody marveled at the intricate intelligence system of the neighborhood. No one had left since he entered. Someone must have seen him on the street. "It's handy enough."

"Handy. That's a good one. Place stinks, it does. Skels to the left and skels to the right. One broad with no teeth. Real class."

"I didn't stop for the company."

"You did, I'd start to worry about you."

"Never knew you cared."

"Tommy wants you to drop by. Failing that, he wants you to call him."

"I look forward to it."

"Thought you might, seeing as how you ain't stupid, far as I can see. How's your building?"

"Bigger every day."

"Me, I'm scared of heights personally."

"Most reasonable men are."

"Like I said, get in touch with Tommy. He's a nice guy until his patience wears thin. Toodles."

Briody nodded agreement and when the cousin was gone

bought one last beer, sliding pennies across the makeshift bar. He realized he needed to be more careful to watch what he said and whom he said it to. He needed even to be careful with Grace. Would he ever be his own man?

gan was a cutup. He sat behind Walker's desk, feet propped, and smoked his cigar doing a dead-on imitation of the Mayor. "A reformer is someone who rides through a sewer in a glass-bottomed boat. More champagne of course. My dear Cardinal Hayes, it's well known that Jesus himself fancied the ladies. Mary Magdalene—case in point."

Farrell did not mind the detective's antics, because at times like this waiting for Walker seemed to be his main function in life, and it annoyed him. "You still haven't found my hundred grand?"

Egan dropped his feet to the floor. "Like it went down a rabbit hole."

"Should I begin to doubt your skills as a detective?"

"Johnny, the lads are working their way through every mug on the West Side. Seems like maybe someone smart got lucky."

"I will just have to sell another bit of the city off to make amends."

"That's the spirit. Or I can cut the boys loose, maybe snatch a bootlegger for ransom."

"Egan, no need for theatrics. We are in a spot to earn like gentlemen."

Farrell sat on a Louis V chair looking out over the kinetic mid-morning on Central Park South. From this vantage point the sidewalk was nothing but hats rising and falling with each step. It looked as if you could walk all the way across town on the tops of those heads like a frog across lily pads. He sipped coffee and worried. The hundred grand was the least of it.

He heard stirring in the rooms behind him and glanced anxiously at his watch. "If I had a nickel for every minute Walker was late I might retire."

"You'd at least have the hundred G's back."

"Thing is I never once heard the merest apology for his timing. It's like he doesn't want to acknowledge that any schedule besides his is important."

"The man does set his own pace."

"At least he's egalitarian about it."

"Easy with the Fordham words."

"He's fair. He leaves laborers, senators, housewives, and foreign royalty standing around muttering while they glance at clocks. He made Herbert Hoover—I mean only the President of the United States—wait for forty minutes in the Oval Office."

"I hear he was two hours late for his own wedding."

"I know eyewitnesses to that spectacle."

"He charms them."

"He got away with it."

"You gotta admire him, in a way."

"He tosses off a quip, a smile, and the audience, never mind the aggravation of the extra hour or two wasted, is his."

"People just can't stay mad at him."

"He's like a roguish child."

Farrell himself was a stickler for time, and the Mayor's carefree manner drove him nuts. He poured another cup of the black, thick coffee and returned his gaze to a *Life* magazine with a photo spread of the Mayor from his second inaugural. There was the pride of Greenwich Village decked out in top hat and tails, and always, that devastating smile. Farrell remembered that morning well. Walker had come straight from a night at the Central Park Casino and nailed a beautiful, rousing speech with ease.

Egan went to use the bathroom, trailing a cloud of smoke. Farrell stood and looked over the pictures framed on the wall, Walker posing with a who's who of celebrity and infamy, many with Betty Compton, his showgirl mistress, at his side, and none of his dear wife Allie, not a single one. Farrell was amazed that the public tolerated his flagrant adultery. But it did, oh how it did.

The steward came in and replaced the empty coffee urn with a fresh one. Farrell resisted. He was jumpy enough without extra stimulus. "Justin, what are the odds his excellency will grace me with his presence anytime soon?"

"That is a very good question, Mr. Farrell. I would say long."

He walked over to the bookshelf, perused the titles. There was a lot of world history, biographies of Alexander the Great, Grant, Jefferson, Thomas Aquinas, the great philosophers, the Greeks. The Mayor was not known to be one for the books. Farrell wondered. He plucked a leather-bound copy of *Macbeth* and flipped through it, recalling his days at Fordham College with the Jesuits, the Shakespeare class taught by Father O'Hare, that feeling of new worlds opening to him through words, possibilities. That feeling seemed so lost to him. Hard to believe it was only a little more than a decade since he had strode onto that campus in the Bronx. He slid the book back in place and looked out again over the park. His nervousness was not a bad sign. It meant he was aware, that he was on guard, he thought, sipping more coffee, that he was alive.

Egan returned. "Johnny, I need to make a call that can't wait. Regards to the Mayor, I'll see you at the car."

A minute after Egan left, Walker, dressed in a navy blue silk robe, came in carrying his sleeping eyeshade in one hand, trailed by his steward. Walker sat and the steward placed the day's papers in front of him in a precise stack and then poured a cup of coffee.

"For such a pretty girl, Betty snores like a marine." He sipped his coffee. He put his cup down and worked through the papers.

"I have a busy day, your honor." Farrell glanced at his watch.

Walker ignored him. "You know, Johnny Farrell, this seems to happen every decade or so. It starts as whispers in private drawing rooms and then it becomes table pounding in opposition clubs and then editors wake to it and off they go with their righteous squawk until it blares from the headlines, a regular reformist howl."

"You worry it might be different this time?"

"Different? Let's see." He picked up various papers. "They're blaming me for unemployment, for speakeasy shoot-outs, for the still-unsolved murder of my 'friend' Arnold Rothstein, for overflowing orphanages, for the price of milk? Isn't that an Albany issue? Oh and this is beautiful—for the sorry state of Wall Street. What chutzpah. The same speculators that brought about the collapse, the ones who fattened on the dreams of the little man, who beguiled pennies away from widows, want me to take the heat for their failings. And daylight machine-gun fire? Did I vote in Prohibition?" He tossed the papers aside. "Different, Johnny? I'd say not. It's a good thing the sun is shining today or they would pin the clouds on me too."

The steward put a plate of runny scrambled eggs before the Mayor and refilled both their cups with black coffee.

"I wonder, though," Farrell said. "My father-in-law seems to think this time is different. There seems more at stake."

"You're an astute politician. What do you think?"

"Some of it is the usual hysteria and hypocrisy. I just worry that with the slump, people want scapegoats. If the goo-goos and the Republicans can frame the debate, can paint us as the bad guys, this time will be different. It will be a lot worse. Heads will roll."

"Heads always roll."

"I agree. But whose heads?"

Walker finished his eggs in silence. When he was done he leaned back and lit a cigarette. "There is more to this than the nattering of your relations."

The Mayor was loath to know details of off-the-books activity. "There have been some look-sees into my operations. Nobody that's announced themselves."

"The police?" Walker exhaled, his face tightening.

"Not ours. Not federal or state as far as I can tell."

"La Guardia's people?"

"The little guttersnipe is not really up to that sort of thing I don't think. What about Roosevelt?"

The Mayor laughed. "Come on now, Johnny. He just vetoed the Republican legislation calling for the investigation into my administration. He may be a Knickerbocker, but he's no enemy of the Hall. I think you're spending too much time in the shadows."

"His eyes are on the presidency. He needs distance. He learned from Smith's humiliation that being tarred with the Tammany brush is no asset in the hinterlands."

Walker pushed the soggy remains of his breakfast around with his fork. "Johnny, you have made yourself indispensable. You know secrets, you make money, and you're a good and loyal soldier. Let me get dressed and we'll attend to some business."

"I only need an okay on one thing right now."

"Can it wait?"

Just then Betty walked through the room, wearing a robe that matched the Mayor's. Her black hair was disheveled and as she waved to Farrell he caught a glimpse of a bared breast. He said, "Good morning," and turned away.

When Betty was gone the Mayor chuckled. "It's all right, Johnny, looking's no sin."

"They want the contract," Farrell said.

Walker sighed. "It's already let."

"They don't care."

"We did not have these problems before the Volstead Act. What about Corcoran, the contractor? He's no shrinking violet."

"They say they'll kill him. After they kill his family."

The Mayor blanched. "Good God. When will they be sated?"

"I am not in a position to say."

"I hate being involved in any of this."

"So do I. I just need to get your okay. I'll spare you the gory details."

Walker stood and pulled his robe closed. He looked out over the street for a moment and then turned back to Farrell. His eyes were puffy and just the hint of stubble brushed his chin. With true sadness he said, "How did it ever come to this?"

"We need to stay ahead of it."

"These are the days when I really and truly miss our Jew."

"Rothstein was all right."

"You could deal with him."

"He had class."

"What he had was a marvelous talent for keeping the animals in line."

"He had real class."

"Killed over a lousy card game."

"That, we may never know." Farrell checked his watch. "Time has come to deliver bad news."

"Give the Colonel my regards. And something to keep him happy."

"I have a thing or two in mind."

"I bet you do, Johnny Farrell."

Walker, his robe pulled tight, wandered back in the direction of his bedroom, calling out to Betty.

Farrell found Egan waiting with the car and sent him on his way. He needed to see the Colonel alone. A block from the Ritz the cool marble lobby of the New York Athletic Club was a respite from the midday glare of the streets. Farrell stood beside the monument that listed the membership dead from the Great War, the twin bronze eagles looking over each of his shoulders. He recalled coming here as a boy to watch Tommy Touhey box older men, subduing them with viciousness. The lunchtime crowd, almost all dressed in fine suits of muted flannel, hurried in and out of the lounge, striding with purpose. Many of them were the Catholic elite of the city and most knew enough to stop and shake Johnny Farrell's hand. Farrell went along with the backslapping, the bonhomie. It came with the territory, but behind his smile, his winks, and his cheer, his unease was growing. The Mayor had been dismissive, which was not unexpected. But that did not soothe him one bit. Something was going on.

Paul Corcoran, tall, white-haired, and built like a barrel set on top of tree limbs, entered the lobby accompanied by a man of equal height but half the girth. Corcoran leaned forward as he walked, creating the impression that he was looking for someone to fall on and crush. He noticed Farrell and steered his companion over to him like a prison guard transporting a convict.

"Johnny. You ever meet Frank G. Shattuck?" Corcoran as usual did not wait for a reply. "Owns all the Schrafft's restaurants. Hires only Irish. What do they say? Off the boat at four o'clock, working at Schrafft's by five. Big fan of the Mayor."

Shattuck nodded hello, then slipped away, toward the lounge, anxious to get away from the bellowing contractor. Farrell waited patiently for Corcoran to let go of his hand.

"You got time, Farrell? Come on, I scheduled us rubdowns. Why not?"

Farrell followed him into the locker room and soon the two of them lay flat on their bellies on adjoining tables while thick-necked masseurs worked them over. Farrell thought the massage sounded like a good idea, but he was having a hard time relaxing. He was wired, for one thing, and while saying no to Corcoran had to be done he did not look forward to it even if he did get a kick out of denying such men things they thought they were entitled to. The muscle slaps, knuckles digging into his spine, the liniment on his skin—all were done to little effect.

After the rubdowns they headed for the heat. Farrell grabbed a manila envelope from his locker and followed Corcoran, who slipped out of his robe and yanked open the pine door of the sauna. Corcoran was a big man who gave lots of money to lots of people, was a minor industry himself. Farrell felt slighter than usual standing next to such bulk. The contractor had led men through blood and fire in the forests at Belleau Wood and as proof his back and chest bore the angry marks of hot steel intercepted in mid-flight. He was unaccustomed to being denied.

As their pale knees turned rosy in the heat, Johnny Farrell said, "Paul, I have good news and bad."

"Spit it out."

"You can't have that sewer contract."

The contractor's rotund gut heaved. "What kind of crap you selling me?"

"Something's come up. There's been a change. Unforeseen."

"That piece of work is mine, fair and goddamn square." Corcoran had the type of voice that could be heard above mortar fire.

"You'll be taken care of." Farrell attempted appeasement. The dry heat burned his lungs.

"Taken care of? Listen to me, you hotshot mouthpiece. For the last time it's mine and that's that. Somebody's got to rein in these goddamn Corsicans. Who let those sons of bitches in the game? Greedy bastards." Corcoran had turned a lobster-pot red.

He was right, Farrell thought. But so what? His ability to control the so-called Corsican criminals had become a lot weaker over the course of his tenure. Theirs was a level of cunning that was hard to compete with. He kept an even keel. He said, "Do you remember Francis Scanlon?"

"Frankie? Hell, yes I do. He was a very good friend of mine. One of the best builders this town ever seen, rest his soul."

"Rest his soul. That is the key phrase here."

"He is dead."

"Do you know the precise nature of his death?"

"They tried to kidnap him and he fought back, got killed in the process. He was one tough son of a bitch."

"All true, in a way." Farrell picked up the envelope by his side. He slid a photograph out from it, handing it to Corcoran. It was a crime scene glossy that showed a corpse with a bullet hole in its head, a vast expanse of naked torso, and then a dark bloody stain where the genitals had once been. Globs of sweat dropped off the contractor onto the picture.

"That's what happened to Scanlon."

"Jesus." Corcoran averted his gaze.

"They took their time."

"The papers, the family, they all said he was shot was all." Corcoran thrust the picture back at Farrell and stared at the far wall.

"We thought it best that it was not known. For the family's sake, and friends'."

Corcoran poured a cup full of water over his head. "You said something about good news?"

Farrell slid the wet photograph back into the envelope and adjusted his towel. "There's three miles of tunnel about to be let for a new subway line." He stood and as he reached the door told Corcoran, "It's all yours—every inch of it."

Corcoran grunted.

"There's just one little catch."

"What the hell now?"

"I'll need a hundred-grand finder's fee."

Corcoran just stared.

"By Monday morning."

Farrell stopped on his way downtown for a haircut and a shave. As he leaned back in the barber's chair he thought, So much for the missing hundred G's. Problem solved.

Briody stood on the boat deck next to a small table on top of which two candles flickered in the warm breeze. He smiled as Grace emerged from the galley and placed down polished silverware, a bottle of wine, and two glasses. Briody indicated the view of Manhattan, the sweep of the river. "This is gorgeous."

"You better hope the mosquitoes stay away. They have a way of distracting you from the view."

"Malaria could not spoil this view."

"Ever have Spanish food?"

"Jesus, eating's always an adventure with you, a regular world tour."

"Once you leave behind the notion that all meals need be meat and potatoes it opens possibilities up a bit." She poured him a glass of red wine. They sat on folding chairs and sipped their wine watching the light river traffic.

After a while she went back inside and returned with a dish heaped with food. "This is what they call paella."

Briody poked through the dish with his fork. "All God's creatures, I see."

"A little bit of everything all right."

Briody enjoyed the dish. He cracked the back of his lobster and tore the sweet meat away, scraped the mussels from their shells with his teeth. He tasted saffron for the first time. He liked watching Grace eat. There was no daintiness to her approach. She ate with gusto, wiped oil off her chin with a napkin. The wine flowed.

"Did you fancy Spain?"

"I liked it well enough. It was like a different planet from home. My God did it get hot. Once I got the language down it was all right. Made me realize what a drab old place Ireland could be at times." She took a nutcracker to her lobster. "I'm not sure I liked the girl I was then. I was angry a lot."

"And now?"

"Now, I have my days like most."

Briody sipped his wine. "You were only young then. What were you so angry about?"

"I'd seen enough to have good reason."

When they finished the paella she served him rich chocolate cake along with black Spanish coffee. Briody felt as if he had never had a better meal. Grace cleared the table and when he rose to help she put her hand on his shoulder and pushed him back into his chair. "Go away now. You're my guest."

She came back with another bottle of wine. He was getting fuzzy-headed, but liked it. He had not felt so relaxed in years.

"What about you, Michael Briody? Are you happy here?"

"Same as you. Actually, I'm truly happy when I'm on the job. There's nothing like it really. Most people might think it's crazy, but I love the work, the men. Climbing up there in the sky, making something that will last long after you're gone, turning empty space into something real and concrete."

"Must be nice to feel that way about work."

"Come on, now. I'm sure you're passionate about your art."

Grace filled their glasses. "Sure. But it's more like something I have to do than want to do." She raised her glass. "It beats cleaning up after people."

"I don't think Johnny Farrell would let you take up a scrub brush." Briody regretted the remark immediately. Still, he needed to know how strong her feelings were for the Tammany man. It was more than just romantic competition. He sensed crossing Farrell could prove unhealthy.

She stared out over the river. "Maybe when you're traipsing around with your gangster pals you can ask what they think."

"That's a long story."

"I guess we both have tales to tell."

Briody ducked his head as he entered the boat. He felt foolish for raising Farrell. The walls of the bathroom were covered with sketches, a number of which depicted construction workers caught in their labors. A small kerosene lamp lit the cramped space. He pissed. When he returned to the deck she was up front, sitting on a bench. He joined her and she grabbed his hand and the feel of her flesh made him want her more than anything.

"Michael." She gestured at the city across the water. "Did you ever imagine this when you were young?"

"No. Even when my father told me his stories, it never came to me like this. I never imagined the scope of it."

"Michael, my association with Johnny Farrell can't be easily ended."

Briody put his glass down. "Will it stop you from seeing me?"

"Honestly? I don't know if anything could."

"Then let's not worry about it for now."

"I'm afraid there's more to it than a boy-meets-girl scenario."

He put his hand on her face and pulled her close. "What did you say to me last time?" He kissed her fully on the lips. "Let's worry about that later." They stood and she led him through the close space of the boat, to her bed.

Illicit love on the dirty side of town: this was great. Egan had his cameraman snap a picture of the big Mick as he stood there talking to the Irish girl. She grabbed his hand—perfect. He urged the cameraman to snap away and capture this betrayal, another tool for him to use, another fulcrum. This Irish girl was going to be very useful to him in so many ways. He sucked on a peanut shell and tipped his fedora back. The Governor would be pleased.

From the sidewalk a hatless man wearing a greasy, tattered jacket and brown pants so dirty they looked black approached the car. "Please, buddy, anything—a hunk of bread, maybe a couple pennies, a nickel so's I can get a square meal. I'm an honest guy."

Egan waved him closer. When the man leaned in, smiling expectantly, Egan punched him in the face so hard that he fell straight down. He reached into his pocket and sprinkled a handful of change on the prostrate beggar.

"Nice shot," the driver said, laughing.

Egan said, "Gotta stay in practice," and pointed forward. They roared north on Kent Avenue as the man, on his knees and bleeding from the mouth, gathered his bounty.

The sky crackled with the soft blue light of dawn. Grace rolled over and melded her body to Briody's, feeling the muscled heat of him. He had mentioned how rarely he slept well but now he was sleeping deeply and she hoped it was because he felt at ease with her. She pulled him closer, wrapping her arm around him from behind. The boat rocked them gently and she lay there for a long time in that silence. She felt herself opening to him, laying herself bare although she had sworn after Milo that it would never happen again. She would not avail her heart to anyone or anything. She had convinced herself it was better to go through life as an observer, not a participant. Yet here she was listening to Briody's even breathing, a lover once again. How, she wondered, had this happened?

In the changing morning light she could see the scars that she had only been able to feel last night. She ran one foot along the back of his calf, felt its thickness. He was all muscle and animal force. His body was so unlike Farrell's. So was his openness. For all Farrell's surface charm, she knew his carelessness was often feigned, was a mask to hide behind. The Tammany boy wonder might be a backslapper and one of the fellows, but he burned with a darker light. He would not take her moving on lightly.

Rising now, she strode into the galley and put water on for coffee. Outside, a fog, white and thick, hung over the water, obscuring the skyline above and the river below. She went out on the deck. The fog was so dense it wet her skin, a kind of white silence, so alien in this city. She stood enjoying the temporary refuge, the sense that she was beyond harm in the nothingness. Suddenly a ship materialized out of the gloom, a tug, passing within feet of her. It came and went in the fog with such stealth that the instant it was gone, she was not sure that it had been real—a ghost ship whispering out of her past, perhaps with Milo at the helm. Chilled now, she went back into the cabin and pulled on some pajama pants and an undershirt.

She sat in that odd gauzy light and drew him, a few sketches of just his head and the slope of his neck, his broad shoulders. Then she drew the length of him, the sheet draped over his loins. There was nothing slack about his body. It was made for work, for action, for doing.

In the kitchen she made breakfast: bacon, a half dozen fried eggs, thick slices of brown bread which she slathered with jam and butter. She arranged it all on a tray and placed it beside the bed. Jesus, she thought, this is one thing she had never done before—bringing a man breakfast in bed. What next?

She pulled her shirt up past one breast and leaned over him, pressing the soft flesh against his cheek. He was awake in an instant.

"I've been woken up with far more terrible things than that put to my face."

"One would hope."

"What's this?" He sat up and indicated the tray.

"I brought you breakfast, you big buffoon."

"I can see that," he said, and pulled her down in the bed, and as they rolled together she felt all the muscles in his body coalesce to a force, one already familiar to her.

They'd done some time together in Sing Sing, whiled away the long stupid days shooting the shit, telling street stories. Madden was already an established force on the West Side, a name. Touhey was up the river for shotgunning two men who had tried hijacking a truckload of beer he'd brought down from Utica. They had ambushed him right on Willis Avenue, three in the afternoon. His victims survived, but one would never walk again, the other was left with half a face. The judge took into account Touhey's war record, commendable he called it, slapped his gavel down on three to seven, the minimum. Touhey did nineteen months and a few favors for Owney the Killer.

Touhey watched the last of the show, the girls high-kicking it, the patrons howling with lust, the waitstaff slicing through the crowd ferrying drinks. There were a dozen men, Rotarians from Sandusky, Ohio, according to their conventioneer tags, crowding the stage, waving mortgage money at the girls. One, wearing a straw boater, the class clown, grabbed his own plump breasts and mimicked the girls, move for move. His buddies roared, falling about the place. Drunk and Out of Town don't count.

When he was paroled Madden had lined him up a job guarding boatloads of hooch coming in from Rum Row. He spent his nights roaring about on the open seas, blasting past the moribund and compromised Coast Guard. Big Bill Dwyer and Owney had quite a partnership. In three years he dumped only a half dozen bodies into the surf, enterprising dagos and Jews whose reach exceeded their grasp. He was a fair-haired boy, a comer. They dry-docked him, moved him up, put him in charge of transportation for the whole far-flung empire. Boats, trucks, taxis, boxcars into the Hell's Kitchen and Hell Gate freight yards, seaplanes. Tough Tommy Touhey kept half of New York stewed. He was making two thousand a week and walked into any nightclub in town like he owned the joint.

But he yearned to be his own man. Farrell, his boyhood pal, lined him up the taxi commission, some real estate in the old neighborhood, a few of the better speaks. He took his bootlegger's stake and went back to Mott Haven. Told Owney and Big Bill, Thanks but I'm going home to the Bronx. He buried two Micks in Hunts Point plus one of Schultz's bagmen to mark his territory, and the whole thing was his. He sold all types of alcohol and manufactured his own beer, cut near beer with bathtub gin, ran boatloads into City Island, trucks down from Canada. He prided himself on his independence but also was smart enough to know the winds of change were blowing through the city, forces were gathering, a combination was being created against which he had little chance of waging effective battle.

He sipped his whiskey and watched the busty man from Ohio topple over on a table attended by six of Owney's shooters. Bad move. Owney's boys were up and cutting into the Ohioans with a demented glee. There was breaking glass, shrieks, and the smacking of skulls as the entire gaggle was shown the back-alley door. The fat man, the reveler, the former college football stand-out, was crawling on his hands and knees after his friends, weeping and bleeding, as a gutter-thin West Sider methodically kicked him in the ass in between sips of beer.

The band picked up the tempo to cover the sound of carnage. The girls danced like demons. A table of squint-eyed off-duty cops watched the action with professional disinterest, drinking to the beat. Their money was no good in any joint owned by Madden. Touhey envied Owney's control in Manhattan, sometimes wished he had stayed with the Killer. Madden covered all bases, left little to chance. Cops, judges, politicos, they were all his. When Touhey left his employ he had envisioned himself becoming the Madden of the Bronx and the two of them joining forces someday, a bullet-proof alliance. He had hoped the new Irish coming in, the war refugees, might be opportunistic, hungry. But no, they were either head-down fearful and willing to toil for crumbs or committed only to avenging their defeats. He simply did not have the troops. So here he was, back, hat in hand, besieged by the very dagos and Jews he had scoffed at in the past. And Owney, to rub it in, was making him wait.

"Tough Tommy Touhey, how the hell are you?"

Big Frenchy DeMange was at his elbow as the girls left the stage to a thunderous, drunken ovation. DeMange reeked mildly of disinfectant, his hair was gelled down like an undersized helmet and his face was fleshy and pink. He looked like a man always on his way to or from a boar roast.

"Frenchy, looks like life's been good."

"Meals, I ain't missed too many."

"Thank God. You missed the little sideshow."

"I heard. Some people just can't hold their liquor. Crying shame."

Touhey was not here for small talk. The last of the patrons

were finishing their drinks, gathering themselves for home. A pair of Filipinos, two men who moved with puma-like grace and might have been brothers, started flipping chairs onto tables. The three bartenders draped towels over their shoulders and started counting out their tills. Presently some of the dancers came out and sipped nightcaps, holding their own weary-eyed counsel.

"How's that gorgeous wife of yours? The kids?" Frenchy produced a silver flask from his pocket and topped off their glasses. "*Salut.*"

"Happy and healthy, Frenchy. Gonna rent a house down the Jersey shore for the summer. Get them out of the city."

"That's the way. Fresh air and all that. I hate the beach myself, that freaking sand, what with the sunburn, all that. Gimme a pool any day, warmed by the sun, a couple dozen broads, cold drink in my hand. That's living. Screw the beach. Nice for the kids, though."

The small talk was starting to annoy him. The lead dancer came out with two more girls who looked right out of high school. They stared him up and down. "Hey, Big Frenchy, who's the stud boy?" A giggle fest. Touhey realized just how much he had exiled himself in the Bronx. A few short years ago he was a known figure up and down Broadway. Now, he might as well have been with the lunks from Ohio.

"Behave. He's a married man, happily. He don't run around with guttersnipes."

When the laughter died down Touhey said, "Owney."

Frenchy squared himself at the bar, hunched his fat head down. "That, yeah. Tommy, Owney got tied up with a piece of business that couldn't wait. He sends his deepest apology. Seriously, he wants to know if you can come back down tomorrow, anytime. He'll make it up to you."

"Yeah, fine. I had something might be of interest to him."

"You want, I'll tell him what it is."

"Nah, I appreciate that, Frenchy, but I'd rather speak to him directly on this thing."

"Make sure you call down. I'm sure he wants to see you, Tommy. He's never got nothing but nice things to say about you, both as a worker and a stand-up guy in general. He's fond of you. This thing could not be avoided."

"Right." Touhey donned his coat and shook Big Frenchy's oversized mitt. "I'll call back. Thanks for the drink."

One of the Filipinos put his broom down and caught the keys thrown to him by a bartender. Smiling broadly, he opened the door and wished Tommy Touhey a nice night. Touhey came up onto Forty-fourth Street as daylight was starting to bleed into the sky. A trio of drunks, arm in arm, wove up the block singing a song of despair. Trash blew on a river wind toward Broadway. Touhey pulled his jacket closed and walked over to where his driver was waiting. He caught a whiff of bacon frying. Down a darkened alley, two stray cats went at it with sexed-up frenzy, sounding as if they'd been lit aflame. It must have rained while he was inside because there were black puddles reflecting the dirty neon. On the entire ride back to the Bronx, Tough Tommy Touhey said nothing.

Briody finished his run with a quarter-mile sprint, feet pounding the macadam, the stoops of Alexander Avenue blurring as he sped past. He bent over on 138th Street, sucking deep gulps of air, his lungs burning. Sweat poured from him, fat drops of it turning black as they hit the street. He checked his watch. He had run for an hour. Up in the apartment Maggie was making dinner and the kitchen was warm and smelled of the pot roast in the oven, onions flavoring the meat. All the kids except for the two babies were out playing. He changed out of his clothes and splashed water on his chest and armpits in the hallway bathroom before dressing. He stared at his face in the mirror. There was a line straight across his forehead above which his white skin seemed to glow in contrast to his tan face. He considered working without his hat, to even out his color. He went back into the kitchen buttoning his shirt.

"You going to see Danny?"

"Aye."

"Tell him to pick up some milk on his way home."

Briody smiled and hit the streets. The warm sun and high blue skies encouraged people to be out and they were, in force. He made his way along the sidewalk, weaving past groups of young mothers rocking baby carriages as they smoked and laughed. Many wore bright lipstick, a new fad that was catching on all over the city. On the corner, a half a dozen men had constructed a makeshift miniature golf course from empty cans and scrap wood and with sleeves rolled up and hats pushed back were betting on the action, drinking cups filled with warm beer. Briody slowed his walk, not anxious to descend into the smoky dimness of the Four Provinces on such a fine day.

Abbate, the grocer, sat on a stool in front of his fruit and vegetable stand shielding his eyes from the sun. His produce was laid out in rows of brilliant color. Briody stopped and bought an orange, pressing a dime into the ungainly hand of the proprietor and pocketing the change. He stood for a minute, peeling the fruit with his fingers, the juice running down his wrist as the elevated rattled and clanked above him. The orange was sweet, delicious. He watched a woman with long brown hair backlit by the sun approach, and for a second he thought it was her, Grace. His breath caught as he wiped the juice from the orange on his pants. But as she neared he saw it was not Grace at all, just another shapely woman with cascading hair. He smiled at his reaction and continued along 138th, the traffic so thick that he outpaced the cars coming back from excursions to the beaches and farther, to the green places of Westchester and beyond. Be nice to leave the city. His mood was good.

That changed when Mannion greeted him inside the door and whispered with sour breath into his ear. Briody felt the acid roil in his stomach. Briody had known this day would come. He nodded his head and walked back into the glare of day. People passed him weaving down the street. A few of the lads from the Transit shouted hellos. Dread came over him with a force, the pleasant blue day suddenly sinister. He considered finding a train to ride to the end of nowhere, getting lost in the wilds of America. A fresh start. This impulse surprised him. He had never wavered before. And he would not now. He was a part of something and he had to follow through.

Still, he took his time, decided on walking down to the Bronx waterfront. South of 138th Street the area was industrial, lined with dead factories and rubble-filled lots. The wind was coming off the East River, cool and clean. The sun was starting its decline. He followed the slope of the street down a block of identical brick warehouses that featured many broken windows. A trio of fat water rats feasted on a moldering dog carcass while studying his approach. He tossed a rock and the vermin chased each other across crushed glass before slipping into a crevice in the side of an abandoned building. On that ruined street there was no other sign of life and Briody experienced a moment of utter desolation. Again, he considered flight, and again he forced himself to honor his commitment. For without loyalty, what are we?

A tugboat pushing a barge laden with scrap metal struggled against the relentless tide. He came upon a row of dilapidated wood-frame houses that had been built before the American Civil War and were the last stand of residences in the area. The industrial revolution had sprung up all around, dwarfing them. The houses were worn and dirty and sagged together like a group of drunks at a wake. He passed them and at the end of the block was one more warehouse that bore a sign, "Kopleman Pianos." He paused for a minute and looked out over the water and the span of the Hell Gate Bridge. A locomotive dragged a string of boxcars from the Bronx over to Queens. Manhattan shimmered in the distance. He spotted the frame of the Empire State rising like a fat thumb from a fist, already the focal point of the midtown skyline. He wished it were tomorrow and that he was there, high in the sky and away from all this, lost in the rhythm and sweat of the job and the work and the hanging of steel. He cracked his knuckles. He knew that through the door was a past he could not escape, not even here, so far from Ireland. He bent to tie his shoe, stalling the inevitable. He stood and knocked lightly on the door, his heart pounding.

Cullen pulled open the door and smiled, waved him in. Cool dank air came out smelling faintly of rot. The main room of the warehouse stretched into the dimness, and scattered about, in and out of crating, some like creatures half hatched from square eggs, sat rosewood pianos with nowhere to go. It was one of the last piano factories in the area, abandoned now, a casualty of the consuming depression. Casey sat at one softly plucking away, the notes of "Happy Days Are Here Again" filling the dusty air, echoing the sound. On the battered remnants of a couch two of Casey's men sat passing a bottle between them. They looked up at Briody's entrance, regarded him with dull eyes and nodded slightly. They looked, as did Casey, like men who had weathered something unpleasant and were happy to be done with it. Briody noticed specks of blood on their shirts.

"You're a bit late, Mikey." Casey stopped playing and grabbed the proffered whisky bottle. He sipped thoughtfully, looking at the far wall. Briody saw a painting there of the Sacred Heart of Jesus, a blond, blue-eyed Jesus of matinee-idol looks and a calendar from 1928.

Casey handed him the whiskey and Briody pulled on the bottle hard, hoping the booze would steel him for what had to be done. Casey handed him a pistol. They all looked to him to finish the thing. This is what all his days at war had done, labeled him a killer, a shooter, a sound man. He was an assassin. He had left a trail of dead men in his wake and now, here in this new land, it was time to up the ante, to render another soul moot. He could not falter, for to show weakness would raise suspicions that might lead to his own end. Casey, their leader, his friend from the old country, put duty to the cause above all else. It was beyond him.

Casey drew a finger across his throat and indicated the back of the factory with a jerk of his head. The others did not even look up at him as he passed, were intent on their drinking, already trying, he knew, to forget what they had done here. As Briody walked along the concrete floor Casey started to pet the keys again, this time a song Briody did not know. The farther back he walked the thicker the dust that covered everything. He pushed open the door. The man, what was left of him, was tied to a chair. Briody knew by the look of him that he had given up all his secrets. He tried to raise his head but could not. One of his eyes was swollen shut and the other was cut and bleeding but managed to follow Briody as he crossed the room.

Briody pushed the muzzle into the soft spot at the base of his skull. He closed his eyes. The man tried to speak but could only gurgle. Unlike in the past, Briody had no real idea who this person was, only that he was an enemy agent from the Free State. It did not matter. He squeezed the trigger, the gun jumping in his hand, and the man's head snapped forward and then back and he was no more.

Briody stepped away and started pacing, the gun a weight in his hand pulling him. His breath came ragged and fast and the air was thick with the stink of blood and shit and gun smoke. His heart pounded again and he leaned one hand on the wall, vertigo making his vision blur, so he shut his eyes but the room started to spin. What was this? He put one knee to the ground, then his gun-free hand, and tried to breathe evenly, to steady himself. In the past, he had always been calm after an action, lucid and at ease. He vomited, his bile mixing with the blood on the floor. He was glad he was alone in the room, out of sight of the others.

Casey was still playing the piano as he passed through the main room, the lost notes drifting up to the pigeon-thick rafters. Briody paused, nodded at Casey. He put the pistol on the piano, the gun-metal clanging on the polished wood, and went outside. He sat on the sidewalk on an upturned milk crate and studied the sunset. The industrial streets were still, cut off from the life of the city. He would never be done with killing.

When it was dark, they loaded the dead man into a small skiff and droned out to the middle of Hell Gate where they hoisted him over the side. He disappeared with hardly a sound.

G race looked up to see Anna swirl into the diner, her shawl trailing behind her, a cigarette holder between her teeth, and her beret at a rakish angle. Her lips were painted the blood red of martyrs and she blew kisses at Stanley the counterman, who perked up at her arrival and regarded her with some Slavic hunger. She plopped down at Grace's table. "How's the Rose of Ireland this glorious day?"

"Can't complain, but if it wasn't for all the gory stories in the press I would about you being what, an hour late now." She folded the paper she had been reading and made a show of looking at her watch.

"That's a lovely watch."

"Johnny gave it to me."

"He probably stole it off a widow's still-warm arm an hour after she breathed her last."

Anna put her cigarette holder in an ashtray and took off her jacket. She arranged herself and waved at Stanley. "Coffee, young man, coffee. Black and lots of it."

Stanley did not move anything but his eyes. He rolled them toward the waitress, who was sitting at a table by the back door eating a meal. Her break now over, she stood, then shuffled over to the coffeepot. She poured Anna a cup without saying a word, then went back to her plate and resumed eating.

Anna sighed. "What personable service. A good stiff prick is what she's lacking, a little barnyard rutting."

"You think so?"

"Look at her. Plus she's Polish; the only people on earth that shtupp less than you Irish."

"Achh, you're terrible. And I don't know if I agree with you. When I lived in the Bronx, my neighbor was Polish and the walls were so thin she sang arias every night to accompany the bedsprings. It's a miracle she could walk."

"Exception to the rule. It's true. I've got some Polish in me and it accounts for my dour side. They can go a year and a half without a single smile. Let me use the loo."

Grace looked over at Stanley and back to the waitress. Stanley smiled at times, but it did appear to pain him. Waiting for Anna to come back, she flipped through a pile of tabloids, a half dozen of them, which seemed to feature nothing but stories of machine-gun death, ads hawking clothing and radios, and editorials screeching for investigations into municipal corruption. There was a long piece about Judge Vitale from the Bronx, who had been caught supping with the artichoke king himself, mobster Vito Terranova. It appeared the good judge also borrowed twenty thousand dollars from racket czar Arnold Rothstein right before the renowned gambler met an early end after being shot during a card game back in 1928. The Judge seemed incapable of discretion.

Crooked judges. Grace could point out a few of those. She knew Johnny was getting more agitated by these developments. She remembered the night at Jack and Charlie's "21" Club, Johnny pointing to Judge Crater and saying, I own that man. She wondered how deeply Johnny was involved. He was always bragging about what a big man he was and how close he was to the Mayor and everyone else of importance but he rarely spoke in specifics. He had mentioned that jurists paid a year's salary up front for their appointments. She wondered exactly how her cash-courier sideline factored in. At first, it was just men in the Organization whose accounts she opened, Tammany men. Now there were more drops to cops and others she could not figure.

Anna returned, grabbed her coffee, slurped, then said, "Listen, I've been invited to an opening on Saturday. You should come along."

"I'm going to see Johnny. He's taking me to a show, then dinner."

"That putz?" Anna pointed to the paper on the table before them. "He'll be in jail soon with the rest of the Mick thieves."

"I don't think Johnny Farrell will be so easily caught. He's crafty in more ways than one."

"What do you care? So you lose your sugar daddy, there's hundred more will take his place in a minute. Besides it's not healthy to limit yourself to one man. Bad for the circulation. I read an article. You get all stale and clogged up like the plow woman over there." She sniffed her coffee and then sipped it. "I talked to my father the other day. He's got connections with the old money boys. They have had it with these ethnics coming in and robbing the city blind. They need something to take everyone's mind off of the fact that they bankrupted the country with their greedy little ways and madcap speculating. Somebody is gonna be hung out to dry."

Grace read from a guest editorial. "Men of large affairs. Blah blah blah incompetent vulgarians are running this town."

"Your Johnny is flying awfully close to the sun these days."

"He might be bent but I don't see him as incompetent."

"I picture him having trouble in the big house. Too much the dandy."

"It's all a bit confusing to me." Grace wondered about her involvement in all this. What exactly was she risking? She simply figured Johnny would protect her. He'd said so time and again.

"Confusing? For a long time everybody was making money so everybody was happy. Now people are losing money that are not happy about it, they're not used to it. They're scared. Scapegoats are needed, and badly. You realize you heard little about the Red menace until the stock market crash? Somebody needs to be held accountable, why not the mysterious foreigner, the swarthy calculator, the Jew, the commie? And why not sweep City Hall of Catholics and Democrats while you're at it?"

"Anna, really."

"Don't be such a donkey. Speaking of which, I saw the Judge last night."

"Judge Crater?"

"Long Shanks himself. God, he bores me to tears the minute he opens his mouth. But when he opens his pants, well."

"I thought you were through with him, despite his endowment."

"I am. Except, occasionally, a girl needs what that man has. And he has lots of it. He's leaving for a family vacation soon and I want to get as much out of him as I can before he goes."

"I guess if it's what you need. You're horrible."

"Don't start with that Catholic girl crap."

"Haven't been to church in years. More or less."

"There's your problem right there. There can be no more or less. Life is too short. You need all or nothing, my dear. That's my credo. Otherwise, by the time you get around to doing things all the way, you're dead and they are throwing dirt on top of you. Life is for the living."

"I do enough living to keep myself happy. Don't worry about me."

Anna picked up the *Evening Herald*. "The good Judge Long Shanks does seem a bit distracted these days."

"You really think Johnny will be dragged into it?"

"Who knows? But you judge him by the company he keeps. No pun."

"Casting stones?"

"Please. What do you say, it's a beautiful day, let's take the ferry down to Sandy Hook and gambol, frolic, drink ourselves silly."

Grace ignored the invitation. "I've been helping Johnny out a bit."

"With a body like yours, I bet you have been helping him out."

"No, I mean, I have been moving money around for him."

"Really? The plot thickens. You're not just pretty, you're sly, my woman of intrigue. What exactly does moving money entail?"

Grace wondered at her confiding in Anna, but she had no one else. "Every now and again he has me bring envelopes to different banks and put them in safe boxes."

"That sounds a bit dull. I was hoping for back-alley rendezvous with dark handsome strangers, fog-shrouded bridges, derring-do. Cash-filled envelopes have been a staple in this town since the days of wampum and naked young bucks. When it gets a little more blood pounding, fill me in."

"I pretend I am the wives of many different men."

"Now you're talking."

"I wear a fake wedding band, dress demurely, and show up with money my husband wants stashed. Bank managers size me up, but they are afraid."

"Do they eye you with lecherous intent?"

"Always. Until it becomes clear that my husband is with the Organization."

"How do they know?"

"I've learned to drop the proper hints."

"You are something. Can I go with you?" Anna leaned over the table and grabbed her hand.

"I don't think our Johnny would be too happy, he knew I clued you in."

Anna sat back, disappointed. "My life is so dull. So, to beach or not to beach?"

"I wish. I need to work. I told you about that magazine assign-ment?"

"Please, that hackwork is way beneath you."

"I like it, and it's a day's pay." The money was not the issue. As a result of her errand-running for Farrell she had more cash lying about than she had ever seen. Even when she was married to Francisco and there was a lot of material comfort, he controlled everything. After he died his parents managed to cut her out of any inheritance.

"Well, your loss. And I wouldn't worry too much about your Johnny. He strikes me as just the kind of weasel who always comes out on top." She waved to Stanley. "Send the plow woman back over with more joe, will you? And, I nearly forgot, how are things going with the ironworker?"

Grace pushed back from the table. "Let's just say he definitely has my interest these days."

"Best news I have heard in weeks."

Grace pulled out a fifty to pay the tab. Stanley moaned, explained he could not make the change. She dug in her purse for a twenty.

"Jeepers, don't ditch Johnny Farrell yet, you're running around waving Ulysses Grant's fat face to everyone."

Back at the boat, Harry was already fishing from his milk crate. Next to his foot was a mug of muddy coffee. He turned at her approach and squinted into the sun. "How they hanging, sourpuss?"

"Wouldn't you like to know?"

"You're damn straight I would. If you ever come to your senses, you and me would make beautiful music together. I do not tell a lie."

"I know, I know, Harry, we'd see the world together."

"The world? The hell we would. We'd be too busy knocking boots to see anything except the inside of my well-appointed stateroom. The old slap and tickle is all I'm after, and I don't feel the need to sugarcoat it."

"Ah now, you're the man of my rose-scented dreams."

"Don't I know it. 'Bout time you dump that fancy ass from New York."

Grace laughed and went inside to make a breakfast sandwich for her neighbor. Harry was right. She should probably find a way to stop seeing Farrell before she was in too far to get out. Or was she already? In the bedroom she pried open her hidey-hole and hefted her pile of loot, which had grown into the thousands. Was it the money that was keeping her with him? Money or no, she feared that after almost a year it would not be so simple. Farrell was smitten with her. She knew Farrell well enough to realize that behind his handcrafted suits and polished manner he was very much a product of the Bronx streets. His silk sheets and connections and high company did nothing to change who he was at heart. Back in the galley she fried eggs and sausages. She sliced the bread thickly, buttered it, and then built a sandwich for Harry.

She knew for sure Farrell would not take kindly to her seeing Briody. Was she deluded and the ironworker was just some creation of her lonely imagination? Men tended to spoil for her on close inspection. Most of them wanted only what Harry was at least honest about.

She settled herself next to Harry, who had a bucket full of fish between his legs. She passed the sandwich to him and he nodded thanks, too abashed in his gratitude to express it aloud. She wished all men were so easily accommodated. They watched the ferries and tugboats battle the currents. When Harry was done he flipped his bucket over and his morning bounty of bottom-feeders flopped and glistened in the sun, dying for breath. One at a time he grabbed the fish and smacked them over the head, then gutted them. He tossed the entrails into the water and seagulls started to gather. They hovered above the slime, bobbing on air currents, before swooping to grab the guts, gorging themselves and then rising, blood dripping from their beaks.

"Scavengers. I'll take the much-maligned pigeon any day. When is that spunky Jewess coming to visit again?"

"Anna?"

"Call her what you will."

"Soon enough, if you're lucky."

They both watched over their shoulders as a black car rolled past slowly, sunlight dancing off the windshield. The two men in the front seat looked them over with no attempt at discretion.

Harry shook his head. "That's three days in a row, the same couple of clowns in neckties and squints, driving by real slow, staring, looking right through me. I hear the city is aiming to crack down on us houseboaters, make us pay some kind of taxes." Harry paused and spit a stream of brown liquid out into the river. "They better come with the cavalry, they want to tax me."

Grace watched the men watch her, two stony faces peering with casual malice. She felt a premonition so powerful she struggled not to get up and run into her boat. "They don't look much like tax assessors to me."

Harry spit again. "Well, they're assessing something."

The car roared off. Grace forced another sandwich on Harry and cracked open two bottles of cream soda. She sipped from hers and looked away, out toward Manhattan, toward all that life and anonymity, and felt utterly exposed here.

B riody caught a glimpse of Skinny Sheehan just ahead on the morning street and jogged to catch him. "Mr. Sheehan."

"Michael, seems like I saw you five minutes ago."

They walked in step across to the 138th Street IRT station.

"The wee'uns let you get any sleep at all?"

Sheehan shrugged. "A few winks here and there. The missus is getting ready to pop again."

"Number eight, is it?"

"Nine's the right count. Last I checked." They descended, paid their nickels.

"Is it a baseball team you're after?"

"And then some."

The Manhattan-bound train barreled into the station, stopped so hard that passengers were sent bouncing off one another, and as the door opened they were still apologizing, as if the recklessness of the motorman was somehow their fault. Briody pushed in and stood by the doors. Sheehan followed. People tightened their hold on the leather straps. Those seated planted themselves a little deeper into the wicker, anticipating a wild ride. They all had the look of people staring into some distance, which was funny, Briody thought, because in the close space of the car there was none.

The train rocked along, plummeting through the dark tunnels under the riverbed toward Manhattan. Briody turned and put his hands on the glass, caught glimpses of concrete walls, of track workers carrying lanterns. His head felt pressure. The motorman leaned into the stick and they shot along all speed, light, and shadow.

He wondered if this was one of the tunnels his father had built during his time in New York, in the Aughts. Briody remembered his return to Cavan. His father came home a stranger to him, having left when he was only two years old. It was his eighth birthday when the man he knew only from a few cloudy pictures and his mother's stories came in and picked him up, pressing Yankee dollars into all his pockets, calling him son. The older sandhogs in the joints around Willis Avenue remembered him. His father made an impression.

Grand Central Station was half empty in the hour before the daily tide of commuters became a flood. They passed through the great hall, looking up to the constellations etched in the vaulted ceiling. A custodian pushed a broom along whistling. A trio of chesty railroad cops in black uniforms leaned against the wall and swapped stories in fading brogues, laughing. He bought a *Daily News* that blared MAYHEM IN MIDTOWN and showed a picture of three bodies sprawled on a sidewalk, a crowd forming a semicircle as cops stood by idly, smoking. He folded the paper under his arm, then pushed out the doors of the station for the brisk walk down to the job.

They darted across Forty-second Street in front of the crosstown trolley and walked past the twin lions guarding the library, then headed south. The Empire State rose high above, taller now than all the buildings in sight. The steel frame peeked out, a dozen stories of it exposed beyond the floors where the granite skin had already been set. As they approached the structure they both let their gaze follow the lines to the sky. "Can you believe we'll hit forty floors this week?"

"Flying right up she is." Briody pointed to the *Daily Worker* tucked under Sheehan's arm. "How many dead do they have listed now?"

Sheehan smiled. "Says we're averaging ten a story. Can't blame them for a little dramatization to make a point, now can we? No worse than the crap that comes over the radio from Washington."

"Fair enough. Can I buy you a cup of coffee?"

They took their brass tickets off the board, rode an empty elevator to the fifteenth floor, and bought two hot cups from the canteen man. They walked out the window onto the setback and sat on the lip of the small parapet wall. They watched below their feet as the legions of tradesmen came to work.

Briody thought about the pickup he was to make that day after work, explosives from the lads building the new water tunnel. They were amassing an arsenal bit by bit, piece by piece. There were times when it seemed futile to him, a fart in the wind. He was absolutely committed to a free Ireland, to keeping up the fight whatever shape it took, but here in the New World—he used to laugh at that term—here he realized that that is what it is, a new world indeed, with hope and possibility, where all the old grudges and hates were harder to sustain. The shooting had him spooked. Still, he was a soldier.

"My cousin the engineer says by the end of the month there will be three thousand five hundred guys working here."

"Seems like that many already."

"It sure does. I can't stand waiting for the elevators anymore."

Briody stood and worked his shoulders up and down, trying to shake the stiffness out of them. His head was still fuzzy and he knew the day would stretch forever. He did not mind. He quickly read the paper. In the cover story on the big shoot-out he came across the name of Tommy Touhey. There was speculation that his Bronx neighbor was settling old scores, though evidence was slight and witnesses were not forthcoming. Sheehan, beside him, was engrossed in his own reading. As the work bell neared he left his perch and walked back through the floor toward the lifts but decided on a whim to climb the stairs to where he'd be working. Sheehan waved him off.

"You're nuts."

The stairs switchbacked every half a floor and he took them two at a time. After five floors he was drenched in sweat; by ten he was winded but kept going, enjoying the burn in his legs. There were no interior walls on any of the floors yet, just wide-open spaces with construction equipment scattered about. Hand-painted plaques at each level announced the floor. Small-gauge rail tracks ran through all the floors to transport materials, to increase speed and efficiency. As he passed floors he caught glimpses of men and material being put to work. On twenty-three, a laughing man pushed two of his fellow masons who sat atop a brick-laden cart toward their workstation. On thirty-one, carpenters smoked quietly waiting for lumber. On thirty-five, he startled a plumber who was studying blueprints. He looked up and Briody froze for a second, the air around him tingled. He waved and the man simply nodded. Briody forced himself upward. The man was the spitting image of the Free Stater they had dumped into the Hell Gate, those same baleful eyes and solid jaw. Jesus Christ. Just a coincidence, that's all.

Finally, on thirty-eight he was on top in the free air. He caught his breath as his mind flashed on the face of the man he had so recently killed. He could very nearly smell the blood. He forced himself to settle. Was he losing his mind?

Four hundred feet above the street the wind was from the south and stiff. Briody pulled on his gloves and nodded as his gang joined him. Armstrong bounced up and down. Sheehan saluted. Delpezzo gulped the last of his dark and bitter Italian coffee and pulled his cap snug. They were ready for another day.

That morning in the wind, Briody was never gladder for the job. He hooked up his rivet gun, watched Sheehan ready the coals. He stripped off his long-sleeve shirt and when the rivets started looping through the air he was ready. In a matter of minutes the noise engulfed him and he worked, hot cinders burning his forearms, but up on that high floor he was untouchable by all the worries of his life back down on the solid earth. Nothing was going to stop this job. Because the men loved the idea of it as much as the bosses did.

After lunch, as Briody waited for the rivets, he watched a story above as a connecting gang guided new beams to station. They worked with studied nonchalance. One of the connectors, Spillane, a man who because of his good looks and theatricality was called Broadway Bobby, was walking steadily along the steel, nothing but air between him and the pavement far below, when he stutter-stepped and then froze in mid-stride. Briody wondered what was wrong. The other men in the gang shook their heads as if to say, There he goes again. What a character. But Briody watched Bobby's face and knew this was no stunt, no skylarking. He'd seen enough fear to know when it was real. Broadway Bobby, his lips pulled back and his eyes round and wet, slowly began to lower his knees, genuflecting for the slim safety of the beam he stood upon.

Armstrong came astride him. "Oh shit. That's bad."

Broadway Bobby finally reached the steel with his hands and he held it with all his strength, his fingers hooked like talons on the beam. He shook with fear and his coworkers moved gingerly toward him, speaking softly, offering comfort.

One of them turned and yelled down. "Get a strap."

Briody grabbed a canvas rigging strap and he and Armstrong rode the headache ball, signaling so they were right above Broadway Bobby Spillane. The other connectors were still behind Spillane but they had to be careful. A wrong movement would send Spillane and any of them four hundred feet to their deaths. Briody worked one end of the strap around the crane cable. They needed to get the other end around Spillane and hoist him to safety. The wind was kicking up worse. Broadway Bobby was just shouting NO! NO! NO! over and over, the sound more animal than human. Briody was lowered to the beam right in front of him. He smelled the fear coming from him, the reek of piss. He got down and cooned his way toward the petrified ironworker while Armstrong was dropped behind him.

"Come on now, Bobby. Take it nice and easy." Briody tried to coax him into looking up, instead of down at all the space between them and Fifth Avenue.

"I can't. I just can't. Don't touch me."

Briody, just inches away, reached out, placing a hand on his shoulder. Spillane was rigid with terror. "It's all right. We'll get you down."

Behind Spillane, Armstrong approached with the canvas strap. When he was upon Spillane he worked the strap under his belly, then, standing upright, threaded one end of the strap through a loop on the other end and quickly hitched it to the crane. He stepped back and gave the signal to lift.

The crane started tugging upward and suddenly Spillane lurched forward and grabbed Briody around the waist, knocking him off the beam. Briody tilted over to the street side, the city spinning beneath him. The only thing keeping him from death was Spillane's grip. He struggled to grab the strap or the cable and hang on. Spillane was screaming, digging his fingers into his sides. Briody felt his shoulders straining like they were being yanked from the sockets. Finally, the crane swung them back over the safety of the decking. They were lowered down and Broadway Bobby's crew came over and peeled their colleague from Briody, and the strap.

Briody, Armstrong, Delpezzo, and Sheehan watched as they soothed him to the point where they could escort him off the tower.

"He's gone."

"No way he comes back."

"I seen it once, I seen it a dozen times."

"Guy's ruined."

"Better him than me."

They all turned at Armstrong's comment, and though they thought it crude, they all silently concurred.

Hard Nose McCabe came up, pointed them back to work. "Some guys just ain't cut out for the high work. It's just takes a while sometimes, before they figure it out."

In the hushed vestibule of the Bowery Savings Bank the manager appeared to be expecting her. He stood with his hands clasped at his waist, rising up and down on his toes. She thought it had to be a coincidence. He looked past her to the street door, then lowered his chin and said, "Oh, Mrs. Sullivan. It's some bright day, is it not?"

"A bit hot." She stared at him. He was a short man and did not seem able to meet her gaze. Tellers looked up from their accounting, stealing glances from under eyeshades.

"I think we should talk. I think that is a good idea for sure." He waved an outstretched hand, indicating a corner of the institution.

She followed him, staring down onto his combed-over bald spot. He walked as if leaning into a strong wind. His office was at the back of the bank and surprisingly small. There were three pictures of wan teenagers on his wooden desk, but none of anyone who might be his wife. He produced a soiled handkerchief and blew his nose so softly she wondered what the use was. The air had the feeling of a mausoleum, of something lost. He pulled out a chair for her and then hurried around the desk to sit opposite her as she sat. There was a faded map of Greece on the wall over his shoulder.

"I think you should know there were some men here, asking about you, your transactions, inquiring." He looked down at papers before him like he had evidence of wrongdoing. He picked up a pen and tapped it steadily.

For a moment she forgot who she was supposed to be since she used a different name at each bank. She ran a hand over her ear, tucking a strand of hair. Mrs. Sullivan, right, that's what he had called her. She wondered if she should try to sound cool or play it indignant. She was getting so good at lying. She decided on the middle ground. "And these men, did they state their concern with my husband's affairs?"

He looked down again. He seemed embarrassed. "Well, no. They did not. They were somewhat evasive."

"And you told them?"

He sat upright, dropped his pen, and waved a hand in dismissal. "Well, nothing of course. We pride ourselves on protecting the privacy of our depositors. How else could we stay in business?"

She stared at him until he looked away. "My husband will hear about this. Did you get names?"

A thin line of sweat blossomed on his upper lip, glistened in the glow of the desk lamp. "As I said, they were . . ."

"Evasive."

"Yes, quite."

"What did they look like?" She asked, but felt she already knew the answer.

"They were medium height, average size, fairly complected. And somewhat, well, threatening."

"Threatening?"

"Yes. They seemed to enjoy, well they seemed to have a habit of—for lack of a better term—browbeating."

"Well, thank you for telling me. I am sure it is nothing—swindlers, perhaps. But please, next time, if the occasion arises maybe you can be a bit better at finding out."

It was his turn to stare at her. His tone hardened. "These men were not swindlers. They lacked the necessary charm that profession requires."

She said nothing. Why was she worried what this man thought? He could do her no harm. She rose and followed the manager down a flight of stone stairs into the vault. He indicated the box and stood behind her, alcohol seeping from him, the smell souring the closed space. It was ten o'clock in the morning. "Thank you." She wondered if he had opened the box for a peek. She guessed he probably had.

When the banker retreated from the safe deposit chamber she opened the container and placed it on a table. She took out an envelope from her bag. The oily aroma of well-worn money wafted up, replacing the stink of booze. She looked at the rows of other boxes and tried to imagine what fortunes and secrets, what baubles and loot they held and whether that strange little man snuck about in all of them. Her stash might just be one of the more intriguing ones. She took out the bills and fanned them on the tabletop before her. They were mostly hundreds. She flipped open the box and saw the envelopes from her last three drops sitting there, apparently untouched. That was usually the case with the boxes she visited. The money sat, waiting for who or what she did not care. She looked over her shoulder at the empty chamber and contemplated pinching off a skim of ten bills, more or less, but thought better of it. She locked the box away.

The Bowery was flooded with harsh summer light, exposing

city dirt and grime, the soot-colored buildings, the gray pallor of passersby. She looked about for spies, studied parked cars, glanced at rooftops, and then felt foolish for doing so. She was beginning to really worry, felt the apprehension in the pit of her stomach, butterflies. First the car in Brooklyn, and now this: men asking after her in the banks. But no, she would not live in fear.

She pushed through the doors back into the bank. The manager was leaning over talking to one of his clerks when she passed. He raised an eyebrow but said nothing. In the vault she opened the box and grabbed the bottom envelope which had been lying there for weeks, fat with bills. She slid it into her pocketbook. Men looking into her banking were men who might be blamed for stealing the money.

She hailed a cab, nearly choking on motor exhaust. The driver wore a cowboy hat and talked in a singsong drawl she could barely make out. As they sped uptown, she gave him a series of turn commands while looking out the rear window for tails.

"What you running from, dahlin'?"

She faced forward, felt stupid, forced a smile. "We're all running from something or other, aren't we?"

They already knew who she was and where she lived. She supposed she should tell Johnny about the inquisitive men. She wondered who they were. Cops? Gangsters? His Tammany overseers? Maybe he was keeping tabs on her himself. With Johnny you could never tell.

There was a spatter of blue paint on the back of her hands that she had missed while getting ready that morning. She scratched at it with her fingernail, but it would not come off.

W hat's in the bag?" someone called from the near gloom. Briody froze. He heard his breath come faster, rasping loud in the silence. The docks were deserted. There was none of the usual racket and movement, none of the pell-mell chaos of ships being loaded and disgorged.

Briody backed up. He turned to make his way to the street but two cops came toward him, guns drawn and level, badges shining in the streetlight, moving on the balls of their feet like men looking for the tiny excuse they needed to justify death-dealing. Briody had no desire to become just another fleeing felon shot full of holes on a New York street.

"Drop the bag, shit heel."

Briody bent down and placed the bag at his feet, then stepped away, raising his hands. He knew the game. He kept his hands high and wide. The two cops above him holstered their revolvers and came toward him, jauntily, swinging their nightsticks, tapping them against muscled thighs. The pier was silent, but he could see a gaggle of men, high above him on the ship's deck, their cigarettes lending a hint of color to their dark faces. He thought of prison and it sickened him.

Out on the river he heard the low drone of a skiff on some nocturnal errand. The two cops affected lupine grimaces, mockeries of smiles. They were out for sport. The one who had shouted was as tall as Briody. He drove his nightstick into Briody's gut like a doughboy making a bayonet charge. Briody bent at the waist and as he was coming back up he was clobbered from behind. A million bulbs flashed across his field of vision, his legs felt like sandbags. He smelled blood, wet and metallic. He staggered to his left and then they moved in, deft, brutal strokes, the odd fist, swift kicks. The night closed in on him and the next thing he knew he was cuffed and being half dragged toward a patrol car. When had they cuffed him? The Manhattan skyline was a jagged blur of lights and shapes. The cops were murmuring, intoning crimes and punishments, jail time and the Sullivan Law. They guffawed, they snarled. They got in the odd smack. As they crumbled him into the backseat his initial attacker grabbed him by the face in his meaty hands and pulled him close. Briody smelled his breath, rancid from bad living and cut-rate beer, saw the dirt in the enlarged pores around his nose, which was swollen and looked to have been cracked a dozen times, a gnarled and battered protuberance. When he shouted, his saliva flew about and his eyes pinwheeled with glee and hate. "You stupid donkey pricko! You're going up the river! Up and away! Bye-bye!" Then he pulled Briody close and kissed him full on the lips.

Briody yanked his head away as the other cops roared with laughter, enjoying their own private theater. As he tried to spit the cop pulled him by the lapels and this time, instead of a kiss, he was treated to a loud crack from the cop's forehead, and another light show.

In the station house he was left in a cell to bleed and worry. Occasionally a cop would pass by and smirk. He made an inventory of his wounds, lumps and bruises, a deep gash on the top of his skull that bled steadily, his nose surely broken. He flexed his hands. There was a little swelling on the left, but nothing thankfully that would stop him from working. That's if he could get back to work. He fought to keep focused, to keep his fear at bay. The clanking of the cell door was an echo of all the others that had closed behind him, a sound he had heard too many times in his life. He thought back to all those places and all that time left to rot. But then, always, he had beliefs to steady him, a cause, and comrades for support, not to mention real enemies close at hand. America was changing that. He considered that he was losing faith, was becoming detached, too comfortable. He had always been able to focus, to do his time and even put up with the abuse. Why was he feeling so anxious now? He was silent when the cops would come by the cell. He asked for nothing. He gave nothing. He had learned long ago the value of silence.

Through the night other prisoners were dumped in the cell with him. Most were vagrants and many of them seemed almost grateful for four walls and a roof. Briody gave nothing of the bench on which he lay. One man, a walleyed Turk, made an attempt at menace. Briody sat up and slapped him across the face so hard the man fell down whimpering. Another, a skinny street drunk of some years, took out his flaccid cock and pissed through the bars, cackling like a hyena. Briody did not, could not sleep. He lay still and imagined what might be in store for him until he was nearly distraught. He pushed away those thoughts and pictured himself back at work, gliding along a beam, laughing with his crew.

At dawn Tough Tommy Touhey and a spiffy man in a three-piece suit appeared at the cell door with a cop jangling keys. He saw that it was Johnny Farrell and for some reason he was not surprised. They all were in good cheer. Briody swung his legs off the bench and stood, trying not to wince. He stepped over the supine, the lost, and the forsaken, tiptoed around puddles of ripe human effluence, stomped on a hand that reached for his ankle, and left the cell to a chorus of derangement.

Touhey said, "You look like a dog's ass after a run-in with a propeller."

Briody said, "You suggesting I stay away from mirrors?"

"You looked better after your bout," Johnny Farrell said.

The cop just laughed.

Briody was led into a side room where he was fingerprinted and photographed holding a plaque with numbers to his chest. He followed the officer back into the precinct's vestibule and was told to sit on a bench that ran along the front wall. The room smelled sour and was painted a weak green to match the odor. Even at that early hour cops were dragging suspects through, slapping their quarry, and shouting at each other. Briody stared at his shoes, which were splattered with blood. He was reminded of Grace with her painter's clothes. But while hers contained a rainbow of colors his were just the fading crimson of a night gone bad.

His two liberators came back into the room with a trio of uniformed officers. Briody was not surprised at Touhey's backslapping familiarity with the cops. But Farrell was really the center of the precinct's attention. This worried him. Farrell indicated silence to him with a thin finger to his lips, signed some forms, and then chitchatted with the sergeant and lieutenant. He overheard the boss say to Farrell, "Come on, Johnny, you know how the boys get carried away. They don't mean nothing by it. Just keeping in shape for the real bad guys. A little bit of the old West Side shuffle." He looked over at Briody and shrugged. "Take him over to Bellevue. They'll stitch him up nice. And hey, thanks for those show tickets. The wife was so over the moon I almost got to see her naked."

Briody eased himself into a car that sped them downtown. Farrell sat beside the driver and Touhey and he shared the soft leather backseat. He stared out the window, felt blood trickle down the back of his neck, hot and wet. Farrell turned to him, his hat pushed back.

"The way things work is we let the case find its way to the right judge—one of ours—and things get squared."

Briody, unsure of his circumstance, kept quiet. Many questions were forming in his mind but he knew from experience not to let his imagination get the better of him. The truth had a way of outing. One thing he was almost sure of—his arrest was not happenstance.

They dropped Farrell off at Tammany Hall in Union Square. As he was getting out of the car he handed Briody a business card; the sunlight danced off his wristwatch as he said, "If you ever need me, reach out, anytime." Farrell appeared to glow with earnestness in the early morning. "Any friend of Tommy's. Good luck."

At Bellevue Briody sat upright while the doctor sewed his head closed. He felt the bite of the needle and the skin being pulled tight. The doctor finished with a flourish. "That makes thirty-eight. Quite a good shellacking." He came around and looked at Briody's nose, fingered it gently. Briody clenched his teeth at the pain. "You want that set?"

Briody waved him away.

"I know, I know. Not the first time, you Irish. You want something for the pain?"

"Never felt better, Doc."

"Clean the wound after a day, stitches out in a week. Stay away from nightsticks."

On the ride back to the Bronx Briody kept his questions to himself. He decided to let his head clear. Touhey assured him things would be "handled."

"I let your foreman know you'd miss the day."

"That's not good."

"Just a day. You're in no shape for it, all banged up like you are."

"That's not it. I work in a gang, four men. One man doesn't show, nobody goes up. I'm taking money out of their pockets."

"Here." Touhey produced a fat wad of cash, started peeling off crisp bills.

Briody held up a hand. "No. I'll handle it."

"You thick Mick."

As Briody walked away from the car the bright morning light burned his eyes. He let himself into the apartment and was glad it was empty. He went to his bed. The light, the noise of the street, and a creeping anxiety kept him awake and staring at the ceiling, unable to escape a basic truth. He had done enough time for one life. He lay still waiting for the peace of sleep that just would not come.

D anny Casey manned the change booth late into the night, sliding nickels to weary-eyed, and for the most part drunk, subway riders. It was the duty he despised most. Locked in the box, he called it. You just sat all night in a booth either too hot or too cold depending on the season with only a dim bulb hanging over your head and putting up with the gripes of everyman. He always felt a bit like the orangutan in the zoo, as if the patrons should offer him a banana during the night. He much preferred the conductor's spot, or track work even, just to be out and about. At least he got the night shift when there were fewer bosses and far fewer riders. Occasionally a local beat cop would stop in and they'd share stories about the old country, which, while boring him to tears, was better than staring out at the wall.

He was relieved at 6 a.m. and was walking to shape for another shift when a Cadillac pulled to the curb. O'Brien stuck his head out the open rear window and said, "Take a load off your feet, lad."

Casey ducked into the backseat and sat next to the lawyer, who poured him a cup of coffee from a scotch plaid thermos. "Long night, boyo?"

"Aye."

"Facilitating the nocturnal movement of the metropolis. Where would we be without the gallant graveyard shift? We can't thank you enough."

"They paid us more would be a grand start."

"Speaking of which, how's your union drive going?"

"Slowly." Casey did not trust O'Brien to be sympathetic of

their efforts to organize transit. He was much too much the capitalist.

"Your good friend was picked up last night on the waterfront. Caught, what do they say, red-handed?"

"Jesus."

"Not to worry. I believe we can pull the appropriate levers, keep him on the streets. Mr. Touhey and his old friend Johnny Farrell, the Tammany man, bailed him out this morning."

"The gear?"

O'Brien sipped his coffee. "Nice to see your priorities are in place. Gone, but they might get lost on the way to the evidence locker. Matter of fact, I'd bet on it."

"How's Briody?"

"A little banged up, I understand, but ambulatory."

The car pulled to a stop at the edge of the east Bronx marshes. It was calm here, and facing toward the water and the far Queens shore, he found it hard to believe that the Bronx and all its grinding life were just behind him. The coffee tasted good.

"This is the second load intercepted now that your good friend was involved with."

"And I am sure he made a point of being caught himself. Come on."

"Well maybe we can turn this misfortune to our advantage. I think we need to change tactics a bit. I know I am on the record as opposing involvement with the likes of Tough Tommy Touhey. And I will stay that way, on the record. But I have given much thought to your concerns. I am not a man incapable of change. I think we can cooperate behind the scenes and I think Briody, who is now indebted to Touhey for his freedom, might be encouraged to assist him from time to time."

Casey watched as the sun broke dazzling over the horizon. The coffee was giving him a welcome boost. He wondered about exposing Briody.

"It's a good thing that he was bailed out by Touhey but you might want to limit your association, for a while. Of course you can bump into him out and about. And I don't want him at meetings for a while."

"He lives with me."

"It's very much a renter's market these days. Arrangements are being made."

"He's a friend."

"That is something I understand. But for now, we need to keep our priorities straight. Friendships need to be subordinated for the cause. He can do more for us now from the outside. If the federals look too closely, they'll see him as the one that went astray. We can play it both ways. He'll work as a kind of double agent. Of course, we'll watch out for him."

"I don't know."

"Casey, you weren't here for the Red hysteria after the war. The Palmer raids. Thousands were rounded up without charge, many shipped whence they came. We do not want or need too much scrutiny from Washington. With the New York authorities nowadays, just about anything can be arranged, the proper strings pulled, records vanished, the right ear whispered into, juries compromised by largesse. We have fear, greed, and the might of the machine somewhat on our side. That might not be the case with the District of Columbia crowd. And I'll wager the heat will be turned up over the next couple of years. We don't want to get scorched in that fire."

The car prowled at a low rumble through the early morning Bronx streets: Edgecombe, Southern Boulevard, Willis Avenue. Casey figured O'Brien was making sense. Still, he could not help but think that the man had arranged for Briody's arrest. It all seemed too convenient. Did O'Brien have that much pull? Was it a setup?

"I'll be in touch." O'Brien extended his soft manicured hand and Casey shook it. He stepped out onto 138th Street as the sun peeked over the tenements to the east. He squinted. Some things did transcend friendship and the cause of Irish Republicanism was one of them for him. Still, he would not let Briody get hurt. They went back too far for that.

. . .

Farrell got jumpy the minute Grace told him about the bank manager. He tried to play it off, making what-me-worry faces, but his fidgeting gave away his anxiety. He worked his tie into a Windsor knot with a quick flash of blue silk and flesh. He appeared to grind his teeth. "Day was this?"

She lay on the bed in her underwear, looking at him upside down, her hair brushing the floor. "Thursday? No, Wednesday." She shut her eyes, imagined Briody, saw him high on the steel, then, better yet, naked in her bed. She smiled, wondered when she might meet him again. Farrell stopped pacing. She could tell by the leather creak that he was rising on his toes, a sure sign he was agitated. Suddenly it bothered her that she knew this man so well.

"It takes you a week to tell me something like this?" His voice clicked up an octave.

There was real disappointment in his voice, as if she owed him what, loyalty? Because they had sex? Men could be so foolish.

"Haven't seen you, Johnny."

He sat on the bed with such force that she bounced up and came back down. "What kind of crap are you pulling on me?" He grabbed her face and turned it to him. "Do you think this is a game? Grace, for the love of God, these people will stop at nothing. Nothing. Do you understand that?"

"These people? I don't know the first thing about these people." She smacked his hand off her face and sat upright. "Don't you ever touch me like that."

Farrell got off the bed, stepped back, and held his hands up, palms out. "Look, I'm sorry." His voice softened. "Please. What exactly did the man say? It could be nothing. It could be something. You need to tell me when something like this happens."

"Go see him yourself if you're so worried, Tammany man."

"Come on, Grace. For the love of God, please, I'm sorry."

To answer she leapt up and went to the bathroom, slamming the door behind her to drown out his pleas. She sat on the toilet, not at all caring what he wanted. Still, his reaction scared her. If he was that concerned, maybe there really was something to worry about. She stood and splashed water on her face and, studying her reflection, noticed red marks from his fingers. Farrell called out to her again but instead of answering she ran the bath, and when it was full she lowered herself into its steamy embrace.

riody and Casey sat high in the bleachers at Gaelic Park surrounded by six thousand fellow immigrants. On the green grass beneath them the hurling final played itself out with typical ferocity, the contestants hacking, slicing, and sprinting about. The crack of camans and the shouts of the contestants reached them easily. Blood was spilled. Beer was sold openly in the grandstands, the dozen or so uniformed cops present sipping from cups along with the crowd. But for the apartment buildings looming beyond the edge of the stadium, it might have been Ireland, not the northwest Bronx. Briody drank his beer from a cardboard cup and listened to Danny with growing unease.

"It's not that he thinks you're an informer, now. It's just since you were grabbed and all, he thinks that maybe you should stay away, keep a low profile, is all. At least until your court case is handled."

"I was led to believe that it would not be a difficult matter."

"Even so, these things take time."

Briody wondered at this. "You're telling me that between Touhey, Farrell, and O'Brien they can't sort me out?"

"Patience, Michael, truly it's a virtue."

Briody set the cup between his feet. He did not trust O'Brien, and obviously it was reciprocal. If the man was floating the idea that he was compromised, it could be very bad indeed. Men were killed for less.

"This has to do more with my time in Europe?"

"Not at all, Mikey, not at all. You're hardly the only one that went and fought in that war to come back and do good things for Ireland. It's just that we been hearing the Brits have sent more agents over, and so have the Free State. It's hard to say who's who these days. They're out to finish us off and they're lobbying hard in

Washington for assistance in getting it done." On the field Cork scored a goal and their faithful roared while the Limerick fans booed. "He's a fierce hurler, that lad. It's not you, Michael. We're all to lay off for a while."

"Is that so?"

"I don't mind myself. I am up to me neck with organizing the lads in the Transit. These company bastards are out to wipe us out, so they are."

Briody, sitting in the glorious sunshine of a Sunday afternoon in the Bronx with the smell of the fresh-cut grass wafting from the field below, realized he was not even sure about Casey. He looked around at all the sun-splashed faces and suddenly felt utterly alone. He wished Grace were there.

"How's all that going?"

"Since it's mostly fellas from home, we're holding our meetings in Irish. Drives the beakies mad, not having a clue as to what we're saying. We've been going around trying to get help. We've been turned down so far by the Ancient Order of Hibernians, the AOH, which stands for asses, omadhauns, and hypocrites, given the cold shoulder by the not so friendly Sons of Ireland, and the boot by the Holy Roman Catholic Church, which is proving to be just as bad here as back home. So much for the brotherhood of man."

"Does that surprise you?"

"Not at all. I am afraid we remind them a bit too much of their own past. They're all Yanks now and wish to wash the stain of the toiling immigrant off themselves."

"They're not all bad."

"For sure, they're not. But you won't guess who's lending a helping hand with the organizing."

"Not a clue."

"Wonders of the world—the Communist Party. Mostly Jewish lads, from Europe."

"And you say you're worried about Washington."

"Well now. Funny how America presents you with things you never would have thought possible back home."

"I don't know. I always figured when a man is stuck with little choice you see what he's really all about."

"You've a better imagination than I."

"Indeed."

"Speaking of choices, O'Brien thinks it's a good idea for you to get a little closer to your friend Touhey."

"My friend?"

"They want you to help him out, guard an occasional card game, do a little driving."

"Why me?"

"You do owe him a favor and O'Brien wants to stay close to him."

"I'll not miss work for him." Briody had grown strongly attached to the job, his crew.

Casey thought for a moment. "Fair enough. And there is one other thing."

Briody watched the center fielder break for the open field at full speed, bouncing the ball on the blade of his stick, fake left, and then smash a goal past the diving tender. The crowd was up, some roaring, others lamenting.

"Out with it, Daniel."

"We need to keep a little distance. He's lined up a place for you in Manhattan, a room."

Briody drained his cup and crushed it. "I'll miss the family."

"Better than being locked up."

"That depends, now, Danny."

"I'd keep that sentiment to myself."

"Ah but sure, Danny, we go back too far not to be able to speak our piece with each other."

"Of course. That's precisely what I mean."

"How'd you leave things with O'Brien?"

"Says he'll be in touch."

They sat in silence and watched young Danny climb the benches to where they sat, maneuvering around the fans. He carried a beer in each hand and strained not to spill a drop. He wore a Yankees cap.

"Will you look at my little Yank? I've a house full of them. Little treacherous narrowbacks they are, each and every one of them. And their mother conspiring against me, Jesus."

"Ah now, things could be much worse."

"You're right there. Come sit between us here, you little sultan of swat, and you can witness a proper sport. None of your grass-watching goes on in this game."

"I like baseball."

"You hurt your father so."

"What do you think, Uncle Mike?"

"I love the hurling. Played it when I was your age. But don't mind your father; baseball is a grand game, too. You're in New York now."

Casey stood and said, "Well, I have to see a man about a horse," and went in the direction of the bathrooms. Briody watched him disappear into the crowd, diminished by bigger men, a true believer, Briody knew, for now friendship might come second to the cause.

Touhey loitered in his Bronx cabstand and wondered if he had crapped out. Twitch McGowan's corpse, bloated and half devoured by suckfish, had washed up on the Queens shore, ruining the morning of a citizen dog walker. It was all the evidence his enemies needed to clarify he was behind what the press were gleefully calling Bloody Sunday. He twirled a mug of black tea on his desk and listened to the front-room chatter of incoming and outgoing calls for cars over the new two-way radio system he had splurged on. A calendar on the wall indicated that it was the 25th day of July 1930. 1930. He envisioned the chiseled granite of his own tombstone reading "1900–1930" and felt anger and disgust with himself. All these years in the rackets—half his life—he should have been smarter. There were choices—some good, some bad—that had him backed into the corner he was now in. What made it worse is that the schmucks who were poised to defeat him were inferior in every way. They were less smart, less strong, less capable, less . . . everything. Except, he knew, bloodthirsty and well armed.

He looked in on the mechanic bays and watched a couple of his grease monkeys pull the motor out of a Packard with an engine hoist. The stand was made from cinder block, consisted of a three-bay garage, a front room where customers might wait on a bench, and his small office, with doors opening to the garage, the anteroom, and the back alley, which led to 140th Street. He dumped the tea in a dirty slop sink and let out a loud belch.

The waiting made him edgy. There would be reactions to his actions, that much was certain. He left the shop and walked down 138th Street, enjoying the weather. He was not going to hide, not going to run and die like some rat. If they had the balls to come after Tough Tommy Touhey down here, so be it. He would not be entering hell on his own. There was no surprise in the way things were turning out. The retirement note, the sluggish response from that weasel Farrell, a heist of his booze here, a phone call not returned there. It all added up. What he did not want was to be caught unprepared.

He ducked into the Four Provinces and went right to the back room, thinking this was his life—back rooms. He had made a pretty good run of it, had never been locked up for more than a night after that nineteen-month stretch. He had stashed over five hundred thousand dollars, enough dough so his wife and kids would never know hunger; he owned half a dozen buildings, fifty cabs, a dozen speakeasies, five thoroughbreds, and more now-useless stock than he cared to admit. Not bad for a Bronx kid born with nothing. He watched a fly circle lazily around the room. He considered more preemptive strikes but knew he didn't have the manpower, or, he had to admit, the resolve.

On the floor by the basement stairs his scarred old tomcat Pepper Felix played with a panicked and doomed mouse, swatting it and clawing it, only to let it go so he might pounce again. He occasionally contemplated a move to milder climes, to a place where no killers lurked in the shadows, but no, the Bronx was in his blood and to flee from it he thought would be a kind of death in its own right.

Mannion came in, trailed by the Irishman Briody. "He says you sent for him, boss."

"Sit down, Mick." He watched Briody cross the room, moving with a fluid ease rare in big men. The Irishman had a definite physical presence, the kind that could quiet a room, but he was no mindless killer like Mannion. There was real intelligence in his eyes and he was the type of man who said only what had to be said. Mannion picked up the cat, which still clutched the beleaguered mouse in his teeth, and left the two of them alone.

"Nice of you to come so quick."

"I figured you came quick enough when I was locked up."

"By the way, I should be able to get to your judge. It should all be worked out."

This is what Briody had been hoping to hear. "Thanks, thank you."

"Least I could do to try and help a fella out in the New World. Time in the joint is no way to start on your road to citizenship. Besides, these are the things we do. The things we can take care of. We stick together."

"I appreciate your help."

"Now." Touhey leaned forward, the bulk of his chest on the table, his head lowered, and his eyes staring straight at him. "Maybe you wouldn't mind helping the guy that helped you. Little back-scratch, an exchange."

Briody could only agree. He just hoped it was something he could reconcile. "Tommy, I do owe you one."

"Please, that is not what this is about. You're like a friend of mine now. I helped you because it was the right thing to do. This is no quid pro quo."

"Whatever you call it, I appreciate it."

"Good, so you can see this is merely a favor, something I need a hand with."

"Love to help you, Tommy."

"I always figured you for a decent kind of guy."

For a minute Touhey said nothing. He just stared at Briody. "You know how they say that when you are faced with sudden death your life flashes before your eyes?"

"So they say."

"Right. But I know for a fact that that is all horse crap. You know what flashed before my eyes? In the war and other times? Never my life. Not at all. I'll tell you what flashed. I had been promising my kid brother Bobby I was going to take him to the Ringling Brothers down at the Garden and I never, ever did. That's what flashed before my eyes. Or I'd think, I'd wonder if my mother got the letter I sent her, or jeez, I always wanted to see the Pacific Ocean. Was it like that for you?"

Briody nodded, said nothing.

"You know, I don't know what it is about you, but I never talked to no one about France, before I met you."

"Maybe because you know I was there too."

Touhey waved this off. "I know other guys—lots, was there too. I am right about that death flashing business, ain't I?"

"For me the past meant nothing, the future less. It was all about that very second, all the screaming and dying going on around you. There was not much time for thinking at all then. It was the majority of the time, the days on end when nothing at all happened and you lived in the mud and the shite and the stink of it all, the rats—the lice—God, the bugs could drive you mad. Then I thought about my life. Problem being, I was only fifteen to eighteen. There was not much to think back on. All I really thought about was how stupid the whole war was. Killing for fat rich men. I thought a lot about that."

"They told us we were saving the world for democracy."

"We would end all wars."

"Gotta admit, I went for the fun of it."

"What fun you thought there'd be."

"Some days, I had fun. Killing came easy to me. I was a pure natural."

"One day on a patrol at the end of things, I came upon a German soldier. He was no more than fifteen. He had caught a round that tore the whole bottom of his face off. He was crying, his whole body shaking with sobs, but of course there was no sound coming out of him. He just kept pointing at my rifle." Briody took a sip, placed his mug down. "So, I finished him. That to me was the whole idiotic war."

Touhey stared. "How long were you there?"

"Twenty-seven months, two weeks, three days, four hours, and thirty-two minutes."

"Jesus Christ. I thought seven months of that was more than enough."

"I'm sure it was. Once we arrived, there was little we could do about it."

"Why'd you come here?"

"Ah, the streets are paved with gold in Americkay."

"Don't give me that horse shit."

"People come for all kinds of reasons. I did not have a lot of choice."

"The Brits?"

"If it was only that easy. They tell you about the pledge?"

"What, giving up booze? All's I know is that and the one of allegiance."

"When we got rid of the English they forced a treaty on us that left a lot of things unsettled. Some of us were not happy about it. So we fought the ones that accepted the treaty. It was not like your civil war. This was truly brother against brother. Maybe six or seven hundred dead, but most of the killing was done close-up. It was very intimate. When we stopped fighting a load of us were locked in camps. Men gave up, went home, but many left as soon as they were able. This neighborhood is full of them."

"That why there so many grouchy bastards hanging around? How long you in the can?"

"Three years, two months, three weeks, a day. Hours and minutes I am not sure about. I was unconscious when they brought me in. Of that, thirteen months was in solitary."

"You kidding me?"

"And forty-three days on a hunger strike to round off my stay."

"Jesus. I did thirty days in the hole at Sing Sing. Nearly ruined me."

"Not something I'd want to revisit."

Touhey stared out into the room for a while, rubbed his thumbs on the table edge. "The things I ask of you, they will be nickel and dime, for the most part."

"I appreciate that."

"I won't ask you to do anything I wouldn't do myself."

"That leaves things a bit wide open."

Touhey shook his head and stood. "Come on. I'll walk you out."

When Briody was gone Touhey returned to his back room and took the card that had arrived that morning out of his inside pocket and read it again. It was a retirement card and on the inside, under the printed farewell, someone had written "LUCKY YOU" in black pencil. The envelope had no return address, only the postmark of the GPO in Manhattan.

Touhey sipped a glass of ginger ale and pondered the origin of the warning. There were many possibilities. It might be from the so-called Schultz, a little putz he knew back when as Arthur Flegenheimer. It could be from Luciano—the Lucky You hinted at that—or the Unione, or any number of dagos slouching about these days. He did not think that psycho Coll had the smarts to use anything but a shotgun as a calling card. Legs Diamond? Madden? Tammany renegades? The cops? He was a warrior. The possibilities were endless.

He hit the street. He walked along 138th wondering, Was a man on the brink of his fourth decade supposed to feel this old? There was weariness in his bones. All he had ever known was violence. He grew up brawling on these streets, loved it. He was big and strong and fast. He knocked out eight grown men in the space of ten seconds when he was fourteen. The neighborhood took notice. He had used his brother's birth certificate to join the army and gone to France with the Fighting Sixty-ninth. And when that craziness was over he came back and took work on the docks, where he bludgeoned his way into the best jobs. He hired himself out as enforcer to the old union bosses. Beat up company spies, collected debts, fought off interlopers. He had a three-year run in the prize ring.

He passed the candy store and handed out dollar bills to a group of kids hanging about. They jumped up and down shouting, "Thanks Tommy," and ran pell-mell into the store to blow their booty. A half dozen housewives, done up in print dresses, their hair just so, pushed prams and smiled widely at him, but their eyes were tired. He tipped his hat. "Ladies."

Fat Walsh the beat cop leaned against the wall of a bakery

twirling his nightstick. He saluted as Touhey passed. Touhey stopped, said, "How's your boy, Walsh? Jimmy, right?"

"Much better, Tommy. We can't thank you enough for that doctor. Knows his business he does."

"I need you to keep an eye on the old meat store on Brook Avenue. Someone told me out-of-towners might be trying to open a joint there."

Fat Walsh smiled and tapped his nightstick on the brick wall. "Not on my beat, they won't."

"I knew I could count on you, boyo."

Clouds gathered overhead, shielding the sun, cooling the air. Touhey crossed the street, entered St. Jerome's, and stood at the rear while his pupils adjusted to the gloom. He and Farrell had served mass here together back in the day. The church smell had not changed: dampness, faded incense, wood polish. He genuflected, crossed himself, and approached the candle area. There were three women, widows, draped in mourning black, worrying rosaries, muttering prayers, and keeping distance from an old saucehead who had found religion but not soap. They dropped coins into the box and continued to offer up prayers for ghosts real and imagined. Touhey stuffed a one-hundred-dollar bill into the slot. He lit a candle for each of the seventeen men he had dispatched to the other world. This did not include the pile of bodies he had left in France. War was war. He fully believed he would meet all of them again. And now that he was being squeezed between enemies from the north and from the south, it might be a lot sooner than he liked. He turned to leave but stopped, and what the hell, lit a candle for the city he once knew, the city of his boyhood that was fading already into the mists of the past.

Armstrong dug around in his lunch bucket and pulled out a deck of cards. "This time I'm taking all your Mick and guinea money, you immigrant mutts. You wanna work in my town, you gotta pay for the privilege."

The gang sat eating lunch at one of the wooden tables on the fiftieth-floor canteen as Armstrong dealt hands of knock rummy, seven cards facedown to each man. The men held cards in one hand and ate with the other. It was cool in the inner shade of the building. The game flowed fast and furious. Behind them the line at the canteen counter wound down, men finding places to eat quickly at one of the cafeteria-style tables lined up in ten rows of five.

"The grub ain't half bad," Sheehan said.

"How'd the baptism go?" Armstrong asked while dealing.

"It was nice, real nice. Right, Mikey?"

Briody had gone to the Sheehan christening the previous Saturday, first the ceremony at St. Jerome's and then the party afterward at the Knights of Columbus Hall. It had been a disorienting experience in the way it placed him back home. The Latin incantation, the largely Irish crowd, the songs and ceremony and the drinking and family made him feel as if he was back in Cavan.

Briody slapped down a winning hand. "It was a great day. I think the highlight was your brothers pounding each other over the cold-cut table."

Armstrong studied his hand. "Which brothers?"

"Brian and Vincent. The usual suspects. They both had to go to Lincoln Hospital for sewing up. My ma was screaming like she was on fire."

"She might have had a reason. What's with you Irish guys?"

"Nobody fights like brothers."

Briody was contemplating a piss-poor hand, nothing but a pair of deuces, when he looked up and saw framed in the open space where a window would go a man hatless and free-falling, his arms flapping madly as if trying to fly, his face contorted by horror and velocity. It was a flash, a flicker of an image like those at the picture shows. It happened so fast he doubted his own vision until he peered next to him and Sheehan made a quick sign of the cross and took off his hat. Delpezzo and Armstrong, their backs to the sky, were engrossed in calculating the odds offered by their cards. They had no idea.

Sheehan shook his head. "That's how it always happens—out of the blue."

Briody and Sheehan got up and started walking toward where

the worker had fallen. Armstrong won and raked the pot toward him. "What's wrong with you guys?" he asked as they passed him.

Pa Kelly, a bricklayer foreman, made his way through the canteen, his hat in his hand, stopping to speak urgently to each group of his men. The masons stood as one and ran for the elevator, leaving sandwiches half eaten and cups of coffee that would go cold.

When Kelly reached them he stated the obvious. "One of our guys went down."

"How is he?"

"He fell from fifty-seven."

The gang looked down to the street where the first ambulance screeched up, lights swirling. Nobody spoke. Hard Nose came off the elevator and strode to where they waited. He peered over the side and made a quick, imprecise sign of the cross. "Let's go men. Nothing can be done. Nothing at all. We need to get moving. You're better off not thinking about it. Come on."

Armstrong spoke sharply. "Give us a minute to pay our respects."

Hard Nose started to respond but stopped, nodded and said, "Fine. I'll see you up top," and moved away.

There truly was nothing they could do, so back to the rivets they went. They secured beams that because of the height now had to be lifted five separate times to reach them, derricks passing the steel higher and higher. The building was halfway done and they all knew the odds. More men would surely die. They spent the rest of the day securing perimeter beams, the most precarious work hanging high above Fifth Avenue. The gang was silent. Briody watched as the ambulance finally pulled away, headed for the morgue. After a few blocks its dome light was dimmed. There was no need for alacrity now. At quitting time the wind kicked up hard and they scrambled to tie down planks that might go airborne. Briody tucked his hat in his belt. When the work was done they locked their tools in the gang box and went their separate ways, each thinking about the dead brickie, and about his family.

. . .

gan watched the Judge, thinking: Booze and broads, two weaknesses worth exploiting. Crater sat at a corner table huddled over a tumbler of top-shelf brown stuff and the *New York Times*. Egan ordered a beer and sipped it slowly. Cozy little bar hidden off the lobby of the American Hotel. The bartender regarded him with rheumy eyes and went down the line picking up scarce empties. It was late afternoon and the place was still. A half dozen sports perched on stools along a nickel-plated bar and only four tables were occupied. There was a mirror over the cashbox and Egan positioned himself so he could spy on the jurist.

He had gone over possible targets and settled on judges. A crooked cop was no story in Gotham, too many, too ordinary. The Vitale case was making waves but he was a dago and a lowly magistrate. Half the city expected them to steal and the other half did not care if they did. But a state supreme court judge, Joseph Force Crater of solid Presbyterian stock, and a Mason to boot, now that had some juice to it. Egan imagined the headlines as the papers hit the newsstands, the gleeful tabloids, the startled broadsheets. Scandal and ruination was now his job.

For weeks he had been studying the Judge and his dark cravings which, from what Egan had witnessed, he could not control. Knew he wore a size 17 collar and was hung like a show pony. His favorite meat was veal; second was Lindy's liver, which he smothered with fried onions and copious amounts of horseradish. Egan ran his finger along the ridge of his mug, popped a peanut into his mouth, shell and all, savoring its salty flavor. The door opened, two worn-down party girls flitted in and, not finding the festive air they desired, retreated, trailing perfumes and giggles. Egan watched the Judge watch them go. The Judge had a wife living on Fifth Avenue at Tenth Street but did not make a habit of practicing family obligations. Just last week Crater had bent juror number seven—a housewife from Kew Gardens—over the desk in his chambers and administered a load of justice.

He wore a size 11 shoe; his suits were custom-crafted for him at Vroom and went for a C-note each. Despite the schlong and shoe size his ever-present panama hat was a mere 6⅞. He had exactly

$137,942 in an account at Morgan Stanley. He favored voluptuous redheads but would screw anything with two legs and a pulse after downing a couple of gin and tonics, his favorite drink. On a professional note, Crater's judgeship had cost him exactly $22,500: a year's salary, which he had placed in a Bloomingdale's shopping bag and handed to Johnny Farrell, Tammany hotshot, while sitting ringside at a prizefight in Madison Square Garden.

Egan downed the last of his beer. The Judge folded his paper, stood, and tucked it under his arm. As he passed Egan smiled up at him, tipped his hat. Crater nodded back and moved out onto the smoky street under the El.

The July heat came on hard, and even the slight river breezes died before they could gather and rise off the water. The smells worsened during the day but this did not deter the boys of the neighborhood who sought escape from the simmering tenements in growing numbers. Grace watched them from the studio on her boat. They came to the river's edge and stripped out of their dirty and tattered clothes. God, they were so thin. They had the pronounced ribs of feral dogs, and many had sores and cuts on their knees and elbows, but still they flung themselves into the rank water. Grace drew them in all their exuberance—pen-and-inks of their mid-flight contortions, the great bridges as a backdrop.

Later, as the sun began to decline in the western sky, she sketched the ever-rising Empire State Building, which now, in midsummer, was more than fifty stories tall, dwarfing all the buildings surrounding it. Even half completed, it altered the crazy jagged skyline of the city, became its focal point. From here, it was only the tower and the derricks waving like mad antennae. She yearned to record it from the inside, to capture all the rattle and hum of its ascension.

After dinner Briody came by, carrying a bottle of red wine. They settled on the deck under the dull night sky. She noticed his face was discolored, a bit swollen, and figured it was from that dreadful boxing. Smoke from the sugar plant, sticky with burning cane, drifted north on a warm breeze. She showed him some of her new work.

"We lost another man on Tuesday. A brickie. They say he had five children."

"That's horrible. I'm going to worry about you."

"Sometimes we just have to do things." He moved his chair closer to hers, took her right leg and laid it over his thigh.

"Your boyfriend got me out of jail last week."

"He didn't mention it."

"So you've seen him."

"I did not say I wouldn't." She took her leg off of his.

"You're not curious about my arrest?"

She did not want to tell him that Farrell had given her the details, bragging about springing him. "I'm not sure what I want to know."

"Maybe that's better."

"Is it?"

"I was caught with a bag of guns."

"Rivet guns?"

"No, guns for killing."

"You're a hunter."

"I like to think I am an ironworker. An ironworker who is falling in love with another man's woman."

"I belong to no one."

"Men get ideas."

"I can't help that."

"We begin to think we should fight for things."

"Things. That's just it, isn't it? It's always about possessing things. About ownership. I can't stand to think about it like that, Michael. I don't need that in my life. Right now I need to keep seeing Johnny Farrell. There are a lot of reasons, reasons I can't go into right now. But one thing I need you to know is I'd much rather be with you."

"The consolation prize."

"If you want to see it like that."

"You're sleeping with him still?"

"It's my business."

He was silent for a while. "Fair enough."

"Come on, Michael, we have both been through enough to know you need to live this life in the moment. Please bear with me. I want you. Not him. I just need to fix things so no one gets hurt."

Briody stood and drained his glass. "Well, that's just it, isn't it?"

"What do you mean?"

"Somebody always gets hurt."

The cattle king, decked out for a rodeo, pushed away from the card table and hobbled past Briody in lizard-skin boots. "Hey fella, I gotta drain the python. Keep an eye on those city boys for me, will ya?"

Briody leaned on the wall near the door dressed in a new wool suit with a .38 tugging down his left side pocket. Touhey had a sense of humor. He liked to rent out room 349 in the Park Central Hotel, the one where Arnold Rothstein had been fatally shot a couple years before, and use it to host his high-stakes card games. Briody was paid fifty dollars a shift to guard the games on certain weekend nights and was always tipped out by the winners. So far this was all that had been asked of him in exchange for the fixing of his case, soft but boring duty that went all night and sometimes well into the next day. It got so he could barely keep his eyes open.

The cattle king emerged from the bathroom and let rip a loud fart. "Damn, where's my manners?" He sat and the game recommenced.

Touhey had arrangements with the hotel staff, and of course the 18th precinct. Most of the players were rich men and often from out of town. Some were famous. Last week Briody had watched John Barrymore, drunk, still sporting spots of greasepaint, lose twenty thousand dollars and then try to get it back by browbeating and bellowing.

Briody went and looked out the window onto Seventh Avenue. A light mist was falling and the night streets were slick and quiet. He pushed the window open to let fresh air in. The smoky room reeked of sweat, booze, and desperation. He turned back to the game and watched the toothpaste scion throw money away. The kid, neatly turned out in a navy blue Brooks Brothers suit, had been up ninety grand. Now he was down twice that and panic had a firm grasp. He tugged at his pearl gray tie and gulped a warm glass of beer. He looked around the table, gazed into each of his opponents' eyes as if searching for mercy, but found there only a collective deadpan. These were beefy men of the illicit night. They gave nothing, displayed neither sympathy nor gloating over the rich kid and his woe. He pushed his glasses back up his nose and stared glumly at his hand.

"My father's gonna kill me," he muttered, and then, "Focus, focus, focus," over and over and over, a mantra. Briody thought he might as well be saying hocus-pocus, for all the good it was doing him.

It was the kid's turn to deal and he called seven-card stud, low spade in the hole, deuces, and one-eyed jacks wild. His choices had been getting wilder the deeper he sank in defeat, as if the widening set of variables might somehow turn the odds in his favor. Briody shook his head. The kid's demise was the one thing keeping him awake. The cards came down. The kid had aces showing and his eyes blossomed with greedy hope since all attempts at a poker face had been abandoned about fifty thousand dollars ago.

Tommy usually sketched the background of the players for him, especially ones that might be trouble. This cattle king had learned to gamble in the last days of the Wild West, had survived saloon shoot-outs, pestilence, and various natural disasters ranging from flash floods to locusts. He liked to spout off about Injun country. He wore the smirk of a man who had beaten longer odds than you would ever find in a card game. The kid clung to the false hope of the doomed.

The chips piled up like pirates' doubloons. The game was called as the kid appealed for more markers and the men turned their lizard eyes to Briody. He said wait and went into the next room and phoned Touhey in the Bronx. Touhey laughed and said let it ride. Briody went back to the game room and when he nodded the assent he saw something flicker in the air, the long knives being sharpened. Briody knew the others relished the idea of carving off a bit of that famed family fortune for their own. The kid smiled a loopy leer at the news and indicated that he wanted more scotch. He was obliged.

Briody went over to the bar and poured himself a small measure of Jameson. Watching the games was dull enough, but it was easy on the nerves, far easier than the gunrunning. He refused to give up the ironwork and Touhey had not argued. The whiskey burned. He chased it with water.

Finally the cards were flipped and the kid's own poison got him. The cattle king was sitting on three deuces and a one-eyed jack, which gave him six kings to the scion's five aces. The rich kid in a huff of relieved excitement waved the three of spades, thinking it was the low spade, and reached for half the pot. The cattle king had one more surprise and when he turned over the deuce of spades the kid let out a wail like a slapped dog and began to weep soundlessly. The other men laughed over the meltdown and called it a night.

The kid yelped and jumped up and ran, as if there was actually somewhere he could hide from Tommy Touhey. The cattle king of Wyoming stuck out his rhinestone-studded boot and the kid sailed into the wall. Briody picked him up by the collar and, his night done, escorted the kid down to the street.

"I'm dead."

"You want a cigarette?" Briody offered but the kid refused.

"You don't know my father."

"I'd say he'd be easier to deal with than Mr. Touhey."

"I promised I'd quit. I promised I'd go back to Princeton."

Briody flagged him a cab. "Time for a new hobby, I'd say."

He watched the cab turn on Fifty-second Street and speed away. He figured the kid's recklessness with his father's money was not so different from his own signing up with the British army to fight in the Great War. Young, stupid, and impetuous is a combination that often finds ways to express itself. He was in no hurry to get back to his new residence. He missed the claustrophobic chaos of the Casey household, the smells and noise and pressures. He walked east a few avenues and then down to Forty-second Street past the squat magnificence of the library with its stone lions, Patience and Fortitude, guarding the entrance. He passed stragglers, most of whom appeared drunk, swaying as they walked. At the corner a man stood and proclaimed, "I am Drunky Drunk! King of all winos!" A mounted cop clip-clopped over and with studied disinterest cracked his nightstick down and the king of all winos collapsed in a quiet, bloody pile.

Briody ducked into an all-night bakery just as the owner was pulling a tray of rolls out of the oven. He bought three and ate the steaming bread as he walked to Muldoon's rooming house on the corner of Thirty-eighth Street and Ninth Avenue, the margins of Hell's Kitchen. Paradise for six dollars a week. On his way up to the fourth floor the sounds of sex like a lament reached him through the thin walls as ancient bedsprings were bent to feverish use. A woman's cries rose and fell. He opened the door to his room and pulled a chain for the overhead bulb. Things scurried into the shadows and then the bulb popped and fizzled to black. In the neon glow of a Chesterfield sign he pulled off his suit.

There was a table, a bed in bad repair, an icebox, a cooker and a couch, and that was it. The spartan grayness of it appealed to him. He stuffed his suit in the bag and laid out his work clothes, the canvas pants, his T-shirt, the bandanna, his work boots. That was really him, not the suit he put on for Tommy Touhey.

He dragged a lamp over from the bedside and sat at the table, trying to write a letter to his mother. In a week and a half he had got no further than Dear Mammie. He had much to say. Lately he had even been thinking of paying her way over, putting her up in a flat in the Bronx. He wondered if she would come. She had never even been to Dublin, and New York would seem like an improbability to her, a kingdom of elusive and uncertain dreams. The place that first seduced her husband and now her son. He stared down at the mostly blank page. No avail, he'd do it tomorrow. He thumbed through the well-worn King James Bible and stopped at the Psalms. He'd made a point of giving it a thorough reading while interned in the Curragh, at first out of boredom and then out of appreciation for the sheer dark grandeur of it. He had weathered solitary far better than most men and he had done it by reconstructing whole stories in his head. The Bible was so old that the pages broke in his hands and yellow pieces fluttered to the floor. He ate the last roll, which still held a touch of the oven's heat.

He unfolded the drawing that Grace had done of him, laughed again at the muscular portrayal: his knotted biceps, his face set and determined as he leaned into the riveting. He had carried it every day since she gave it to him. He traced her florid signature in the bottom right corner. There was something strong, bold, in the way she wrote as in the way she walked and painted and talked. He thought about her and Farrell. It was something he simply had to accept for the time being. He could barely wait to see her again. She represented some kind of hope to him, some possibility of a different life, and he wasn't even sure why. He stretched out on the bed and tried to ignore the oppressive stench of mothballs and the buzz of a scavenger fly. From somewhere the music of the never-ending New York night reached him. He imagined her out there, perhaps dancing, or tossing her head back to laugh at a clever re-mark amid the clink of glasses. He fell asleep. He did not dream. When he opened his eyes it was morning, Monday morning, and he was going to work—his real work.

Egan watched the Governor lick chicken grease off his fingers thinking, An aristocrat should have better table manners. Egan had refused lunch. He believed firmly in not mixing business with pleasure, but he did accept a soda water to wash down his peanuts with. They sat at a table in the Governor's downtown of-fice. The man from Hyde Park was taking a long time looking over the photographic evidence, his wide pink face bent over the com-promising shots.

"Interesting stuff, Egan. You're a motivated fellow. Good God, is that Justice Andersen with two—boys? John, John, John. Well that certainly explains his dumping not only a first wife but a second as well." Roosevelt studied the picture, shaking his head. "Problem is I appointed some of these judges."

"Irrelevant sir. You merely followed the lead of the Tammany bosses."

"Doesn't exactly describe great leadership."

"You're an honest man duped by corrupt officials. You are appalled."

"Still, what does all this do for us?"

"We need to create the right climate. We need outcry. We need a mood in the city that provides us cover to do what needs to be done."

"Which is?" The old Knickerbocker smiled.

"Launch you right into the Oval Office."

"You are a man of grand vision, Egan."

"The only way you get where you were born to be is to play Tammany two ways. In the hinterlands you will be seen as the great agent of a long-due cleansing—a righteous purge. Here, you need to be seen as the guy who, let's face the facts kids, had no choice."

"Born to be."

Egan watched him chew on that phrase, savor it.

"A cocktail, Egan, a little libation? How about a Bronx?"

"Never touch the stuff, sir."

"How is the money trail?"

"Growing."

"Well. Follow your nose, man, and keep me posted."

Egan stood and started to gather the papers and photographs.

"You can leave these."

Egan raised an eyebrow.

"For my own files."

"Just burn them before you move to Washington."

"I'll burn what needs to be burned before Washington, Egan. You can rest assured."

Egan left the Governor and returned to his East Side apartment. His three rooms were small and stuffy with the oppressive summer heat. He cracked open his windows to little effect and pulled a beer from the icebox. On his kitchen table sat Johnny Farrell's satchel holding Johnny Farrell's hundred grand. Egan pushed it aside and spread the *Tribune* open. When he finished the beer he went and lay down on the couch. It was time for a nap. He needed his rest because, as usual, he was going to be awake all night, hunting.

ewis Hine, squat, strong, and dressed for rough labor, treated his camera like an extension of his body. Grace watched him set his press Graflex up for a shot, coaxing settings, nearly stroking the black box atop a tripod as he peered across the expanse of sky at an ironworker straddling a beam. But for his round silver glasses, he might have easily passed as one of the several thousand tradesmen hustling around the site. His concentration was as intense as that of the young man balancing sixty-five stories above the street.

He had greeted her at his studio at sunrise with a grunt, a nod, a cold "Oh, you're the painter," and that was all, and had gone back to his various rituals. Even the great agent of urban reform knew there were certain allowances to be made to the machine. He handed Grace a large supply box to carry and she struggled silently to keep up. Two assistants, graduate students from Columbia University, glum and earnest at dawn, had not been in any hurry to assist her. He barked commands at all of them and they were soon driving uptown from Canal Street to Thirty-fourth and Fifth Avenue in a battered panel truck.

Once they had passed the security post and unloaded she found herself pleasantly ignored by Hine and his minions; by morning coffee she realized that Hine was her entrée to the job and no more, and she wandered around the floors where he was shooting, staying within shouting distance in case someone challenged her right to be there. She was surprised that she was not the only woman on-site—she spotted canteen girls and several nurses in crisp uniforms. She could not believe the intensity of the work. Every floor was like its own factory. Small-gauge rail wound through each floor and the material, brick, block, pipes, cable, was snatched by the various crews and instantly put to use. The men seemed intent on working harder and faster than everyone around them. Their faces dripped sweat and large stains darkened their clothes. One laborer stood and wrung the bottom of his shirt until a small stream of water fell from it.

She quickly found there was no way she could paint because she had to stay on the move to stay out of the workers' way. She carried her sketchbook and paused whenever she caught a scene that intrigued her. She drew what Hine shot, sketching different angles, focusing on certain men, certain movements. She spent an hour working on the muscled arm of a mason who hung one panel of Indiana limestone after another, sliding them into place with grace and ease. She sat on an upturned bucket and worked fast and sure. She felt the building surging around her—all the commotion and industry, the force of human labor pushing skyward, the men teeming and bent to an exact task, skilled and purposeful, all their energy making the structure alive to her. The floor vibrated beneath her, the men shouted and sweated, pounded and hauled. When she sat on the lip of the floor she could see the derrick men on the far side working to rig loads of beams for hoisting to the next level. The sun was hitting her square now, her face warmed by its heat, and rivulets of sweat snaked down her sides but she dared not take off her canvas work jacket. She flipped the page on her sketchbook and started afresh.

After the morning coffee break she watched Hine load his camera onto a small cage hooked to a derrick cable. She walked over and knew this was the shooting platform Briody had described. The one assistant, tall with a puff of blond hair and a skinny mustache, brushed past her, handing Hine a box of film. Grace figured it was time to be bold. "Mr. Hine, would you mind very much if I went along?"

The photographer looked up, his face stern. She felt the bristling of the college boy beside her, appalled at the intrusion. Hine stood straight and looked at her for a long moment. "Fine" was all he said, and she stepped onto the cage.

The signalman said, "Letting the dame go. Wow."

Hine reached around her and pulled a small waist-high gate closed and nodded to the signalman, who leaned over the side and, looking up, made a circular motion with his forefinger. Suddenly they lurched away, swinging out into the air sixty-five stories above the street. Grace staggered back, grasping for the rim of the cage, and Hine grabbed her from behind, steadying her. "You need to be careful, miss." Grace, looking out over the city, was too stunned to reply. Her knees locked and all she could do was gape at the view as they rose even higher. They were on the east side of the building and she could see across to the Brooklyn shore where her boat was and all the way out to the sea past Rockaway, dozens of church spires poking the sky. To the north the Chrysler Building caught the sunlight, looking near enough to touch, and to the south the downtown temples of finance clustered at the bottom of the island, like a giant medieval fortress. How many people, she wondered, had ever been so high? Coal-powered generating plants belched blackness into the clear sky and rows and rows of apartment buildings led to the water, where industrial structures hugged the shore. Past Staten Island she saw a dirigible floating like a silver cloud off the Jersey coast. One thing her vantage proved. The city did end. There was a limit to it. Out in all directions it was a blue vastness whether of the sea or the mountains.

Hine pointed to her pad. "Put that away. You'll be helping me up here."

The cage was mesh and below her feet the city streets shimmered. They were higher now than the steel, higher than any of the men. She was giddy from the heights. She folded her sketch pad and put it in a bucket.

Hine pointed to a man straddling a column, reaching out as a derrick swung a beam toward him. All that held him was his left arm wrapped around the steel. "Just watch that. How can you put a price on the ability to do that, on fearlessness? You know how much he's being paid? Two dollars an hour if he's lucky. Two dollars to risk everything."

"It's beyond belief."

Hine steadied the tripod. "Why do you want to draw these men?"

"I feel in a way that if I don't, someday all that they did here will be forgotten. What do we know of the men who built the Pyramids? Or the great cathedrals? Or the aqueducts of Rome?"

He seemed pleased by the answer. "Obscurity. We will rescue them from obscurity, perhaps. Unfortunately it won't change the facts of their lives, the danger. It won't stop some of them from dying."

They sat on buckets suspended above the city and ate. He relished his knockwurst, biting into large chunks of the pink meat, which he cut with his folding knife. He used his handkerchief to dab small bubbles of grease from his lips. A squall kicked up and they began to sway in the breeze. Her stomach clamped around her meal.

"You get used to it, in a way."

He took her sketchbook, flipped through it quickly. "You have real talent."

"Thank you."

"I mean that. These are uncommonly good. Where did you study?"

"Jesus, that's a good one! I didn't."

"This is even more impressive. I like this one the best." He showed her a picture she had done from the building across the street, one of Briody perched on a plank hanging over the street driving a rivet true with his gun.

She smiled. "I like that one the best, too."

After shooting another hour Hine signaled for them to be brought back to the deck. As the cage swung back toward the frame Grace stared out over Brooklyn and Queens. Hine stood close. "It's funny what they tell you. They say, Don't look down, just look at the end of the beam, or just imagine you are five feet up."

"Instead of hundreds."

"Like it's something anyone can do."

Grace stepped gingerly onto the platform. When all the gear was packed they carried it down the temporary stairs and waited for the lift. The elevator operator smiled and pulled the door closed. They dropped at amazing speed and as they passed each floor she caught flashes, scenes of men at work, or faces waiting for the cage. No floor, it seemed, was empty. In the subbasement they loaded the gear into the truck.

"Can I have the boys drop you somewhere?" Hine seemed to have warmed to her.

"No. I just have to walk to the ferry. I'll be fine."

She waited for Briody and followed him across Thirty-fourth Street. When he was walking alone she came astride him, saying,

"Why don't you spend some of your big ironworker money on a girl like me?"

Briody grabbed her in his thick arms and lifted her and twirled her in the street. "I could think of nothing better to do with my hard-earned Yankee money. Jesus, you're as dirty as I am."

"Ah, come on. You like a filthy girl, don't you?"

"So what did you think? Is it everything I said it was?"

"Jesus, Michael. It's altogether wild. How can you stand those heights? I was petrified."

"I guess you can either handle it or you can't."

They walked in step for the ferry. While they were waiting for the light at First Avenue a sedan pulled to the curb beside them. A face pale and hard she remembered too well leaned out. She froze. "Excuse me, can you tell me which direction is Tammany Hall?"

Briody turned to Grace but the man said, "Just kidding," laughed, and pulled his head in the car as it roared away.

"You believe that eejit?" Briody asked.

"Silly, that's all." But Grace felt her mouth go dry, her joy vanishing.

In her room they never managed to get undressed. They were silent, hot, and dusty. Pulling at each other's dirty clothes, they stripped away just enough so in the humid heat of late day they could make love with their work boots on. After a while, she straddled him and, fueled by a creeping terror she could not escape, moved up and down on him with strength until they collapsed, sweat-drenched, in a tangle of limbs. While Briody dozed she stared out onto the Manhattan shore, afraid to think of what dangers lurked there for them.

They stood at the urinal, dicks in hand, the prince and his factotum.

"Johnny boy. How's tricks?"

"I am starting to think we might have more than a little problem."

Walker sighed. "I was hoping you and Grace would join Betty

and I for dinner and a bit of carousing tonight. That was fun last time, but too short. We'll go somewhere quiet."

Farrell thought it odd that he did not mention the shooting that had taken place after he left the Cotton Club. "Somebody has been nosing around our banking system."

"I figure we'll start at the casino, then maybe hit Jack and Charlie's. Top-notch lamb shank."

"It's not, obviously, the NYPD."

"Seems like we don't get out enough, just the four of us."

"Plus, I hear they might be going after more of our judges."

"Betty is quite fond of your colleen."

"This won't stop with that moron Vitale. All they need is one judge singing the wrong song."

"They tell me Cab Calloway is the best thing to hit this town in a decade."

"It's only a matter of time before someone starts talking."

"I was thinking we need a ticker-tape parade, Johnny. Any suggestions? I think the people deserve a little pomp and circumstance, some light revelry to ease their troubles."

"I can't figure who and why yet. But I think we need to—something, circle the wagons."

"Maybe we'll bring Lindbergh back for an encore, or find some prince from Europe, a current and popular hero from the sporting world."

"Your honor. It's different this time."

"Those Jesuits got to you, didn't they?"

Farrell, his stream spent, shook, tucked, and zipped. He went to the washbasin, cleaned his hands, and smoothed back his hair. The Mayor took a while. When he was done he too washed and tended to his hair. Walker was not oblivious to the coming crises, despite his refusal to acknowledge the stress. Farrell took note of the deepening of Walker's crow's-feet, the lines in the recently smooth brow. Faces never really lie.

They emerged together from the restroom of the Union Club. Farrell saw his wife standing anxiously with a few of her tea club cronies. He took a list of people who should be acknowledged from his pocket and handed it to the Mayor.

"I'm not taking this lightly. It is different."

"Different, Johnny Farrell? Well, you're the troubleshooter, Johnny Farrell, the political fixer, the Tammany man. I'm merely the Mayor. I am sure you can handle it."

Walker entered the main hall and was engulfed by a crush of rectitude and uprightness, by women turned out in the season's stylishly muted fashions, cut to fit in the Fifth Avenue boutiques or snapped up on excursions to Paris. Diamonds twinkled at him from necks and ears, subtle perfumes and tea breath. Stiffness gave way to demure smiles. He angled his way to the lectern and smoothed out his notes from Farrell. He made a fifteen-minute show of the acknowledgments—the wives of the prominent, the good reverends, the executives and trustees of the most powerful corporations and foundations. He had a habit of doing so, often spending as much time acknowledging as speechifying. The way they sat up, a little preening, that feeling of importance he bestowed. He also enjoyed ignoring those who annoyed him. They would fidget, waiting for the ego salve of official recognition, like a pack of puppies waiting for a teat. He liked to toy with them at times. Look at them as he read the list of names. Here it did not matter so much. He had no real enemies here, none that might harm him, although the quiet assembly was an opposition camp. He knew his effect on them, was fully aware of the power of his charm. He also knew it was a fleeting temporal power. When he was in their presence it worked, but the moment the door swung closed on his back it turned off like an electric current, a switch thrown. They went back to disparaging him over their bread pudding. How he loved democracy.

He leaned on the lectern and smiled out at the crowd. "Some of my staff suggested I not come here today to meet with you fine and upstanding women. They reminded me that my vote totals in precincts thickly habituated by members of your good and decent society were alarmingly minute. But, I said, how could that be? Are they not for good and decent legislation to ensure the dignity of childhood? Are they not against the savage buffoonery of the Ku Klux Klan? Are they not open to the ideals of a free and pluralistic city where those of all colors and creeds and philosophies mingle? Oh sure there are differences. I don't mind a little bubbly while perhaps you might prefer a nice cup of tea. I prefer the night and you, I am sure, the day. While I am at a ball game among the braying multitudes of hot-dog aficionados you are on the way to an opera where they might nibble on Vienna sausages at intermission. And sure you might not have endorsed boxing, or baseball on Sundays. But I assured those in my employ that these are merely questions of style and not substance and what is important is that we are all fervid supporters of this great metropolis and all its varied inhabitants, whether they come from *Mayflower* lineage or back alleys in Naples, whether they toil in the downtown temples of finance or sweep the streets of that very same district. I pointed out, dear ladies, that they, my staff, surely underestimate the charitable nature of your hearts. And just because your husbands write those naughty editorials attacking my able administration"—a pause for polite applause—"doesn't mean you are not independent thinkers, one and all. I'll bet you don't subscribe to those errant points of view. After all, it was Tammany that supported suffrage long before the editorial boards of most of the august newspapers in this town."

From the back of the room a woman with battleship gray hair, eyes, and dress stood and shouted, "Liar!"

The Mayor drew back from the lectern in mock horror, then retorted, "Now that you have identified yourself, you may sit down." The good ladies roared their approval.

On his way through the lobby he was accosted by a man wielding a notebook.

"Your honor, is there any truth to the stories of a widening judicial scandal?"

"Who employs you?"

"*Daily News.*"

"Well, you're new so I'll excuse the rudeness. Scandal? Don't be silly. One bad judge doesn't spoil the bunch. We have the best judges in the nation."

Where the hell was Farrell? He ignored the reporter and signed autographs for the blue-haired ladies of good fortune. Chin up, old girl. Smile and a wave, smile and a wave, Gentleman Jimmy Walker is your humble public servant. He yearned to be back at the hotel with Betty, an afternoon romp. Her flesh wrapped around him ensconced in her bounty. All concern faded away, his stomach quieted, his heart lifted. Betty was a respite, a refuge, a perch on a different reality. My sweet Betty. He walked through the doors and out onto Gramercy Park.

He waved Farrell over and jerked his thumb at the offending newsman. "Deal with this, Johnny, deal with this." He walked toward the waiting car. Two of his detail whisked him through the crowd to the backseat and closed the door behind him. "Lights and sirens, Jacko. Let's give the old girls a thrill."

As the car sped away he settled back and to no one in particular said, "Ah, but this is a reckless age."

F arrell watched the Mayor go and wheeled on the reporter.

"McDermott, is it? A nice Irish boy. Where's your loyalty?"

The reporter pulled back, shocked by the question. "My loyalty is to the story. And to what the people have the right to know."

"An idealist. Fine. I'll call Boyle, your editor. He's a personal friend."

"Bill Boyle sent me out here."

It was Farrell's turn to be shocked. "Great. No more comment for you. Beat it, Skippy."

"Is it true that judges buy their appointments?"

Farrell turned and walked over to his wife. He waited while she helped an elderly woman into her car.

"Well done, Johnny. Everyone was thrilled."

"Good, Pamela."

Farrell stared at his wife and there in the soft dappled light of Gramercy Park he remembered back to when they met and a time when he was in love with her. A time when it wasn't about her money or her family connections, a time before trench warfare of the heart when she was a young Vassar graduate who wanted to make the world right and he was rising in the machine and still convinced of all the good he might do. They were just steps from the rooms where he often carried out his sweaty betrayals. He realized just what a beautiful woman his wife was. He kissed her. Right there and on the lips and squeezed her tight, but when he pushed back he was Johnny Farrell and he had to go. At the corner he paused and looked back. He held his hand up and gave a slight wave, but she just stood and stared so he turned the corner and walked quickly toward the Italian part of town.

He worked his shoe leather hard. The sidewalks were crowded with mothers and children and on the stoops men sat idly, staring at their feet or making small talk. Farrell considered the future of the city, who would run it, who pulled the strings, who was on the way out. The rackets were spiraling. There was no sanction, no control. The floodgates on cash and corruption were shattered. Everybody howled for their piece of the action. All the structures they had erected to corral the graft were tumbling. Where was the discipline? Every street punk with a heater was forming a kidnap gang. Half the rookie cops thought their badge was a license to steal and shake down. Beer-war shoot-outs erupted almost daily. It was bad for business.

Judges. If they went after the judges the whole thing might collapse. Bill Boyle, a friend, was sending out reporters to go after them. Another very bad sign. If this kept up two things were very possible. Walker was a goner and the entire machine might topple. Farrell needed the streets to be consolidated. He needed chains of command. He needed chaos corralled. For the past few years he had taken the measure of the underworld princes. It was time to get behind one horse.

Farrell was met at the coffee shop door on Avenue A by a gregarious Sicilian who towered over him. He was ushered inside and the Dago rose from his table and greeted him with open arms. "Johnny. So nice to see you. Welcome. Please, sit."

The Dago stirred his coffee in slow circles. He wore a gray three-piece suit and an expression of such studied calm that it was hard to believe his reputation. Farrell decided to match his feigned indifference. He drank his coffee, said nothing.

"I want to thank you for that contract."

"It's going all right?"

"Yes. But now I want you to help me with something else. Something grave."

Farrell raised an eyebrow, waited.

"I need to be able to reach some of your judges."

Farrell held up his hand. "I'm not sure what you mean."

The Dago sipped his coffee and smiled. He looked at his watch, a slow grace to all his movements. "We are both busy men. Are we here for business, or no?"

"I don't think I can help you."

"This would be unfortunate. I have a particular case in mind. One of my best men has been charged with a killing. He is surely innocent. He is surely not getting fair treatment. A gun was planted."

Farrell set his cup down quietly and leaned in to speak softly to Vamonte. He took a pen from his pocket and a business card from his wallet. He slid them across the table. "Write his name down. I'll see what I can do. No guarantees."

"Why do you say this—no?"

Farrell considered a response.

"You don't have this power? Do I need to address someone else? Is that what you are saying?"

Farrell looked around the small space, breathed the unfamiliar odors of a Mediterranean kitchen wafting from nearby. There was nowhere to run, nowhere to hide. The Dago still smiled but he felt as if something unspoken yet sinister had transpired. He tried to swallow without being noticed. He turned back to glance over his shoulder at the street.

"Write his name."

The Dago stared at him. Not a word, not a gesture, nor the batting of an eye—he just sat with that creepy stillness. Farrell realized he was relishing the scene, had been aiming for this for years. Well, he was still a gutter thug and always would be. The Dago might think he was making headway toward power, but he'd find out soon enough.

The Dago bent and scratched a name on the card. "I think we both have the same aims. Stability. If we want a good business climate, we cannot have this, this is not Chicago. This is a great city."

"I could not agree more."

The Dago indicated a tabloid that lay open on the table. "Speaking of judges, I see this as your number one threat."

"We're keeping an eye on it."

"Can these men be trusted to be discreet?"

"Most are smart guys."

The Dago nodded. "I would make sure you impress on them the hazards of talking to the wrong people. Come, let's walk."

It was not a day for walking. The air was thick, gritty, and hot, malarial. Still the streets were busy. He heard shouting in Italian, an odd snatch of Polish, babble in Yiddish. Farrell had been in every corner of this city, had seen neighborhoods change hands like disputed civil-war territories, and had done business, political and otherwise, with all types, but he still felt ill at ease on streets such as these. The Dago walked with his head held high. The Dago walked like he owned the street. He had a stately bearing and despite his lack of years he was greeted as a village elder by everyone on that block. Widows came up to him, children stared in awe, young Turks lurked in doorways hungry to be noticed by him. They crossed Avenue A. A few paces behind and a few ahead, two men dressed oddly for the season in long dark overcoats continually scanned the street.

"That business uptown, a seven-year-old boy gunned down like a pig for playing on his doorstep. That is messy. That is messy and it is wrong. How can a city prosper when it is under siege by animals? That is why these old-timers must go. They look backward, they solve everything with blood. They live for petty vendettas. You and I come from a different generation. We look forward, no?"

The man made sense. How much of it was an act, a performance for his benefit, he did not know. They walked past cheese shops, a bakery, and a *salumeria* where long sausages hung sweating in the windows. People smiled and waved. It was not unlike walking with the Mayor, Farrell thought, except the Dago did not respond with smiles and handshakes. He glided through, merely nodding, sometimes offering a slight raise of a hand, like a cardinal granting absolution for sins not yet considered.

They entered a butcher shop near Twelfth Street in front of which sweaty men in gray overalls unloaded goat carcasses from a new truck. Farrell followed the Dago, skirting the counter. He listened as they all spoke rapid-fire in Italian. There were hugs, manly kisses to both cheeks, Mediterranean affectations, a flashing of hands and a wad of money. The owner, a stout man with a comical mustache, tried to wave it off, but the Dago was quietly insistent. Farrell got the gist of it. Meat for every household on the block.

In the back room men with knives and cleavers and saws worked, flicking and slicing and hacking, their aprons stained with fresh gore, like ancient hunters bent over the kill. Piles of guts and trimmed fat glistened in the stark light. Blood pooled on the floor. Flies gathered.

"These old men are fools and their time has passed. I will deal with them. What I need from you is someone inside the machine, the Organization. We would be partners. Favors will be our commerce."

He spoke with conviction. Their arrangements had been mostly one-off deals, construction contracts where Farrell profited nicely by lining up work for the Dago's front companies. But Vamonte was hinting at bigger things, a stronger alliance. He was not your garden-variety street monster like Tommy Touhey. He was still smarting over Touhey's treatment of him at the Cotton Club, but at the same time, when bullets flew, it was Touhey who on instinct dragged him out of harm's way. Still, Touhey was what? The king of Mott Haven?

Farrell had set his sights much higher than that. He had no qualms about working with Italians and that might just give him the advantage in power struggles to come. Many of the old-school sachems were vociferous in their small-minded hatred of the other. All you had to do was the math. The Irish were waning while these others waxed.

In the back cooler hanging among the carcasses of goats and pigs and dead cows there were three men trussed, their faces covered in congealed blood dusted white with frost. Little puffs of breath escaped their nostrils. Their eyes stared, like empty black holes, but they were alive, yet. Farrell fought off the impulse to vomit, biting his tongue to hide his retching. No one looked, no one even acknowledged them. They moved through the freezer and came out into a courtyard. The light dazzled his eyes. He swallowed hard. Should he say anything, laugh? Make a joke?

They sat at a small table draped in a red cloth and shared some wine. For thirty minutes the Dago made small talk, cutting thin slices of sausage and cheese with his folding knife. After a while he was led through another building and out onto Avenue A again. He wondered if he had imagined the men hanging in the freezer.

"The last time we spoke of a man in the Bronx."

Touhey. He needed to commit one way or another regarding his old friend. "I am trying to negotiate that. Make it better for everyone."

"Make up your mind. I am a patient man but there are others who want to make alliances that don't have your reservations."

Farrell shook his head. Said he'd get back to him, then got out of the neighborhood as fast as his feet moved. He decided to walk to get the chill of death and of that meat locker out of his bones. On Fourteenth Street he bumped into a classmate from Fordham.

"Johnny Farrell, kid. I see you all over the papers, whispering in the Mayor's ear. You done all right for yourself there, kiddo."

"Yes . . . George Swatchka?"

"Donnie Schweitzer."

"Of course."

"Jeez, Johnny. You okay? You're looking a little peaked there, good buddy."

"I had a bad piece of meat for lunch. I'll be fine."

"You gotta watch what you eat. I notice you're coming from the guinea part of town. They aren't known for their hygiene. I got two sisters married to them so I oughta know."

Farrell palmed off a business card and walked toward Union Square. He was burning up and the sweat poured off him. Jesus, how deep was he in now? Had he just made a fatal blunder? He realized he was next to the Consolidated Edison building, the spot where the old Tammany Hall had stood. What would the old masters have done? One thing he knew, they would not have let the bastards in the door to start with. He hurried back to the Hall, passing without a word through the lobby and up the marble steps to his desk.

"This came for you." Alice, the secretary, stood before him, her hair pulled back so tight it made her look Asiatic. She thrust a package at him.

"When?" he croaked out, swallowing fear.

"Just a minute before you walked in."

When she left he stripped away the manila wrapping paper to find a handsome rosewood box. It featured an engraving of a donkey being ridden by a man of unmistakably Mediterranean features. He put his ear to the box, then his nose. The cloying smell of fine cigars. He laid a trembling finger on it. He nudged the brass latch open. It was nothing but fat cigars laid out and a small card with a note that read "Look forward to doing business with you."

Farrell dropped the note in the trash and lit one of the cigars. It was a fine deep smoky tobacco grown and aged in the tropics. He exhaled luxuriously, thinking, Not a bad cigar at all.

On their way off the site, Hard Nose McCabe came along and handed Briody a letter. "This was dropped off for you. Now I'm a goddamn postman to boot."

Walking west, Briody read the letter four times before it fully registered. His mother was dead. He stopped, let the sea of pedestrians wash past him, felt his heart race in his chest. His mother, dead? It was not possible. She was only forty-nine. On reflex he ducked into Holy Cross Church, made the sign of the cross, knelt in a pew at the rear, head bowed. He had not seen her in eight years. Her disappointment at his involvement in war, in any war, had estranged them. He thought of the distance between them, a great gulf, and how close they had been when he was young. She never made an effort to hide the fact that he was her favorite. He always assumed that one day he might make amends. Now it was too late.

The church was quiet in the afternoon, light filtering down through the stained glass, the vaulted ceiling dark above him. The marble altar was draped in linen, ready for a mass to come. Two priests walked past him holding a conference of murmurs. He was too much in shock to indulge in his usual anticlerical thoughts. He felt truly homesick for the first time in years. She would be long buried by now in the parish cemetery alongside her husband and four of her babies. All of her children were dead or scattered around the earth; only his sister Maureen had been there for the end.

After a long quiet time he lit a candle for her, the sulfur and burning wax bringing back his own days as an altar boy. His mother used to wake him for the early mass and see him on his way, having to push him out the door. He returned to the pew and prayed on his knees for the first time in many years. The church's stand against the republican war efforts had been the final push for him. He recalled the priest coming around during the hunger strikes to admonish him and his colleagues, refusing to give them the sacraments, the excommunications, and the irony of the growing respect the men had for the Protestant chaplain, who seemed much more sympathetic to their ideals, or at least to their suffering. Briody knew that even his mother, utterly devout, rejected the church's stand on that issue.

He bent his forehead so it rested on the top of his clasped hands and recalled his mother so vividly there in the pew of Holy Cross that he might have been hallucinating. She would ride miles on her bicycle each day, her hair always trailing in the wind behind her. A woman of her time and place but with a sense of humor that carried her through any trials, through hard times and dead babies and years' absence of his father, the unwanted advances of neighboring men, drunk and thinking licentious thoughts about a woman on her own. He remembered her facing up to the landlord's belligerent son, her newborn clasped to her chest. But always the day started and ended to the sounds of her laughter. She told all her children that they were not to go to bed angry or sad, for they would be haunted through the night by any unresolved differences or grudges. In that New York church he could see her and smell her and feel her touch as surely as if she were there with him, as surely as he used to watch her in her dress in the late evening of the long summer nights tracking through the fields calling his name.

He stood, shakily, considering how far he was from both his home and his now inconceivably dead mother. He backed out of the church making the sign of the cross once more. Walking down the steps, he knew that there was only one place he might find true comfort. On Forty-second Street the day hammered and swirled, car horns brayed and the rush-hour crowd swarmed. Insults were yelled back and forth by red-faced drivers through open car windows and he realized with sadness that her death affected nothing here.

Grace walked up Broadway ignoring the wolflike leering and taunts of men. The mere fact of her attire—pants, work boots, a man's shirt—emboldened them to display their true nature. She was preoccupied with Briody and happily ignored the imbeciles. She smiled with the knowledge that not one of them would even look sideways at her if she was by his side. The day before a young Irish boy had handed her a note from Briody announcing that he would come by tomorrow. She was beside herself with anticipation. She had had a great day sketching, first in the park, and then she moved around drawing the Empire State Building from a variety of perspectives: coming up the subway stairs at Thirty-third and Eighth Avenue, from the corner of Mulberry and Spring, from Bryant Park where a man with a telescope sold peeks of the building for a nickel each, and from the ferry dock at the East River. There seemed no corner of New York that did not offer a view of the skyscraper.

She bought fish sandwiches and met Anna at Isabel Bishop's studio. The three of them ate sitting around a large round oak table and swapped notes and tips on style. Grace licked her greasy fingers and took her time touring the studio, which she had not seen before. There was light from every direction, even from the roof where peaked skylights let the sun wash the wood floors and plaster pillars of the open space. She decided it was her new favorite room in all of New York. Isabel was doing a series of sketches of the shopgirls who gathered in Union Square for lunch on fine days. Grace felt an unusual stab of envy. She would never be as good.

Anna was trying to talk her into taking more classes at the Art Students League.

"Isabel, you like studying with Miller, don't you?"

"Kenneth? Sheer genius. Listen, everybody is crazy about Picasso, cubism, all this nonsense. It's all fine if that's what you fancy, but I see it as a passing fad. Painting takes real talent, not just an eye for color. Nothing has changed since Caravaggio, talent will out. I think Miller will love your work."

Grace was flattered. The taking of classes seemed like a frivolous extravagance right now. On the way out, she and Anna walked across the park, past Tammany Hall. "Do you want to visit your beau in the Temple of Doom?"

"I think I am working on a new beau for the moment."

"Maybe you are smarter than you look."

They parted and Grace walked east along a crowded and exuberant Fourteenth Street. Young boys ran in and out of stores, chased by tight-faced shop owners. Housewives hunted bargains. At Third Avenue a drunken man stood at the bottom of the El stairs and warbled a song in a forgotten tongue. Grace dropped a quarter in his cigar box. She turned south at First Avenue where she purchased the plumpest chicken she could find, a string of garlic, and a bunch of rosemary. She ducked into the fishmonger and picked out a pound of briny mussels. She went around the corner on Twelfth Street and entered a store on Avenue A where an old Italian man sat doe-eyed at a counter, his thick drooping mustache lending him an air of inescapable melancholy. She told him she would like two bottles of his best Italian grape juice. He considered her for a moment and then nodded. Presently a woman came from the back with a sack containing her wine. Grace realized the man must have a buzzer behind the counter. Next door in the *salumeria* she selected Italian sausage and some homemade mozzarella that dripped milk.

Out on the street she shouldered her way through the crowd

and waited for traffic on the corner. Two boys in short pants engaged in a mock boxing match. She looked across the street and saw someone who looked a lot like Johnny Farrell walking with another man. She stared for a second and realized with a start that it was Johnny. She turned away quickly, making as if she was window-shopping, and watched them in the reflection. They walked trailed by two other men and were talking intently. What was he doing down here? She faced the street and recognized his companion. Vamonte, the Dago. She had worked once briefly in a club he owned. Thank God Farrell had not seen her, but his connection to Vamonte was disturbing. She hurried east toward the river and the ferry home.

She was surprised to find Briody already there, sitting on the deck. He stared out across the river and before he turned at her arrival she knew that something irredeemable had happened. She put her groceries down and stepped onto the boat and he came over and embraced her. She felt his breath in her ear, and as he squeezed her he said simply, "My mother's dead."

He showed her the letter. Then they just sat on the chairs holding hands, silent as the chicken went uncooked and the day turned inexorably to night.

The grief over his mother's passing stayed with him, a heavy presence, for days. His sister had not explained anything. Her letter merely said that his mother had died after a brief illness. He wrote back pressing for more details. He felt guilty, examined his life, the choices he had made that led to their estrangement and his being so far away from her for so long.

The job consumed him and the crazy pace still quickened. Hard Nose McCabe announced at the beginning of the month that the goal for August was twenty-two floors, one for each working day, and anyone who failed to pull his weight could go and enjoy the beach for the rest of the summer. That was the quota and it would be met. The men took the challenge as a point of pride. A few grumbled, but others sensed that this was beyond the usual and that decades from now, generations would say with pride that they were of someone who built that building—the Empire State Building.

On a Thursday of suffocating heat and dead air Briody smashed a finger between his rivet gun and a steel beam. He had turned away for a second as a seaplane roared past, could see the pilot clearly, two passengers behind him, their faces framed in portholes, grinning maniacally. The pilot, out for sport on a summer day, waved a hey-ho. Briody grimaced as blood squirted onto his shirt, ran down his arm. He cursed and examined the wound. There was a slice, as if made with a scalpel, that exposed the gray meat. The tip was smashed. The pain was so intense that it went numb. He felt a wave of nausea. Sheehan looked over at him.

"Mother of God, I bet that smarts."

Briody muttered curses under his breath.

"Go see the doctor. Now."

He climbed down and as he made his way across the floor to the elevator, Hard Nose McCabe came up. "Going to Coney Island?"

"Doctor."

Briody held up the hand. McCabe took it, turned it over, holding the mangled finger close to his face. "A doctor. Get a bandage on it and get back to work."

"Right, boss." He went to the infirmary on the fortieth floor and took a seat next to a carpenter with a nail stuck in his foot, and they made small talk while the doctor attended to a brickie who had been struck with a tool of his trade. The brickie's face was a mask of blood. His eyes were vacant, dull. The doctor stared into his eyes and shook his head. "Get this man off of this site and over to Bellevue, now."

Briody watched as the doctor used a pair of pliers to pry the nail from the carpenter's foot. After he cleaned the wound and covered it he sent the man away and turned to Briody.

"What can I do for you?"

Briody held up the finger.

"That's nice." He grabbed the finger and held it out, pouring alcohol all over it.

Briody clenched his teeth at the burn. The doctor plunged the needle into the torn meat of his finger, yanked the catgut through. Briody winced, bit on his cheek. The doctor whistled while he stitched. When the sewing was done the doctor wrapped the wound in gauze and taped it firmly.

"I bet you go right back to work."

"Can't let the boss man down."

"The faster they go the more men get mangled. Besides, you're all working your way onto the breadline."

"Ah, but look what we're accomplishing."

"What's that? The biggest empty building in the world? Who do they think will be able to afford to rent? I say they make it into free housing for the homeless."

Briody watched him fill out a form. "Something tells me that's not likely. Seven stitches?"

"Nine. This country. My land of liberty, what's it becoming? A paradise of fools and the deluded, sadly deluded."

A man was brought into the infirmary supported by two coworkers. He yelped as they set him down and hurried back to work.

"Nine stitches, a crushed fingertip. You're headed back to work right now?"

Briody waved his bandaged hand about. "Good guess, Doctor. Somebody has to pay the bills."

"Eighty dollars a week really worth risking your health?"

Briody examined the bandaged finger, his trigger finger. "I've risked it for far less than that."

The doctor waved him off. "Go on, I've got to work on this gimp here. It looks like he won't be dancing for a while."

Briody made his way back to the work floor. In his absence the crew had been idle and fallen behind. They sat on a beam smoking. When he approached Sheehan was the first to come to him. "You all right?"

Delpezzo was behind him. "That's gotta hurt."

Armstrong slapped him on the back. "Let's hit it fellas. Those squareheads went flying by us. No way I'm playing second fiddle to those Swedish clowns."

Briody fell back into position. The sky had clouded and thick black thunderheads were piling on the horizon. They needed to hurry, to beat the coming storm. He did his best to isolate the finger, but every time he swung his rivet gun onto a burning bolt and pulled the trigger pain screamed up his arm. He said nothing. The crew needed him. He would get used to it.

hings are changed, Tommy. Why not come on board? Why not play in the big leagues?"

Tough Tommy Touhey rolled a couple of dice over and over, the ivory cubes clicking softly in his palm. He said nothing. The noise from the Four Provinces reached them through the door.

"We can still run the show," Farrell went on. "We'll let the Dago help us achieve what we always wanted and then, when the time is right, we'll get rid of him. It's just a temporary thing, a marriage of convenience."

"Something you are familiar with."

"Guilty as charged."

"Self-knowledge is a beauty to behold."

"We're in on our terms and we're out when we want."

"You make that sound easy."

"Why does it have to be hard?"

"You have no idea what you're up against." Tommy rolled the dice on the table. Snake eyes. "What's in it for me?"

"You're outgunned, Tommy. It's only a matter of time."

"You come out on top. Fancy Johnny Farrell, cock of the walk."

"Tommy, it's not like that. It's a way to move toward the future together."

"The future. You talk about it like it's something you can predict."

"Maybe not, but I figure we can shorten the odds."

"So, you're doing me a favor, is that it? I give up my half of the Empire State Building rackets so that little weasel guinea gets even fatter?"

"Tommy, I can't stop these guys, they're too big. So I say, hey, come in. If you can't beat 'em, join 'em."

"The greaseballs."

"These guys are different. They're the new generation. They're no way like the old-timey zips. We're all in the same game."

"You're gonna be a water boy for these guys, Johnny?"

"Tommy."

"They snap a finger, you come running?"

"It's more like a partnership. A business partnership."

"What happens when youse disagree?"

"We work it out."

"You think so?"

"Tommy, they need us more than the other way around."

"Us?"

"I told them, I'm not hooking up without you. They understand it's a package deal."

"Great. I get tossed in the river tied to you. The two of us, glug, glug, glug."

"I have no interest in dying."

"Sometimes what might interest you is not so interesting to others, Johnny Farrell, savvy?"

"Tommy, there's no rush. Take a day or two. Think on it."

"I might. But just remember, Johnny Farrell, I know where a lot of things are buried."

Farrell rose to leave. "This, I know."

"You know, Tammany man, I seen your mother the other day. She's still living in that walk-up. She's getting old, Johnny. Her hip is shot. She coughs blood."

Farrell's face bloomed red. "I've been trying to get her to move for years, Tommy. She won't budge."

"I'm only saying, she's getting old. Says a lot about a guy, how he treats his mother."

Once Farrell was gone, Tommy thought it over. The Italians needed Johnny, the Jews did too. He brought the Organization into the picture, which meant the politicians, the judges, and the cops—real power. He was their entrée to the truly Big Time and a way to rise from the streets. Whereas Touhey knew he himself was expendable. He never thought things would come to this, but they had, and he'd make an accommodation, buy some time. It was all he could do.

E gan belched loudly. "Damn, those hot dogs are murder."

Farrell sat between him and the Mayor drinking stale stadium coffee. On the bright green diamond before them, the Yankees were dead even with the visiting Red Sox in the bottom of the eleventh. Babe Ruth was on deck, standing just a few feet away, idly swinging his warm-up bat, sweat dripping from his brow.

Farrell's stomach was in knots. Since meeting the Dago he had been gripped by a constant fear of losing control of all he had built up, of his whole world coming down around him, of chaos and disgrace, death perhaps. No matter how much he believed that they needed him more than he needed them, he felt that he had set something in motion that was irrevocable and unstoppable. He tried to focus on the fact that without him and the machine, without the Hall, they were nothing but gutter thugs. He finished the coffee with a wince.

Egan leaned over and spoke across him to the Mayor, who was enjoying a coffee spiked with Jameson. Whiskey in the heat. "The Great Bambino. I get a call, three maybe four years ago, a disturbance at the Plaza. Room 1214, I remember right. The house dick is an old pal of mine from the academy. I grab a couple of the boys and up we go to this suite and my pal, the house dick, lets us in with a passkey. What a sight. All the windows are busted out and the baseball god here is running around the room buck naked, a hoo-er over each shoulder, a top hat on his head, chomping on a foot-long Cuban, and there's gotta be another six, seven broads naked strewn about the place amongst the broken furniture. Turns out we interrupted a little absinthe and gin party Babe was having with a dozen of his favorite hoo-ers, maybe a little cocaine too. God forbid."

The Mayor shook his head. "You didn't haul him in?"

Lary doubled off the wall. Ruth shouted encouragement, then grabbed his regular bat and lumbered to the plate.

"The Babe? Hell, no. The minute he sees we're the law he drops the hoo-ers on the couch and tries to buy us off. Starts stuffing C-notes in all our pockets, while we try to coax him into some clothes. I mean, it was some terrible thing, seeing your hero in his birthday suit."

Ball, low and away. Ruth stepped out of the batter's box, took his time so the rookie pitcher might think over what he was up against—the Great Bambino in the house that he built, game on the line.

"You refused, I'm sure."

"I mean, a guy wants to stuff things in your pockets. It's not like we ever put a hand out."

The Mayor smiled, acknowledged a "Hey Jimmy" from the crowd with a wave. "My faith in my police rewarded again."

Called strike. Ruth let the end of his bat drop on the plate and glowered back at the umpire. Farrell laughed along with them and pulled his tie loose. He kept seeing the bodies in the freezer. The Dago's display had spooked him, no question about that. Not because the men were dead or dying, but because of the dark genius of their display.

"Matter of fact, after he ran out of hundreds he sat on the couch—naked still—and started blubbering like a baby."

"He was chagrined."

"He was truly."

The next pitch came high and tight and Ruth stepped away from it, turning to face them. He spotted the Mayor and made a comical scaredy-face. The crowd oohed in amazement that the fresh southpaw on the mound had the stones to buzz the Babe.

"Nice to see that even the celebrated can understand the parameters of good taste."

"That they know shame."

"It's Johnny Farrell's job here to keep me from such predicaments."

"Sometimes I act before the fact, sometimes after."

"He always acts."

The Babe swung from his toes and the ball rose, a majestic display sailing far into the upper deck while the crowd stood as one, screaming, and the Babe nonchalantly made his way around the bases in the hot sun, then stomped on the plate. As he passed into the dugout he pointed and cocked his finger at Walker and winked. The Mayor shot back.

They made their way up and out of the stadium to the usual cheers. It was baseball and it was Sunday and the only reason any of them was here was that Walker, over the objections of those high-hat snobs in Albany, had made it possible.

Farrell checked his watch. He was to meet Grace downtown.

Briody checked his watch. The Italians were late and this made him anxious. He wanted to do the job and get back to Brooklyn, to the boat and Grace. He leaned against the light pole and watched the idling procession of people taking in the air and the sunshine. It was a pleasant afternoon and no one seemed in much of a hurry. A woman in a white dress with blue flowers passed and he caught a whiff of the same perfume Grace wore, which smelled of roses, of summer. He brought his wrist to his nose and inhaled Grace's scent. He thought of their coupling and smiled at the vision. He wondered where it was all going, what she meant to his life. She was not what he had expected. He'd hoped to see the building through and then slip out somehow from under the influence of Touhey and maybe even the lads, start things new and fresh, leave town if he had to. But now she occupied most thoughts of the future.

He checked his watch again. This too was work for Tommy Touhey. Just a little favor for our Mediterranean friends. Just go and help them out a bit, get them in the door was all. No real dirty work. We'll see, Briody thought. He had come somehow to trust Tommy Touhey, to trust him more than Danny, and that was strange indeed. So here he was standing on a street corner dressed in his best imitation of a Mick detective, complete with fedora on his head and a badge in his pocket. He had turned down the offer of a service revolver. No thanks, Tommy, enough gunplay in my past thank you.

The sedan pulled up and one of the Italians pushed the door open. "Get in" was all he said. Briody looked up and down the length of Broadway and while ducking into the backseat said, "And a lovely day to you too, fellas."

There were three of them, hard-faced and wiry, and when he sat they turned to him briefly as if to size him up, then looked away. Briody was along for the ride but they were silent, grim with some nefarious purpose. Briody kept his mouth shut, but all the same he was not going to let them ruin his fine mood. As they motored through the busy streets of the metropolis, of his new city, he pulled his fedora down and leaned back, closing his eyes, the smile still on his face. The two in the front exchanged phrases in broken Italian, trying, he surmised, to keep him in the dark.

After a time he looked up and noticed they were crossing into the Bronx on the Willis Avenue Bridge. Yankee Stadium stood in the near distance. Presently they pulled in front of an apartment building on the Concourse, one of the new ones of tan brick and art deco flourishes—aluminum spandrels, gleaming windows. The lobby was cool and clean and lacked the lived-in reek of the older tenements. They took the elevator to the fourth floor and the skinny one, who seemed to be in charge, pointed to a door. 4B. Briody knocked three times.

"Who the hell is it?" An angry bark.

"Racket squad," Briody answered as instructed, pushing his badge toward the peephole. There was scuffling and cursing as three bolts were thrown open. A man pushed his head out and, looking at the four of them, said, "What's the problem? You talk to the Inspector?" His face was bright red and topped by a wave of silver hair. He wore boxer shorts and a T-shirt, black socks. He smelled of whiskey and his watery blue eyes were hard, suspicious.

When Briody didn't respond the man's eyes narrowed and he said, "Who's the greaseball?"

The Italians were through the door in a flash and beating the man down with lead-filled saps as he tried his best to fight them off, grunting and moaning. The wife came in screaming in Italian, which surprised Briody and seemed to anger the others, who spit back at her in her native tongue. She pulled one arm from behind her back, brandishing a pistol, and the skinny one let her have it with the sap, right across the face, and, clobbered, she went down all twisted. Briody stepped back and closed the door. He wanted no part of this. He watched as the Italians dragged the man by his ankles into the kitchen. He leaned against the wall. This kind of violence embarrassed and sickened him. The skinny Italian, the one that had hit the woman and smiled, struck a match and lit the gas on the oven. The other one lifted the man by his shoulders and shoved his head in the gaping door, then laughed and turned the flame all the way up. Briody walked to the back of the room and stared out the window at the courtyard between the buildings. There were a dozen or more lines of bright white laundry stirring lightly in the breeze. A young boy of about three sat on the ground and with a stick fashioned as a gun he was taking aim and shouting bang, bang at pigeons that lined the railing.

The man came to and screamed, bucking to get his head out of the oven while the Italians struggled to hold him down. In the process his boxer shorts slipped off and his bare white ass, marbled with fat, was all Briody could see of the man. The smell of burning hair filled the room, a grotesque perfume. They kept working him over while quietly explaining that the Empire State Building policy was no longer to be shared with him.

When they felt they had made their point they walked out, leaving the man lying on his kitchen floor, blubbering with his eyebrows singed off, bald from the flame. He looked like a giant cooked baby. In the hallway the wife was crawling toward her husband weeping, her mouth hanging open slack at an unnatural angle, the mandible snapped, blood trickling down her chin. As they passed her the skinny one turned, shouted "*puttana*," and kicked her so hard in the ass that she was lifted a foot off the ground. Her scream was choked up in her broken mouth. The Italians paused and burst into laughter, the violence passing like a dark cloud clearing the sun.

Outside on the street, Briody was surprised to find the sky just as blue as they had left it. The skinny Italian, still smiling, waved him into the waiting car. Briody stared at him hard and said, "No. I'll be taking the IRT. But thanks." He watched the smile leave the man's face, which darkened like his eyes. Briody fought the urge to punch that face right through the window. The man muttered something in Italian back over his shoulder, and as the car sped away all Briody could make out was the word "Irisher," spat like an epithet.

Grace worked off a scaffold until her arms ached and her shoulders were swollen from the effort. The mural work was her favorite. She had called Briody's friend Casey and the men who ran Tara Hall, the new Irish center where various fraternal organizations were to meet, hired her on the spot. It was easy to know who they wanted, their immortals, their martyrs and fighters and dreamers and madmen who aspired to only one thing, a kind of freedom. She thought many of them were lucky to have something to fight so fiercely for, to be removed from the mundane fate of so many others. She liked to wonder what these men would have become had they no tyranny to oppose, no battle to join. Would they live dull lives or make messes of everything around them? Could they have settled, the ones from the country as farmers, the city boys as clerks? Did they need to set the world on fire? Did circumstances make the man or was it the other way around?

She had used pencil to sketch an outline. The large north wall she worked first. Easter 1916, the most famous of all the glorious failures. She remembered her father glowing with pride as word of the uprising swept through their village, causing people to come out and chatter about the news slowly drifting to them. Many of their neighbors were put off by the violence at first, had considered the Dublin crowd to be reckless buffoons. She worked intently trying to capture something of their doomed energy, a quickened sense of the fear and adrenaline. She tried to imagine the taste of black powder, the scream of the shells, the keen of the wounded. She wondered at their second thoughts, the awful feeling of monumental blunder, of self-destruction. She remembered reading somewhere about an American Civil War battle of satanic devastation and how so few of the thousands of weapons recovered had actually been fired. All the chaos and slaughter perpetrated by so few of the combatants, the ones, she figured, with a taste for blood. She had trouble imagining violence on such a large and impersonal scale. Her violence had always been personal and direct, singular in its effect.

As she worked she tried to telescope the raw scenes of action, to let each of the men have his own response to it. She knew enough about tribulation to know everyone reacted individually to it. She stopped to make some tea and was amazed to find it was four o'clock. The day had just evaporated on her. She cleaned her brushes and stored everything on a bottom shelf in the custodian's closet.

The man Casey came in and stood back, looking at her work. He was short but had a forceful presence and she knew the type. He was a true believer and no one or no thing might deter him from whatever cause he had taken up. The Irish countryside was full of them. Some became priests, some the ranting drunks, and a few, like this one she guessed, became something else entirely.

"Michael was not exaggerating a bit. Not lying about you at all. It's amazing stuff." Casey gaped at the mural and Grace had the odd feeling that he was picturing himself enshrined there among the rebel greats, like a boy putting himself in the middle of a radio play.

Another man, dressed in a suit, his white hair perfect, came and stood next to Casey. There was something about the man she did not like. He stared at her, not the work. He merely looked impatient. Then he said, "How do you know Michael Briody?"

It sounded more like an accusation than a question. Grace was not sure what to say so she answered, "From home. From Cavan."

"Is that so?" Again, a question like an accusation.

She shrugged, thinking she had already said much too much to this cold-faced man. But oddly, she did feel as if she had known Briody for a very long time. She gathered her sweater and left the men admiring all their dead heroes.

. . .

A h Monkey. I wish I had the zeal of youth to combat these men. I'm no match for them, none at all. Maybe I never should have sought reelection."

"Ah Jimsie, don't talk like that. I can't stand to hear it. You're the best mayor this city has ever had. Second to none."

"You're a kind, kind girl. You would think all I ever did was make myself and a few fat men rich. Where is all my money? Ah Monkey, if they had any idea at all."

"Ah Jimsie, I hate when you get all morose. That sourpuss kills me. Let's have a good time. Things will work out fine. You're the Mayor, and that's one thing they can't take away from you. What are they gonna do, un-elect you? They can't. It would be down-right un-American."

"How do you know, my little Canadian?"

"Knock it off. The people love you. They're crazy about you. Everywhere we go all they want to do is be near the great Jimmy Walker. I see it all the time with my own eyes."

She straddled him on the couch and put her hands inside his robe. "I know, let's go to the racetrack, drink champagne and play the ponies."

"Come on now, Monk, it's Sunday. You know where I have to be."

"That cow." She leapt off him and stormed into the other room, where there followed a series of door slams, shouts, and curses.

Walker smiled. Women. He took off his robe and proceeded to dress. He looked forward to seeing his wife. Through all the years she had stayed a very dear and close friend, understood him in a way that neither Monk nor anybody else ever would. She knew him before he put up screens, locked parts of himself away from the world. And as much as his very open relationship with Betty hurt and shamed her, she chose to remain his friend. He knew that if the roles were reversed, forget it. He put his tea down on top of the ed-itorial. They had a point—the city was certainly in the hands of racketeers. Imagine the horror it would provoke in their cozy offices if they knew the extent to which it really was.

Finished with her tantrum, Betty came back in and adjusted his tie, fussed over his collar, and rubbed her perfumed fingers through his hair, marking her turf. Walker stared at his face in the mirror, seeing the lines and furrows. He missed the Tin Pan Alley days when he was the hot-stuff songwriter, the Broadway sport. God, it seemed like centuries ago. Even in his years in Albany as a legislator, when he stood before the gallery and speechified, turned words into action, a sort of poetry. He was never cut out to be a boss, to have to make all the ugly decisions that required. He was an accommodator, a showman, the guy who loved to deliver the good news. When he signed on to run for mayor, Charlie Murphy was still alive and the title of mayor did not include the duty of boss. That was Charlie's job and he was a master at it.

But the buffoons who had succeeded Murphy were not up to the task, and somehow Walker had to make up for their shortcomings. Unfortunately, he found he was wholly inept at the art of saying no. People took advantage. All these bums he had made, all their successes they owed to him and his connections—once they got a taste of largesse they forgot everything. All they did was come back with outstretched palms. More and more and more, gimme, gimme, gimme. Where was their loyalty? There was none.

He loved this city, and despite what the howlers for his scalp said, he believed it was a far better place now than when they were running it and the ghettos were filled with offal and filth and child prostitutes. They sat in their plush chairs uptown and railed against everything, but where were they when it mattered? They urged their Republican lackeys in Albany to fight every single advancement he and his colleagues proposed, anything that might allow the poor to have an easier time of it. What did they come up with? What was their grand solution to the problems of the poor and the exploited, the destitute? Why, Prohibition. And now that bodies were piled to the sky they still howled like the damned over a man enjoying a night out and a little booze. They were fools and, worse, hypocrites. He fastened his cuff links and pulled on his jacket. He checked the mirror again and made sure his hair was just right. He hugged Betty, who was reading a novel on the bed, and set out.

He had to admire them, these bootleggers, and in a way give them their due. They had started life as guttersnipes, not a one was given anything by this life but a good kick in the pants. Now they were partners in running the great metropolis, and he suspected their power would grow because it was based on the two black gods of fear and greed. One or the other could accomplish just about anything, could motivate the most obstinate or righteous of men. He'd like to see his more prominent detractors fill his shoes for a day and deal with the beast they helped to create.

On the way downtown, he ordered the driver to stop at Bergdorf Goodman, where he had had the manager summoned to open for some private Sunday shopping. He selected a diamond bracelet for Allie. It was a false offering, he knew, and his guilt cut like a knife. Still, he wanted to show he was thoughtful and appreciative.

There was a car sitting in front of his town house on St. Luke's Place.

A police captain, grim and severe in his uniform, approached him. "Seven dead." He stared at his shoes and continued, "Includes a five-year-old boy."

Walker felt all the joy go out of the day. "Booze?"

"What else?"

"How?"

"By the looks of it, a hijack went wrong."

Church bells pealed as women in summer dresses walked hand in hand with their children, going to and from houses of worship. The trees that lined the street touched over the block of town houses. He stood holding the gift. "Get a statement to the press. Express the appropriate outrage. Assign a dozen of the best detectives to bring these hoodlums to heel."

The captain stepped back and saluted crisply, then jogged to his car. Walker took out his handkerchief and wiped his face clean of sweat. Seven more dead. When would it end?

Allie, thick around the middle, dressed in a plain brown church dress, waited on the steps. Good old Allie. He forced a smile for her. She'd have the Sunday dinner cooking, let him put his feet up and smoke his pipe. Her sitting room was like a little cocoon, a place where he might hide from the world. He made out to Betty that this was a chore, some hard duty he was required to perform, but in truth he took great comfort in it. He turned and, bearing gifts, made his way to the warm embrace of his oldest love.

S ome crazy business, killing kindergarten kids, isn't it, Mrs. Conklin?"

"What is this city coming to?" Grace answered, then stepped out of the Bank of the Metropolis on Forty-fourth Street into swampy summer air. Yesterday's beer-war bloodshed was splashed in black ink on the front page of every paper in town. Over breakfast she had not been able to read about it at all.

It was lunchtime and men out for breaks had pulled their ties loose against the heat and carried their jackets slung over their shoulders. On the corner a shaved-ice monger offered a choice of coconut, chocolate, lemon, or cherry for a penny apiece. She chose lemon and decided to continue on downtown and visit Isabel Bishop's studio. At Times Square army trucks dispensed tepid soup to lines of bedraggled men who stared at their feet or the backs of heads in front of them, as if even conversation was too much effort in the heat. The Camel cigarette sign blew smoke rings that immediately fell apart in the fat air. The entire city seemed to sweat: the buildings, the statues, even the cars and trolleys and trucks that rattled past spitting black smoke. Still, Grace did not mind it. After summers in Andalusia and Cuba, this heat was bearable.

At Thirty-seventh Street a man in a khaki suit and white fedora hooked her elbow and, squeezing hard, said, "Keep walking, sister, and we'll all get along just fine."

Grace dropped the remains of her ice and felt her knees buckle as she was dragged along the sidewalk. She caught a profile of the man's face and knew exactly who it was. She had been expecting this moment for some time. A car rolled slowly beside them, keeping pace. Sunlight played off the window, making it impossible to see the faces of those inside. She made out shapes of hatted men in the front seat. But they made no movement toward the car. The man squeezed her arm harder. She forced herself to be calm.

"You might be scared, you ought to be. You are in over your head. Now, who am I? you might wonder. That is not of great concern. You will know when you need to. Just consider me a duality of possibilities. I can be either your best friend or your worst nightmare, savvy? That choice is yours to make."

He steered her through a brown steel door into a half-lit room where several men perched on barstools gaped at the wall. No one paid them any mind. He sat her at a table and took the seat across from her. He waved off the glum waiter. He spread a handful of peanuts in front of him, popped one in his mouth, shell and all, and continued, "I'm not after you. I am not even after your boyfriend. Either of them. That's right. I know more about you than you want to hear."

"I don't do anything."

"Oh, but you do. You sleep with men who are not your husband. You paint pictures. You befriend winos and degenerates. You parade around dressed like a man. You do all these things, none of which concerns me. But what you do that I am interested in is, you spend a lot of time in banks, don't you?"

Grace assumed that he had limited knowledge. He might know what banks she went to, but she doubted he knew what went on inside. She decided to play along, to give him enough to make him go away for now. "I put money in boxes."

"You put money in boxes."

"That's all."

"Good. Then you have nothing to fear from me. We can help one another. We can be pals, best of friends."

"So why should I help you at all, if I have nothing to fear?"

"I was referring to your boxes, the ones you put money in. I got you six ways to Sunday. On top of it all you're running around with that pack of commies. You keep doing what you're doing, give me a list of names, names and places, and don't get cute with me. 'Cause you want to act wise, and best-case scenario you're on a boat back to potatoland, worst, and they find your remains twenty years down the line. I'm the last guy you want to toy with, got me?"

Grace nodded her head. At a casual glance he was nondescript, mild even. But a close look and she saw it. It was in the eyes and the set of the mouth. The pockmarks, the slight but sinewy build, a coiled malevolence. Here was someone who had been done wrong and had let hatred become part of his bone structure, his being. There was a darkness in him, a danger, and of all the nuts and killers and psychos she had encountered since moving to New York, this man scared her more than any of them.

"I got you," she told him.

"I am not out to destroy you. I'll give you a number. Once a week you call and give me an update on your boxes and the money. This is all I request. I want to know what you know, and if I do, I will protect you. Because, sister, you are in way over your sweet little head. My name is Jack, that's all you need to know."

Grace looked at the table before her. It was polka-dotted with cigarette burns and notched with so many initials that they canceled each other out, so there was no record of any of them being here. Someone in a back room played a saxophone badly. Jack studied his nails. His flesh was pink and hard and his eyes looked right through her. She had trouble meeting them. She figured it best to play along. Was this someone Johnny would worry about? She knew there was no way anyone could know what went on in the vaults. She could feed him a series of lies and deceptions. She was in control, if only she let him think otherwise.

"Please. This has come as a shock to you. Take a night to sleep on it. Call me tomorrow with your answer."

She wanted to be out of there. The air was stale and hot, and the few patrons had the look of corpses, pale with sunken eyes and lost hope. She nodded, attempted a subservient smile.

"And sister? Your hotshot has a lot of juice, but this is beyond him. Trust me." He slipped her a card with a number on it and indicated the door. She was free to go.

On the street she took in great gulps of air and walked east as fast as she could. She passed crowds of window-shoppers and merchants standing in their doorways to comment on the weather. The city was alive with color and movement and she was glad to be out of that fetid room and among the truly alive. At Park Avenue she turned north. Outside the new Waldorf a line of hansom cabs waited for the tourists that did not seem to be coming to the city anymore. The reek of horse piss cleared her head and she turned the corner and crossed to the Shelton Hotel on Lexington Avenue, Johnny's new choice for their trysts.

She went in past the smiling doorman and took the elevator to the top floor. She paced the room trying to calm down and figure the best course of action. She decided on a swim in the basement pool. It would help her focus. In the women's locker room she pulled on her suit and tied her hair up, covering her head with a bathing cap emblazoned with the hotel emblem. The tile floor was cold under her feet but a slight steam rose from the water's surface and the smell of chlorine burned her nose. There were lounge chairs around the perimeter of the pool, but only two were occupied, both by big women reading fashion magazines and smoking cigarettes. The attendant watched her as she stood on the edge of the pool, curling her toes. She dove. As she cut with easy strokes through the blue water she knew. A plan took shape. She was going to put together a stash. She willed herself to believe that she was going to come out on top. It was up to her. She did not need to flounder anymore, she would keep doing what she was doing, make the calls to this Jack, and keep Farrell in the dark. Then, when the time was right, she would run. The only thing she feared was Briody not going with her.

When she pulled herself out of the chlorine-rich water the pool boy stood holding a towel for her with a hunger in his eyes. "I ever tell you, that Houdini guy, he was underwater here for an hour and thirty-one minutes. I was on duty that day, case anything went wrong. Maybe his magic don't work."

"We could all use a little magic, can't we now?" A disappearing act, that's what she needed.

"I guess that's on the level."

Back in the room there was a note from Farrell saying he would be late. It was just what she wanted to hear.

. . .

After a long night of guarding another Touhey card game, Briody nearly ran to the site, happier than ever to be back to honest labor. As he passed into the belly of the building he caught up with Armstrong.

"Hey Mickey. How they hanging? I'll be glad to get up in the air today. The only thing that cleans my head out anymore. How was last night?"

"A little bit of good and a little bit of bad."

"That's life."

"So it is."

They joined the gaggle of men waiting for the lift. It was a brilliantly clear day. He did not think he could work on one of the crews inside the building, the plumbers or electricians or carpenters, because to him that was nothing more than factory work. As the cage ascended the din started up and Briody winced against its force. When they arrived at the upper deck Sheehan and Delpezzo were waiting for them.

They took turns riding the headache ball up to their stations, which were two stories above the derrick platforms. As Briody clung to the cable and rose above the city he felt an exhilaration he knew few people could imagine: the metropolis lay beneath his feet, dozens of stories beneath him, the cars and people antlike now in their distance. Here, in the sky, he felt most at home. He joined his crew on the scaffold. Just below them, the riggers were waiting with the first beam of the day. The derrick plank floor was all set and the connectors idled above them, anxious for work. Sheehan checked to see if the rivet forge was ready. He nodded and Armstrong signaled to the derrick men. Briody watched as the connectors secured the next beam. He turned back to his own gang, and as soon as Armstrong bucked up he was hammering away with the rivet gun. Up here nothing could touch him, not the screams, not the lousy work he did for Tommy Touhey, not the problems with Danny and the Clan-na-Gael. No, nothing reached him here, not even the muck and blood and horror of his past.

At lunch they stayed put on the beams, toasting their sand-wiches on the rivet forge. Sheehan talked with a full mouth. "Re-member we was working on 40 Wall Street when they had that crash. I seen a guy crawl out on the window ledge. It's real narrow, those streets, and the guy, he can't be more than fifty feet apart from where I'm standing. He's blubbering like a baby. At first, I had no idea what the hell was going on."

"You think he was out there, what, cleaning the windows?" Armstrong was pulling onions off a roll and flinging them out into space. They caught the sun as they floated over the city, little glow-ing disks fluttering on the jet stream.

"What do I know? You guys were down at lunch. Anyway, he looks me straight in the eye and it starts to dawn on me that this mope is gonna fly. I don't know what to think 'cause he's staring at me like he's looking for advice. I just shake my head no. He shakes his head yes. I shake my head no and off he goes, splat. I look down and there's blood all over the place. It looked like he was lying on a red blanket—except one of his legs was about a half a block away. Then this big crowd gathers round to see him."

"What'd you do?" Briody asked.

"Me? I finished my sandwich and go back to work. What else could I do? I spend all day making sure not to fall and I need to see some joker do it on purpose? The poor slob, the last face he looked into before he dies is me. Ha! What a way to go."

"I would have jumped, too," Armstrong said.

"Well, it's not too late."

Armstrong took out a pocket flask and tipped his head back, taking a long pull. Briody caught the whiff of whiskey on the rising breeze. Delpezzo shook his head and pulled his gloves on. They went back to work and bent themselves to nailing down the last story of the week, the fifth in five days, a pace never even attempted until now.

Briody's hands and forearms were numb when the bell sounded and the paymaster finally reached them. Hard Nose McCabe waved them down. "All right ladies. We're done for the week."

The paymaster waited for them to climb down to the decking. "You monkeys don't think I'm gonna come up there to give you your money, do you?" He handed out pay envelopes. "Don't spend it all in one place now."

Armstrong locked up the gang box and waved his pay envelope in the air. "Come on, let's go pay our dues and drink and fight and screw everything that moves."

Briody was glad to go along. Touhey had given him the weekend off for covering a Thursday night game, and he knew that Grace was tied up with the lawyer Farrell. Jealousy was a tough thing to keep at bay, but he was managing, for now. Besides, he had a week of hanging steel behind him and the release of a crowded barroom and laughter was enough to look forward to.

Men spilled out of the site. Most took the cages, others raced down the stairs, some rode down on headache balls and still others jumped from as high as the third floor, hitting sand piles with thumps and shouts as they picked themselves up and brushed off the sand. Briody thought passersby might assume that the building was about to collapse the way the men hastened out of it. They were bouncing on the balls of their feet, a week's work behind them and thirst money in their pockets. The shadow of their monument was larger and longer than it had been on Monday and they were closer to the dole lines, but these facts did nothing to dampen their zeal to build faster than anyone ever had.

Briody moved along with all of them, the immigrants and native-born; some, the young and lithe, moved easily, while others walked stiffly, wearing the accumulation of past jobs and the wear and tear of their labors, scars and nicks, mended bones, and creaky joints. A few peeled off to head home but most did not. It was time for drink and release.

They spilled through a nondescript wooden door behind which was a beer hall half the length of a football field. Until a few months earlier it had housed a publisher that churned out turgid pamphlets and texts calling for the violent demise of capitalism. As a rebuttal, federal agents had hired a goon squad to bust the place up. In the aftermath a trio of sharp college men had calculated the thirst potential of the nearby wonder of the world and decided it would be silly not to create a way station for the men. The saloon had prospered beyond even their ambitious estimates. Such success creates notice, and soon underworld kingpins took the three on as partners. The entire operation strived to redirect as much of the Empire State payroll as possible. The men referred to it as the Cave.

Briody and his gang elbowed out a niche at one of the two bars that stretched the length of each wall. Tradesmen tended to drink in cliques, plumbers with plumbers, tin knockers with tin knockers, and so forth. The beers came fast and frosty and they all slapped money on the wood before them. Briody noticed a man sitting at a round table toward the back of the room, men forming a line to see him.

"Let the fun begin." Armstrong made a habit of dumping a shot from his flask into each mug. Soon, a quartet of doors at the back of the hall sprung open and dozens of party girls poured through and made their way to the throaty roars of the men. The workers quickly made their hungers known. Some snatched the first girl that came by and took them to the upstairs rooms rented in twenty-minute allotments. In alcoves on either side were gaming tables crowded with men eager to chance their week's pay. Men shouted and waved greenbacks, anxious for the big score. Others were content with the booze. Presently Armstrong led several women to their square yard of bar and introduced them all around before taking one, a brunette with sad eyes, and escorting her toward a third of an hour of blissful commerce.

Sheehan and Delpezzo, being dutifully married, played and flirted but declined the upstairs interlude offered by their perfumed friends, who soon moved on. Briody enjoyed the spectacle, but even knowing Grace was with Farrell, he could not think of another woman's embrace. He was besotted and there was nothing he could do about it even if he wanted to. He certainly would not belittle that by consorting with one of these made-up and desperate women, a number of whom he knew were selling themselves only because of the times. He smiled and laughed at their come-ons but turned his back to them.

Armstrong returned grinning, holding up his arms and making muscles, the pirate after a successful pillaging. "You nancy boys don't know what you're missing."

"What's that, a dose of the clap?"

"You got these dames all wrong. That one was saving for the college. Gonna be a teacher, too."

"Providing scholarships these days, huh?"

"I provided all right."

Briody watched as three men in suits and fedoras came through the door and headed directly for the man sitting at the table in the rear of the room. The slenderest of the three led the way. The other two flanked him and their eyes moved over the crowd with steely deliberation. As they approached the table the man stood quickly and smiled and as he extended his hand he bowed his head perceptibly, his manner turning instantly from one of dominance to one of subservience. The slender man extended his hand not so much to shake the other's as to allow him to touch it. After homage was paid they walked as a group through a door that closed behind them, leaving the man at the desk to continue his business.

Armstrong had been watching the procession in the mirror. "You see this shit? The greaseballs took things over and now we got to kick back, just to keep our jobs."

Briody raised an eyebrow.

"Jesus, you dopey donkey." He leaned in closer, his head almost resting on Briody's shoulder. "That's THE DAGO," he said in a stage whisper.

"The gangster?" Briody played dumb. One of the men with him was the nasty one from the Bronx, the short Italian that had taken such pleasure in torture.

"Yep, King Guinea himself. Wannabe lord of the underworld."

Briody ordered them more beers. He said nothing of his connection to Touhey and Touhey's connections to the man who had just walked through the room. He nursed his beer and considered the imminent weekend. He was planning on a nice quiet one. He'd promised to take Danny's kids to the zoo.

They went as a gang to the back of the room where a man sat at a table with two hard cases standing behind and to either side of him. A line of workers made their way one at a time to the seated man and placed money on the table before him. He wore black-rimmed glasses and a short-sleeve button-down white shirt that exposed thick, hairy arms. His bulbous nose was crooked and smashed in the middle. Some men on the line paid off gambling debts, others placed bets, but all paid the new tribute, a kickback for being able to work while so few had jobs. It was a straight ten percent of your pay, like it or not.

"Will you look at this piece of shit? Maybe if I had to pay a whiter man it wouldn't bother me so much." Armstrong's hot whiskey breath hung in the air. "You know the difference is when you Mick creeps were running things you took money from the guys that gambled, from guys wanted to give up their money. These Africans force you to pay whether you want to or not. That's a whole different thing entirely."

Briody looked over at the man. "He looks white enough to me."

"Yeah, well, looks can be deceiving."

"That so?"

"Yeah, well I know." He looked at his arms and stared into the mirror. "One hundred percent white, one hundred percent American."

Delpezzo made like he had not heard him and Sheehan shook his head.

"Worse than all that is look at this beach ball. Three minutes of work would kill him and he sits there getting rich off of all of us, all my hard work."

"That's the way it goes." Sheehan was trying to douse his ire.

"Bullshit it is."

"It's all the same. Just the cost of doing business. Would you rather be out of work?" Delpezzo was resigned.

"I could break that pudgy creep over my knee. Taking the workingman's money like somehow he's owed it."

Briody's turn came and he placed a five-dollar bill and three dirty singles on the table before the man. The man looked up at him, expectant.

"Briody. Ironworker."

The man nodded, peering over his glasses, made a mark on a

sheet. Briody stepped back and to the side, keeping an eye on Armstrong.

"Hey, how are you? Working hard today?" Armstrong asked the seated man.

The man looked up, a hint of a smile on his face. Armstrong was laughing, appearing good-natured. The man sat back and looked side to side at his muscle, who went from their heels to the balls of their feet.

"Oh. Right." He dug in his pockets. "I suppose I owe you something. Chubby."

The air got a little tighter. "Hey, you take a joke? A ha-ha? Way I look at it, you take my money, least you can do, fat boy, is take a little joke with it." Armstrong dropped a five on the table and when the man leaned forward slightly and reached for it Armstrong grabbed his hand and pulled him easily out of the seat. The goons moved off the wall, but Armstrong had his fingers firmly on their boss's throat. "Come on, another step and I snap his neck like a pigeon. A big fat pigeon." He pulled the man close and, leaning down, said, "I just want to ask you, fat boy, you ever work a day in your life? Have you? Come on, have you? You got the balls to sit here and take money from each and every one of these guys who break their asses all week long?" He ripped the man's shirt off, exposing his white belly, topped by fat breasts.

Briody placed a hand on Armstrong's shoulder. "Come on, let him go."

"Just say no. 'Cause I know that's the answer."

The man let out a whimper of a no and Armstrong dropped him to the table, then tossed his five on top of him. "There's your money for nothing."

The two goons came around the table but Armstrong, backed by a large group of workers, stood his ground. The man gasped threats that no one could make out and Briody grabbed Armstrong by the elbow and led him through the crush and out to the street.

The gang stayed together until they were back at the site and sure they weren't being followed. Sheehan and Delpezzo moved off, shaking their heads in mutual disappointment and worry over Armstrong.

"I'm gonna go back upstairs and shoot some craps. You wanna come?"

"No, John. I'm off home."

"You spot me a sawbuck?"

"Don't you think you should go home, too?"

He nodded to the building. "Who you kidding? This is my home. Just like it's yours. We ain't like those other guys with wives and kids and responsibilities to go to at nights and weekends. This is where we belong. The job is everything to us, Mick."

Briody handed him a twenty. "Forty hours a week suits me to the ground. I'd stay out of the Cave for a while. Those fellas don't like to be messed around with."

"Weasels and wimps, I'll take any five of them at once, make that ten."

"I don't think you're bulletproof, man."

"I'm an ironworker, Paddy. I'm invincible. Just like you." Armstrong bent his knees and wrapped his arms around Briody's waist, lifting him easily into the air before setting him down.

"One can only hope." Briody watched Armstrong disappear back into the building, then joined the pedestrian traffic heading west. He knew the type of animal they were dealing with. To save Armstrong he would have to go to Tommy Touhey and ask a favor that he was not sure even he could grant.

A s the summer heat deepened they just fell into the rhythms of each other's lives. She would meet him after the day was done at a café and they would share a meal. Sometimes they went back to her boat, others they lay together in the cramped and dark space of his room, like drifters on the run, tracing the outlines of each other's bodies, always, it seemed, coupling.

She worried about facing Farrell and about his wrath. She started to entertain notions of flight, of leaving New York altogether, but reeled herself in. Farrell was increasingly caught up in his various machinations and summoned her less often and for this she was grateful. A couple of times a week she would go by the hotel and there would be envelopes waiting for her. She did her banking and called the man Jack and told him lies. She never knew she was so good at it.

On a sweltering Tuesday she lay entwined in the sheets and while pretending to sleep watched Briody dress for work. First he stood naked for a moment, staring out onto the river. Then he quietly gathered his clothes, pulling on his socks and underwear, his muscles milky in the dawn light. He stepped into his trousers and pulled his T-shirt over his head. He sat on the edge of the bed and laced his work boots tight. She closed her eyes as he bent over and bussed her forehead lightly so as not to disturb her. The soft touch of his breath gave her a chill. Then the boat rocked and he was gone into the day.

She was falling in love with Briody and worried at the prospect of being vulnerable. She got up, dressed, and after a cup of strong black coffee sat at her easel. She mixed dull earth tones and painted from drawings she had made at the Empire State site on an overcast day when the only bold colors were the bandannas some of the men wore. The piece described the bowels of the building, where a nonstop flood of heavy trucks passed through, disgorging block and brick, cement, wire and pipe, windows by the hundred, the raw materials for the site. Since meeting Briody she was painting better than ever and she doubted it was a coincidence.

Later, past lunch, she put the painting aside and cleaned her brushes. She picked up a stack of life drawings she had done of Briody. She spread them on the floor in front of her and stared at the likeness of the man who had come so fully into her life. How had she let this happen? She noticed that despite the physicality of him, the muscled assuredness, his eyes described something else, something she had repeatedly captured without being conscious of it: he had the eyes of one who saw too much, the eyes of a poet. She smiled but then she thought how he contrasted with Farrell. Edginess about the Tammany man and about his dirty money cooled all enthusiasms. She had told Briody none of it, and was beginning to feel as if she was betraying him. She gathered up the drawings and lay down on the cool sheets of the bed. She could smell him still on the pillow, but it could not comfort her, for she knew a reckoning was coming.

In the gym, Tommy Touhey came in and watched him train.

"I need to be able to get ahold of you."

"I go to work every day."

"You say that like it's a grand achievement."

"Take a look at the skyline."

"It's hard to miss, but it don't get your case dropped."

"I thought it was a done deal."

"The Judge is playing cute. Says some well-dressed men—educated guys—from the State Department have been to see him. More than once."

Briody could suddenly taste the hot dead air of the gym. He turned and beat a rhythmic tattoo on the speed bag, ignoring Touhey until the round was over. "What do you need?"

"They only hold so much sway over a state judge. He's more ours than theirs. Turns out there's a guy missing. The way they're after him he must be related to the Queen or something. I told you they were fanatics, your donkey pals. They're in America and they still want to fight some lost and old war. The Irish. Me, I am a pragmatic guy. I'm looking to make everyone happy, let everyone think they got at least part of what they want and most of what they need."

Briody picked up a dumbbell. Touhey stood beside him, his foot on the ring apron, and watched two middleweights go at it while Briody squeezed off curls.

"And another thing. I know you're making time with Johnny Farrell's girl."

Briody stopped and dropped the dumbbell. It crashed to the floor and rolled away all the way to the wall where it hit with a loud clank. He looked hard at Touhey.

"Hey, I'm okay with that. He's on my bad side anyway. Just, you need to know, this city, it runs on information, it runs on knowledge, and nobody seems able to keep a secret. Because these secrets they're a kind of currency that people trade back and forth. A barter system. Anyway, like I said in the past, I like you and right now I don't like Johnny Farrell so very much. My boyhood pal. I think you are a lot better at understanding the notion of loyalty."

"I just need to understand enough to keep healthy."

"Now Farrell, he's a pip-squeak, but he's a dangerous pip-squeak because he looks out for number one and that's it. I need you to get out of the girl what he does and who he sees, as much as possible. I think my old pal might just be trying to arrange for my departure from the scene, and less than peacefully. That's something I need to avoid."

"We don't spend much time talking about Johnny Farrell."

"No, I doubt you do. I'm just telling you what you don't want is Johnny Farrell ever talking about you. He likes to hold on to what he thinks is his, right or wrong."

Briody shrugged and pulled his bag gloves back on. He felt the need to hit something.

"I know you're a tough guy, but this won't be a Marquess of Queensberry-type situation between you and little Johnny Farrell. He has a lot of unpleasant friends and lately he's made a few more. You've seen them in action."

Briody decided to play along. He told Touhey about Armstrong manhandling the bagman at the Cave and asked that he intervene.

"I can probably handle that."

"Good, I'll see what I can see."

"Compromise, the great American way."

Briody nodded and watched the gangster leave. Johnny Farrell was a concern but it was the other thing, the Feds nosing around and asking about what had become of the man from the Free State, that bothered him. Love might be a deadly thing, but nationalism, now that was something that knew no reason. When the bell clanged he turned back to the bag and pounded his doubts away.

. . .

God, the heat was still awful. He stood in the night shadow of the El as a downtown train rattled overhead reading the latest news from home in *The Irish Echo*, waiting for Danny to come along. The evening had brought no relief from the hot wet air and he yearned for a cold beer but was afraid of letting his guard down. He was at the center of too many dangerous intersections and could not help but feel exposed, as if he might fail in many ways. His talent lately seemed to be in making enemies, real and potential.

Danny skipped down the stairs and grabbed him by the arm. "O'Brien told me. It's not something to worry about. They are putting together a little list, some intelligence. They are looking for ways to turn someone around."

"Are you saying this is not about yer man landing on the bottom of the Hell Gate?"

"A mere detail they want to clear up, no doubt. But nothing is any different here than in Ireland. They want to know who we are and what we are up to. But here we have as much leverage as they do and certainly as many friends. They can't harm us here, Michael."

"Touhey tells me these are men from Washington."

"The appeasing of foreign governments is a bit of a hobby for the federal men. I am not worried about them and neither should you be. Look at Prohibition if you want to judge the effectiveness of the federal agencies. Speaking of which, why are we meeting here and not at a cozy and cool saloon, a place where we might slake our thirsts?"

Briody was tempted. He needed to put up some walls but he hoped he could still count Danny as a friend and ally. "I need to meet someone else, so I'll have to pass. How's the wee ones?"

"They miss your company."

"Give them my regards. Tell Danny I'll be taking him to a baseball game soon."

"You too, with the baseball now."

"How's the union going?"

"It's a dirty little war. We should be thankful that the Irish so-called Free State and the Brits are not as resourceful and underhanded as these rail companies. Fierce bastards they are with a spy network the envy of the Raj."

"I'll wager they've met their match."

"Let's hope."

"I'm off now." Briody pushed away from the shadows.

"Michael, keep well. All this intrigue will sort itself out soon enough and remember we go back a long, long time and I will always be looking after you."

Briody crossed the avenue and ducked down the stairs for the train downtown. He believed Danny, he truly did.

Touhey had sent his family down to the Jersey shore, and with them out of the house he took to sleeping in different rooms each night. During the hot and long days he made a point of being visible, to not be seen as a man who feared. Still, he had men stationed at key intersections, on rooftops and in the windows of shops lining the main streets of his embattled domain, watching. He carried his gun at all times, its cold steel reassuring against the small of his back. The stress, the heightened animal level of alert, induced nostalgia. He played out the days of his youth like a film reel in his mind flickering with the light and shadows of the past. He indulged in great suppers at the steakhouses of the neighborhood, savoring meats and debating a last meal in his head. He settled on a T-bone, potatoes with cheese sauce, and sweet corn, then changed his mind to rack of lamb. He considered the pros and cons of a bloody last stand. He doled out cash and favors like a man without worry. He slept with his clothes on.

He awaited the message, a blow that would be the opening salvo of negotiations. He had given them some, but he knew it was not enough and just the act of compromise meant he had shown a weakness they would seek to exploit. It would never be enough and that is what Johnny Farrell could not see. His old buddy had sold his soul to the new boys in town and was blind to the facts. Tommy Touhey was getting used to the idea that his reign might be over.

On a steamy night he was jolted awake by the explosion. He grabbed his gun and ran barefoot down to the street. The Four Provinces was ablaze. Glass from several adjacent storefronts littered the street, reflecting the fire like burning embers. He slipped the gun into his pants pocket and watched as the firemen arrived and a crowd gathered. Neighbors hung out of windows, propped on pillows. Residents of damaged buildings, some naked but for sheets or towels, were led into the street. Touhey wondered whether they understood the significance of the attack, whether they knew their lives were changing.

Mannion showed up, his one constant. The oversized killer stood staring at the ruins. Touhey thought he might cry. "What are we gonna do, Tommy? Somebody has to pay."

"Oh, they will. Mark my words, they will." Touhey did not have the heart to tell Mannion that it was all over for them.

After the fire was out the street ran with cold, blackened water. Touhey sat for a while on the stoop of his building and squeezed his pants cuffs dry. It was time for plan B. He had thought it out long ago. He'd let the beer routes go. It was a lot of work for not enough return. He'd keep his whiskey and sell the high-end stuff like a boutique operation, his fighters and of course his cab company, the card games. He decided on optimism. It was merely a tactical retreat from business that had become too volatile, too hot. Hey, he was alive.

ough Tommy Touhey, I mean what the hell is the world coming to?"

Johnny Farrell sat with Egan in the steam room of the NYAC letting the heat stew out the booze. He shrugged at the Captain's question. "The only constant is change, Egan. You seen enough of it."

"I don't see him, of all people, going without a fight."

"Tommy's no dummy."

"He's no pushover either."

"Those who don't bend tend to break."

"You don't seem too concerned. I thought he was your Bronx guy."

"There's a lot of guys in the Bronx."

Apart from him and Egan the room was empty except for a skinny man he knew in passing about the club. He had been picking up a lot of snippets of bad intelligence, little nuggets of whisper and rumors of storms gathering. He did his best to sift through these and attach appropriate significance to each bit of information, to assess threats, to dismiss the cranks and pranks. He bent over so he was staring straight at the ground and the sweat poured off of him. He sat back and leaned against the tile wall, running his fingers through his hair.

"I need you to do me a favor. It appears someone is nosing around. It might be nothing, it might be something. My girl, Grace. She has been doing a little banking for us. Someone has seen fit to tail her. We really do need to know who and why. And we need to see they desist."

"Got you, boss. Who do you see replacing Touhey?"

"You'd be surprised how many men are waiting to try."

They stopped to get their shoes shined in the lobby. While the bootblack worked his magic Farrell opened the paper and there was Touhey's joint in the Bronx, the front collapsed onto the street. He was not surprised, really. On both sides of the bombed-out bar there were boarded storefronts, and trash littered the streets. The old neighborhood was starting to look like crap. He tipped the old Italian a sawbuck and admired the gleam of his shoes. Outside, on Central Park South, he stood with Egan.

"What about Roosevelt? Who else stands to gain so much from a Tammany scandal or the Mayor's downfall?"

"I'm just a dumb Mick copper. I leave that politicking to you college guys."

"I mean Roosevelt's a great party man, but he always tried to keep some distance from the Hall. Why not muddy the waters and then take the moral high ground? He might avoid the anti-Tammany flak that destroyed Smith in '28."

"Personally, the Old Patroon don't strike me as being so shrewd."

Farrell flagged a cab. "Best advice Silent Charlie Murphy ever gave me."

"Don't ever underestimate an opponent."

"You got it." Farrell ducked into the cab, barked instructions to the driver, and wondered where his Grace might be on such a fine day.

Egan watched Farrell's cab roar westward. He stood in the splendor of a late summer day and had to laugh at the thought that he had just been ordered to follow himself.

Just another tale of lust and deceit in the big town, the Judge thought. He had a tough time keeping his eyes open while the lawyer for the defense droned on about the gross injustices inflicted upon his client. He looked over as the accused, dressed in a cheap suit bought off an Orchard Street pushcart, tried to retain his dignity. He checked the case file. It appeared that the defendant had thrown his young bride out the window of their tenement apartment after finding her in a lewd embrace with the building superintendent. The wife survived but she would always walk with a limp. Crater considered that in most societies she would fare a lot worse and the aggrieved husband would never be dragged into court. He might even rise in stature. The Judge had made up his mind. The poor fool was an upright citizen, a taxpayer and a clerk for Consolidated Edison. If the jury returned a guilty verdict, which seemed likely, he'd give him, let's see, three years, suspended, let him get on with his life.

He checked the clock, willing it to speed up, to reach the magic of cocktail hour. He stared hard at the wife. There was a pleasant heft to her bustline and he wondered what she looked like unclothed. He wished he could spy her ankles. The ankles never lied. She looked up at him and away quickly. He knew his face inspired anxiety in defendants and counsel alike; it was the most judicial thing about him.

Finally the summations were polished off and the case adjourned so the Con Ed man needed to stew another day. Summer recess was just three days away, and while he relished the time off he would be forced to endure several weeks of country living with the solitary company of his dear bride, God bless her. Unfortunately, he would be far from the string of gamines and their charms that he kept sprinkled about the city. Good God, three weeks. He planned to indulge enough in the next few days to hold him over for a while.

Crater nearly leapt from the bench and in the passage to chambers began unbuttoning his robes. He ran through a list of possible dates for his nightly carouse, pictured each naked and writhing, mentally noted varying flesh tones, depravities, and curves. He chuckled at his good fortune. He was surprised to see two men waiting in his chambers.

The one he knew, a Mr. Touhey, shut the door behind him and smiled in a way that reflected no warmth.

"Your honor."

Crater paused, then hung his robe on a hanger. "Mr. Touhey."

"Judge, you look great. How the hell do you manage to keep that tan when you work inside?"

Crater sat at his desk. "Well Tommy, little tricks of the trade."

"That's great. Tricks of the trade. Speaking of which, my pal here has a case you were supposed to dismiss."

Crater thought the man with Touhey looked familiar. But this was beyond anything he had dealt with before. No one ever approached him in chambers.

"His name?"

"Briody, Michael Joseph."

"Right. Well, it seems there are complications."

"So, un-complicate it."

Crater was in no mood to be bullied. He stood and splaying his hands on the cool mahogany before him, shouted, "The unmitigated gall. There are higher powers than you, fella. Your friend has managed to make some powerful enemies."

"Powerful?" Touhey smiled and picked up the Judge's gavel. "Some federal clowns show up in our city and you bow to them? Do you forget who made you?" Touhey twirled the gavel, slapped it in the air, a mock dismissal.

Crater said, "I think you should leave now."

"I leave when I am ready, Judge."

"You want to keep this up, I'll call the Hall."

"You'll call the Hall. You hear this, Mike? He'll call the Hall."

"My patience is wearing thin, gentlemen."

Touhey stood and slammed the gavel down on Crater's outstretched finger, moving so quickly the Judge only had time to blink his eyes before he let out a howl and pulled the bloody digit away. He sat grimacing and wrapped his shirttail around it, the cloth mushrooming red.

"Guess you won't use that finger to dial the Hall with. You want me to work on the other nine?"

The door flew open, a court clerk rushed in, saw the blood, and looked from Touhey to Briody, then back to the Judge.

"It's all right, Donohue, the damn window caught me."

Donohue stood his ground. "You sure?"

Crater used his good hand to wave him out the door. The color came slowly back to his face.

"That's nice, Judge. Your tan is coming back. You went a little pale there."

"What do you suggest I tell the feds?"

"For one, kick them out. You are the judge, not them. If they have a problem with my friend here, where is their case? I am surprised at you, Judge, letting those idiots bully you."

"I don't know."

Touhey shook his head. "I mean really, your honor, who can hurt you more and who can help you more? You're a smart guy, went to two colleges they tell me. So I gotta figure you acting so dumb, it's an act, a little vaudeville number you conjure up, time to time, see how the other half lives."

Crater sighed. "I can't schedule it until after the summer recess."

Touhey stood. "Fine with us. We are not unreasonable men, are we, Mike?"

"Not in the least." Briody shook his head.

"It's been a pleasure doing business with you, Judge. Take care of that finger. I am sure one of your bimbos will nurse it back to health for you."

On the way out of the courthouse Touhey pointed out an old man who walked through the plaza with the help of a cane. "This guy's a legend. He's one of these old-timers that watch trials for entertainment. He's one of your guys from the old Five Points. They knocked down his whole world, built on top of it, and he's still here. I doubt he'll ever die."

They came astride the man. He was less than five feet tall and was dressed entirely in black. Large ears stuck out from under his hat. Touhey patted him on the back. "Hey Sully, any good cases?"

It was an effort for the old man to crane his neck and take in the two tall young men. "Tommy Touhey, is it? The usual. Cheating women and murderous husbands, a fine kidnapping trial just last week. They let the lot of them go, one technicality after another. Great country, Americkay. You can rape and pillage and still be set free to have at it again."

"I got one of your countrymen here, Mike Briody from Cavan."

"Mean bastards, Cavan men."

Briody laughed. "Where are you from?"

"Do you know the Kingdom?"

"Kerry, I do."

"Do you know Tousist?"

"I was there."

"What would a mean Cavan man be doing down in Tousist?"

"I was hiding out there during the Tan war."

"Did they treat you well?"

"Aye."

"I was reared there during the hunger."

Briody looked at Touhey and did some math. "When did you come over?"

"In '51."

"Jesus. What age are you?"

"I lost count of it." He smiled without the help of teeth.

"Tell Mick about when you met the Chinese."

"Oh Jesus. Promontory, Utah, in the spring of '69. Hot, hot, hot, and dusty. We built from the east and the Chinese lads built from the west. We met in the middle and what a party it was. Then we started throwing rocks at each other. A real Donnybrook."

Tommy slipped a hundred-dollar bill into his hand, saying, "It's the one without the President."

"The one Burr shot?"

"Nope."

"The mad fella with the kite?"

"Bingo, Sully."

As they walked on Tommy said, "He's ninety-two, I think. Let's face it, Mick. The two of us will never come near that old."

Under a darkening summer sky, Briody knew better than to disagree.

G race and Briody strolled through Central Park with a basket she had prepared that held cooked ham, soft cheese, a baguette, grapes, and a bottle of deep red wine. They found a spot near the banks of the lake and reclined on the cool grass. They sipped the wine and ate and she asked him if he ever thought about leaving the city.

"No. I don't think so. It just seems like the place I want to be. Despite its complications, I'm comfortable here." He also considered there were at least two men, Touhey and O'Brien, who might take offense to his waltzing off. And while he hoped that his connection to the two of them might end soon enough, he felt there was little he could do about it presently. "I had my way, I'd keep building that building all the way to the moon."

"You're gonna hang steel the rest of your life, are you?" She held out a hand as if she wanted to stop that thought and said, "Not that there's anything wrong with that."

Briody sat up and looked out over the lake. Men in short sleeves rowed their dates about, plying easily under the hot sun. He listened to their laughter, the barking of dogs, and the faint strum of a guitar. So far, he had kept his various entanglements from her, more or less. "It might seem hard to believe, but I love the job."

"I'm sure that you do. It's just I worry sick about you, all the way up in the sky. Remember, I have been there, too."

"It's not so bad. You keep your wits about you."

"Men die."

"Men die in their sleep. They die walking across the street."

"It's not the same."

"What would you have me do?"

"Nothing at all. I'd keep you around to pleasure me night and day."

"I guess that might be preferable to hanging steel."

Grace was silent for a while. He poured more wine. When she finished her glass she pushed away from him on the grass and turned so they were face to face. A man wearing a monocle walked a poodle past them.

"You know, Michael, there's some things about me you should probably know."

He stared at her, said nothing.

"I maybe should have told you sooner. I'm not just a girl who draws and paints. I've gotten myself involved in some of Johnny Farrell's business."

He said nothing, waiting for her to continue. A biplane droned overhead and she watched it head south. He had grown very sick of her involvement with Farrell.

She sipped more wine. "I carry money for him. I put it in banks around town. I masquerade as the wives of various officials." She moved closer to him, draping her arm over his shoulders. "Say something."

"How does this story end?"

"I don't know. I feel like it has gotten beyond me. I should have known better."

"You should have, all right."

"Sometimes, we just don't know. Sometimes, well—easy money."

"Can you walk away?"

"I'm too scared to."

"Do you really want to? You seem in no hurry to distance yourself from Johnny Farrell." His tone was hard.

"Michael, you have to believe in me."

302

"You're just a courier. You're replaceable."

"I know too much."

"What use is it to know things? It's the telling that matters."

"It's worse. I've been skimming some of the money."

He shook his head, stood, and walked a few feet away. "Jesus, Grace. Do you realize what these fellas are capable of?"

"I've been around long enough."

"What if they find out?"

"They?" She stood, trying to close the distance between them, but he backed off a step at her approach.

"You don't suppose this Farrell is his own man."

"You'll save me." She laughed.

Briody was somber. "What if I'm not able to?"

"I'd have to run off without you then."

"Where would you go?"

"There's lots of places a girl could go with a big bag of money."

"They'd find you."

"Don't be so optimistic."

"Grace, these are very bad men."

"Even bad men have weaknesses."

"I don't know if you have a point. I don't know if you really know what men are capable of."

"Really, Michael? I've seen men at their worst. Trust me on that."

He took her by the arm. "I'm not after arguing with you. I'm worried, Grace. Real worried. These men are stone killers, the lot of them."

"What do you think I should do?"

"Well, why don't you try to not steal any more of the man's money. It's only a matter of time before someone notices."

"It's my ticket out, Michael."

"Maybe we can figure something else out. In the meantime we wait and hope nothing happens. Do you still have the money?"

"Most of it."

"Good. Don't spend any more. I really wonder at your recklessness."

"I wonder at it too. Are you going to run away from me?"

"I am a hopeless bastard. Probably the opposite."

The sun declined, moving beyond the tops of the fabulous new apartment houses on Central Park West. She looked up at him and that August light splashed her face, flaring her hazel eyes toward gold, softening her pale skin until it was flawless. When she smiled she seemed to glow on her own, luminous, and he could not escape the feeling that no matter what happened to them he would always remember how she looked this day in the sunlight in Central Park. He pulled her close and pressed his cheek to hers and simply felt the heat of her.

They packed the remains of their feast and headed back to Briody's room. After they made love Briody lay awake most of the night considering what he was capable of when it came to her. At dawn he left her sleeping in that rickety bed and walked to work afraid that anything was possible.

This was not how his vacation was supposed to go. Egan, that horrid cop, had him backed against the wall in the dayroom of his house by the sea.

"It ain't a matter of what you think is right, what you think is fair."

Crater tried to sound firm. "Can't it wait? I mean what could possibly be so important?"

"You're asking me? I'm just the messenger, pally. But the Organization beckons, you come. You don't dither, you don't dally, and you don't turn your snot-nosed face up at them. Got me?"

"I am going to have to insist it wait until after the recess. I have family obligations."

He watched the wiry Egan smirk. "That right?" he said, and made a face indicating that he understood, that he could empathize.

Crater hoped his wife would not chance home and see him browbeaten.

"Family," he heard Egan say, "obligations," and then he saw stars and his head was ringing. He did not see the slap coming but in its echo he knew Egan had smacked his face hard like a teacher hitting a glandular delinquent. "You got till Saturday. If I have to come back and drag you down out of here, you're going to wish you had used some sense."

Crater watched him go, choked down a sob. When Egan's sedan had disappeared onto the main road he turned and stared out through the window at the wide expanse of water and wondered what the hell he should do. He rubbed his jaw, felt it swelling, tender. Farrell wanted him back in town. The investigation was widening and they needed to meet and devise a strategy. The Judge poured himself three fingers of scotch over ice and paced the room sipping the whiskey. He had known all along that it might come to this. The screen door slammed and his wife hurried through the room, her dress waving in the breeze.

"Joe darling, will you swim?"

He regarded his drink. "Not today, sweetheart."

"What is it?" She pressed against him and he squeezed her hard, holding on to something already past him. She was beautiful but she had never been enough and this sickened him now. He might need her very much and he knew he did nothing to deserve her support.

"Work."

"Ah Joe, don't be silly, you're on holiday."

He managed a smile. "If only life were that simple."

He watched her trot down to the water's edge and onto the pier. The sun was high and the air fresh. He wondered if things might get truly bad. He wondered at public disgrace and humiliation, the inside of a prison cell. That would not do. It would not do at all. He was going back to see Farrell. He had no choice. His wife cut gracefully through the cold blue water, her arms flickering like gold in the sun. He turned away and poured another scotch.

That evening he feigned illness to avoid joining friends for dinner, sent his wife off. He made slurred calls to several of his girls around town and drunkenly professed love for those for whom he felt only lust. For surely rutting and laughter were all they had—cavorting and coupling like deranged animals. When darkness was complete he sat all alone on the dock and considered a time back when he was young and bright and ambitious. A time when he was *clean*. He recalled walking across the common at Columbia clutching his law degree as if it were a sword that he might use to slay dragons, to make things right in the world. How had he let his hungers get the best of him? He looked into the bottle—by now he had forsaken the pretense of a glass—and he wanted to say, You did this to me, but no, he was not that much of a fool or a liar. It was time to face the music.

Briody sped north along the Hudson, winding through clapboard villages dominated by church spires. He did his best not to look in the rearview mirror. Touhey had sent him to drive Grace and Farrell to the Saratoga racetrack in upstate New York, saying, "Keep an eye on that clown for me." Farrell, in the backseat, was babbling and happy and seemed not to notice Grace's obvious disinterest. Briody considered throttling him, but instead focused on the road. Farrell's Cadillac drove with luxurious ease. They stopped for a drink in Poughkeepsie and Briody chose to wait outside.

He leaned against the motor-warmed hood in the shade and watched the traffic zoom past. He looked at his hands, the rows of calluses and the black burn marks like pepper along his wrists where the rivet cinders had sprayed him. Other cars pulled in; it seemed everyone was dressed up and headed to the races. Then a pair of young men arrived in a smoke-belching Model T missing a roof. They nearly fell out of the car and Briody could smell the whiskey on them from a dozen paces. They eyed him with the country man's disgust for the city slicker and entered the tavern. Briody smirked, wondering what he was becoming to earn a look like that. After a while the happy couple came out, carrying glasses and a glistening bottle of champagne in an ice bucket. They scrambled back into the car and crossed the Hudson on the new bridge. Briody marveled at how much the landscape resembled home. The green rolling hills and fields, the lakes, all of it could have been Cavan. The only difference was the ungodly heat and weight of the air.

They arrived in Saratoga just before supper and the streets, lined with big houses fronted by porches, were thick with sunburned revelers. Marching bands played and everywhere American flags undulated in the breeze. All the women were done up in fantastic outfits capped by floppy hats while the men sported blazers, tan slacks, and covered their heads with straw boaters. On the long front lawns of the side streets people sipped iced drinks and played croquet. A stunt biplane flew overhead trailing a sign for a local clothing store. This seemed to Briody to be more like the America he had imagined as a boy than New York was.

The hotel was an old wooden structure with a wide porch on which several dozen people were congregated, sipping large tumblers filled with ice and juice and booze. Even here, Johnny Farrell seemed to know everyone. He had lit a cigar and was busy hugging and backslapping. Briody stood off to the side and Grace came up next to him. He could smell her, the mix of perfume and her sweat from the hot drive up. She brushed against him and squeezed his hand. She whispered, "Don't worry, he won't last long. He can't handle his drink these days." And then she moved past the promise and placed her arm through Farrell's. They made a smart couple, Briody thought, young and accomplished, polished in that American way he felt he could never pull off. He turned away, looking out at an antique fire engine pulled by a team of horses.

At least Farrell did not ask him to carry the luggage. Instead he flashed a chunk of green at the bellhops, who raced one another to do his bidding. Grace climbed the stairs, pausing to look over her shoulder at him and wink. He fought the urge to follow her. The Tammany man sidled up to him with that easy smile of his. "Me and the girleen are going to have a nice romantic supper for two. Here." He grabbed Briody's hand and pressed a bill into it. "That ought to get you through the night, old man. Thanks for the driving."

Briody watched Farrell follow Grace upstairs. He glanced down at the bill—a hundred—and was tempted to pass it off to the bellhop. Instead, he slid it into his pocket, and after checking into his room hit the streets in search of a drink. He would use his own money.

• • •

She came to him at midnight and led him to a field of thick dark grass on the edge of town, where under a fat August moon they made love and then stared at the stars. Briody pulled her close so her head lay on his chest.

"I can't stand to see you with him."

"I can't stand to be with him."

"Then why do you do it?"

"Michael, if I could walk away no bother, I would. I just need some time. I don't want to cause you any trouble."

"I'm not worried about him."

"You should be."

Briody slid out from under her head and sat up.

"If it makes you feel any better, I haven't slept with him in weeks."

"That solves everything."

"Michael, you knew what was going on before any of this started."

"I guess it's my turn to come clean."

"Is it a flock of mistresses you've stashed around town?"

"I'm still involved in the war."

"What war?"

"Our war."

"War without end, amen, is it? It's not my war."

"We send money, guns. Sometimes explosives get shipped home."

"Why do I need to know this?"

"You're not the only one stuck into something."

"You have doubts now?"

"I don't know why. Maybe life in America. Maybe the job. Maybe you."

She paused. "You know, they killed my father."

"Who's that?"

"The IRA."

Briody stared at her. "I'm not sure what to say."

"Well, at least you didn't say you're sorry. I'm sick of people saying that."

"Did you know about me?"

"It wasn't much of a guessing game. You're of an age and an attitude. Besides, Johnny Farrell makes it his business to know all about everyone. I hear more than I am supposed to."

"Well I'm glad to see it hasn't put you off me."

"Maybe it's vengeance I'm after."

"If so, I'd rather you decide my fate than anyone else. What happened with your da?"

"They came and were trying to burn down the stables. My father went out to stop them. Now, he was as republican as they come. But he did not see all the big-house people as the enemy. We all worked for the Bells and they had always been fair. It was early on a Sunday morning, still dark, and the air was warm, strangely warm for that time of year, and a mist was rising from the fields. I ran out after him without my shoes, the grass was cool on my feet. One of the men held a torch and the light was flickering, casting them in and out of shadow. I could hear them arguing and then I saw a flash and heard the shot. The men all ran away and as I got closer I could smell the gunpowder and my father was lying there trying to hold his stomach in and the ground was all wet and dark around him." Grace was silent. "He held my hand and then he died."

"Christ. I'll not defend that."

"Who could, Michael, really?"

"You must know some of them running around claiming to be this or that were just bully boys."

"If I didn't understand that on a certain level, we wouldn't be talking this minute."

"Fair enough."

"Later, they sent my mother a note of apology and some money. I think she was angrier that day than when my father was killed."

For a while they said nothing. The cicadas filled the air with their mad song, a symphony heralding derangement. "Sometimes, Grace, what I do is much worse than running guns."

He knew by her look that no further description was needed.

"It's a long way from home to be fighting a war that's supposed to be over."

"I won't argue that. Not tonight, not here. Let's try to stick together, see if we can both put the past where it belongs."

"I'd like nothing more than that, Michael. Nothing at all."

At the top of the street they separated, and in the humid hour before dawn he watched her walk down that lonely road to the hotel, alone.

Hey sport, you have any of that money left, put it all on Jim Dandy."

Briody, his clubhouse breakfast interrupted, looked up at Farrell, who smiled, then glanced down at his racing sheet. "A hundred to one?"

"Trust me. A little bird told me." Farrell winked and turned as Grace came up beside him. She stared at Briody, a smile coming to her lips.

Briody was glad for the pretense to get away from them. He shouldered through the jovial crowd to the betting window. He had not slept but somehow was not tired. He unfolded the crisp one-hundred-dollar bill and slid it across to the teller. "On Jim Dandy. To win."

The man looked at the bill, then back up at Briody, and laughed. "You're betting against Gallant Fox, a Triple Crown winner, and on a hundred-to-one shot?" He laughed again. "Choose your poison, boy."

Briody wandered through the grandstand and found a pole to lean against. He looked out over the lush beauty of the track and was reminded of the time when he was small and his father, fresh from America, took him to the racecourse at the Curragh of Kildare. He loved the track as a boy, even as his father grew angrier at every losing horse.

He watched the bettors, first the clubhouse crowd, who all seemed to be tan and at ease in fine clothes, and then the grandstanders, many pale and carrying a sheen of desperation, especially in their eyes. Briody saw their hunger for the big score—for the thing that might ease the drudgery of their lives and free them from the claustrophobic rooms they'd left behind to come to this oasis in the country. He was dismayed to see O'Brien glad-handing his way through the crowd toward him.

"Enjoying the sport of kings?"

"That's one name for it."

O'Brien straightened his maroon tie, which already was knotted and hanging precisely. In the hard light Briody could see he had missed a spot shaving, just below the ear. "Thought that might appeal to you."

"Is that so?"

"What with your service to the Crown and whatnot."

Briody looked around. If not for all the race fans about he might just have given the man a good smack.

"It's a joke, lad, a bit of mischief. Relax. It's good to see you. It appears we have mutual friends."

Briody did not respond.

"Johnny Farrell? The Organization's man for judges and jackhammers. An ambitious lad he is, that Farrell."

"Friends may be a stretch."

Briody excused himself and wandered through the green and white pavilion, stopping for a lemonade. He turned to see O'Brien had followed him. He felt his stomach go sour.

"Listen, it is fortuitous, us meeting here. There is another matter that needs seeing to. I was about to alert Casey. You were to be summoned."

"A matter."

"Much the same as the last time. You recall your boat trip onto the waters of Hell Gate."

"Not easily forgotten." That's all these killings were to O'Brien: matters and boat trips. He kept a comfortable distance from bloodletting, from pain. He'd probably be in his box at the races when it went down, when another life was snuffed out. Briody simply nodded in agreement. His pulse quickened. He had begun to dread the violence. He looked around, trying to spy Grace through the garden of women in floppy hats and the men, the high rollers, sporting bespoke suits that secreted heavy wallets.

O'Brien fixed him with that stare of his. "I'll follow up with the specifics, they come known."

Briody felt his teeth clenching. The light around them seemed to dim. O'Brien tapped him in the chest with his *Racing Form*. "Go with Gallant Fox, he's a sure thing."

Briody forced nonchalance. "No fun in that, betting favorites. I'm going with Jim Dandy." He waved his betting slip.

O'Brien laughed. "A hundred to one. You don't strike me as the long-shot type, Briody."

"Well, maybe you don't really know me at all, now do you."

They watched in slack-jawed amazement as Jim Dandy rounded the last turn hugging the rail, in the running. So far it had been all Gallant Fox, the Triple Crown winner, and the cofavorite Wichone, until suddenly Wichone faded, looking lame, and now Jim Dandy was gaining on the famous colt. Baker, the jockey, was riding high and using his whip with vigor, beating a vicious tattoo timed with the thoroughbred's stride. Suddenly Gallant Fox in the middle of the track was slowing, having burned his speed on his main challenger. Jim Dandy closed hard. With a furlong and a half to go he caught the Triple Crown winner and shot past, barreling along until he was a length, then two, now three ahead and moving with astonishing power. Farrell leaned over the rail, Grace and Briody beside him, and they all shouted in a chorus of excitement. There was a murmur around them as racing fans sensed something extraordinary in the offing and many who had backed other horses started to shout encouragement at this incredible long shot. The rich smell of the sun-warmed turf mingled with the stink of cigars and dozens of splashed-on perfumes. Farrell's heart beat so fast he began to gasp for air. Jim Dandy thundered past chased by all the mares and colts and geldings who were supposed to be superior, crossing the finish line eight lengths ahead of the prohibitive favorite. The crowd went mad.

Farrell jumped up and down and hugged Grace, then Briody. "Holy Jesus, a hundred to one. I'm rich."

Losing bettors passed them, offering congratulations and wonderment at how the hell you had the chutzpah to bet on a hundred-to-one shot at all.

Farrell looked down at his ticket and read the number of the race and the number of his horse, Jim Dandy. A hundred to one. He felt the rush come up from his toes, a giddiness flooding him like warm blood. A hundred to one. He was going to walk away from the track with fifty thousand dollars. There was no other way to explain it. The Dago had pulled this off and Johnny Farrell had backed the right horse, indeed.

He turned and hugged Grace and then clasped Briody's shoulder. "Hey Brady, a tip like that, not bad hey? I'd say you owe Johnny Farrell one."

"Who's Brady?"

"Right, Briody."

"Sure, I owe you one, Johnny."

They cashed in their tickets under the bewildered gaze of the track master. Farrell had to take a cashier's check to cover the extent of his winnings. They declined an armed escort. They paid a stable boy to drive the car back to New York, then went to the train station and purchased first-class tickets home. As the train rattled south they feasted on oysters and champagne.

Briody put the thick stack of hundreds and five hundreds in his jacket pockets and wondered if ten thousand dollars was enough to buy Grace out of any trouble coming from her brazen fleecing of Farrell and his cohorts. Outside Poughkeepsie, Farrell got up and, swaying from the bubbly, made his way through the crowded cars cajoling other passengers, bragging about his horsemanship, his uncanny great luck. Grace leaned back against the window, smiled at Briody. She rubbed his leg.

Briody took out a stack of bills and slapped her across the thigh. "Maybe we can straighten out your problem with this."

Grace reached over and squeezed his arm and kissed him quickly, full on the mouth. She did not want to ruin the day but she knew freedom from Johnny Farrell was not going to come so cheap.

The day was clear and bright and started with cigars. Sheehan had spent most of the weekend looking anxiously over a midwife's shoulder as his ninth child was born. "This fellow did not want to come into the world. Forty-one hours of labor." He passed the smokes around, then brandished matches.

Armstrong lit his cigar, puffing hard. "Why don't you leave that poor woman alone?"

The gang stood on the temporary decking eight hundred feet in the air. Briody smoked. "I have to agree with Armstrong."

"For once."

"Nine is plenty."

"After five, my wife says no way." Delpezzo laughed.

Sheehan looked out over the city, waved his arm. "We're nearly done here. I just wonder how the heck I'm gonna feed them all."

"Something will pop up."

"Armstrong, that's easy for you bachelors to say."

The sound of the work horn drifted up to them. "Come on, let's get this steel slapped together."

It happened just before lunch. The air was calm, the wind easier than on most days, when out of nowhere a blast of wind hit them and Briody pulled back, slapping his hat down, and he saw Sheehan, a few feet ahead of him on the beam holding a plank, rock to his left and pause and then, realizing it was smart to drop the plank, did just that. But his weight now was too far forward and he was motionless, stuck in a place between will and gravity, and he pawed the air and then screamed. Briody dove along the beam, the steel cracking against his sternum, and all the air went out of him reaching for Sheehan, but he was off and freefalling, not a sound coming from him now, and as Briody followed his descent he could feel the velocity the father of nine was gaining as he smacked off the edge of the setback and spun wildly out over the street, and when he hit the ground he was nothing but a speck so far beneath them as to be unrecognizable. Briody was gasping for air and behind him Delpezzo started to cry quietly and Armstrong was cursing and beating his spud wrench off the metal so hard sparks were flying. Briody pushed himself up and sat for a long minute staring out into the void, the sky blue, the sun still holding a lot of heat. The word spread up from the place where Sheehan had landed and down from where he had fallen, so in a matter of just a few short minutes men were dropping their tools and huddling on the edges of all the floors and taking off their hats and making the sign of the cross. The job fell silent, and my God, Briody thought, that silence was an awful sound here on the greatest building in the world, as men who had not been to church in decades bowed their heads and prayed for all those children with no father.

The gang rushed down to the street and helped load the scant remains of their friend into a canvas morgue bag. They watched as the ambulance pulled away and then, no longer a complete gang able to work, they embraced one another and then all took the train to the Bronx to Sheehan's apartment.

They were led by the oldest boy, Jimmy, into the back bedroom where his mother was recovering from the childbirth. The room was small and hot. The minute she saw them she started to scream. Briody sent Jimmy, who looked so very much like his now-dead father, to fetch the doctor. After the man sedated her the ironworkers left, except Briody, who sat alone with the sleeping woman until her sister came. In the dark night he walked down the street to the train considering that it was no longer going to be the greatest job in the world.

Grace paused over the lobster, her appetite waning. She had come tonight with every intention of telling Farrell she did not want to see him any longer and that she was calling it off.

"Can you believe that Jim Dandy?"

"Some horse."

Farrell reached in his breast pocket and pulled out a long thin box covered in black velvet. "I figure you were my lady luck, back up there at Saratoga." He slid the box across the white linen, sat back, and smiled expectantly. "A token of thanks."

Grace stared down at the box. She knew this was it. This was the perfect opportunity to tell him that they were no more, that they were over. She looked around the room at the crowd of high-hat swells supping in the Manhattan night, murmuring over rich food. He would not dare make a scene here, would not risk his reputation. She could slip out and run, get Briody. She felt herself begin to sweat.

"Don't be shy, baby."

She put her hand on the box. She wanted to push it back across and gain her freedom. Instead she picked it up and creaked it open. There was an emerald necklace of dazzling beauty.

"Here." He grabbed it, then got up and stood behind her, draping it around her neck where it hung like an iron collar she could not break.

She picked up the empty bottle and waved it like a surrender flag at a passing waiter who was back in a flash to exchange a glistening new one for the spent. For the rest of the night all she said was "Sure Johnny," and he never once asked for more than that simple validation.

The good judge got down on his knees and opened the Meyer Brothers safe, cast iron and lead-lined; he swung open the heavy door and pawed through his cash and bonds and stocks, taking all the money and half the securities, their bright colors somehow indicating riches. He knew better. The pile of paper was worth a fraction of what it had been worth just months ago. He left the jewelry, stuffed the uncounted cash and paper into his bag, and stood, nudging the safe closed with his toe. He had made up his mind. Run. He figured a few years would do it, give him enough time for it all to blow over. He understood statutes of limitations, knew the law, could estimate the shelf life of a scandal.

He moved through his apartment for what he knew would have to be the last time. The living room was elegant, reflecting his wife's good taste, the latest in design, the sunken living room, parquet floors, a rug woven in a dusty corner of Persia and purchased on a shopping spree in Paris, all this financed by racket money of origins he did not desire to contemplate. That morning he had cashed two separate checks for six thousand dollars each. All he had to do now was stop and clear out an account that held another fifteen and all told that should get him started nicely on his way to a brighter clime.

He looked in on the bedroom, a joyless place for longer than he could remember. It was quiet and sun-drenched in the meat of the afternoon, the four-poster bed taking a direct hit from the daylight streaming through the tall windows. The bed, on its pedestal, was an island in that vast room of blond oak floors. It was the kind of setting that invited mad frolic, but his wife was no fan of his sexual appetites and the bed, covered in white cotton and down, might as well have been an ice floe for all the heat they generated there. He felt a moment of anger at her refusals and saw it as justification for his sexual escapades. Still, the guilt won out as it did more and more often. He closed that door deliberately, padded down the silent hallway to the living room.

A dagger of sunlight caught a photograph on the nightstand so it shone like a mirror. He walked over and picked it up. It was of himself and his youngish bride, the two of them in the Poconos back when they were in love, back when the future was theirs. He went to place it in his bag, but thought better of it. He needed a clean break, a fresh start. He stood it on the end table again. He paced the length of the room and then went and stared out the window at Fifth Avenue. The heat was forcing people indoors, into shadows in search of relief. Five years was enough time for the felonies he had committed to lose their bite, another five and those who worried about what he might say should no longer care. He would return after that decade, a man of fifty-one, still vibrant, still able to entice a showgirl or two, still alive.

All his weaknesses were plaguing him. His father had warned that someday he would pay the piper. Pay indeed. Still, all he needed to do was play it straight for a day or two. Make the right arrangements and off he'd go. He looked out again onto Fifth Avenue. He would certainly miss this town and its temptations. But he knew places where the sun shone most days and no one cared about the past, about who you had been or what you had perpetrated. He stood before the mirror and adjusted his dickey bow, spit on his fingers and slicked his hair down. He placed his panama hat squarely on his head. He was an actor more than a judge and all he needed was to see this last act through, a couple of scenes of his own design and he was gone.

First, he'd see Johnny Farrell and yes the man to death. Yes Johnny, no Johnny, whatever you say old boy. Farrell would hold the hounds at bay just long enough for him to escape. He passed through his lobby, holding the bag filled with lucre and bare necessities, traveling light so as not to raise fears of flight. He'd leave it at his favorite hotel, make his rounds, and then make his move. He tipped his panama to two passing ladies blessed with golden hair and great gams. Thank God he had been blessed with an escape artist's cunning. Catch me if you can.

Without asking her, Egan had ordered hamburgers for the two of them. Grace watched him devour his burger, the grease dripping down his fingers, eating with a deliberation that suggested satisfaction over the death of the cow he was ingesting. When he finished, he attacked his fries, and did not lift his head until he was done. She sipped her cola, her unease settling in the pit of her stomach.

They sat in a luncheonette booth on Queens Boulevard. She stared out onto the street while he looked over the notes she had made. They were lists of fake names, false bank deposits, a fictitious mirror accounting of her underworld doings. She had sprinkled in enough truth to make it all sound reasonable. She forced herself to sit down and meet with Egan once a week. The man unnerved her, but she figured that was a good thing. It complemented the image she wanted to portray, that of an innocent, weak, and frightened girl in way over her head, desperate to do the right thing.

She watched the riders coming down the stairs from the train and sipped a glass of water the waitress placed before her. Egan murmured to himself, a pair of reading glasses perched down his nose lending him a professorial air, except when he looked at you with those eyes. He plucked the glasses off his face, snapping them closed and sliding them into his inside jacket pocket all in one move.

"Looks like you're a good girl after all. That's good, that's smart."

"I don't want any trouble."

"Trouble? They'll be no trouble for you, missy, as long as you keep playing along."

She nodded her head, looked down at the table as if she was afraid to meet his gaze, which in truth she was. Those creepy eyes, all watery blue and cold, pitiless, like the dim lights of hell.

"Tell me about your Irishman."

"There's nothing to tell." Grace heard the edge in her voice and tried to tone it down. "He's an ironworker. He builds buildings."

"That right? What is an ironworker doing accompanying a known racketeer to shake down a supreme court judge?"

Grace shook her head.

"He tell you about his arrest and indictment for running guns?"

"No."

"You need to watch out for yourself."

"I do. Watch myself, that is."

"You seem like a decent sort."

"I try."

"He tell you he's a suspect in the disappearance and apparent homicide of an agent of the Irish government?"

"Never mentioned it." Grace said nothing more. She leaned back in the booth, folded her arms across her chest, and wondered if he was lying. She figured probably not.

"Interesting hobbies, your ironworker has. No?"

"I guess you never really know someone, do you?"

"That's why you need me."

"Really?"

"I'll bet you're a small-town girl. A farm girl. You show up in the big city and you are vulnerable, you're an easy target for creeps like Farrell. Then maybe you're homesick so you're open to the old-country charms of this duplicitous ironworker. I understand. By the way, I've checked your ironworker out. Checked him out stem to stern. He's got quite a history. Why don't you ask him about it?" Egan stood, dropping a fiver on the table. "I worry about you, Grace. You're a sweet kid." He took her notes, stuffed them in his pocket, and left.

Grace waited a good long time in the booth, nursing another cola. She was not really that surprised. She knew that Briody had a republican background and that he had been to war and that sometimes wars were not fought on battlefields. He had told her as much. Still, in a way it made her feel better, because now she need not feel so guilty about her own dirty secrets.

She found him in his room and joined him on the bed. He was fresh from work and just out of the shower, smelling like soap. She laughed at the different colors of his body, the neck, face, and arms browned by the sun, the torso and legs luminous and pale.

He showed her one of her drawings, pointed to the man on the left. "He died."

"Oh, Michael."

"His ninth child was born the same day."

"What happened?"

"Nothing really. He just went to work and then there was some wind. I mean it was a perfect day, clear, calm. Out of the blue it was. A gale. It was like the hand of God knocked him down."

For a long time they said nothing. Grace went and came back with sandwiches. They ate sitting on the bed. "A man came to see me today."

"What kind of man?"

"A man that told me stories about you. A man that seemed to know a lot about you."

He pulled her across the bed, putting her head to rest on his strong chest. "Jesus. You're quite the intelligence agent. We could have used you back home."

"Sounds like you could use me right here and now. Is there danger of prison?"

Briody stood and pulled an undershirt over his head. "Supposedly, none." He laced his boots.

Long after dark, they decided to catch the last ferry to Brooklyn. They walked across town, the night air heavy with summer energy. He held her hand and as they approached the Empire State Building lightning started to cleave the night sky, lacing it with blinding light. The air was electric, but there was no rain. The building served as a lightning rod and when they were a half block away a long jagged bolt struck a derrick on top of the building, causing a blue flame to undulate down the sides of the building like waves coming onto a shore. For a second the whole structure glowed with that blue light. They felt their hair rise on end and then it was gone, the air suddenly crisp and clear. Briody turned to look at her. "Did you see that?"

They walked tentatively over to the building and reached out to touch it but the stone was cold. "I never saw such a thing."

Briody hugged Grace and they laughed, then walked on to the ferry dock, glancing back when they saw lightning, but no more bolts hit the building. Thunder rolled over the city like an artillery barrage. On the river the clouds finally opened, a midnight thunderstorm, and they reached her boat drenched from a steaming rain.

They hung their clothes up to dry and sat in her room. He watched as she pried open the floor and lifted out a metal box. She opened the box and he saw a pile of money, and beside it a leather-bound journal. He peered into the floor hole and saw two pistols.

"I've a list of every drop I've made. I also feed information to this man Jack. Only some of that is true."

Briody picked up the journal and looked through it. Dates, places, names, amounts, all listed in meticulous print. "So what's it all mean?"

"The way I've been able to sort it out, it's Farrell's way of distributing the loot throughout the whole system. From what I gather, most of them are real men: district leaders, police captains, various politicians, gangsters, the odd lawyer, even a reporter or two—all those that fatten on the business of the metropolis."

"Jesus. They don't even bother to use aliases."

"Why would they? They are the powers that be."

"Then who is this man Jack?"

"I'm not sure. Maybe from the federal government."

"Could he be a journalist?"

"Not with eyes like he has."

"Grace, I think you are in a lot of danger. There is too much at stake here. These men would kill for much less than this."

After she fell asleep he sat outside and stared into the gloomy river night. A lone barge whispered past pushed by a fat tug. He wondered if he had it in him to kill again, for it was then that Briody considered he might have to kill Johnny Farrell.

Farrell awoke in his Fifth Avenue apartment when his son crawled into bed with him and plunked a peanut butter jar on his head.

"Hungry, are you?"

He followed young James into the kitchen, where his wife sat leafing through the morning *Times*. She did not look up to speak. "I don't suspect you would like to accompany your family on a picnic?"

Farrell stood at the counter smearing a glob of the peanut butter onto a fat slice of bread. He handed the sandwich to his son, then licked the rest from the knife blade.

"Pam, are you kidding me?"

She stood and grabbed the boy by his hand. "Kid you, John? Is that even possible?"

When they left he showered, dressed, and inhaled several cups of coffee, perused a half dozen newspapers. It was the dog days and the crime blotters were influenced by the prevailing weather pattern. Sloppy homicides, neighbors brawling, drownings—summer mayhem. He was glad he no longer practiced law. He could imagine the type of imbecile he might have to defend. In the hallway he riffled through the mail and found a bill from Saks for four thousand dollars. He dropped it on the dining room table thinking, We fight our wars with whatever means we can.

His meeting with Crater had gone well and he felt he had certainly shored up the firewall surrounding the judge scandal. Crater was no dummy. Like most men, he found the idea of a bloody and premature exit from life unappealing. They had met in the dining room of the NYAC and the Judge had practically kowtowed to him. After the meeting he had sent a coded note to the Dago expressing that all was well.

In the polished lobby the doorman stopped him. "This came for you first thing today. They said not to wake you up." He handed Farrell a card and a set of keys, then pointed to a Dillon coupe parked curbside.

"You sure got some nice friends."

Farrell read the note, "With regards, your partner."

He walked through the open glass doors of the building and looked at the automobile. It was the exact model and color of a car he had pointed out to the Dago with admiration at their last meeting. He walked around it, studied the lines, the body gleaming in the sun. It had the appearance of moving while sitting still, as if it was accelerating toward the next curve. He laughed out loud. What a gesture. He pulled open the driver's door and sat inside and the buttery leather was cool even in the great heat. He gripped the wheel. He decided on a drive in the country, knew just the spot. Maybe Grace would join him. It was up along the headwaters of the Wallkill River, outside New Paltz. They'd pack a lunch, chill some wine, swim under waterfalls, and then make love in the warm sun, just like the old days.

He was about to get out, to go and grab some things for his jaunt, when something in the rearview mirror caught his eye. Curious, he stared and then turned around. On the backseat was a hat, a mistake, he figured, left by whoever delivered the car, and he should return it to its owner. He got out of the car and ducked his head into the backseat. He could not picture any of the Dago's men wearing a panama hat, chuckled at the idea of it. But the chuckle died in his throat. Farrell stared with disbelief as the street, the entire world, faded from his consciousness until it was nothing but that hat that seemed to glow with its own wicked light. He stood transfixed. Finally he reached out for it and grabbed it gently by the brim as if it might be booby-trapped. He turned the hat slowly in his hands. It was of top quality, a tight and professional weave. He flipped it upside down and saw that it had been worn for some time, a swiggle of sweat lines on the band. He reached and flipped down the sweat band and there, stitched into the crown, was the monogram JFC. He mouthed the letters, once, then twice, elongating the consonants until he was certain his eyes were not lying, and then he felt the weight of his entire existence dragged over a cliff. Joseph Force Crater. He dropped the hat and staggered back into traffic, where he was grazed by a speeding taxi.

The doorman snatched him from harm's way and said, "Mr. Farrell, you look bad." He bent and retrieved the hat from the street, handing it to Farrell.

Farrell stared at him for a long minute. "Maybe he ran away with one of his sluts."

"What's that, Mr. Farrell?"

But Farrell was moving back into the cool of his building, the hat like a smoking gun in his hand.

The Buick had just been cleaned and simonized and as Briody pulled in front of the building on West Forty-second he sat enjoying the smell of lemon oil in the sun. Tommy Touhey, fedora pulled snug and dressed in his best navy suit, came out of the lobby trailed by a fellow Briody had met only once, a tall man with a hatchet face he knew as a shooter from Cleveland. They slid into the car, Tommy in the front, the shooter in back, and Briody pulled away, easing into the eastbound traffic wondering who the target of these killers might be. He made the left onto Eighth Avenue and they were tooling north on a summer day, all of them assessing the multitudes of women strolling along at their lunch-hour leisure, when the windshield cracked. Briody felt the car rock and then he looked to his left and there was a man leaning out the window with flames jumping in his hand, and Tommy yelled, "Punch it Mick, let's go," and then the back window was gone in a sun-shower of glass.

Briody noticed they were being fired on from the other side as well by men in a black Ford that rolled and spit bullets at them, and now he knew Tommy and the hatchet face were returning fire out opposite sides because of the smell of the cordite that filled the car. He saw a man in the left car as his hat flew off in a pink wet mist. The man dropped his machine gun and hung half out the window, trailing muck and blood along the side of the car. Briody sped between two delivery trucks, scraping the quarter panels of each. Tommy was shooting and cursing and the hatchet-faced man was reloading and cursing. Pedestrians flickered past as images caught in a thousand attitudes, some faces slack, others taut with screams he could not hear, others diving, flattening themselves on hot sidewalks. He jerked the wheel to the right and they scraped the Ford; sparks shot into the air and Tommy let rip with a quick burst. Briody stole a look at the faces in the other car, pasty and close enough to spit on. He hit the brakes and they flew past him and he made the hard left, ramming the other car into a light post on the corner of Seventy-second Street, shocked to realize that the shooting and screaming had been going on for thirty city blocks already and more surprised that the black Ford had made the turn wide and was closing fast. He spun hard onto Riverside Drive and watched in the mirror as a man eating a hot dog stopped as if in a picture, his eyes going wide with surprise; and the Ford clipped him and he was in the air cartwheeling through the beautiful day, airborne from the force.

Briody felt the blood pounding hot through his entire body, his feet moving deftly up and down—clutch and gas and rarely the brake—and Tommy still screaming, more out of joy it seemed than anything else. He obeyed the barked command to make a right on Seventy-sixth and then a left and they were back up on Broadway. Calm descended on him. He saw everything clearly, could anticipate the movements of everyone and everything around him. The bullets were coming again but meant nothing, because they were destined for bodies other than his. He swung out wide, braking for a second so he fishtailed away from two girls licking ice cream cones as they crossed the street. More concussions rattled the frame. Tommy leaned across him and emptied a revolver so close to his nose that his face was burned by powder, and now his ears throbbed with a ringing he could not shake. Then they were alone and speeding through Central Park flatlands with smoky shantytowns on either side.

The chase was over so Tommy told him to slow down and just get them back to the Bronx. It felt silly all of a sudden to be driving so orderly, like someone out for a Sunday cruise. There was no sound from the backseat and as he passed the squat museum he knew there was just the two of them now.

M ick, can you keep a secret?"

"I've a few stashed away already."

"That's me." He pointed to the bullet-riddled Ohioan, whose face was now a chunk of bloody meat, unrecognizable as human. Tommy saw the corpse for what it was—his ticket out. He would draw up a will and date it a month ago. He'd pick out a place in California, fashion an alias, maybe open a cab business or sell cars. He'd leave this city because he wanted to live and if he stayed he would die. He could not win. Farrell's defection was the last straw. Johnny Slick. He considered killing him as revenge but he knew that he had gotten what he wished for. He'd be lapdog for the Italians until they were done with him.

They drove down to the abandoned stretch of factories along the Hell Gate and Briody was seized by dread remembering the man they had killed there. He pushed that memory away and worked along with Touhey, who was busy erasing himself from existence. He watched Tommy slide off his rings and watch and dog tags and fit them on the bloodied and dead shooter from Cleveland. Tommy took one of his pistols and placed it on the floor at the man's feet, then stuffed his wallet into the dead man's pants, pausing to take out some bills and his mother's holy card. He nodded and Briody took a can of gasoline from the trunk of the Buick and spilled it all over the corpse and on the seat cushions of the car. Tommy struck a match. "Say so long to Tough Tommy Touhey. He had a nice run," he intoned, then dropped the match and a roar of heat and flame jumped into the Bronx sky. They paused for a minute and watched it burn. Briody saw in the distance the job, over seventy stories now, and once again he wanted nothing more than to be there. They got back in the other car and he drove a dead man on to his new life.

Touhey sat with his hat pulled over his eyes on the ferry to New Jersey. The sun was lying flat over the tops of the Palisades, turning all the passengers' faces a soft golden color. A wind kicked up, and the boat rocked gently on the tiny whitecaps that dotted the lower river and the harbor. Briody stared at the Statue of Liberty and recalled the feeling it had inspired upon his arrival a year ago now.

Touhey indicated the statue with his chin. "Most people see that, they figure they're home-free I guess. Me, it's the opposite. I'm home-free going the other way." He fell quiet for a moment and then went on: "Listen, tell nobody but my wife. Tell her to wait six months and I'll send for her. Everything's gonna turn out swell. Six months, things will have changed so much, I'll be a forgotten man."

Briody doubted Touhey would ever be forgotten by his friends, or his enemies. When they started down the Jersey Turnpike Briody noticed an immediate change in Touhey, the tension flowing out of him so that his entire carriage visibly sagged with relief. By Trenton, his face seemed to have dropped a decade of worry.

"You believe the stones on the creeps, thought they could take me out? I could stay and fight. I'd start with little Johnny Farrell, hang him from a lamppost, but hey. Thing about guys like Johnny, they always get what's coming their way."

They rented a room off the highway in south Jersey and bought a quart of whiskey from a local shop owner, who looked them up and down, shrugged, and then returned with the bottle wrapped in newsprint. The room contained two beds that squeaked and groaned with every movement and they passed the bottle back and forth over the space between them. Touhey's good mood had faded, and as they drank he grew somber.

"I should have been smarter, Mick."

"How's that?"

Touhey swallowed some whiskey from the bottle and ran his hand through his hair. "I should have stayed working with Owney and the boys downtown. I just hated having to answer to anyone, wanted to be my own man."

"You can't worry about the past. The past can't hurt you, Tommy."

"I wouldn't be so sure of that."

"All we can do is live for the here and now."

Touhey laughed. "Well we're here and we're now and look at us, like two hoboes drinking piss water."

"At least we're here and now."

"I'll drink to that."

When the whiskey was done they faded to sleep and it was Touhey up first and shaking Briody by the leg. Touhey shaved and when he came out of the bathroom he was holding a pistol by the barrel. "Here. I don't think I'll need this where I'm going."

"You sure about that now?"

"One can only hope."

Briody took the gun, as much to help Tommy be rid of it. "When was the last time you went about without one?"

"Good question. Before the war, I guess. When I was a kid."

They drove down the coast to Wilmington, where Touhey sent Briody into a department store to buy him some clothes for his journey. At Union Station in Washington Touhey purchased a ticket for Memphis. "From there I'll head west. My mom has some people south of San Francisco." At the platform he extended his hand. "Hey Mick, thanks. And keep your eye on Farrell. He's got a lot more on the ball than he lets on sometimes. He's an evil little prick. Take that girl and get out of that city. It just ain't the same town it used to be."

He stood on the bottom step and turned. "You know, Mike, that time you were pinched with the guns?"

Briody nodded, sensed he was about to hear something he would rather remain ignorant of. "You were set up. I don't know by who, or why. But Farrell called me that afternoon, to make sure I'd be around. Keep your wits about you. And listen, you find yourself in a jackpot, go see Mannion. He ain't the sharpest tool in the chest, but he's a capable guy when things are going bad. Good luck."

Briody watched the train slowly pull from the platform, clouds of steam billowing out and obscuring the view. He wondered at Touhey's information, what it might mean. Who would want him arrested and why? He stood for a moment and let the crowd of people rush past him carrying suitcases, grim and determined to be somewhere. He looked up at the board and considered all the places a man might go. But he knew he was going back to New York, to Grace, to the job, and even to Danny and the lads. For better, or worse, it was now home.

A l Smith yanked the covers off Walker, who covered his face with a silk pillow. "A judge, Jimsie? A goddamn supreme court judge?"

Walker groaned and waved Smith away.

"Have you lost your mind? Get up, you stupid son of a bitch. We have to talk. This is nuts. This is going way too far. A judge can't just be made to disappear. This is America. How do you think that looks? We have enemies, dammit. You don't know what it's like out there. Didn't you pay any attention in '28?"

Walker spoke around the pillow. "Nineteen twenty-eight? He's asking me about 1928?"

"I'd roll into town at night, out the window of the train, there'd be rows of burning crosses, Jimsie, men in hoods, Klansmen gathered in the fields. They burned me in effigy, burned the Tammany tiger, railed against us as gangsters and stooges."

"Now if they burned you, you'd have a real complaint."

"I spend my entire life trying to make something, to stand up for us, for the Irish, the Catholic, the immigrant, the Jew, the tenement dweller. Now what happens, a judge, a dirty rotten supreme court judge, goes to a play and then whammo presto, he's gone?"

"Gone where?"

"Gone where? Do you know what our enemies will make of this? What the hell is going on in this city, Jimsie? It's your watch. You're in charge. Do you have any control at all? Is it that far gone, are the racket boys that much in ascendance? For the love of Pete, how did this happen?"

Walker slowly pulled the pillow off his face. "You still here, Al? How about fixing me a drink? Come on, Guv. You haven't been out of the Fourth Ward that long."

"This is not a joke. Do you know what this means? All we have done, all the legislation, the child labor laws, the workmen's compensation, the, oh Christ. All of it will fall in the shadows of this crap. It will obliterate every good thing we have ever done."

Walker sat up, swung his legs over to the side, felt the cool wood of the floor on his toes. God, his brain hurt, and now this intrusion. Who the hell let Smith in? Heads would roll. "Not to mention hurt your chances in '32?"

Smith's face darkened, took on a tinge of blue. He sprayed saliva when he shouted. "You got some nerve! This is bigger than me, it's bigger than you! This is beyond us, Jimmy. You run around with showgirls, you embarrass your family, the Irish, the party, your church. You think a smile and a quip will get you by every time. This is different. Mark my words; you have given them the weapon to destroy you with. To destroy all of us. Here." Smith stalked over to the table and grabbed a bottle of wine and tossed the bottle on the bed. "As long as little Jimmy Walker is happy."

"Algie. Do you know how difficult it is to explain things to the Happy Warrior? I want to be able to make such things not happen. I want to live in the shining city on the hill, a place of virtue. Well, with maybe only a little clean vice. I'm no profiteer. Sure, I accept favors now and again, but Christ, if I was half the thief they make me out to be, I'd be swimming in millions and not having to accept the handouts from well-to-do friends and acquaintances. There are many more complexities to being mayor than governor."

"Horse crap."

"You know, Al, for all your political genius, sometimes you miss the subtleties." Walker rang for his servant, who came in with a pot of black coffee and a pitcher of mimosas. Smith refused both.

"Al, you think I can stop these people? Crater was no choirboy. He got himself in over his head and now he has paid the price. I have my best detectives on it, and so far we have kept it out of the papers, which you know is no mean feat in this town."

"Who would do this?"

"For all we know, he just took it on the lam, Al. There is no body, no crime scene, no evidence of foul play."

"Which is worse. If he had been gunned down we could have blamed it on a jealous paramour, a love triangle turned ugly. His disappearing without a trace is a worst-case scenario. It smacks of a professional job. No one will talk. No one will come forward. Jesus, the brouhaha over Rothstein is just dying down and that was two whole years ago. And he was a criminal. No matter what we know about Crater and his vices, the public will see him as a judge, a man above the fray. This is going to be bad for us, Jimsie. This is too, too much. You have to put the pressure on. You have to reel in these elements that are running amok. Decent people have a right to believe in their government. Do you remember the little man, the average joe?" Smith stood and leaned over him. "Or are you too infatuated with the high life to give a good goddamn?" Smith spun and took his leave, slamming the door so hard the windows rattled.

Walker looked out the window and watched Smith, a bit stooped now, cross the street, bent to the fight. There was a beast loose and no, he had no idea at all how to stop it. Why did they turn to him? The truth was the racket boys scared him. Just a year ago, Smith had come to him and urged him to drop out, to take a bow and go and enjoy life. He figured the gold-toothed crusader was just trying to get him out of the way so he could make another go at the White House with a little less Tammany baggage. He sighed. Where oh where would Alfred Emanuel Smith be without Tammany?

He understood a Roosevelt keeping his distance. He was a man from another world entirely. But Al Smith needed to remember he was only anything other than a Lower East Side schmuck because of the likes of those he was now trying to deny. He walked back over and crawled into bed, pulling the covers over his head. Just what the hell had become of the good judge? He honestly had no idea.

He wondered at Smith's thinking he still had a chance to become president, as if those yahoos and bigots in the hinterland would not resume their attacks as soon as he reared that ugly head of his a second time. Or as if the party might see fit to anoint him for an encore debacle. Fat chance, Al.

He threw the covers off and went and ran a bath. Where the hell was Betty? He would have to see Johnny Farrell. The man had his ears to the ground on these things. He lowered his bony ass into the steaming tub, thinking, Jesus, where was it all to end?

Egan figured it was time to roll the dice, to stir things up, as the Governor said. He pulled Farrell aside at a gathering of potbellied men of commerce. "Boss man. I got bad news and I got worse."

Farrell grabbed him by the elbow and they moved outside. The sidewalk in front of the Commodore Hotel was quiet on a cool night. Farrell lit a cigarette. "I hear we're in for a bad winter, according to the *Farmers' Almanac*. What's your take on it?"

Egan flipped up his collar. "I'd say it's going to be a bad fall, before we ever get to winter."

A downtown bus docked curbside with a screech of brakes. The door opened. No one got on, no one got off. Egan studied Farrell. He had always considered him weak, but now, in anticipation of what he knew was bad news, he seemed resolute, calm. Sometimes you just can't judge.

"I'll take the worse news first."

"I could be wrong. It's bound to be a matter of opinion."

"Perspective is everything."

"Your Irish lass has been skimming from her drops."

Farrell inhaled deeply, then dropped the cigarette and crushed it under his heel. "A lot or a little?"

"All I can say is that a few of the captains have called, wondering, Hey, what the hell is going on."

Farrell exhaled. "And so, Captain, what's the bad news?"

"She's, well, she spends a lot of nights with a certain Irishman."

He turned and grabbed Egan's lapel. "Which Irishman?"

"An ironworker named Michael Briody."

Farrell felt his knees buckle. First Crater, then Touhey, now this? His ears burned with the heat of betrayal. How stupid was he? He spun away from Egan back into the hotel ballroom, where he retrieved his coat and hat. Men called out to him, waved at him, sought his attention, but he paid them no heed. By the time he hit the street again clarity of purpose was descending on him. After all he had done for Grace, this was how he was repaid? By robbing him and running around with some potato-eating immigrant? Why was he so blind? Because of love? He ducked into his city car and barked an address at his driver, who, sensing the boss's anger, drove quickly with his siren keening out into the city streets.

Egan enjoyed the walk over to his apartment on East Fifty-fourth Street. He nodded at the superintendent and took the stairs. At his kitchen table he jotted some notes to pass on to Roosevelt. Farrell's bag still sat there, bursting with money. He had planned to use Grace, but he wondered if Farrell himself, put in a position of need, of desperation, might be used against Walker and the machine. He poured himself a glass of beer and toasted the city night outside the window.

.   .   .

riody stood at the back of St. Jerome's as the priest praised Thomas Touhey's lavish generosity to the parish. He marveled at the American Catholic way of ignoring such details as multiple homicides so long as enough cash was waved around. For even the most rectory-bound priest must have known exactly who and what Tough Tommy Touhey was. The church was packed so thickly with mourners that there seemed to be almost no air in the place, and he unbuttoned his suit jacket to ease the stifle. He listened as Tommy's oldest boy read from the Apocrypha. "He who pleased God was loved; he who lived among sinners was transported—snatched away, lest wickedness pervert his mind or deceit beguile his soul."

That is one way of looking at it, Briody thought. He wondered what effect all this was having on the children. As far as he knew, the wife had told no one and the grief was real.

He considered the corpse, the dead shooter from Cleveland, and wondered what his own family might be thinking. They would spend the rest of their years not knowing, waiting with diminishing expectations of his ever walking through the family door. In his experience even the hardest of men had somebody somewhere who wished him to come home safely. This one was doomed now to spend eternity in another man's grave, perhaps visited on another man's birthday, collecting flowers until even Tommy Touhey was forgotten and joined the gone in these huge American cemeteries set far away from the places where the dead had lived.

When the priest descended from the altar to lead the procession Briody stepped outside. A crowd of several thousand was gathered to watch the coffin being loaded into the hearse. The day was sunny and many shielded their eyes to watch as the doors swung open and the crucifix, held aloft by a pimply altar boy, caught the sun and gleamed like a sword of light. Among the attendees were those who loved Touhey, some who feared him, and even a few who hated him. Briody watched Touhey's children pass him and follow the casket to the waiting car and wondered how they were going to react to their father's coming back from the grave, a modern-day Lazarus.

After the burial at the cemetery in Castle Hill, the mourners came back to the neighborhood and filled the bars to overflowing. They drank with impunity. Briody was in no mood for booze so he walked around to the Caseys' apartment and found Maggie on the stoop. She greeted him with a smile and a strong embrace.

"Michael, you're looking well."

"A sight yourself." And Briody meant it. There was something about her that he had always been attracted to, something that transcended the physical, although her face and beautiful hair made her pretty enough. He'd always envied Casey for having her, and the family, the solidity of all of it. As much as he loved Grace he never saw her being the steadying force in his life. That would be his role in hers.

"So, the king is dead."

"Have you ever seen a funeral like it?"

"God no. Quite the spectacle. I made a point of avoiding the man. Did you care for him?"

Briody fought the impulse to reveal the man's true status. "Honestly, I did. He wasn't a bad sort. I had the good fortune not to be his enemy."

"I guess it all depends on your perspective."

"Where's himself?"

"Away at work. And the kids are scattered about the blocks at their Yank games." She adjusted the newborn on her lap. "We miss you, Michael. It's not the same with you gone."

"I'm sure the extra space is a good thing for you."

"I'd rather have the company. He broods a lot these days. You brightened his mood like no one else."

"He has a lot on his mind."

"Well, I've got six and counting of his children on my mind, and body, and back, and in my hair. It's America, he can move on like the rest of us."

"Are you sure that's how you feel?"

"It is. What's the use of it? I mean, nobody at home wants to keep fighting, why should we?"

Briody had caught himself beginning to think the same thing. He shrugged.

"I can't find the romance in losing that he can."

"He'd say it's better to fight and lose than to surrender."

"My hero. Please, Michael. When we were still back home and the Tans were kicking down our doors, fine, I agree. But this is no longer about us. It's about the children. Things can be rough here, but there are choices. I'm never going back, no matter what happens, and neither will my children if I can help it. I'm through with that place."

Briody turned his face up to the sun. "I'm not sure I could ever say that."

"Have some children, Michael. That will change your mind fast enough."

Briody stood. He put his fedora on and laid a hand on her shoulder. "Tell Danny I won't be making the meeting, and that I need to talk to him. I'll be at my room all day tomorrow. He can call the house phone and they'll come get me."

"Look at you in your fancy suit and your gangster hat. You're a fine man, Michael. Find yourself a nice girl and settle down."

Briody doffed his hat and laughed. "Finding the girl seems to be the easy part of that."

He walked down Alexander Avenue with the sun shining in his face. As he neared the corner of 140th Street a black panel truck came up the block, followed by two police cars. The stickball players scattered to the curbsides. A man got out of the truck and conversed with a city marshal, who was pointing up into a building. The cops emerged from their cars and stood looking forlorn as three stocky lads followed the marshal and the landlord into the dark vestibule. Briody heard the screams. Presently eight children sat on the curb while their parents pleaded with the cops, who stood shrugging and shaking their heads. In no time their belongings were piling up on the sidewalk around them. Three beds, a set of drawers, a kitchen table with three spindly chairs. Briody saw a framed picture of the Pope, a carton with some tinned food, a pile of clothes that looked like rags. Suddenly the Bronx seemed too much like home. He dug in his pocket and pulled out what he had, two hundred and thirteen dollars, and walked over to the husband. The evictee wheeled on him, another man in a suit, and Briody grabbed his hand and pressed the money to him.

"Just a little gift from Mr. Touhey."

He was away and down the stairs of the subway before the man could manage a thank you.

G race, lugging paints and rolled-up canvases, led Anna down her pier. The sun was declining behind Manhattan, flaring the sky blood orange. Still, the river was busy. Black smoke trailed from the stacks of hard-charging tugs. Seagulls hovered, caught on salty updrafts, barking madly. Anna followed her, wrestling with two overstuffed grocery bags. Grace used her free hand to open the door and bent to shift her load and help her friend. She was looking forward to cooking the fish they had bought, drinking some wine. She wondered why Harry was not there to greet them.

"Where's your nutty neighbor?"

They entered the boat and when an answer came from the dimness of the living area they both jumped and dropped their packages. Farrell sat in the shadows waiting for them and when he turned on the light both she and Anna gasped at the sight of him. Grace did not say anything but she knew it was all over. His face was held so tight and pale that it looked more like a phantom version of Farrell than the real thing. "Hello, Grace." His voice, which in its tautness was unrecognizable to her, scared her even more. She was suddenly very afraid for herself and for Anna. Was it the money he had found out about or was it Briody, the man Jack, or all three?

"Your nutty neighbor?" Farrell nodded and two goons who had been lurking by the galley door ducked into the bedroom and came back dragging the bloody and mumbling Harry. They dropped him on the floor at Farrell's feet.

"He's very protective of you, Grace. Very loyal. We should all enjoy such total commitment."

Grace was torn between the impulse to run and the need to help her friends. She made a move toward Harry. Farrell shook his head and one of his men backhanded her and she bounced off of Anna and the two of them crashed to the ground. When she tried to get up the man kicked her in the stomach so hard that she lost all her air. She lay writhing and gasping, fighting to breathe, while her vision dimmed, blurring everything at the edges so Farrell's gaunt face looked to be a melting wax mask. She felt like she was drowning. She could not get her wind.

The other man, the chubby one with the bright red face, grabbed Anna by her hair and, dragging her across the floor, snarled, "You're under arrest."

Anna yelled, "For what?" Grace was proud of her defiance but if she had been able to speak she would have told her not to provoke these men, for she understood now what they were capable of.

"How's prostitution sound?"

"That's a crazy lie."

But the man punched her in the head and she dropped to the floor, silenced.

Slowly, in sharp gasps, Grace regained her breath. Farrell was squatting beside her, wiping the blood off her face but not in a way that indicated any concern. "You're a clever girl who has played me for a fool. You will live to regret that. I want the money, Grace, and I want it now."

"It's in the banks."

"Oh. It's in the banks. I guess I was wrong about you." He pointed with his toe at Harry's prone form and the chubby man pushed his hat back and smiled in a way that filled her with terror. He brushed aside the bag of groceries and picked up the can of white spirits. He rolled Harry with his foot and took out his handkerchief, waving it like a man about to wipe a park bench for his beloved to sit on. He squatted and placed the cloth over Harry's mouth and nose and opened the can with his other hand.

"No, don't. It's here." The cop, just for fun, poured a squirt and Harry came to, choking, and spun onto his belly, puking blood and groaning.

"Please. I'll give you the money. All of it."

"Really, Grace. That is very considerate. Then we need to have a little chat about your friend."

Grace felt a shock of nausea. What would he do to Michael? "What friend?"

Farrell laughed and then smacked her face so hard her eyes burned with tears she refused to let go of. "All right, we'll get to that. Now, give me my money. I am very disappointed in you, Grace. You let me down. You let me down in so many ways. And now, you will have to pay for doing that to me."

She led him into the bedroom and she pried open the floorboard and started digging out the cash from the hole, passing it to him a handful at a time.

"I gotta say, Grace. You sure had me bamboozled. You sure had me hoodwinked."

When the money was all gone she nudged the locked box which still held her journal, sliding it farther under the floor, out of sight. The two thick black guns lay there. She stared for a moment at the heavy revolvers, could see the brass edge of the shells nestled in the cylinders.

"Grace, is that all you have in there?"

She said, "Just this," and grabbed one of the guns, turned, and waved it at Farrell and pulled the trigger. The explosion was deafening and the gun flew up and back out of her hand. She saw a hole ripped in the wall just an inch over Farrell's shoulder. For an instant everyone froze. Then the man who had kicked her was across the floor in two steps, his hands around her throat. She dug her nails into his arms, but he simply smirked and held her motionless.

Farrell's mouth hung open for a second, as if he was stuck in mid-thought. He spoke calmly. "Feisty. I like that, Grace. Real sass." He gathered up the rest of the cash.

She watched through the door as in her studio the chubby man whistled and sprinkled turpentine about. She tried to pull away but she was taken out, dragged by one arm and her hair, kicking at air.

On the deck they pitched Harry into the river and put Anna in one of the cars. Then they made her watch as her boat went up in a great roar of flame and white smoke. All was gone, her paintings, her mementos, her life, a conflagration against the backdrop of the city.

What, she wondered, would they do to Briody? Why had she

stayed? Why had she not fled when the chance was hers? Was there something in her that needed disaster? She was thrown in a car and forced to lie on the floor of the backseat. One of the cops stamped his feet on her spine, holding her in place, and soon she was speeding toward what kind of hell she could not imagine.

She awoke in a bedroom somewhere, a girl's bedroom: the walls were pink and stuffed animals were stacked on the shelves, staring down at her. They must have sedated her. She stood up and then felt the pain, the stiffness in her back, the aches and bruises where the men had held or hit her. A hard light came through the windows and she figured it must be the next day. She tried the door but of course it was locked and so were the windows. Outside, a long emerald lawn led down to a choppy sea where bright sails caught the September wind. The chubby man sat on the porch sipping lemonade. She returned to the bed and pulled the covers over her head and sobbed, wanting to get all the sorrow out before Farrell came to see her.

Hours later, in the deep night, she woke to find Farrell sitting in a chair at the foot of the bed, smoking a cigarette in the gloom. He did not speak for a long time until finally he stood and said, "Grace. If you leave, or even try to leave, I will kill him. It's that simple."

Briody walked heel to toe, a trapeze act on the uppermost cross-beam, his eyes focused straight ahead, ignoring the nine-hundred-foot drop on his left side. The wind wasn't too bad but the air had a real bite to it. When he reached the corner he squatted and unscrewed a shackle from the beam, then retightened it at the end of the cable. He considered that at that moment there was no one anywhere in the entire world who stood higher on something man had made. He raised his hand and signaled up and away to the derrick man. The cable swung away.

Grace had not come by in three days. He was beginning to worry. It was rare that he went two days without hearing from her. He lowered himself, sliding down to the derrick platform, and joined the gang warming their hands and toasting sandwiches over the rivet forge.

"I miss Skinny," Delpezzo said.

Briody missed him too, his easy ways, his enduring good humor. He still could not believe Sheehan was dead. Armstrong spit onto the coals, the saliva hissing into mist. Briody knew he was more affected by the death than he was letting on. Armstrong rarely even broke balls anymore. He seemed to be just waiting out the end of the job. "The thing that gets me the most is he really was the nicest guy in the world. You hear guys say that about guys, but this guy, it was true."

Briody nodded, finished his sandwich, licking mustard off his fingers. Since Sheehan's death they had fallen off the top gangs in terms of production, and there had been a couple of missed rivets dropped. Luckily, no one below was hurt. Even Hard Nose McCabe did not bring it up. The topping off was coming. The new man, Johnny Doerr, was a good hand but knew better than to chime in when the talk was about Skinny. He just stood and stared off into the distance of Jersey.

Briody wondered why Grace had not called yet. He went over to the east side of the building and looked out toward Brooklyn and her boat, which even from on high he could usually make out. Something was wrong. He looked down at the Williamsburg Bridge, then worked his eye back along the shoreline to her pier. Feeling a creeping dread, he went and dug Sheehan's telescope out of the gang box, training it at the Brooklyn shore. Her boat was gone.

After work he hailed a cab and fidgeted anxiously in the backseat as he directed the driver to the Williamsburg waterfront. He found Harry sitting on an upturned milk crate, his face battered and swollen. Harry watched him approach without a word. Grace's boat was not missing at all but was burnt down to the waterline, a smoldered black floating wreck. That's what he had seen from the building. The fire had stopped abruptly at the river. He was seized by dread, was almost unwilling to ask what had happened to Grace.

"I tried my best. But I'm just an old man. That's it, just an old man."

"Grace?"

"They took her, I guess. Where to, I am in the dark on."

Relieved that she was at least alive, Briody nodded to Harry and carefully mounted the wreckage, picking through the remains. There was not much left that was recognizable. Out of the black refuse he gathered a shirt with one sleeve burnt off, several photographs singed and melted at the edges, the subjects just ghostly shadows. Her paintings were reduced to splashes of congealed vivid color amid the blackness. There was a painting of the Empire State Building that had survived somewhat intact and a photograph of Grace as a girl in Ireland. The smell of ruin sickened him. He carried what was left of her life onto the dock and stood alone and watched the river traffic. In the distance the Empire State Building stood starkly against a gray sky. The wind came from the north, the first hint of winter out of the Canadian wilds.

"I warned her about that asshole. Many a time I warned her. You can't trust a man wants to be pretty."

Harry offered him a drink and Briody took the bottle and sat next to him. The homemade whiskey was clear and burned his throat but was no worse than most of the pocheen back home.

"I knew from the get-go that it would go bad for her with that fella. Funny how people don't want to listen to reason, don't want to see what is right in front of their faces."

"Did they hurt her?"

"I don't know. I was too busy trying not to drown. She had her friend with her."

"Anna?"

"The one and only." Harry drank and shook his head. "I miss that Irish girl. She made life around here bearable. Life is so full of horse's asses."

"I know how you feel."

"I suspect you might."

Briody took another sip. There was nothing much he could do. He went back on the boat and tried to imagine the layout before the fire. He walked the three steps from where the bedroom door would be and bent low. The wood was all gone but in the pile of ash he saw something smooth. He went to his knees and brushed away the soot and burnt wood. There it was. He tapped on the metal box. Its handle was deformed from the heat, but it was otherwise intact. He took it over and asked Harry if he had anything that might open the box. The old man scurried into his rickety boat and came back, waving a nail bar.

"This do her?"

Briody took the tool and snapped open the box. There, still whole, was her ledger. Briody picked it up and turned through the pages, and perused the scribbling and accounting. Most of the names meant nothing to him. But next to each were bank locations, numbers, and dates. He took a last sip of whiskey and thought, just maybe this was a map to freedom for them. He stuffed the journal into his waist and ignored Harry's question about what it was.

You killed the Judge?"

The Dago did not respond immediately. He regarded Farrell with that infuriating hint of a smirk.

"You like to wager. How much would you gamble that no judge will speak ill of us again? I could think of no better way to show the city we are serious."

"Us."

"Partners, right?"

"He's a judge."

"Is he? Or was he?"

Farrell was too frustrated to respond. He was in no mood to speak in riddles. "And Tommy Touhey?"

The Dago said, "That was a man with a lot of enemies. I think you might be at least as big a suspect as me, no?"

"I don't kill people."

The Dago laughed. "No, maybe not. But you do seem to benefit from all the dying going on."

Farrell wondered then if he was truly lost. The Dago was right. He had set something in motion and now he was powerless to stop it. He was sure to benefit from the deaths of Crater and Touhey. He just needed to make sure his own corpse was not added to the pile. And he had to figure out a way to get rid of the Dago when he was no longer of use.

"I see it as we're both doing just fine."

"Good. It is important we stay together in these troubled times. Partners." The Dago raised his glass of deep red wine and Farrell obliged him, the clinking seeming to echo like the tolling of a bell.

Briody entered the Art Students League and took the stairs to wait outside Anna's office. After a while, Anna came down the hall talking to one of her students, a girl with short hair and bulging eyes that lent her the look of a fever victim. She hung on every word Anna said and it was not until they were at the stairs near the door that Anna broke free. When she turned to enter her office Briody stood in her way. She stepped back, shocked to see him, her hand coming across her heart as if to still it.

"Michael. What are you doing here?"

"Where's Grace?"

"Oh, Michael. You need to stay away. You don't know what you're dealing with. They'll kill you, they'll kill her, they'll kill anyone they want, and there is no stopping them."

"I don't care."

"What are you going to do? Call the police? They are the police. They are the judges and the juries. Look what happened to Crater. You think they would have trouble with you, an unknown immigrant?"

"I need to see her."

"You sad man. Come in."

She led him into an office so crowded with stacks of books that he had to work his way sideways to a desk with two chairs. Every inch of wall was covered with drawings and paintings, some black and white, others riotous jumbles of color. He sat in the chair next to hers and their knees touched. He slid his seat away an inch.

There was an ashtray piled high with butts and she immediately lit a cigarette and offered him one. He declined.

"She won't see you, Michael."

"She won't or she can't?" He noticed her hands seemed to shake—nerves, or just caffeine and tobacco?

"They told her they will kill you if she sees you."

"Who's they?"

"They is they."

"Farrell?"

"Among others. They arrested me for prostitution. For prostitution! I was dumped in the Tombs and then dragged to Jefferson Market jail in leg irons. It was four days before my family found me. People did things to me, Michael. It was a living hell. They'll stop at nothing."

Briody waited for her to calm, then pressed his case. "How does she contact you?"

She stared hard, shook her head. "Fine." She blew a long plume of smoke upward and rose, taking an envelope from the shelf above her head. "You know Grace. She's clever. Apparently they keep her at a house in Long Island, near the sea. She charmed one of the grounds boys into delivering a note to me saying she was all right."

Briody stared at her. "Was there anything for me?"

"Don't take it the wrong way. I know she wants you more than anything, but she knows what they are capable of."

"Can you get a note to her?"

"Do yourself a favor, let it pass."

"Anna, I can't do that."

"Well that's a very sad thing, because it means you are dead. I am talking to a ghost, an apparition."

"Can you get it to her?"

"Honestly, I don't know. If the boy comes again, I will try."

Briody took a pen and wrote on the back of Grace's note asking her to call or write. He included the address and phone number of the rooming house. He finished by writing, "I found your favorite book, safe and sound." He folded it and gave it to Anna.

When he stood to leave Anna handed him two pictures. One

was a sketch of himself and his crew, the other a nude drawing of Grace, sitting on a chair looking to the side, her long hair flowing over her right shoulder, obscuring her breast. It was perfectly rendered. He felt the air go out of him at the likeness.

"I figured she might want you to have these. If I hear anything, I'll call you." She escorted him to the door. Her hand shook as she grabbed his arm. "But please, Michael, be careful."

"I'll be whatever I need to be to get her back."

She shook her head sadly. "You fool."

"I really can't help that." He took the elevator down and flagged a cab on Fifty-seventh Street. On the way back to his room he sat with her picture opened on his lap. There was no way he could let her go.

He was not surprised to find O'Brien waiting in the small dim lobby of his rooming house. The Clan-na-Gael man clasped a leather satchel in his hands and rocked up and down on his toes. Briody wondered if he was worried about the dirt on the floor.

"I've been waiting awhile. Interesting clientele, here at Muldoon's flophouse."

Three men sat sleeping on a worn couch, heads back and mouths open. All wore scuffed boots and empty tool belts. The hotel manager peered out from his booth regarding O'Brien's fine clothes with suspicion.

"Workingmen, mostly. Are they strange to you?"

"Workingman hardly describes what you are in this world, Briody. Can we find somewhere private to talk?"

Briody led him up the slanted stairs to his fourth-floor room. He swung the door open and dropped Grace's pictures, rolled, onto the table. O'Brien dipped into his satchel and produced a photograph. He held it aloft. "I believe you two are acquainted. He made quite a name for himself with his interrogation methods, what the lads tell me."

Briody felt his face go hot. Brannigan. "So he did."

"He will be a guest of our fair city while meeting with local agents of the federal government." O'Brien reached into his bag again and this time produced a pistol and then a suppressor which he casually married to each other. "He arrives two weeks from Sunday. He will be checking into room 947 at the Shelton Hotel." He tossed the gun on the bed. "A wonderful piece, that." O'Brien leaned over and looked at a picture of Grace on the desk. "I hear she left you, your hometown girl."

"If you're finished, there's the door."

O'Brien dipped a final time into his bag. "Here is a passkey. He's traveling under the name Smith, clever fellow."

When he was gone Briody stared at the face in the photograph. Brannigan. He was the man they would turn to when answers had to be gotten. With Brannigan breaking men was not just war, it was cruel sport. When the sides split for the civil war Brannigan continued his work for the Free State forces and his former comrades became the victims of his ghastly methods. Briody took the pistol and placed it in the drawer. If anyone deserved to die it was truly Black Jack Brannigan.

I t was in the air, the feeling that finally it had all gone too far, that all the crazy scams and schemes that had been played out over the last decade had coalesced into the unthinkable. In the fading light of a summer evening a state supreme court judge was snatched and wiped off the face of the earth. Judge Joseph Force Crater was subtracted, killed, disappeared as surely as could be. A month after he vanished the story finally broke, all the whispers and innuendo became roaring fact, and the papers were in all their bold-typed glory shouting and yammering away at the powers that be. There was to be a reckoning, an accounting, a righting of the scales of good and evil. But for now there was a relentless hunt for clues to the man's disappearance, feverish speculation in offices and speakeasies and at kitchen tables. The racket boys killed him, he ran off with a gamine or two, he was hiding from real estate partners bent on his destruction. Witnesses were produced. Kooks and cranks came forward in droves. Detectives chased down leads as far away as the rocky California coast.

Farrell knew now that all was changed in ways he could not have conceived. Anything was possible. He made the rounds of his sleeping children's rooms, bent over and kissed each one of them lightly on the cheek, feeling the reassurance of their sweet breath in his face. He wondered about them growing up, becoming adults without a father. He closed the door and padded down the hallway to the library, where he shaved ice and poured himself a tumbler of scotch. He sat and kicked his shoes off, sipping the whiskey, letting the ice numb his teeth. Well this was what he had aspired to. A level of control they had achieved, no one could stop them now. Crater was simply a message to anyone who might try. He heard the quiet hum of traffic out on the avenue. He walked and looked out over the park to where the glow of the casino was just beyond the trees. He thought about strolling over, but no, tonight—it was becoming a habit—he would drink alone. His wife and kids had unofficially moved upstairs to the in-laws' apartment and his children barely acknowledged him when they passed in the hallways. They came down to stay with him one lousy night a week and he would let them run amok and when they tired he would read them to sleep.

He did his best to deny any knowledge of Crater's fate to Walker and Boss Curry and the rest of them. Did they believe him? Did he care? At the oddest moments he was tempted to blare it out, to shout it to strangers, to beat reporters, cops, to his wife and kids, to his Tammany cohorts, Guess what—I know—I can tell you what happened to the Judge. That's right, me. It was a strange mixture of dread and a surreal sense of power that his complicity in the biggest mystery of the new decade produced in him.

The Dago, outwardly placid as ever, took the opportunity to preside over the slaughter of a number of old-school Sicilian chieftains. Most were quiet little assassinations that barely made the papers, so crowded with the Crater story. Farrell truly saw the dark genius of the man. Still, what had been the reasoning behind getting rid of Crater if only to keep the how and why a great secret? Farrell had come to the conclusion that he was an audience of one for this grand and public act so he made a simple decision. Don't return any of the Dago's calls. Cut him off, totally and finally. He had every right to, every reason.

And of course Tommy Touhey. Farrell shaved more ice, poured more scotch. Touhey's murder hit him on an even deeper level, as if he had been cut off irrevocably from those forces that had shaped him. Touhey, for all his violent impulses and criminality, had been a good man, a stand-up guy who had a set of values that, however twisted his actions, were a guiding force. He truly tried to hurt only those who deserved it, other outlaws who knew the game. Out of guilt Farrell sent a package of twenty thousand dollars to Touhey's widow and a condolence card explaining that he had been out of town the day of the funeral. A lie. But he felt better anyway.

When the bottle was dry he walked dopily down the hall and collapsed into bed, pulling the pillow over his face. He wished for a moment, before passing out, that tomorrow, all his mistakes would be unmade.

Without Grace, work was truly everything now. Briody ate his lunch eighty stories up, legs dangling, his back to a beam, watching the antlike to-and-fro of people far below and eyeing birds that floated past on the jet stream. After lunch they were resetting their scaffold when out of a clear blue sky white flakes began to fall, landing on their hats and shoulders and covering the plank floor beneath them, a sun blizzard. One of the inspectors happened along and after examining the flakes from the curious storm declared it barley, probably from Owney Madden's nearby brewery, caught in an updraft. The men laughed, the men picked up the pace.

Briody squeezed the trigger of the rivet gun unthinkingly, over and over and over until his whole arm was numb. He squeezed it until the riveting was done for the day. Coiling the air hose, he understood that he had never known true longing. He felt more alone than he had in the hole, and if it wasn't for the crew he did not know what he might do.

The weather cooled but the pace of the job never slowed and he gave himself to it. His days were work and then the retreat to his room where he waited for something, anything, to happen. He felt helpless. Small fears started to fester and grow. He felt powerless. His past revisited him and he had trouble sleeping. The street noise of the New York night was his only company. At least at work, they were so far into the air that the rest of the world was remote, distant, and even the screech of Manhattan life could not reach them. Briody cherished his solitude in the clouds. It was all he had.

On the appointed Sunday of Brannigan's arrival, the first in October, he stood on the sidewalk outside the Shelton Hotel, pausing just for a moment. Traffic rushed past, drivers working their horns. Neon signs glowed in closed shop windows. He looked up and down Lexington Avenue, searching, alert for all that looked wrong. A light rain began to fall, lending a sheen to the street. The gun weighed in his pocket, heavy as a stone. Satisfied, he fingered the passkey and then pushed into a quiet lobby, lit in soft gold light. Neither the countermen nor the bellhops in their beige uniforms reacted to his passing. He stepped into the elevator and was whisked to the twelfth floor. As soon as the doors closed behind him he went to the stairway and walked down three flights of stairs. He padded along the carpeted floor and placed his ear gently to Brannigan's door. Hearing nothing, he slipped the key into the lock and let himself into the room.

He stood in the gloom, listening as the sounds of the street floated up. The room was empty. He took a quick look about. Brannigan had not checked in yet so he sat in a chair, watching the skyline, his ear attuned to noise in the hallway, waiting for his target to come to him.

He remembered back to when they were comrades and Brannigan, desperate to find out who had tipped the Brits about an arms shipment, had buried the two prime suspects, a lobsterman and his son, buried them alive, slowly filling in their graves as the men cried their innocence until their lungs filled with dirt and they could scream no more. The fact of their innocence meant nothing to him. He had used the murdered to send a message about collaboration, called the dead men true patriots. Brannigan had only gotten worse during and after the civil war.

As he sat, time seemed to stand still. He checked his pistol, tightened the suppressor, made sure there was not yet a round in the chamber. How many times had he waited in dark rooms to deal death and pain?

At ten o'clock Briody heard them in the hallway, Brannigan and a bellhop. He slipped into the closet and listened as Brannigan tipped the boy and asked him to come back with a bottle of whatever he could find. When the door shut Briody stepped out and leveled the pistol. "Hello, Black Jack." Brannigan turned, actually jumping off his feet and stumbling back on the bed, his hands up to ward off a bullet strike.

"Jesus, are you that surprised? Your eyebrows nearly flew off your head there, Jack. What did you expect to find in New York, of all places? Come here and take a load off." Briody used his foot to move the chair away from the writing table. "Scared, are you? Black Jack Brannigan, the fearless one?"

Brannigan walked over, his hands still up before him. He sat on the chair and Briody took a pair of handcuffs from his pocket and, holding the gun to Brannigan's head, cuffed him tightly to the chair. He then leaned against the desk inches from his captive. "This ain't like Dublin, or London."

"Michael Briody." Brannigan shook his head. "So this is how it has to be?"

"The great Black Jack Brannigan meeting his fate?"

"The war is long over, man."

"A bit concerned that your past has caught up with you?"

"You're one to talk about the past, Briody."

"A flash of defiance, is it?" Briody put the point of the pistol under his chin and lifted his face up with it.

"I was following orders."

"I saw you. You made the rules up as you went along."

"You were right by my side."

"The Tans were one thing, they had it coming. But our own lads, and then after the treaty." Briody felt himself becoming angrier than he wanted to for this. "I mean, Jesus, women even."

"It was the only way to end it quickly. Before more died."

"Terror has its uses, is that it? How very thoughtful of you. Let me ask you just one thing. Whose idea was it to tie those men to the mine in Kerry and detonate it?"

"Does it really matter?"

"We always believed it was you."

"I won't change your mind, so why bother."

Briody walked over to the window. All the nine men killed that awful day had been close friends of his. He had escaped capture because he had gone to Killarney for a meeting. On his way back he had watched from the roof of a farmhouse as they were blown into little pieces, blown beyond recognition as animal life. He strode over to Brannigan and jabbed the gun into his forehead. "It very much matters to me."

"Goddamn you, Briody, are we going to sit here and debate what side was more cruel than the other? Are we going to go over the details of every killing, of every operation?"

"There are degrees."

"I'm sure the dead will be pleased to hear that."

"We targeted the leadership. We used sound methods."

"You shot men like dogs."

"We didn't torture and we sure as hell didn't kill prisoners for sport."

"Just fecking do it."

Briody pulled the trigger and there was a loud click. Brannigan sobbed. He looked up and Briody saw fear in his eyes. Who is to say which of us is worse? He chambered a round. For a minute he kept the pistol pressed so hard to Brannigan's forehead that blood began to trickle, snaking its way down the contours of the man's face. But Briody knew what he had intuited long before he came to this room. He could not kill. Not for this. Not anymore.

Moving the pistol a few inches to the left, he squeezed off a round, the bullet exploding a pillow on the bed, causing a cloud of feathers to swirl in the air. He slid the pistol into his belt and grabbed Brannigan by the hair. "When the boy comes back with your whiskey tell him the key is under the bed. They want you dead. Run, or they will have you dead. You can't hide in this city.

When you get out, leave through the delivery dock and keep running till you get back to Ireland. America is no place for the likes of you."

Briody left him stunned and sobbing in the chair. He took the stairs down and walked through the lobby and out onto the darkened street. He looked about, assuming he was being watched. As he moved along that cold wet avenue he hoped Brannigan had the sense to disappear. Briody knew it was the only thing that might buy him time. When O'Brien found out, he needed to be gone.

The trees were on fire with autumnal colors, a glorious flaring of red and gold and burnt orange against a blue Long Island sky, but she managed to turn the scene, to paint it sinister and full of foreboding so it held the threat of a bleak and sustained winter. Her easel was set up on the patio at the head of a lawn that stretched the length of a hurling pitch down to the sound. Pleasure boats cut through whitecapped water. Farrell was rarely there as of late but always present were his men with weapons, usually two or three, sporting hard faces and polished gunmetal. They always seemed bored.

She drew her captors for fun, putting rodent features to their faces and handing the sketches to them as she finished, watching as they shook their heads and stared at the likenesses. She heard them muttering about her, calling her the wacky dame and worse, but always at the edge of hearing and never when Farrell was around. She knew they could not hurt her, not because they did not want to, but simply because they were not allowed.

She had recruited one of the boys who worked on the grounds as an accomplice, a message carrier, and had sent a series of notes to Anna. But when Grace read the note from Briody she started to cry, because she knew he would come for her and that he would probably be killed, and she sent back a lie, trying to let him down easy but mostly to assure him that he would never find her. She needed to get out on her own without anyone else being hurt. After that she did not send the boy to New York anymore. She cut herself off from the world beyond that long lawn.

When Farrell was around she was always smiling at him. In fact, she was just pulling her lips back away from her teeth, but he did not know the difference. But this was good. This was okay. She was slowly suckering him, baiting him, working toward a moment's respite, a lowering of his guard, and then she would be off and running and there would be no stopping her this time. She would find Briody and they would keep running forever if they had to. She was adapting to her role as prisoner, was biding her time. The day's rhythm was always the same. Up early and back to bed soon after dark. They gave her books, and lately Farrell even allowed her paintings and etchings. At night she dreamed of violence, of smoke and death.

Farrell came out to her with a pitcher of lemonade. He stood behind her for a few moments and placed his hand on her shoulder. "Now that's a pretty picture, Grace. Beautiful."

"Thank you."

"Crazy weather this late in the year."

She put down her brush and joined Farrell at the umbrella table. They sipped the sweetened drink and made small talk. His anger at her betrayal was waning, mostly because of her acts of false affection, but also because she continuously downplayed her feelings for Briody, calling it a fling and no more. She wondered if Farrell was stupid enough to believe her act. She thought he just might be, and that he had better be because she was counting on it. His ego was so big he had had a hard time believing she had betrayed him once, and must have figured it could not happen to him a second time. She was grateful for this.

"How's things in the city?"

She sensed an instant deepening of his mood. He stared out over the water for a time before saying, "Great, Grace, just great." And he was so obviously lying that she felt obligated to comment on it but kept her mouth shut. She hoped that the more his troubles increased the less he would focus on her.

"Is there anything I can do?" She placed her hand on his shoulder, and although her concern was a fiction, in a way she felt for him and for all that his crazy ambition had wrought. She imagined there had been a time in his life when those flashes of charm and decency were much more constant, before all his strivings and conniving had darkened and hardened him. They sat for several hours as the sun swung overhead and fell, turning the sky the color of the trees. The air cooled and she packed up her easel and she stopped in the kitchen and poured herself a glass from the tap. For a second she was alone and she opened the first drawer she could and there it was, a long sharp knife for carving meat. She took it quickly and slid it inside her easel to the hilt, which she concealed by carrying it between her arm and side. She would be free of the place and Farrell before winter, one way or another.

nna?" He found her outside her father's Riverside Drive apartment walking a small dog. She pulled up the lapels of her coat and hunched her shoulders as if she was trying to disappear into the folds of her clothing. She was drained of all her usual cockiness.

She held up a hand, palm out, and did not meet his eyes. "Listen, I don't know what to tell you. I just don't know. They're always watching me." She looked past him, both ways up and down the street. "I am going to Europe until all this craziness blows over. You had a brain you would be heading out of town too."

"Why hasn't she called?"

"I don't have an answer for you, Michael. I know she was crazy for you but I just don't know."

"Did she get my letter?"

"Here." She dug a sheet of paper from her pocket. "I didn't think you really wanted to see this."

He read her response. "Dear Michael, I am sorry for this trouble, but please, I can no longer see you. I wish you all the best. We had quite a fun time of it, didn't we? Yours, Grace."

Briody let his hand drop to his side and watched a number of grim-faced women get off the crosstown bus carrying empty sacks. They headed north into the park, and although they traveled as a group, they did not speak to one another.

"Housewives." Anna said. "Every day, they come. Scavenging in the dumps for scraps of food. That's what this country has come to. I can't imagine they would put up with this anywhere else. This dog eats better than they do."

"I'm not so sure."

"About the dog?"

"What other places might put up with."

"Right. I forgot you were from someplace else. Listen. These men will kill you, Michael. You have to understand. You need to be afraid."

Briody looked at her. She was tired now, a woman whose most vibrant years had been misspent. He knew she was absolutely correct. But he also knew his need for Grace was greater than his fear. "When are you leaving?"

She glanced at her watch. "In three hours." She pushed past him, then stopped and yanked the dog. "I hope things work out, Michael. For you and for her. She's the best friend I ever had."

Briody read the note again. Was it truly what she wanted? He looked around on the street, watched as another platoon of scavenger women debussed, as others walked over along the side street down from the tenements along Amsterdam Avenue and Columbus, others up from Hell's Kitchen. It was a bleak scene but it could not compare to the starkness he felt in his heart.

There's doubt about him, Danny, doubts that go all the way back."

Danny stared out onto the street. Behind him his children tumbled about the worn furniture.

"So, it's me or him?"

"Not at all. But it is a war. We cannot allow ourselves to be compromised."

"He's a good man."

"Good men make mistakes, good men weaken."

"What's your proof?"

"I don't believe in coincidence."

"It happens."

O'Brien twirled his hat. "I did not want to have to do this, but do you remember his safe house in London? He either has the worst luck in the history of insurgency or he is an agent. The choice has been made. The order came straight from the top. I wanted to extend to you the courtesy of prior knowledge. It would behoove you not to abuse that courtesy."

"That's very kind of you."

"This is not easy for any of us."

"I ran through shite and blood and fire with that man. He wasted away over forty days on a hunger strike for the cause and you want me to believe he sold us out? Can I ask you what you have ever suffered for the cause?"

O'Brien studied him. "All the suffering in the world is one thing. Betrayal is another. It happens to the best of men. But in a war hard choices need to be made. Don't confuse things, Danny."

"I'm not confused at all, O'Brien."

"All right. Here it is. After I gave Briody the location of the last target the man suddenly decamped back to Dublin. Briody was seen going into the hotel and leaving. He let Black Jack Brannigan, of all the murderous scum, walk out of here alive."

Casey blew out breath and looked up at O'Brien. "Maybe something else spooked him."

"As I said, I don't believe in coincidence."

Casey walked O'Brien down the stairs and out onto Alexander Avenue.

"Remember, man, discipline and loyalty are our greatest weapons."

Casey nodded and watched as O'Brien slipped into his car and drove off. When he came up the stairs his wife stood in the door-way to their apartment, shaking her head. She stared hard at him. "Nothing good will ever come from that man."

Casey pushed past her into the close air of his living room and his children swarmed around him.

．　．　．

H ow's your inamorata?"

They were in the apartment above the seafood restaurant and he was slightly nauseous from the stink of rotting fish. Farrell had made the mistake of telling the Dago about Grace and her transgressions and now he tried to play it off, to wave it away as nothing but idle chatter. As angry as he was, he did not want her falling prey to the Dago and his band of cutthroats. God forbid. "Women. She's a frisky one but I have her under my thumb."

He sat waiting for him to do what, say more? Farrell forced himself to stay quiet.

The Dago leaned forward. "I find that they only understand strength. Women are like children and dogs. When they transgress they need to be punished, to be taught there are consequences to their actions."

They sat in the front room overlooking the crowded street and sipped wine brought to them by one of the Dago's two favorite minders. He could not keep the names straight, but one was lumbering and appeared to be thick except for the eyes, which were obviously bright and full of quick wit to go with his animal strength. The other was a wiry fellow no taller than your average jockey, and despite his scant physique projected an awful menace. Farrell never knew when they would or would not be there and he had the feeling that the Dago kept the two of them guessing just as much.

"Maybe I should introduce her to Pasquale, here. He has a way with women."

The Dago actually laughed, which was a rarity, and the slight Pasquale smiled with such leering glee that it seemed an obscenity.

Farrell shuddered. "No, no. I have it handled."

Pasquale asked, "You so sure?" and Farrell could only imagine what kind of old-world hellhole might produce such concentrated malice.

"Yes. I'm damn sure." Farrell's voice rose more than he wanted it to, but the thought of that animal going near Grace was still horrifying. He saw something cross Pasquale's face and knew he had just been lodged on the killer's blacklist. It was a mistake to respond. He was on equal footing with the Dago and should not even bother with the likes of Pasquale, who was nothing more than a nasty street urchin. The look chilled him to the bone, because he knew that it would not be forgotten. The Dago, amused by the interaction, did nothing to discipline his underling. He waved the two of them out.

"Pasquale is an eager soldier. Don't take him so serious. He will only do what he is told."

"I'm sure he serves his purpose."

"True. I was sorry not to hear from you last week, or the week before."

"I have been busy. Crater's vanishing is causing me a lot of problems. We should have talked about that."

"Sometimes talk is not worth much."

Farrell watched Vamonte walk over to the window and sit on the sill, the light from the street backlighting him so he could not make out the features of his face. He had broken his own promise by coming down here, but felt the right thing, the manly thing, was to let the Dago know face to face that it was time for, at the very least, a hiatus.

He attempted an assertive tone. "We can't run amok, there are rules. There is a system, a structure, in place. You yourself always go on about how violence is bad for business."

"Is there any evidence the Judge, he met with violence?"

It was Farrell's turn to smirk. "Please."

"I read the papers. Many people believe he is on the run."

"No one that matters believes that." Farrell stood. "I think we need to curb things for a while. Let the air clear over this—let a little time go by. Then we can move forward." He put his hat on.

The Dago nodded. "Maybe you know best."

"I know how these things play out. I've been around a long time. We need to let this thing fade. Everything is too hot right now. I'll get in touch when things are a little cooler."

He extended his hand and the Dago said, "Cooler?" and let the hand hang out there for an agonizing length of time before he shook it.

Farrell felt his resolve waver. "For a time."

At this the Dago merely stared. Farrell turned and walked out the door, feeling the eyes on his neck like hot breath. He hurried down the stairs and when he crossed the street he turned and looked up at the window. At first he looked at the wrong floor and then when he got it right there was the Dago staring down at him with that same blank, pitiless look, and in the next window was the evil elfin profile of Pasquale. Farrell, walking sideways, bumped into a street cart, knocking tomatoes and eggplant onto the sidewalk. The vendor cursed him in a strange singsong tongue. Farrell bent to help him but the man pushed him away with his hand so Farrell righted himself and walked on, making a great effort not to look back a second time.

In the instant Briody came awake he was certain he was not alone. He rolled on his side and reached for the pistol to find it gone. He sat up, the fear washing away all his fatigue. He made out the shadow of a man with a gun.

"Relax, the name is Egan. I think we have a mutual interest."

The light clicked on and Briody rubbed his eyes. "What might that be?"

"To see Grace live to become a grandmother."

Briody figured this must be the man Grace spoke of. "I don't know you."

"I know you."

"Why should I trust you?"

Egan handed him back his pistol. "Ah, but how do I count the reasons? Let's take a drive."

Briody had fallen asleep in his work clothes; now he threw some water on his face and followed Egan downstairs. On the street two hard-eyed men stood smoking against a Chrysler. At Egan's approach they tossed off their cigarettes and looked up expectantly. Egan dismissed them with a wave and jumped behind the wheel. Briody joined him in the car. They made a left on the corner and headed east across town in the hour before dawn.

Briody was still agitated at being taken unawares. It was the kind of slip that could easily get him killed. But lately he seemed incapable of focusing. He was weakening and outside of his working day he simply was not really among the living. His retreat to his room was automatic. He no longer went to the gym or ran, or joined the men for a drink. Grace's note had unnerved him and he was unsure of how to act, what to do. Was she just trying to protect him? As much as he loved her he was not sure. There was something unfathomable about her that he figured time would smooth away. He lived in limbo. The building was almost done, and then what?

On the Queensboro Bridge he asked the obvious: "Who do you work for?"

Egan maneuvered around a slow-moving truck and, hitting the accelerator hard, answered, "Grace and I have a working relationship."

"That's not an answer to my question."

"Let's just say the good people of New York and leave it at that."

"So you're a cop?"

"Of a sort."

"Not of New York City."

"Yes and no."

"Are you from Washington?"

"Not there."

Briody was not in the mood for games so he sat silently as they passed through Queens, anxious to be shown where Grace was being held. Then he would be that much closer to getting her back. He would figure out the how later. Right now the where was the most vital thing he needed to ascertain.

Presently they crossed the city line and Briody was surprised at the hilly beauty, the lush estates which seemed impossibly grand. They turned down a lane and passed one house after another that was on the scale of a palace. One was surrounded by hedges so high you could only see the top floor. In the widening light Egan said, "That's where your love is being kept."

As they rolled by the driveway, Briody looked in at the vast grounds, which led to an Italianate mansion. "Arnold Rothstein had the place built to resemble an estate somewhere in Tuscany. Strange for a Jew, I always thought."

"I wouldn't know about that." Briody had no interest in a history lesson. Now that he knew where she was, he felt his resolve returning. "How do I get her out of there?"

"You promise to help me, I can get her out of there for you."

"What do you want?"

"I want her to testify."

"I can't say what she'll do."

"We can keep her safe."

"Like Judge Crater safe?"

"The Judge was not on my team." Egan pulled away. "We don't want to dally too long here. There'll be eyes on us."

Briody studied the street intently, planning a mission in his head. As they neared a bend in the road he saw the water and realized all the houses backed onto the sound. That was good, another avenue of attack.

On the way back to New York Egan drove hard, constantly roaring past slower cars. He kept his window down so the two of them had to shout to be heard. Egan defined himself as some kind of civic avenger bent on taking down the corrupters. Briody suspected there was more to it than that, that a power was lurking unseen behind this man. Near Corona they passed a huge pair of eyes staring from a billboard.

Egan hit the brake, cursed as the car fishtailed to avoid a woman on a bicycle. "You should know I have Grace's interests in mind."

"Why don't you go and get her yourself?"

"Things are complicated."

"Nothing is what it seems?"

"We are not yet ready to make ourselves known."

"In the meantime . . ."

"Grace has heart, Grace has spunk."

"You can't go forward without her?"

"I wish I could. She knows all the right things."

"I might be a greenhorn, but you really believe you can take down the powers that be?"

"The time is right. We have the will."

Briody let it go at that. Crossing the bridge, they came to a standstill in early morning traffic. He wondered if freeing her from Farrell and handing her to Egan was such a great idea. From the apex of the bridge he could see the Chrysler Building spire, and behind it, higher now, the Empire State, which glowed as if on fire halfway up, the new windows reflecting the rising sun. He instructed Egan to head for the site.

When he got out of the car Egan promised he would stay in touch. Briody did not like the sound of that. He missed Tommy Touhey's knowledge of the underworld. What if this man was not who he said he was? Briody did not mention the ledger to Egan. Now that he knew where Grace was, it was up to him. For the first time in weeks, he felt fully alive.

Armstrong was standing on the sidewalk peeling an apple with a pocketknife. "You sure do keep strange company for a greenhorn."

"Ah, just a Yank cousin, is all."

"Yeah, and I'm the king of France." Armstrong slapped Briody on the back. "Welcome to your last day as an ironworker. Today is the day. We top off and it's hitting the bricks for us. The party's over."

Briody followed Armstrong to the hiring shack, where they picked up their brass IDs. They shoved onto the elevator and the screen was pulled closed. The operator yelled, "Seventy-five express," and leaned on the lever. They whooshed skyward at 1,500 ear-popping feet a minute.

Up on the steel the air was so cold that Briody's face went numb. They worked at a leisurely pace, securing the last beams. The men took turns dropping down to the deck and warming their hands over the molten heat of the rivet forge. Their time in the sky was over. Briody watched as the last rivet gangs climbed up to them along with the connectors and the rivet punks, the various foremen and superintendents. Grace's photographer, Hine, worked setting up his camera on a tripod. Briody could scarcely believe six months had passed.

Hard Nose McCabe held his hat down with one hand and rode up on the headache ball. They carried a flag up and unfolded it and it started to whip and snap in the wind, wrapped around Briody, shrouding him in the stars and stripes. Armstrong laughed. "Look at you now, Paddy, a true Yankee, all right."

Briody laughed and then the picture was taken that would forever show him there, behind Armstrong and just to the side of Hard Nose McCabe, who was reaching out to hold the lanyard that secured the flag as it whipped violently in the wind. He said a quiet prayer for Sheehan and the other men who had died. A flask was passed and they drank and looked out over the city, not a single derrick waving in the sky, and they had to wonder if this was the last time any of them would ever be this high above the streets.

Briody took his time climbing down and wandered around the top floor, stepping over tools and buckets and planks. He could not believe it was over. They had thrown up so much steel and now he stood on the pinnacle of all that labor and wished it would go another hundred stories. He went over and took the torch and, hanging over the open spaces of the city, seared his name into the back side of a beam, marking his participation.

Out on the north river, another of the huge passenger liners was being nudged to dock by a quartet of tugs. Briody watched for a minute wondering what her next port of call might be. It seemed from this vantage that he could just step out on the deck and go.

He took off his gloves and laid them on the plank where they had eaten their last lunch and then whistled for the crane. When the ball spun out he hopped on and rode down to the seventy-fifth-floor setback, then made his way inside to ride the elevator down. He was the last of his gang to leave the site. As he walked out onto Fifth Avenue he knew something he would miss as much as the men and the work. He would miss the structure the job gave to his life, the sense of purpose.

They hit the Cave with a rush of adrenaline and drank like men trying to drown, celebrating the topping off with mad exuberance. The drink was free and the bartenders worked as fast as they could to keep the men happy. At the end of the shift the rest of the trades came in and joined the ironworkers, who were well on their way. Briody carried on with the best of them, drinking hard and telling the tales; already they were entering the stuff of legend, they would be talked about for generations and he was in the thick of it. But a part of him was not there at all. In the small hours, woozy from the booze, he left. As he passed the building he leaned forward, pressed his face against it, and kissed the cool product of midwestern quarries, then walked on. He felt there was a reason that the job had ended and he had found where Grace was on the same day. There was no choice to be made.

Farrell came downstairs and gave the doorman the usual backslap and wink. He had not heard from the Dago in nearly a week and assumed the gangster was getting the message. Farrell had been stern at their last meeting, he thought, had demonstrated the need to keep their distance, to go their separate ways. A clean break for the time being, he had said. The Dago had surely smirked his usual half smirk and nodded his head, but had not disagreed, had not put forth an argument. And so far, nothing. Maybe he was in the clear, the Dago intimidated by his standing in the city.

Out on the street he looked for his children and was surprised to see they had walked down in front of the next building where a slight man was bending over, patting their heads. Farrell did not recognize him as a neighbor and when he called out the man stood and smiled and Farrell felt his blood run cold, a wave of nausea. It was Pasquale and he was smiling and for a moment Farrell wanted to run back into the building and hide but his children were staring at him so he was unable to move and as Pasquale passed he tipped his hat and said, "Beautiful babies," in that rotten English and walked on, turning the corner backlit by the dazzling sun, which blinded Farrell when he looked after him. His kids ran to him, waving bright cherry red lollipops.

Farrell rubbed his eyes and wondered, had he even seen Pasquale? He bent to hug the children and they thrust the candy at him, saying, "Daddy, look what your friend gave us." He snatched the lollipops and threw them into the Fifth Avenue gutter, then dragged his children, screaming now, into the imagined safety of their building.

arry held a steady course up the East River and through the Hell Gate, the inboard motor droning with a steady hum. The wind was cold and sharp and there were no other boats out at the late hour. Briody sat next to the captain's chair holding the gun Tommy Touhey had given him, the gun he had been meaning to throw away but was now glad he had kept. He spun the cylinder and then inserted bullets into each chamber. He flipped the pistol closed and then slid it into his waistband and as they made their way along the Long Island shore he jiggled extra slugs in his hand like a dice player. Harry, unusually quiet, was intent on his piloting, so Briody went over the operation in his head, a habit from his IRA days, when he was known as a meticulous planner, a man for detail. He never sent men on a mission that he had not orchestrated himself, and as he thought how things might go, he knew this was not a job he would send anyone else to do.

He knew the basic lay of the land, knew what room she slept in, and knew Farrell was in the city for the night so she would be alone. There was a guard shack at the end of the long drive where at least one armed guard worked all night. That was the sum of his knowledge. He was going in blind. There were too many variables, too many ways things might go badly. He was desperate. And desperation always led to recklessness. As they passed through Throgs Neck he convinced himself there was no other option. Even if Egan was able to get her out he would want to keep her under wraps and force her to testify, something Briody was certain she had no intention of doing.

As they rounded the shoulder of Long Island Harry stayed close to shore and Briody listened to the sound of the wake lapping the rocky coast. The houses grew larger and better lit as they passed by Queens. Briody wondered at the lives being lived in those golden rooms. He shifted the pistol to the small of his back and moved to the side to escape the trail of Harry's cigar smoke. When they spotted the pier at Great Neck, Harry killed the boat's lights and tossed his cigar overboard, cutting the speed down to a slow steady rate. Briody pulled a watch cap out of the bag at his feet and tugged the scratchy wool down to his brow.

"All right, Harry, hold at anchor, and whatever happens, don't leave the boat."

The old man nodded and stooped to retrieve something from below the wheel. Briody saw that it was a Tommy gun and said nothing.

"I got a trick or two up my sleeve. Go get her, Mick."

Briody nodded and slipped over the side of the boat. He sloshed through water knee-deep and cold. Then he took a step and he was falling in over his head and he beat his arms and rose to the surface, gasping for air. They must have docked on a sandbar. He doggy-paddled a few feet until he found a firm footing and climbed up the bank. He made his way, dripping wet, along the rocky beach fighting his fear and now a bone-cold chill. He wondered if the gun would fire. He moved on the balls of his feet. Some of the houses were dark for the season; from others yellow lights splashed squares onto lawns that stretched to the water's edge. Dogs barked in the distance. He found the seventh house in and then scaled the fence, lowering himself into the yard. There was no moon and he waited until his eyes adjusted to the gloom. Ahead lay a sparse grove of trees and then an expanse of lawn that ran to a patio and then an enclosed deck. He took several deep breaths and then took off, hugging the fence.

Halfway up he pressed his back to a fat oak tree to collect himself, to steady his nerves, to listen. The wind moved through the trees, shaking the dying leaves, and the cold was through him. He snuck along the side of that huge house toward the front drive until he was behind the guard shack, where he was relieved to find only one man sitting. Briody saw that he was reading a newspaper, so he swung around the booth and punched him through the open window. The blow caught the guard square and Briody, to make sure he was not going to be a problem, crowded in and belted him three more times, savage shots that ripped the skin of his face, splattering blood about the booth. The man collapsed in a heap and Briody yanked out the phone wire. He found a gun on the table and tossed it far onto the neighbor's lawn.

He hurried back along the side of the house to the backyard, crouching as he passed below windows. At the rear door he knelt and, finding it locked, used electrical tape to crisscross the windowpane above the handle. He tapped it, breaking the glass, and pulled it out, then reached inside to unlock the door. In the kitchen he squeaked across the tile floor on his soggy feet, the sound seeming to roar his presence.

In the left hallway he found the one that had to be her room, because there was a chair next to the door and it was locked from the outside. He slid the bolt and when he pulled open the door he saw a flash of white coming at him and he grabbed her and the steel blade went past his chest.

"Michael, Jesus. I nearly gutted you."

"Well, I could not really call ahead, now could I? Let's go."

He looked back at the trail of water he had left, then heard two men speak. As they turned the corner he pushed her back into the room. He smiled and held up his hands to show he was not armed. The two men started and then rushed for him. He hit the one in front with a quick, hard right and the man fell forward and Briody caught him by reflex. Jumping back, he pulled his gun out and pointed it at the other man. He heard something behind him, but before he could turn he felt a pistol jammed to the back of his head.

"All right, smart guy. Drop it."

Briody considered an elbow, but then the other one would have time to pull his gun and he was pretty sure he would not hesitate to shoot. He held his left hand out to the side and let the gun drop and it clattered along the floor and then he was seeing stars and as he went to one knee he realized he had been smacked with the gun, but not hard enough to be knocked out. He felt blood start to trickle hot down his neck and then he heard the door slam open, and the guy behind him screamed and fell on top of him and it was Grace yelling, "Grab the gun, Michael."

The other guard turned and ran and Briody realized he must

not be armed but had to be going for a gun. "Come on." She was pulling him up and he turned and the one from behind him was crawling along the blood-slick floor, a knife buried to the handle in his back, crawling to God knew what. Briody picked up the man's gun and they pushed out through the glass doors and ran onto that impossible lawn. They were halfway down to the water when floodlights came on and suddenly it was midday and there was nowhere to hide and he heard the crack of pistol fire so he aligned himself behind Grace to block her from any bullets that might find a target. A second shooter had joined in and now he heard the boom of a shotgun and even before the sound registered there was a burning in his shoulder and scalp and he smelled scorched flesh. The shots were honing in and he knew the second shooter was the more skilled of the two. He cut left and grabbed her by the hand and in the artificial light he briefly saw her face and was amazed that there was no fear in it, it was determined and grim. They hugged the tree line and rested for a minute in the scant shadow.

"Nice to see you, Michael. What took you so long?" And she was actually smiling.

He did not want her to know the true answer to that question, for while she was apparently fearless, lately he was full of fear.

"Come on now, it's up and over." He interlocked his fingers and gave her a boost up. He gave her a few seconds to get clear and then he jumped, grabbing the top of the fence, but pain spiraled down his back and he could not hold the grip, sliding back down. His only option was to run because they were charging down the lawn after him. He pulled the gun out of his waistband. He was losing blood and could feel dizziness come over him. He squeezed off two shots in the direction of the house, purposely high and wide, and then took off out of the shadows, sprinting, tossing off a third shot. He was again a running target, but now out in the open. He made the gate and shot the lock but it did not open, knelt and fired again and still it held. He could smell his own animal fear, could hear his heart pounding in his ears. Bullets cracked through the fence inches from his head, tore up the grass by his feet. He had one bullet left. He turned and fired and then kicked the gate with all the strength he had left, once, then twice, and finally on the third try it swung open and he was through it. As he ran down the dock, bullets snapped the air around his head. He dove into the frigid water, the shock of it bringing him totally back to focus. The boat was beside him and Harry was laying down a suppressing fire with the Tommy gun, the fat hot bullets churning up the fence, sending splinters and wood shards into the air while Grace pulled him onto the boat. He heard a few more pops and suddenly it was silent. Harry pulled off the empty drum, dropped it, then scampered to the wheel, slamming the throttle open so hard they all fell back as the boat roared away from land, and then they were going full tilt, the speed surprising to him now.

Harry steered easily and they cut through the channel for Silver Beach, where Mannion had a safe house set up for them. Harry angled the boat to the pier and Briody jumped off. He helped Grace out and then they watched as Harry pushed off, spun the boat, and hit the gas hard, leaving an angry white wake.

Inside the cottage Briody built a fire, then sat in front of it, shirtless, while Grace dug shotgun pellets out of his shoulder with a hot knife, plunking them into a tin cup.

"That's eight. I don't think there are any more. Least not ones I can get to." She ran her fingers through his hair, feeling the scalp for pellets. "I think the head wound is just a graze."

She found some gauze in the medicine cabinet and after cleaning the wound wrapped it tight. "This place is well stocked."

"Tommy's man, Mannion, says they have a half dozen scattered about the area, all set up for those on the run."

"Maybe we can just stay here, wait things out."

"Movement might be better."

"Why did you come for me, Michael?"

"I didn't think I had a choice, really."

"I was hoping you wouldn't." She stared for a moment. "But wishing you would. If that makes any sense at all."

Briody did not answer. He stood and pushed the chair away and then pulled blankets and pillows from the bed, and then used his good arm to ease Grace out of her dress. They lay in front of the fire unclothed, letting the heat bake the chill out of their bones, holding each other, sleep impossible despite their fatigue. It wasn't until the sun from the east turned the room full of hard light that they were able to drift off.

Farrell arrived at the mansion and listened to the report in grim silence. Once again he had been played for a clown by this woman who had professed love and devotion to him, all along knowing it was nothing but a ploy to deceive him. He felt stupid and weak, like a moronic schoolboy tricked by an ingenue. He saw in the eyes of the men that they thought him a fool. She was only a woman, after all, and wasn't the world full of them? He noticed the knife sticking out of the dead man and wondered if it had been meant for his own chest. Probably. Her little prison break had saved his life. He knew now he should have listened to the Dago. He should have killed her. She knew too much, was a danger to too many.

He figured it was the Irishman who had come for her and he was surprised. He did not think the Mick had it in him. He stepped over the dead man and walked through the emptiness of that great house and slid the glass doors open to look out at the sound. She was out there on the water, slipping away from him. He had no choice now. He had to find her and he had to kill her, to silence her forever. The wind picked up and the soft lights on the far shore twinkled out one by one as the darkness pressed down. He sat, alone, and sipped from his flask, letting the whiskey burn all the way to his gut.

. . .

race woke first and propped her head on her elbow, studying Briody as he slept. He had lost weight since she had seen him last and his tan was gone. She watched his eyes twitch with some dream, muted sounds coming out of him. She hoped his wounds would heal all right, without infection. From her knees she bent and kissed him softly, then pulled on a shirt and went to the kitchen and made tea.

The view out the window was stunning, a New England seascape of boats in various states of repair, masts bobbing gently, denuded trees, a rocky coast. The water was a hard blue. You would never guess you were in New York City, waking up to these sights. She stood on the back lawn, the grass wet beneath her feet. Off in the western distance she was surprised to see the skyline of Manhattan. From her perspective the Chrysler Building lined up perfectly with the Empire State standing behind it, looming with much greater mass as if you could easily fit the Chrysler inside of it. The kettle whistled so she went back inside. She took her tea and sat in a rocking chair and waited for Briody to come back to her. He stirred and when he turned to her his face was chalky white, the hollows so pronounced around his eyes that she saw there a death mask. She took her tea and went out onto the deck.

When she finished she went back in and the light in the room had softened and now he was just a man asleep. They needed to get out of town and they needed some money to do so. After all she had been through she was not leaving broke. Outside the sun was already falling. She put more wood on the fire. Briody began to wake up. She watched him, feeling ashamed that somehow she had become a prize that men fought and died over.

For the next few days Grace and Briody rarely strayed from the cottage. There was an ample store of food and they cooked elaborate dinners, read books, drank hot tea, and rested always with an ear to the road above the house. Grace tended to Briody's wounds, which were healing without problems. After breakfast on the fourth morning Grace propped the singed journal on the kitchen table. "More than seven million dollars in forty-one different accounts. I never realized it was so much."

Briody sipped his tea. "I figure it's the only way out for us. He needs to know what we have."

"I'm not so sure. I'm scared, Michael. Maybe we should just go."

"You can only run so far before the past catches you. It's better if we can leave clean."

"I don't know if this is enough." She closed the book.

"I think we need to take the chance."

They went back and lay on the bed, which overlooked the sea. "You know, despite everything, I hate the idea of leaving New York. It's the first place I ever truly felt at home."

She ran her fingers down his side, pushed her head further onto his chest. "I feel the same way. But things have a way of working out. I'll wager we'll be back someday, when they are all gone."

"I doubt they will ever be gone."

"Nothing lasts forever. Especially not in this city. If I've learned anything it's that."

He kept quiet on the other *they* that worried him as much or more. He needed to talk to Danny, to see where he stood. That was a group he saw forever fighting, forever settling scores. He felt a wave of guilt as if he was abandoning what he most believed in, but in truth were they not really forsaking him? O'Brien, he suspected, needed to define himself by enemies real and imagined. He just hoped Danny and the lads saw him for what he was.

"I'm going to Tammany Hall."

"Michael, don't."

"The man is no killer."

"How can you be sure?"

"The one place he will least expect to see me is his sanctuary in Union Square."

. . .

gan, we cannot afford to let her get away." Farrell stared across his desk at the Captain, weighing whether to tell him that he had involved the Dago. He thought, No, not yet.

"She's an amateur."

"I wish I could agree."

"I have my best men scouring the train stations, the bus depots. I posted roadblocks at major city byways and bridge and tunnel entrances. We're turning this city upside down. Don't worry, John. We'll reel her in."

"She knows far too much."

"I ain't gonna say I told you so."

" 'Cause you didn't."

"But you get a woman that's going around behind your back, she's capable of just about anything."

Farrell felt the heat come into his face. A lecture he did not need. "She's not in here, Egan, so go." Farrell fluttered his fingers toward the door.

"Right."

When Egan left he stared at a picture on the wall taken in Saratoga, at the Travers. He remembered Briody's connection to the lawyer O'Brien and decided it was worth paying the man a visit. First he leafed through the day's mail. There was the usual stack but one was a thick envelope with a return address in the Bronx. He sliced it open and dumped it on his desk and stacks of bills tumbled out. He picked up a handwritten note. It was from Touhey's widow and read, "No thanks you creep. Tommy told me everything." The last word was underlined three times. He shook his head, exhaled slowly, and then crumbled the note and pitched it over his shoulder into the bin. He gathered the money back into an envelope and stuck it in his desk drawer.

On his way out to the street he thought it funny how twenty grand seemed nothing more than pocket change to him these days, and how money, his obsession for so long, was now literally the least of his worries. There was a massive demonstration in the park and he questioned the wisdom of moving the wigwam here, making it a target of convenience to every pack of loonies that decided to come to Union Square and air their grievances. He took one look out the front door, turned on his heels, and made his way to the side entrance, passing unmolested down Seventeenth Street to Irving Place, where he flagged a cab.

He was shown right into O'Brien's office and the spit-shined attorney met him on the soft carpet and shook his hand with such sustained vigor that Farrell felt it going numb. "John Farrell. You're looking grand, boyo. Please have a seat."

Farrell sat down and massaged his hand under the desk. He had met O'Brien while attending a seminar the man taught at Fordham Law and they had hit it off, both being Bronx Irish. Since then Farrell had been in the position to occasionally toss the man some valuable city contract work. O'Brien did not forget a favor.

"Amazing what's going on in this city. Crater pulling his Houdini act. Must be driving you guys nuts."

Farrell accepted a proffered cigar. If you only knew. He lit the cigar and sat back, puffing hard. He wondered how forthright he might be with his old professor.

"So, lad. I'm usually the one coming to you, hat in hand, looking for a bit of work or a favor. To what do I owe the pleasure?"

Farrell had the odd feeling that O'Brien had been expecting him but dismissed this as another manifestation of his increasing paranoia. "I'm looking to find someone. I thought maybe you might be able to help me."

"Why not?"

"Your friend the Irishman, the boxer."

"Briody?"

Farrell nodded yes.

"Is he in some kind of jackpot?"

"He's not making any friends in high places."

"You know a bit about me, John. He's a valuable part of our fraternal organization."

Farrell smiled at the euphemism.

"I can't afford to lose any top-quality men."

"I got a call today from the Commissioner of Finance. There is a new city issue to be offered. What with these being hard times we need some bonds to keep things going. I thought I might recommend your firm for a slice of the pie."

"Now would this quality fellow be missing on a temporary basis?"

"The word is it will be for a very long time."

"I hate to inflict my fraternal organization with any inconvenience."

Farrell took in the sweep of the office, the Fordham and Harvard degrees on the wall, the Harvard displayed with much more prominence, his military commission, and pictures of O'Brien with Calvin Coolidge, Eamon de Valera, and Charlie Chaplin of all people.

"I need to call the Commissioner back. I'm thinking such a worthwhile firm as yours, with such keen legal minds, I don't see why the whole pie can't be yours for the taking."

"Well, I think I can help you find what you are looking for."

Their business done, they reminisced about the old days, swapped stories of their golden years on the streets of the Bronx, although Farrell never bothered to point out that his Mott Haven streets were a very long way from O'Brien's shaded green streets of Riverdale.

"You really need to stop by one of my dinner parties, Johnny. The family would love to see you. Plus, we get quite the mix of guests, it's a real fine time."

O'Brien relished his cigar. He'd wanted to get rid of Briody for a long time. He could never fully trust an Irishman who had fought for the Crown. Besides, he saw a certain slackness coming into the movement, a lessening of discipline and resolve. Briody's warning off Black Jack Brannigan had been nothing short of treasonous. Doing away with Briody might be just the thing to snap his men back into a proper focus. And now his solution had just walked in the door. He was a firm believer in the theory that things always work out for the best. When his cigar was done he gathered his jacket and briefcase. He needed to send a telegram to Dublin.

. . .

E gan heard the word go out along the underworld wire, could feel the streets buzz with the news of five-thousand-dollar rewards. Grace Masterson and Michael Briody, five G's apiece. Every hood and bent cop for miles was out hunting such lucrative bounty. He chewed silently on a mouthful of peanuts, digging from a bowl before him on his table. He turned the radio down to cool the ranting of some disaffected preacher man howling from the hinterlands. Grace was crucial, Grace was critical.

He needed her safe and stashed away until the investigation became official. He needed her on the stand to back up all the data she had collected, not stretched out in the morgue. Egan realized he should never have shown the Irishman where she was being held, because his plan to use Briody to help convince Grace to testify had backfired badly. At least with Farrell she was ultimately accessible, but now she might be anywhere. He looked at his watch. The Governor wanted to be debriefed, and what was he to say? The most important piece of evidence was missing? That was unacceptable.

He took his jacket and pulled it on as he bounded down the stairs. He needed to start working other avenues, to pressure others to testify, but they were a seamy cast of characters that crawled through the sewers of the metropolis and they hardly made credible witnesses. Grace—attractive, smart, articulate, clean—she was the perfect witness. Plus, he knew that sooner or later his men would start bumping heads with the city cops and that this was bound to prove irksome. Time was crucial. As he passed through the door to the street he intercepted a messenger coming in the door. He took the envelope from the boy and signed for it. He stood there on that busy street and opened it. There was a note from Grace saying she would enjoy seeing him soon. He smiled. She was still in play.

. . .

Harry moved along the Brooklyn waterfront in the gathering dusk. The wind had changed and was coming out of the north now, cold and malevolent, the first spit of winter to come. He loped along with his eyes on the ground, scouring for bits of wire and tin. He, like many, had been reduced to a scavenger. He passed boarded-up factories, latched-down warehouses. Some were patrolled by dogs, others by low-paid guards, dregs, riffraff fresh from upstate prisons who rejoiced in spilling the blood of the hungry. Other buildings were simply abandoned to the vandals. He felt a presence and looked up toward the street. There was a dog slouching along, a four-legged mirror of himself. Then another and another; they gathered and watched him, sniffing the air, gauging his vitality, his ability to ward them off. There had been several attacks of late; an old woman was set upon just last week and fatally mauled.

He picked up a rock and threw it in their direction and yelled, but they stared sullen and did not back away. The toss set off the pain in his ribs. He still ached from the beating they had given him the night they grabbed Grace. He never bothered with the hospital and wondered if that was a mistake after all. He had been passing blood. He looked across to the island, which he had not visited in more than five years. That was where all his trouble was coming from. Below him Norwegian rats, plump, battened on corpses, slithered along the river muck. He moved faster, outpacing his canine shadows toward the pier and safe harbor. He noticed the car, black and new in the lost light, noticed the outline of two hatted heads. They paid him no mind and he reciprocated. They were there every night and day now, watching, waiting. In his dilapidated cabin he lit a fire and warmed his hands. He dug out a bottle, the last of his stash. He nodded off while sitting up, his back against the stove, so his bones stayed warm.

When he woke there were three of them standing before him and he knew that this time they would finish the job. What scared him the most was the smiling; for them it was not about anger, which sooner or later is always spent. These men were going to be patient in their doling out of misery. It was Mr. Fancy Pants from New York and two goons, they looked to be Eyetalians, not Irish.

He leaned forward and spit out his false teeth so he would not choke on them. He wished he had more whiskey and he wished he had more ammo for the Thompson and he especially wished that Grace would somehow learn that on this night he did his best. Just before the end, in a fever dream of pain and blood, he worried that the words Silver and Beach were pried out from deep within him.

On the trolley across the Bronx Briody pulled his coat around him and worried over any male old enough to be a shooter. He avoided eye contact and thought about work to keep his mind clear. Already he missed the job and the camaraderie and the intricate dance high above the streets. The day was crystal-clear and cold and when he changed to the IRT and passed under the South Bronx he imagined the Casey household. He missed them and knew he had to try and stop by to say goodbye before he left town.

He mingled with the demonstrators in Union Square, staring at the Hall, willing his fear away. His mouth was dry and he took a piece of chewing gum and slid it into his mouth, but it was like chewing on cotton. A black Pierce Arrow pulled to the curb and Farrell got out and dashed into the building, his driver moving on. Briody shouldered past men carrying signs denouncing Herbert Hoover, men gray-skinned and gaunt from hunger and lack of prospects. There was a mustiness to them that brought his prison days to mind. Briody went around to the side entrance of the Hall, worked the lock open with a pick, and let himself in.

He climbed the stairs and walked down a corridor lined with portraits of men with mustaches and steely gazes that seemed to say, I went out and made my way in the world. And you? What have you done? The polished floors were buffed to perfection. No one was around. Briody found Farrell's office and pushed his way in. There at a desk, his feet up, puffing on a cigar, was the Tammany man.

Farrell pushed back away from his desk and jumped up. "What the hell?"

"If I was here to kill you, you'd already be dead."

Farrell stared and then pulled himself together, sat down again. "You gotta be kidding me." He sipped from a tumbler of whiskey. "I gotta admire a guy like you. Some set of stones you must have for a donkey. You come walking in here to see me when I have half the cops and all the robbers in town hunting for you."

"I just wanted to thank you for getting me out of jail."

Farrell stared at him as if he did not recall. "What makes you think I can't have you put back in? And your little whore of a colleen? She left a dead body in that house."

Briody decided not to take offense at the epithet. "Because if you do, you'll be sharing a cell with us?"

"Wouldn't that be cozy?"

"I'm here so we can come to an understanding, so we can all get on with our lives. We just want to be left alone."

"That's sweet." Farrell started to smile and then broke into a chuckle, and then a laugh that progressed in intensity until he was giddy. He wiped his eyes with a handkerchief and shook his head. "That's terrific." He opened a drawer and placed a bottle and an extra glass for Briody, then proceeded to pour three fingers of Jameson into each, capped the bottle, and used it to nudge one of the glasses over the desk to Briody. "Drink up, boyo, while I explain the ways of the big city to you."

Briody sipped the whiskey.

"You see, I have a lot of say in a lot of things, but the word is out. You will be killed, as will Grace. It is beyond me. I am not a killer, as much as I'd like to be. I can unleash it, I can benefit from it even. I certainly have recently. Unfortunately in my despair over the way your friend has been acting I may have blurted out my dissatisfaction with her, her betrayal, and worse, her insane meddling in the affairs of dangerous men, many of whom have no qualms about killing. So you see, you better start running and you better not look back. My hands are washed of you, but you have more enemies than you can imagine."

Briody produced a few pages he had torn from Grace's journal, placed them on the desk. Farrell picked them up and quickly flipped through them. He shook his head. "Grace, Grace, Grace. My God, I am a fool." He crumbled the pages up and tossed them at Briody. "But you are a bigger fool. You came here to threaten me but you are powerless to do that. Even if you had what you think you have you don't know a thing about how this city works. Maybe you'll find a judge or a prosecutor we don't own, then you can try, try, that is, to sit a jury we can't tamper with, which might be a first. Then even if you get a case going you need to hope there is a public that we can't satiate with largesse, or that we can't conjure up a bigger and meaner bogeyman for them to hate. But even if all goes to plan what will happen? What will you get? You'll get me, Johnny Farrell. My head. I'll be ruined, destroyed. I'll be the sacrificial lamb. And as soon as the story is out I will be described as a mid-level operative, a political hack who got greedy, a maverick. That's right, that's how it goes. It was a risk I was willing to take. And the Organization will endure."

Briody stood and turned to leave.

"You have nothing! The beast is loosed and you are going to be run down and gorged on. I can't save you, and I can't even save her. But hey, Irishman. Tell her something for me."

Briody stopped at the door.

"Tell her that I wasn't lying. Tell the little whore I love her."

When Briody left Farrell worked the bottle hard until it was bone dry, then snorted the vapors. Tears streamed down his face. He opened the drawer and took out this time not a bottle but another vehicle to oblivion, an old revolver he had kept well oiled all these years—just in case. He turned the gun in his hand, read the markings, pressed it to his temple, feeling that steel, then shoved it in his mouth and tasted the tang of metal and oil. He cocked the hammer. He wrapped his index finger around the trigger, dropping his elbow, and angled the barrel so the muzzle was now pressing the flesh on the roof of his mouth; he rubbed a spot where he had scalded his mouth on a molten coffee at lunchtime, and the metal cooled the soreness. He closed his eyes and counted to three, started the count a second time and then a third.

He opened his eyes and was looking at the picture of Silent Charlie Murphy, his dead mentor and hero glaring at him in the heavy frame, and he could swear Silent Charlie shook his head. Suddenly he felt like a complete horse's ass and he dropped the gun to his desk, crossed to his couch, and passed out.

When Farrell came to, the Honorable Jimmy Walker was standing over him with his arms folded across his chest, his lips pursed. Beside him was Grover Whelan, the fat-faced Police Commissioner on leave from his wife's department store chain holding the pistol in one hand and the empty whiskey bottle in the other, which he handed to Walker. Whelan was the outside appointee, the man sent to deliver the PD from its natural tendencies toward graft and corruption. He hovered, projecting gravitas, and if Farrell had not felt so bad he would have laughed in his face. Farrell sat up too quickly and felt the blood drain and the bile rise so he grabbed the couch to steady himself.

Walker shook his head. The Commissioner tsk-tsked his low regard for Farrell. The Mayor put the bottle and pistol down and sat in Farrell's chair. When Farrell was able to glance up, he saw that the Mayor was not studying him but looking over at the picture of Murphy.

"We could use old Silent Charlie now."

Farrell grunted in response, stared at the Mayor in profile, the fine line of his nose, the Adam's apple, a wisp of a man who seemed to be losing what ballast he had.

"Silent Charlie told me the first rule of survival in this game was to spread the wealth. He reached out to the Jews, the Italians, the Germans, the Swedes, the Chinamen, and the colored. What enemies you can't charm, buy, what ones you can't buy, bully. He had that sense of calm; never let it be known that you have a problem, keep a straight face."

Walker smoothed the crease in his pants. He rubbed his jaw. "Johnny Farrell, I am having a hard time following that advice. I remember you, a fresh-faced kid from the Bronx, wanting to get in the game. We were all impressed by someone of your generation, you reminded us of our own younger selves, Johnny Farrell. You reminded us how far we had come because we strove to ascend. We encouraged you and you played the game like the best of them. We turned a blind eye when you cut corners. You made us proud, some of us rich."

Farrell wondered if he had any more whiskey stashed about.

"Crater is not coming home, is he?"

"I honestly don't know."

Walker seemed to take this badly. Farrell knew it had nothing to do with sorrow for the jurist, just what it might foretell.

"How's the family, Johnny?"

Farrell shrugged, and not from indifference. He did not have an answer to the question.

Walker stooped to fix his spats. "I don't need to tell you that Crater is a Pandora's box, Johnny Farrell. We're counting on you to keep a lid on it." Walker tapped him on the knee, a fatherly gesture. "But first we need know everything, John. Who you are involved with and how—all of it. So take your time. Start from the beginning, the truth is all that matters."

Farrell nodded, asked for a glass of water, but he knew it was far too late for the truth.

Briody moved through those crowded city streets trip-wire anxious. If Farrell was right, there were many people hunting for him and Grace. He slipped into a pharmacy phone booth on Fifty-seventh Street and called the one true friend he had in America.

He heard the steps approaching the hallway phone.

"Michael?"

"I need to get out of town."

"I bet you do. There have been men looking all over the neighborhood for you. Some are cops, others, I don't have a clue, but they are not a pleasant bunch. It's not safe for you here. Meet me at the Lantern, on Decatur, above Fordham, at six. We'll sort you out."

"Thanks a million, Danny."

"Please. It's the least I can do. Whatever you do, be careful."

Casey hung up and stared at the phone for a long time. He looked down the hallway into his own sitting room, at his children huddled around the radio. His wife was in the kitchen and the smell of the roast beef reached him. There was laughter and warmth. He cursed himself and he cursed America.

Grace, bored and nervous, was compelled to sketch, to do something, so she took her book and walked to a flat rock where she sat and drew a dry-docked single-mast ship. There was something so forlorn to her about a sailboat out of the water. Briody was late, and she was trying to calm her nerves by focusing on the work, to compress her fears into something manageable. They were only hours from escape and she needed to stay calm. She finished a drawing and was turning the page of her sketchbook when she heard the low murmur of several cars and the closing of a number of doors. The wind was blowing hard and she strained to make sure she was not hearing phantoms. She moved a few feet up toward the house and caught a glimpse of men walking across the front lawn, through the windows of the house.

She ran, grabbed the bag with the diary, and scurried crablike along the coast. She rounded a bend in the seawall and slipped on algae-slick rock, cracking her head on the way down. She pulled herself into a sitting position, waited for a second while her head cleared. She considered swimming for the far shore, but the water was too cold and the currents sped through where Long Island Sound met the East River. It was suicide. Voices came to her from up on the lawn and she gathered herself and with her head still woozy started again along the coast. She looked back up and three men were coming down the grass with guns in their hands. The rocks stopped and there was a short stretch of sandy beach and she ran along it as fast as she could, her feet sinking above her ankles so that she seemed to be running in place. Her lungs burned. At the end of the strand was a pier and as she climbed onto it she heard the first shot and now she was truly afraid. This time, they were going to kill her.

She ran along the pier and up a small embankment to the bluff overlooking the water. She heard another shot, then three more. She looked about quickly at quiet streets lined with bungalows and cottages, the houses all abandoned for the winter. There was no one to help her. The three men were up on the pier behind her now so she ran down between two houses thinking, Do I try to hide, or keep running? She cut through three more yards and came onto a street. She stopped for a second to catch her breath and suddenly there was a man behind her, so she took off running along the street until a car rounded the bend ahead of her, up on two wheels, a man on each running board hanging on with one hand and waving a gun with the other. She was trapped. For a second she contemplated her defeat but then she turned and ran back between two cottages, dashing blindly, fear moving her on at speed so the world was just a blur until she was out the back and onto a street and she tumbled into the path of some men and she was down in a tangle of limbs, trying to pull her hands free so she could cover her face from attack, to ward off the blows.

Instead of blows there were careful hands and soft words as she was lifted to her feet. She looked around confused at two dozen young men, all bright-faced and eager, dressed in gray sweat clothes with the letters NYMMA across their chests. "Who are you?"

"We're from the Maritime Academy, ma'am. Are those men trying to hurt you?"

Grace looked back up the road and her pursuers were sliding their guns into pockets and belts. They stared sullenly and then turned and got back in their cars. They sped off, leaving her there safe for the time being.

"They were, yes."

"Come on, we'll see you get home all right."

Grace moved along, surrounded by her saviors, more worried than ever about Briody.

B riody had the cab drop him off two blocks up from the rendezvous and for twenty minutes he studied the door, the street, and the passersby. His senses were kicked up, his fear lending clarity to his sight, his smell, his hearing. There were no cars parked, no assassins worth worrying about. From a radio somewhere in an apartment above him he heard Bing Crosby crooning "Black Moonlight." In a kitchen somebody was frying onions. A boy with angry splotches of acne came up the block toward him, bouncing a ball. Briody forced himself to be calm, then he crossed Decatur Avenue, walked the two blocks south, and ducked into the windowless Lantern.

The room was empty. A ruddy bartender with a shock of greasy black hair nodded as he took a seat, dropping a coaster before him.

"What's your choice?"

"Beer." Briody drank it slowly. He felt the reassuring weight of the gun in his pocket.

A phone rang and the bartender answered, listened, and then hung up. The bartender leaned over the bar and, though no one was anywhere near, spoke softly. "Are you here for Danny?"

"I am."

"Go on up the block. You know the stair street?"

Briody nodded, left some change on the bar, and pushed back outside. He wondered for a second about the skulduggery, but no. He was sure Danny was going to be there and he would have money for him and a place to run to. And if anything was going to happen to him it would surely be in the bar and not out on a public street.

He heard the trains hammering past Fordham a couple of blocks away. He stood at the bottom of the granite steps and looked up. There was a small clump of oaks but they were bare now. He started up the steps, looking around. As he got higher he could see into windows of adjacent apartment buildings. There was life going on, suppers being served, routine. At the top of the stairs was a tiny park containing a small square of grass and a concrete path along which several benches sat. A trash can, filled to overflowing, was attended by a trio of pigeons. There was no one there.

He stood in the chill and was surprised that even here above Fordham Road he could see the Empire State Building, spotlit, like a totem in the New York sky. Where the hell was Danny? He had started to think about leaving when he heard Danny call to him from the bottom of the steps. He walked toward the top stair and, looking down, saw his old friend. He let go of the pistol in his pocket and raised his hand, waving to Danny, relief coming over him, when suddenly he felt something like a punch in his back and he dropped to his knees. He had not even heard the first shot, and when the next two came they did not sound to him like gunshots at all but more like someone clapping. There was no pain, just dizziness and confusion. He struggled to his feet and craned his neck and there was a man he did not know standing on the top of the building pointing a gun at him. Looking back to Danny, he saw, undeniably, shame in Casey's face. Then his old friend was running away down the Bronx street. Briody tried to call out to him but then the last shot came, this one loud and unmistakable. He thought of how he had disappointed Grace, how a life they had imagined together was not to be, and then he fell, tumbling over and over again to the sidewalk below.

When Briody failed to show up, Grace called Egan suspecting the worst. She left a message and then took a taxi to Riverside Drive. Anna's father stood at the door and nodded, but let her in immediately and offered her a plate of food which she declined. Her boots were muddied and she did not notice until she sat down and saw the trail she had left on the polished wood floor. A servant brought them tea.

"Anna is in Paris. I am sure she would be happy to see you."

Grace looked around the parlor. It was a warm room, filled with pictures of family. This is what she no longer had. She was adrift in the world, alone. Anna's father was a modest man but you could tell by the way he spoke that he would sacrifice anything for his daughter.

"Do you need money for passage?"

"No," she lied.

"I would put you up here, but they still watch the house from time to time. I think it is best that you leave as soon as possible."

"I plan to."

"These men will, well, you know better than anyone I'm sure."

At midnight, Egan came with a car full of men and escorted her back to the Bronx, to Our Lady of Mercy Hospital. In the basement morgue, she stood back a step while the attendant pulled a sheet off of Briody. They left her alone in the room. She knelt, crossed herself and said a prayer from her youth, finished, and stood. She leaned over the body and placed her hand on his face, waxen and cold, so utterly unbelievable to her even now with the proof before her. There were two gaping exit wounds in his chest, meaning they had shot him from behind.

In that cold tile room of stink and death she let herself have a long cry. After a while, she wiped her tears away and then leaned over and kissed him softly on the forehead, and the eyes, and then the lips. Before she backed away she slid his scapular medal off and dropped it in her pocket.

She stood straight and smoothed her dress front and then walked out to the back alley where Egan waited for her, smoking in the dim light. He opened the door and left her to her thoughts as they drove along the length of the city from the Bronx, crossing over the Willis Avenue Bridge and roaring down Second Avenue. They waited in his apartment till morning and then got back in the car. As they curved around the bottom of the island the Statue of Liberty rose in the distance.

"I used to dream about that when I was a girl."

"Dreams ain't all they're cracked up to be. My father used to take us there when we was kids. Every year, rain or shine, on the anniversary of his coming to this country. Now it just reminds me of things that went wrong."

"How could that be?"

"My father died. Me and my brother ran for it. They caught us trying to take the ferry. Then they stuck me on a train, sent me to live with some very bad people in a place called North Dakota. The statue reminds me now of that day."

"Is that why you turned out this way?"

"I don't mind how I turned out. I think I learned the right perspective on humanity."

"What's that?"

"Given the chance, nine times out of ten people will do the wrong thing."

"I wouldn't go that far."

"Oh no? Look at the fix you're in."

Grace stared out the window at the bustling downtown streets. "I want him ruined."

"That, lady, may depend heavily on you coming back to testify."

"What good will that do?"

"It's not so easy, town like this. But it will help. There's going to be a general housecleaning going on in this town. It's not likely that your boy will be left standing."

"When will it happen?"

"Levers are being pulled, investigations are being arranged. When these people fall, the noise will be heard near and far."

"Can you do it without me?"

"You make my job so much easier."

"I'm scared. I mean I'm really scared. Look what they have done already."

"You're scared, but you're tough. You ain't the average dame. I need you on this."

"I won't rule it out."

"That's my girl." Egan leapt out of the car and ducked into the Broadway booking office of the Cunard Lines. Presently he came back and slapped a ticket on her lap. "*Mauritania*. First class to Southampton. Leaves in . . ." He checked his watch. "One hour."

At pier 82 Egan flashed his badge and escorted her up the gangway to her cabin. When she settled in he took a brown envelope out of his coat pocket and handed it to her. "I don't expect something for nothing. That's a down payment on your testimony. You come back like I know you will, you get the other half. Don't be modest. I stole it from Johnny Farrell, if that makes you feel better."

Grace hefted the envelope and slid it under the pillow. She strode to her terrace door, opened it, and stood outside in the chill air. She stared at the skyline that had become as familiar to her as the stone ruins in the fields behind her house growing up. She was going to miss New York City.

Back inside Egan stood, hat in hand. She walked over to him and squeezed his arm. "Thank you for what you have done. I'll do my best."

"You know, Grace, for some reason I believe you. And I'm a cynic from way back."

Later, as the great ship cut through the narrows, the morning sun broke through the clouds and lit the Empire State like a tower of gold. It dominated the skyline. She knew she would go there when she wanted to be near Briody, that the cemetery was no place to honor a man like him. As the liner surged on the city receded until far out at sea all that was visible was that building, rising like a beacon, calling her back one day.

·

ACKNOWLEDGMENTS

These men died building the Empire State Building:

Giuseppe Tedesci	Laborer
L. DeMonichi	Laborer
Reuben Brown	Ironworker
Sigus Andreasen	Carpenter
Frank Sullivan	Carpenter
A. Carlson	Carpenter

They should not be forgotten.

Empire Rising is a novel. Some of the characters in it were living people; some of the events actually happened. They have been given places in a work of fiction. It is my story, in other words, and I'm sticking to it.

Still, no novelist really works alone. I am grateful to my Aunt May Delpezzo (née Mary Kelly), whose tales of immigrant life in the Bronx were the inspiration for the book. She passed away on November 16, 2004, at eighty-five years of age. She'll be missed dearly.

Two other books furnished details of the Empire State Building's construction: *Building the Empire State*, edited by Carol Willis, and *The Empire State Building: The Making of a Landmark*, by John Tauranac.

I am blessed with a great agent, Nat Sobel, and an incredible editor, Paul Elie. They may not always agree with each other, but I almost always agree with both of them.

At FSG, Kathryn Lewis, Liz Calamari, and Susan Mitchell are the best in the business.

Angela Cioffi is a beautiful woman with the biggest of hearts. I should be so lucky.